The Last Word

The Devil's Bed

Doug Lamoreux

To Jenny
without whom nothing matters

To Jack, the Sac, and AC,
whose efforts allowed the dead to walk.

I - The Legend of The Dead

One

"And now, *messieurs et mesdames*," the tour guide said, "we pass through the centerpiece of the most terrifying legend in all of France and one of the world's most horrifying stories."

Brandy had been waiting for this for over an hour. And, as it had been a long time coming, she intended to enjoy it.

As for the others in the group, the guide's speech was having its effect. With the mood established by the remnants of the ruined castle, looming behind him and above them, and the additional gloom cast by the forlorn chapel on the opposite side of the courtyard, they were of a mind to be horrified.

"From this spot," he continued, "the Templar knights set out on horseback. Rich and greedy for more, bloodthirsty, hated and feared. They raided the countryside, stealing, murdering, then returned with their captives. *Oui*, the Templar's sacrificed virgins to the Lord of the Flies, here, at the insanely named *Château de la liberté*. Castle Freedom; the castle of death."

Finally, Brandy thought, finally some death!

Her elation was because they were well into the tour and, until that point, the guide's schtick had all the horror flourishes yet sadly lacked emotion. His flat delivery was spoiling the show. Brandy was neither weird nor ghoulish. She recognized hopping from one European graveyard to another was not the vacation most would choose. But they weren't writing a Master's degree thesis entitled 'Burial Practices Around the World and What They Mean to Life' and she was. So, despite the gorgeous autumn weather in the green, rock-strewn hills of the Languedoc-Roussillon region of the south of France, amid this group of tourists clothed in their own explosions of color, Brandy followed, notebook open, pen at the ready, eager to collect facts about. . . the dead.

Brandy Petracus was a compact brunette, easy on the eyes, and approachable when she wanted to be. Everywhere she went she carried her bag o' plenty (named by her fiancé), a massive purse made from an old carpetbag to which she'd added a duffle

4

shoulder strap. In it she carried all of the accoutrement needed to exist on this hostile planet; food, First Aid and farding material. Oh, and her brain worked. More than once an intimidated male had called her 'a computer'. She could live with that.

Like a computer Brandy had been in 'sleep' mode throughout the bus trip from the village of Paradis, where she, her fiancé Ray and Ray's sister, Vicki, were staying, to the remnants of this 14th century site. She remained uninvolved throughout the cursory look at the grounds, the decaying outbuildings (a chapel kept up, a stable partially so, a guard house not so much), and the ruins of the castle.

Put away all fantasy notions. Neither white knight nor fair princess would be putting in an appearance. These were the ruins of a nine hundred-year-old fortress, subjected to two hundred years of battle, then abandoned. Seven centuries of exposure and vandalization followed. Not to mention bombardment. The chapel and stable had been occupied by the Germans during World War II and those few portions of the castle untouched by time, the elements, and ancient armies surrendered with the Nazis to several well-placed Allied cannon shells. What remained consisted of a western wall, the ground and first floor of the keep, the ground floor entrance to the main hall... and a descending staircase barred by a *NE PAS ENTRER* sign (DO NOT ENTER, Brandy imagined) leading to a spoken of, but unseen, dungeon.

The tour guide, Felix Bussey, droned on. In his mid-twenties, pale and blonde, Felix was so obviously uninterested in his own patter it defied logic he kept his job. His desire to be elsewhere was palpable. His only displays of interest came with repeated glances at a startling red-head on the fringe of the group.

And what a group. Besides the red-head, there were two tall Nordic men who looked sorry they'd come, and several Asians having the time of their lives. There was a French-speaking coterie led by a stick of a woman intent on proving her education, at least, was well-rounded. She conducted her own tour in spite of Felix. An Irish couple trailed the group; she annoyed with him, he with everything. When Felix said something he doubted, the Irishman muttered "Fek." When he did, his wife jabbed his ribs and barked "Language!" There was a Don Juan look-alike who'd apparently taken the tour a thousand times. And Brandy's future sister-in-law, Vicki.

Brandy hung in, watching the stick lady lecture, watching the Irish pair spar, watching the tour guide watch the red-head. The exercise offered its amusements but was wearing thin. If the tour guide didn't get to the morbid stuff soon, she feared she would have a fit.

Felix droned on as he led the group down the stairs. "The Templars introduced the 'keep' to French military architecture." They spilled into an open area that once had been the foyer and he moved on to the differences between a castle and a Château. Then amused himself by pointing out the *Château de la liberté* was in fact neither. It was a Stronghold. Pen poised, with nothing to write, Brandy bit her lip not to scream.

Victoria Kramer was not having a good time. While the tour wasn't all Brandy had hoped for she at least had moments of excitement. Vicki languished. Brandy's insistence they remain at the front of the pack hadn't made it any easier. The stunning blonde was failing to hide her creeping boredom. It was not the vacation Vicki imagined when she'd first heard Brandy's sales pitch. The local hotel was clean and modern. But it was hardly the Château of which she'd dreamed.

And having a room across from Brandy and Ray didn't help. She and Brandy had been friends a long time. She'd introduced her brother, encouraged their relationship, and was looking forward to a best friend as a sister-in-law. But suddenly Brandy and Ray were fighting and, while it was none of her business, it made life uncomfortable.

Vicki's greatest fear was winding up a third wheel. And that's exactly what happened. She'd been feeling superfluous throughout and here she was, tagging along again, on Brandy's death tour. Meanwhile Ray, the jerk, was off doing whatever younger brothers did when no one was looking.

Life wasn't fair. She was an attractive, single woman at a castle in the south of France... and did she have a knight to save her? She had Brandy taking dictation from the endlessly droning tour guide.

"During the reconquering of Europe, many castles were built to protect the villages of France from the Muslim Moors and Christian Castilians. Military Orders, particularly the Templar Knights, defended the Kingdom."

Felix led them out the arched doorway and into the courtyard. Vicki was swept along without enthusiasm.

Across the space stood a forlorn chapel and its shadowed bell tower. A stable leaned in the grass off the courtyard to the left and their tour bus sagged in the grass to the right. Further to the right, unseen beyond the wall, was the dry moat and drawbridge they'd crossed coming in. Vicki longed to cross it again – going out.

Out. . . to a hot bath in a comfortable hotel room (even if it wasn't a Château), in the village of Paradis, in the valley below this crappy old castle. Somewhere, outside of her head, the tour guide was still talking.

"This is where they lived. And this is where the terror began. . ."

Two

As advertised, the tour finally got around to the blood and black magic. When 'virginal sacrifices' came up, despite the cool of the day, the glowering red-head began a slow burn. Brandy decided she was either an angry virgin or she knew Felix personally.

Either way, Brandy's patience was eventually rewarded. Felix got round to the gore and Brandy came out of 'sleep' mode. She lifted her notebook, poked her ill-fitting reading glasses back on her too-short-by-a-smidge nose, and began scribbling. Soon she found herself whispering to Vicki, "Isn't this fascinating?"

"Fascinating. I always said virginity was overrated."

"What... oh, virginal sacrifices... I get it." Brandy said. "I agree. The Halloween stuff is silly. I was hoping for more historic details, the executions, burials."

"Yeah, Bran." Vicki shook her head. "That's what I meant."

Brandy ignored the sarcasm and returned to her notes. Meanwhile, Vicki sighed, yawned, and drifted toward the back of the group.

Felix droned on. "It was upon this spot where the Templar's reign of terror came to a terrible but well deserved end."

Vicki wondered what *she'd* done to deserve this. Unable to pin-point the sin, she dropped the query and began to mentally list the dozen places she'd rather be. She came up with eight then realized, sadly, each had the same thing in common – you could smoke. The whole damned United States had stopped smoking. But she was at Castle Freedom. *Viva la France*. Surely this mausoleum had a corner into which she could duck?

It was then Vicki felt a cheek against her flaxen hair, lips brushing her ear and, in a whisper she heard, "You appear nearly as bored as I, *mon cher*."

She turned, taking in the olive skinned speaker; the man Brandy had whispered looked like Don Juan. ("Don't look!"). Vicki looked now and saw brown-black eyes, a thin mustache, amazingly white teeth, in an expensive blue suit. "Excuse me?" She was

12

buying time to catch her breath, though she hadn't realized she was breathless.

"Forgive my rudeness. I merely said you appear as bored as I. My English is. . ." He waffled his hand fluttering manicured nails. "If I caused offense. . . ?"

"Not at all. And you're right, I am bored. When you've seen one medieval castle. . ." She hesitated and he laughed. Relieved, Vicki joined him.

"Loup," he said, introducing himself.

"Victoria. My friends call me Vicki."

Loup Wimund took her offered hand. "Let's be friends, Vicki."

"It was here, *messieurs et mesdames*," Felix thundered, with an animation unseen until now, "that Jacques de Molay, Grand Master of the Order, and seven of his Temple knights were burned to death for their transgressions against God. For consorting with the Devil. From this spot, Francois de Raiis, head of Castle Freedom, as the flames ate away his body, shouted his curse of vengeance."

Brandy scribbled with relish.

Felix clasped his hands behind him as if he were bound. He stared menacingly into the crowd with insane eyes and screamed,

"You who murder us... know this. We shall not die! We shall return from the dead to exact our revenge upon you!"

A nervous giggle from the crowd, a "Fek!", one of the French women gasped aloud. The stick lady, with strategically aimed elbows, made her way to the frightened women's side offering comfort.

"Revenge," Felix continued mercilessly, "upon you... and your children..."

The woman appeared near fainting. The others were, in their turns, unmoved, delighted, getting jabbed, and glowering.

"... and your children's children!"

Loup whispered in Vicki's ear. "And your children's, children's, children?"

"And their kids," she whispered back.

Both laughed. It was lost on neither that their lips were nearly touching.

Felix, monotone again, gestured. "If you will all... turn." They did – to take in the gloomy chapel across the courtyard. "We continue. The Templars were renown for their signature round chapels."

It was an odd segue. The edifice looked like every chapel Brandy had ever seen; river stone, brick, mortar like the castle, scant windows (a few shuttered, most boarded over), three steps to the heavy front door, a bell tower, rising fifty or sixty feet into the air, looking 'added on' to the north

14

(their left) corner. And, seen earlier, a balcony on the outer north wall. But it wasn't round and, being Brandy, she said so.

"The original chapel was," Felix explained, "but it, and its replacement, were destroyed. Finally a more traditional, less expensive chapel was erected. And added to over the years."

Felix led them in and out so quickly they might as well not have gone. Brandy's disappointment was nearing anger. Felix moved on – oblivious. He led an arc into the grass on the chapel's south side. "Your tour continues off the beaten trail or, if you will, off the courtyard onto the trail."

Lagging, Loup extended his hand. Vicki weighed the consequences of grasping it. What the hell. It was her vacation too. She took hold; surprised to find it rougher and delighted to find it stronger than she'd imagined. Hand-in-hand, Vicki and Loup followed after the tour.

"Here rest the old dead of Castle Freedom and the countryside."

The small cemetery, south of the chapel, looked much like any graveyard; stone markers, teetering and weathered, some newer, polished marble and granite. It was, admittedly, spooky.

"The old dead?" The fainter asked. The stick lady was still at her side.

Felix nodded solemnly. "This is unused for some time. Today's dead are buried in the village cemetery."

"These graves are abandoned?" Brandy asked, pen poised.

"There are no longer burials here. It is still tended by our caretaker."

"And the Templars? Are the Templars buried here?

"There are several knights buried here, *oui*," Felix said. "But not, I think, the ones you mean. You are referring to the knights of the curse? The executed knights? Their graves are further on." He pointed toward a dark timber across a field to the east. "That is our destination... If you dare?"

Amused, he started away. The tourists followed warily.

They crossed the field of tall grasses, wild flower plants (with little in the way of flowers) and jutting boulders by a well-worn cart path. It sloped gradually down from the chapel for a hundred yards, inclined uphill for another hundred, and ended in a grassy berm before the timber. They mounted the berm and the burial place of the Templar knights came into view.

It was a tiny, ancient cemetery, untended, forgotten. Weeds and autumn-browned wild flowers grew as tall as the rusted wrought-iron fence surrounding it. A raised stone sarcophagus sat inside the gate and, on the far, slightly uphill side, a second sarcophagus made the plot symmetrical. Bookended between the two were six other graves, at ground level, covered with heavy stone lids. Eight forlorn, overgrown tombs in all.

Felix raised his hands to silence the nervous murmurs in the group. "Because of their crimes they could not, of course, be buried in the chapel cemetery. It is here, in unhallowed ground, where the Templar knights are interred. Whether or not they rest...?" He shrugged.

"The ankh crosses engraved upon their tombs, Egyptian symbols of enduring life, signify the black gods to whom they paid homage. And, for those of you literate in Latin and French, the writings etched on their stones tell of their sins."

The tourists lined the fence leaning to see, and craning their necks to read, the graves. Seven of the lids were as described, chiseled inscriptions, coptic crosses, and the names and date (all the same) of death. Strangely, the eighth, the sarcophagus at the end of the plot, was devoid of these markings. A name and matching date of death decorated the lid but nothing more.

Felix was relieved. The tourists had what they'd come for and, other than getting them back, his day was over. Then the dark-haired American girl began asking questions. And, *grande Dieu*, they were the real thing. Felix fielded several then, realizing he was in over his head, attempted to cut her short and move the group along.

Brandy balked. "Wait a minute. You're leaving? Can't I go in?"

"Go in?"

"Yes. I'd like to see the graves up close. Make some rubbings of the inscriptions?" She rifled her monstrous purse looking for chalk and paper as evidence of intent.

"No, no, no, no." Felix waved the idea away. This was all he needed, some-body who really gave a damn about this stupid tour. He didn't have enough trou-bles. Fournier's standing orders regarding tourists was 'get them in and get them out'. "It is not allowed."

"This is why I came. To see the burial site. I can't go in for just a few minutes?"

"Mother of God," Felix exclaimed in mock terror. "No!"

Rule one in dealing with trouble makers was to use the colorful, somewhat colorized, Templar legend. With that in mind, he followed his horrified look by crossing himself, spectacles, testicles, wallet and watch. "It is an accursed place."

The Irishman muttered "Fek!" His wife barked "Language!" The poor guy got his ribs jabbed again, but Brandy was on his side.

"I don't believe in curses," Brandy said. "And I'd really like to see the graves."

Felix sank inside. 'No' was a perfectly good answer. Why wouldn't she take it? The American left him no choice. If bogus curses would not move her, perhaps a bogus law would. "I'm sorry. It is protected. Historical. No one is allowed."

Brandy looked at the supposedly protected, completely unkempt, graveyard and knew he'd lied. And, as the tour guide began to herd the others away, knew also there was nothing she could do about it. Angry and cheated, but resigned, she fell in and headed back. In her disappointment, Brandy failed to notice Vicki and her new companion lagging behind.

As the group sank over the berm and out of sight, Vicki leaned against the iron fence smiling at Loup. "When I was a kid, we lived beside a cemetery. My brother and I grew up using it as our playground."

Loup leapt the fence and landed in the tall grass inside the cemetery.

"What are you doing?"

"Being a kid." He held his hands out in invitation. "Let's play."

Three

Vicki looked after the tour but saw only the berm and a sky collecting angry clouds in the west. They were alone. And being alone with the dark Frenchman was, she had to admit, exciting. She giggled to vent her nerves and allowed Loup to help her over the fence. Safely inside the graveyard, Loup kissed her - and she let him. Then she pushed him away and wandered toward the graves.

"I'll never forget that cemetery," she said. "One night, we'd gone to see a vampire movie. . . "

"*Ah, vous aimez des vampires? Très intéressant!*"

God, that's so sexy. . . "Whatever you said." Her smile faded, replaced with a shiver at the childhood memory. "Maybe it was because I was a kid. I sat there, terrified, with my sweater over my head. Then we had to walk eight blocks and through that cemetery to get home. I thought I'd die"

"You do not believe in the, eh, living dead, do you?"

"I have enough trouble with the living. . . living."

Loup's eyes shined as a subtle change occurred in them. What she had taken for concern suddenly registered as amusement. He bellowed a laugh.

Strangely unsettled, Vicki turned away. The nearby raised tomb came into view and just then the Templars seemed as good a diversion as any. She pointed to the sarcophagus lid where the inscription was bisected by a crack running across its stone face. "What does it say?"

Loup followed her gaze. "Francois de Raiis. Died – 18 March, 1314. Murderer."

"Nice epitaph."

"There's more," he said, reading on, "Heretic. Idolator. Witch."

Vicki bit her lip. Loup saw her discomfort and smiled. "Oh, *mon cher*, he was not what you would call a. . . bad fellow."

Vicki looked a question at the handsome stranger.

"He allowed me the top of his tomb to deflower my first maiden."

"Really." Vicki was aghast. "How romantic."

Loup changed. There was no physical transformation, but she couldn't help but feel something menacing had overtaken him. His child-like giddiness disappeared. His handsome good looks seemed suddenly frightening. The mouth that had so tenderly kissed her was now framed in thin lines. His nostrils flared. His eyebrows were lightning bolts, his ears pointed, and the deep black pools of his eyes were suddenly tunnels leading - Vicki didn't know where.

"Romance?" He grunted. "She was a pig, eighteen to my fifteen. But couple a fat whore with a curious youth, add a stolen bottle of vodka. . . Heaven."

Vicki wordlessly turned to leave. Loup grabbed her wrist and pulled her back.

"Where are you going?"

"I'm getting out of here."

"*Mais amour*, we are at the gates of heaven."

"You've got to be kidding me?"

"I could not be more serious." Loup pulled her to him. He pressed his mouth against hers so fiercely it hurt and forced his pointed tongue between her lips.

Vicki pushed him away. "Jesus, we just met."

"And what a delicious meeting it has been."

23

Loup jerked her to him, so suddenly a muscle pulled in her neck. Vicki pushed back but he was having none of it. "I am not kidding," he said through clenched teeth. She pushed again and Loup shook her. "I am not kidding!"

Vicki slapped him hard across the face and Loup's eye reddened. He viciously returned the slap. Vicki fell back against the sarcophagus striking her head with a boney thud. Loup threw her legs apart and ripped her blouse. Crying, her consciousness slipping, Vicki stopped fighting.

The adult skull, twenty-two puzzle-like bones joined by rigid sutures, was a marvelously designed container. Directly beneath lay the protective membrane *dura mater* (tough mother). Together, they could take one hell of a wallop. But when Vicki's skull slammed against the stone they cracked and tore; the puzzle pieces scrambled.

As suddenly as he'd begun the violence Loup stopped. His eyes widened as a deep red pool grew on the lid of the sarcophagus beneath the girl's head.

"Damn it. Damn!"

He climbed off, staring at his handiwork, and cursed. A smear of her blood marred his hand; the bitch. He wiped it on her blouse. He straightened his suit and looked

around, suddenly afraid. Then he ran...
leaving Vicki alone.

———†———

The battleship gray bus sagged in a fading
patch of shade inside and just up the curved
drive from the castle's gate and just at the
edge of the stone courtyard. White muslin
banners with *Tour de Terreur* splashed in
red (and Marcel Fournier Tour's Ltd in
smaller black) were tied from windows on
each side.

The red-head, brooding as the approaching storm clouds, climbed aboard first and
took her place, right of the aisle, behind the
door. She eyed the driver's seat like a falcon
watching a rabbit hole.

Outside, Felix stroked the air urging the
others to board quickly. "*Messieurs et Mesdames*. Everyone, please."

Seemingly from nowhere Loup joined the
group in line. The tour guide grimaced to
see his reddened eye but Loup trumped Felix's look with one of his own; smarmy self-
importance. He paused at the door, whispered, "Don't say a damn word," to Felix,
then boarded the bus. He found a seat alone
at the back.

Brandy, note pad and glasses stored in
her bag o' plenty, scanned the courtyard for

her friend. Vicki was nowhere to be seen and, as the others funneled past, she grew concerned.

The Irishman bought her some time, holding up the line to ask, "Do ye' have tours at night?"

Felix looked sharply up from his clip board. "*Ce qui?*"

"Ye' know... tour's after dark. T'would tink yer speech would be more effective in the dark."

"No sane man will have anything to do with Castle Freedom after nightfall."

"Ye'd tink t'would be a gold mine."

"Tell me, *monsieur*, what can a dead man buy with gold?"

The Irishman ran his hand through his carrot hair. "Fek."

Jab. "Language!"

Felix stared the Irish couple past with terror stricken eyes - and grinned once they were aboard. His smile vanished when he saw Brandy loitering.

"Please. There is no time to waste." He interrupted her attempt to speak and gently pushed her up the stairs. Brandy had no choice but to board. Felix took the wheel, fired the engine and shifted the gears.

"Hold on," she shouted. "Stop!"

Felix hit the brakes.

"My friend isn't on the bus!" Brandy said. "My sister-in-law, she isn't here."

Felix looked to the others, in their places with worn out faces. He looked outside the bus and saw what he always saw after a tour; the castle caretaker, Anibal Socrates, waiting for their departure. He looked past Brandy to the scowling red-head and assured her, with plaintive eyes, he wanted none of the American girl's trouble. Out of places to look, Felix returned his gaze to Brandy and shrugged helplessly.

"That's it? You can't just leave her."

The tour guide sighed and reached to open the door.

"Felix!"

The rear view mirror displayed Loup storming the aisle. Another uninvited swimmer, Felix thought, pissing in his pool. Loup wore a hateful frown, but then, Loup always did. An argument ensued that, for those who spoke French, went:

"What the hell are you doing?"

"Her companion isn't on the bus."

"It is not our problem. We cannot wait."

"But we..."

"Her companion is not our problem!"

The red-haired girl chimed in only to be ignored. Loup ordered Felix to drive the bus.

"Who are you anyway?" Brandy demanded. When Don Juan ignored her too,

27

she said, "Fine. Let me off. I'll find her my-self."

"I said let's go!" Loup repeated. "If you want your goddamned job, drive!"

Felix set the vehicle in motion nearly knocking Brandy and Loup off their feet. Grinding the gears, revving the engine, he stuttered the bus to the castle gate, under the arch and over the drawbridge.

Following on foot, the caretaker closed the gate as the bus disappeared down the road. He secured the chain, grateful they were gone. The sky to the west was growing dark. If the ache in his knee and the pains in his feet were indicators, and they were, a storm was on the way.

He'd been in the midst of a long overdue job. And poor Zorion, his faithful mule, was still harnessed to the cart waiting. Socrates needed to finish. He took a last look at the sky. A storm was surely brewing.

Aboard the bus, Brandy was fuming. She'd expected the return to the village to be a return to 'sleep' mode. Instead, she was wide awake and kicking herself for fail-ing Vicki. And she was enraged at Felix and creepy Don Juan, whoever he was. How dare they? How dare they?

God, she wished Ray had been here. Why wasn't he? He'd come to France but hadn't come along on the tour. All the benefits, none of the bull. Where was he when his sister needed him? Where was he when she needed him? As she sank back into the bus seat, Brandy found herself growing very angry with her fiancé, Ray Kramer.

Four

Brandy would be pissed. Ray ogled the myriad designs covering the walls of the little shop fully aware that, if she knew he was there, man, Brandy would be pissed.

'There' was *Art dans le Movement* a tiny, obvious tattoo parlor (garish lighting, graffiti paint job) with no logical reason to exist in the quaint French village of Paradis. So, when he left Chambon, the immense village park, where he'd killed off a ham and pastrami on rye, a bag of chips, and an hour, and after passing a cobbler's shoppe, a cheese shoppe and a bakery, the last thing on earth Ray expected to find was a tattoo parlor. Maybe it was fate.

The place was decorated with the expected wall to wall tats and, unexpectedly, an amazing collection of bleached animal skulls. Rats, cats, dogs, birds. The artist had personality.

"That's bad!"

Ray, a monstrous 'biker' of a man, turned and again saw what he'd expected, a heavily tattooed and pierced shop artist standing in a back room doorway. What was unexpected was the British accent - thick as cut-comb honey.

"The tats! Bloody hell, they're baaaaad! I like, mate."

"You're English?"

"You mean British? Nah." He saw Ray's confusion. "Believe it or not, mate, I'm French, actually."

Ray bit his tongue. Six weeks of Anger Management and still his first thought was, 'Is this guy fucking with me?' If he was French he was keeping it a secret from his voice. It thought he was British.

The artist laughed nasally then raised his hands, signaling for peace. "Honest to God, I'm not mocking you. I was born here, three blocks away. But I was raised in the UK. A political brat. My father was in the Foreign Service, diplomatic messenger, ambassador to Her Majesty, a member of the EP. Misspent my youth in Nottingham and the rest in London. Came home last year to open shop." He stepped forward to shake. "Jerome Rousseau," he said. "Despite this bloody accent. . . I'm pure Frog."

He laughed again and this time Ray joined in.

"You've got a bit of an accent yourself. *Americain, n'est-ce pas?*, as the locals would ask."

Ray nodded. "Red, white and blue. Ray Kramer. By Wyoming, out of Illinois."

"Wyoming? A cowboy?"

"Yeah, with a steel horse. Hog rider."

"Fucking-A, mate. I like bikes. I also like tats, if you don't mind my getting back to business."

"I don't mind." Ray examined his own left arm without enthusiasm. His muscular bicep sported an inky hooded executioner, ax in hand, before a shadowed castle with a bat flitting past a faded yellow moon. "I'm getting tired of them."

Ray considered Jerome but, beneath the art, there was little to see. Five-six maybe, emaciated, with an ice blue complexion. His bald head resembled a bag of doorknobs, his teeth a sagging fence, with silver, gold and amalgam pickets. Over-sized, blue plastic glasses. But that was the canvas. To compare himself was silly. Ray could snap Jerome like a dried twig. To compare their body art was the reverse. Ray's didn't hold a candle.

The word 'psycho' ran, in crimson, from ear to ear across Jerome's throat as if it had been slit. Inky barbed wire encircled each wrist. Letters marred his fingers but he fidgeted so Ray couldn't read them. Beneath his fishnet tank top, a werewolf howled on his right breast, a demon screamed on his left, and an undetermined creature from hell jumped a Harley through a flaming hoop across his back. Those were just the big tats. Around them ships sailed, cars raced, animals pounced, weapons fired, blood spurted and skulls, lots of skulls, grinned as one tableau ran into another across Jerome's body. To say nothing of the piercings.

"I'm thinking of getting away from the spooky stuff," Ray said, scanning the walls. "I don't know. Maybe an animal. . ."

Jerome clicked the metal stud in his tongue. He closed his eyes - even his lids had tats – and got an idea. "I could cover that with a buffalo or a bear. Either would kick ass."

Distracted by thoughts of a bison on his bicep, Ray didn't see Fournier's gray battleship pull up at the Bus Stop across the street.

Brandy marked time waiting for the others to disembark. It took a moment and she suffered Don Juan's glare as he passed but, excepting Felix and the red-head, the bus finally emptied. Brandy shouldered her bag and headed for the front. Felix saw her in his mirror and sank visibly. She knew the feeling.

"Please, you've got to help me."

"There is nothing I can do, *mademoiselle.* If your friend chose not to ride back with the bus... We are not responsible."

"You are," Brandy said. "Vicki's never been to France before. There's no reason for her to stay at the castle. Why would she do that?"

"She is your friend. I have met many strange women."

"*C'est comme ça,*" the red-head chimed in angrily. "What women?"

"*Ça n'a pas d'importance,*" Felix told her. Then, in horror, added, "No, no, no. No women. That is not my meaning. I have met no women!"

"Vicki isn't strange," Brandy cried, trying to reclaim the driver's attention. "I don't appreciate what you're implying."

"I imply nothing. I am sorry, please. Do not appreciate it... from the sidewalk." Felix rose from his seat, giving Brandy no choice but to back down the stairs and off the bus, then closed the door in her face.

Brandy scowled through the bus door window. Inside, the red-haired girl barked at Felix. He raised his hands in surrender and climbed back into his seat. The girl kept talking. Brandy kept staring. He ignored both and pulled away from the curb.

———+———

Jerome's suggestion had settled and Ray, despite knowing better, found himself studying a wall of tattoos. He pointed to an eye-catching bison. "How much?"

Jerome twisted his lips in thought. "I'd have to have five hundred."

Ray sank. The vision of a new tat faded, replaced by one of Brandy beating him to death with her carpet bag. He'd promised not to add any without their talking first (like he was a kid). It wasn't the art; she was cool with his body. It was the money. Ray looked the shop over again. "You do any bartering?"

The tattoo artist felt a sale slipping away. He had limited interests which were, pretty much, on display. Still. . . what the hell. "I'm into skulls."

Ray smiled a wide 'I'm getting me a new tat smile'. "Well," he said. "My brother's a taxidermist and I don't see a bear skull here."

Jerome's own grin burst from the riot of ink and metal that comprised his face. "Bloke," he said, "I'd do that fucker for a bear skull!"

Ray could not have been happier – until he looked out the window to see Brandy standing alone across the street. "Balls!" Ray hurried for the door assuring Jerome, over his shoulder, he'd be back.

The others tourists had returned to their lives; disinterested, happy as clams, sour as lemons, dishing verbal abuse, or returning physical abuse as was their lot. Brandy, opposite her nature, simply stood at the Bus Stop across from a tattoo parlor (good thing Ray wasn't here!) and down the street from the Fournier Tour office (where the heck was Ray?). It was, she guessed, near sundown but hard to tell as clouds churning a storm in the west cast a gloom over the village.

A gloom settled over Brandy as well. Where was Vicki? And where, in the name of heaven, was Ray?

She and Vicki were best friends before Ray entered the picture. That Ray and Vicki were siblings only made things more fun. Her relationship with Vicki's little brother had begun with lust and moved to love. And a six month engagement left them, where, Brandy wondered? Their most frequently exchanged emotion now was anger. Hers, more than his? She didn't know that either. Why had she asked Ray with them to Europe when she was so angry with him? Why was she so angry with him?

"Hey, baby, you look lost."

Brandy was startled to find Ray beside her. "Where were you when I needed you?"

Ray glanced at the tattoo parlor, then quickly back. "I just got here."

Brandy threw her bag. Ray grunted as he caught it and complained, as he often did, that no one carried a purse anymore let alone her monstrous tote.

"I don't care what other people do," Brandy said, uncharacteristically riled. "I don't care what they think. And I certainly don't care what they think of me."

A blind man could see her mood - and Ray wasn't blind. "What's that matter? Didn't you two. . . " He stopped, looked around and, feeling stupid, wondered if he wasn't blind after all. "Where's Vicki?"

"I'm not sure."

"What do you mean you're not sure?"

"She wasn't on the bus. Somehow. . . we left her back at the castle."

"Left her at the castle? What are you talking about?"

"I don't know, Ray. She didn't get on the bus."

"Where the hell's my sister?"

Brandy's eyebrows arched over her reddening face. "Look, Ray. You're not going to yell at me like some nasty biker skank." She snatched her bag away from him. "I was busy doing what I went to the castle to do. We got separated during the tour, lost track of one another. When we were leaving, she wasn't anywhere around. The driver wouldn't hold the bus. Said it wasn't their responsibility." Brandy took a deep breath. "I don't know where Vicki is."

Five

Vicki stirred slowly, holding the blood-matted hair at the back of her head. "Oh, God," she whispered, saliva running from the corner of her mouth. She was groggy; her head swimming laps. She wiped her tears, her hands filthy with dirt and blood, making matters worse. She felt horribly sick and fought not to retch. Between bouts of dizziness, she climbed down and took in her surroundings.

She'd been lying on a tomb! She stared through cloudy eyes at the gray stone splashed with what looked like blood. Hers? Vicki had no memory of what had happened there, no clue what she was doing in a cemetery.

She staggered to the wrought-iron fence, grabbed it for balance and vomited. She was glad she'd skipped breakfast. The returning coffee was disgusting enough. Then it dawned, she remembered skipping breakfast! She'd had a cup of terrible coffee. European coffee was abominable, that she remembered. But was it a recent memory? She hadn't had a decent cup since leaving America. Yes; they'd left America, Brandy, Ray and her. Now they were in France. And the coffee was terrible.

Ray hadn't wanted to go. No, he hadn't! "That's fine," Brandy yelled across the room. No, across the hall, to another room. "I'll get more done without you grumbling."

Brandy had been with her. But where was Brandy?

Vicki lifted her head and everything rolled. Dear God, where was Brandy? What, in the name of heaven, was she doing in a graveyard? She followed the fence to an old gate, only to find it too encrusted to budge. Despite her head and stomach, she had no choice but to climb (fall) over the fence to freedom. Rising, Vicki stumbled away.

The pool of blood she'd left behind mothered streaming rivulets, propelled by gravity... and maybe something darker, that flowed past the ankh symbol carved in the tomb's lid and into the large crack in the stone.

It seeped inside the sarcophagus and, building there, dripped onto the mummified skull of the Templar knight lying interred.

One slow, thick drop at a time as it oozed through the fissure. A drop on the void once covered by a nose. A drop that struck the taut papery skin of the cheek and ran away into the depths of the grave. A drop on the toothy grin. Another. Another. Vicki's blood eked through the teeth, fell into the black pit of a mouth, landed on the dried tongue...

The blood dripped.

People would be amazed to know the time and work required to care for a ruin. Anibal Socrates, the caretaker at Castle Freedom, had been meaning to get at the big stones buried at the edge of the courtyard for years. Today had been the day. The stones were out, piled on his cart and, after securing the gate behind the last tour of the day, ready to be hauled away. In reward for his effort his back was killing him.

Socrates had always been a powerful man, a rich baritone, a bull, with a great mustache that arrived well ahead of him. But the years, the work and the disappointments had taken their toll. He was still boisterous but the joy was gone, still large but more gross than grandiose. His mustache had gone gray and his fleshy nose now led the way.

His power was gone. Thank God Socrates still had his mule.

Zorion, a thousand pounds of might, was stronger, more patient, sure-footed, durable in the sun, less sensitive to the rain, more intelligent and ate less than any horse. He could carry 400 pounds for fifteen miles without resting. With his long ears and short mane the mule looked like his donkey father, but had the height, body and neck of his horse mother. And, despite his gray sire, Zorion had the wild coat, black, bay and sorrel islands on a sea of gray mule hide, of his Appaloosa dam.

Socrates led his loaded mule cart past the castle's out-buildings. The wood and wire wheels shrieked on the courtyard; a noise to which Socrates was accustomed. Then came a series of new sounds, the rumble as the piled stones fell, the snap of the rear gate, thuds as the rocks hit the ground. Socrates hollered, tugging Zorion's reins, and the cart came to a stop. He stared in disbelief, swore in Portuguese, and sighed deeply.

Then followed a ballet of despair:

Socrates rounded his cart, hiked his trousers and bent over the largest rock.

Sixty yards behind him, wounded and disoriented, Vicki staggered into the courtyard. She fell to the ground and weakly called for help.

The caretaker lifted the stone with a grunt - hearing nothing but the crack of his joints. He maneuvered the rock onto his cart with a thud, the scratch of stone on wood, and his own labored exhalation.

Daylight was fading. With the coming storm the wind, too, was picking up. Socrates groaned. He bent over a second stone, grunted, thumped and scraped it aboard with the others. Then again. And again.

Vicki struggled to rise; her head throbbing, her vision blurred. Was she actually seeing a man? And a horse and cart? "Help." Darkness swallowed her.

The caretaker clicked his tongue, snapped the reins and Zorion started forward. The wheels grumbled from the grass, shrieked on the courtyard, and grumbled back onto the grass. His cargo rumbled, shifted, but stayed aboard. Socrates still had the stable to muck. Poor Zorion deserved that after his hard day's work. He'd need to be quick or he'd be doing it in the pitch; certainly he'd be caught in the rain. Still his mule deserved that at least.

Socrates had named him Zorion; meaning Full of Joy. "You give me joy," Socrates said as he led mule and cart away. "I give you nothing but misery. If only there were something I could do for you."

Off the courtyard, sixty yards away, Vicki Kramer lay unconscious and unseen.

———+———

In the fading light, with growing frustration, Brandy rapped on the door of Fournier's Tour Shop. Again she received no answer. She shook the knob, also not for the first time, and found it still locked. She looked up to find Ray, done with his assignment of peering through the dark windows, staring with a smile she wanted to erase with an emery board.

Then he made it worse. "You push elevator buttons that are already lit, don't you?"

Brandy shifted her huge shoulder bag, ignored the question, and asked one herself. "Did you see anything?"

"I didn't see a bus, if that's what you're asking."

The witty banter might have gone on forever but Ray went suddenly tense. His smile vanished; then returned cut completely from whole cloth.

"What's the matter?"

"There's somebody watching us. Don't look around. At the corner of the building, behind me. Keep talking. In your normal voice. Ask me something."

"Eh, shouldn't they be here, yet?" Uh, too loud and stilted. "I... I don't understand where they could have gone. The tour just ended, you know. Where could he have gone?"

Ray was no better. He returned to the windows with his hands cupped around his eyes. That seemed goofy to Brandy. The approaching storm featured neither sun nor glare. (Nonchalance was harder than it looked). Staring through the glass, Ray moved sideways down the building.

"Would they take the bus to get something to eat?"

"This isn't New York, Brandy," Ray said as he reached the suspect corner. "He probably drives the freaking bus home." He reached around. Something squealed! He jerked it to the sidewalk and stared into the ink and chrome face of Jerome Rousseau.

"Easy, mate," Jerome yipped, hands up on either side of Ray's beefy arms. "I'm a hemophiliac!"

Even at dusk the tattoo artist was a sight. Seeing it for the first time, Brandy couldn't help but ogle. "What are you doing spying on us?"

47

"Spying?" Jerome was deeply offended. "Spying?"

"Men only repeat themselves when they're thinking up a lie," Brandy declared. Both men stared. She ignored Ray's and defied Jerome's. "Well?"

"I don't lie. And I was not spying. I came to help you."

Ray let him go. "Help us how?"

"To warn you." Jerome started fidgeting. "Look, it's not my business, indeed, but trust me, you don't want to be caught here."

"We're just looking for the bus driver."

"You're not going to find him here, love, not at this time of the day. And you don't want to be here either."

"I'm not big on puzzles," Ray said. "We have business with Fournier."

"You don't know anything about Fournier's business. And, if you're smart, you don't want to. Marcel Fournier's a bad chap."

"What do you mean?" Brandy asked, stepping in to cool Ray's rising temperature. Not that she blamed him. The little weasel's twitching was getting to her too. Why was the guy so jumpy?

"Just a friendly warning," Jerome told Ray, then added, "Because I want your business."

Brandy saw the 'Oh, Christ!' in Ray's eyes.

Ray tried to cover. He knew Jerome's next sentence and tried to wave it off. The artist didn't get the drift. "Did you still want that tattoo?"

Winter came early. Brandy looked a question at Jerome then stared daggers at Ray. Jerome saw it and retreated, squeaking, "I was... I'll just... eh, later, mate."

When he was gone, Ray turned to Brandy. "Look, baby, I..."

She held up a finger and Ray shut his mouth. "I'm going to change the subject now."

'Okay,' he mouthed without speaking.

"Do you think we should go to the police?" Seeing his confusion, she barked, "Focus, Ray. Your sister's missing, the car rental is closed and we can't find the bus driver. Now... do you think we should go to the police?"

Ray sighed. "I hate cops."

Six

Inquiring on the street Brandy and Ray collected a good many smiles, a few grunts, several blank looks and, eventually, directions to the police station located on a poorly lit side street. With the sun already gone the building was almost invisible. Orange slits stole out beneath drawn blinds in windows twinning the entrance. A frosted globe layered with dead bugs glowed from the stoop ceiling beside a sign reading: *Gendarmerie Départementale*. Little about the place inspired confidence.

"Are you ready?"

Looking as faded as the building, Ray shook his head sullenly. "I hate cops."

"Think of the novelty," Brandy said, leading him up the steps. "How often do you go into a police station through the front door?"

They'd barely cleared the threshold when both were paralyzed by a shout from a small office within. "Stay there!"

On the far side of a counter, through a doorway, stood a middle-aged man holding a weapon. To Ray, it was a .40 caliber SIG. To Brandy, it was a GUN! He had it pressed against his own temple. "Do not come closer," he shouted, in English, with a heavy French accent. "Or I will blow my head off."

Ray grabbed Brandy. Whether from instinct or testosterone she didn't know, but she didn't like it. With an armed madman loose Brandy preferred control over her own movements. She yanked herself free.

In the office, the gunman suddenly lowered the weapon – and laughed. "So... I told this *Américain* idiot, 'Go ahead, *monsieur*. Shoot. You will solve my problem and improve your looks.'"

A chorus of laughter betrayed others in the room. The gunman relished their admiration, until he saw the couple in the reception area. He frowned and tossed the gun into a basket on the desk. He wagged his head.

One of the listeners, younger, dark too, but less threatening, stepped from the room with a smile. "*Puis-je vous aider?*"

His blue uniform was pressed and polished; pant cuffs tucked into black military boots. A badge was embroidered on his left breast and his name, Petit, embroidered on his right. A blue ball cap and white leather gun belt completed his accoutrement.

When their only response was to stare like deer caught in his headlights, Petit repeated his question in English. "Can I help you?"

"Uh, my, uh," Ray stumbled, recovering. "My sister is missing."

Petit smiled. "*Américains?*"

"Yes," Ray said, "we're visiting from the States. My sister is missing."

Petit's smile disappeared, replaced by sober concern or, at least, its professional equivalent. "Her name?"

"Vicki. Victoria. Victoria Kramer."

"She was last seen where?"

"At the castle," Brandy said. "With me. We toured Castle Freedom this afternoon, but she didn't come back on the bus."

"This afternoon?" Petit looked at his watch. "The afternoon tour could not have been back for - thirty minutes."

"Right. But she wasn't on the bus."

Two others abandoned the office and disappeared through the outer door. Then the gunman stepped out to study Brandy and Ray over Petit's shoulder. Only then was Brandy certain he was one of them.

His medals suggested heroism, his brass doo-dads rank. They were pinned onto, and he was squeezed into, a threadbare uniform matching Petit's. While he plainly commanded, the buttons over his gut appeared insubordinately ready to go AWOL. His thick black hair had a shock of white just left of center and his chin had a day's growth of beard. He addressed Petit with a voice that sounded like a load of gravel being dumped.

To experience the moment as Brandy did:

"*Quel est le problème?*"

"*Américains. Leur soeur était sur le tour de Marcel Fournier avec celui-ci et n'est pas revenue sur le bus.*"

"*Le dernier tour?*"

"*Oui, Colonel.*"

Through the babble, Brandy detected a word. The brass, ribbons and humorless attitude apparently made the unkempt guy a Colonel.

He stepped to the counter and made it official. "I am Colonel Mael Blanc," he said. "In charge of this Department, eh, this Region, for the Gendarmerie. Your sister, she has been to the village before? To the Lozere Department? To southern France?"

Brandy met all three questions with one on-going shake of her head. "No. And she's Ray's sister."

54

The Colonel nodded curtly and turned to Ray. "You are?"

"Raymond Kramer. This is my fiancé, Brandy Petracus. No, none of us have been here before. We've never been to Europe."

"Married?"

"What the hell does that have to do with anything?"

"Your sister... she is married or accompanied by a gentleman?"

"No. She's single and she came along with the two of us."

"I'm writing a thesis about burial practices around the world."

"Charming," Blanc said dismissively. "Your sister is not missing. No tourist who has gone unseen for..." He too looked at his watch. "An hour? Is missing. Perhaps she will walk back from the castle."

"My sister tried to rent a golf cart at a mini putt."

Blanc furled his brow looking, with his white streak of hair, like an angry dog. "I am sure that was clever, *monsieur*. But the meaning I do not know." And apparently didn't care because he turned from Ray to Brandy. "She was with you?"

"Yes. We were taking the castle tour."

"She did not return on the bus?"

"No." She seemed to falter, then decisively repeated, "No."

Her hesitation only sharpened his tone. "When did you last see her?"

"I'm not certain. I was listening to the tour. I was taking notes, formulating my paper in my head. I don't remember when or where I saw her last."

"Did she meet or talk to anyone else?"

"I don't know. Just those in the tour."

"We have a single woman, her first time in Paradis?"

"Her first time in France."

"And, most likely, less interested in Fournier's tourist trap than yourself?"

She hesitated, feeling foolish, then managed a weak, "I suppose." Brandy felt suddenly defensive. Everything the Colonel had said was true. Still. . .

"If I were you, I would look for her to show up at your hotel later tonight." He smiled greasily and added, ". . . or perhaps tomorrow."

Ray leaned over the counter toward the gendarme officer. "I don't like what you're suggesting."

Blanc's brow furled again and the dog, secure in his own junkyard, reappeared. The Colonel leaned on his side meeting Ray face-to-face. "You are a religious man, M. Kramer? You and your traveling companion? I have offended?"

"No," Ray admitted through gritted teeth. "And no."

"Ahh, but your sister, *monsieur*, she is a nun?"

"You son of a bitch!" Ray balled his fist.

Before he could use it, Petit shoved his sidearm - with no uncertain meaning - into the big American's face.

Ray froze, staring down the blue steel barrel. It wasn't fear that stopped him. He'd lived a colorful life and this wasn't the first gun ever waved his way. But he knew that when a cop was doing the waving your options were limited. He stretched his fingers wide and eased his hands to his sides.

Amused, Blanc issued an order and Petit returned the weapon to its holster.

"I gather, M. Kramer, you are a bit. . . impulsive?" He wagged his finger. "Permit me to warn you. How would your Judy Garland say? You are not in Kansas anymore."

"He didn't mean it," Brandy said.

"Yes, *mademoiselle*, he did."

"Your officers just pull guns on tourists?"

"We are not police," the Colonel said. "The *police nationale*, the former *Sûreté*, patrol the cities of France. They have no jurisdiction in the countryside. The rivers, the coasts, the villages; these are ours. We are the military police, the Gendarmerie. Do not confuse the two."

Brandy nodded her understanding.

His point made, Blanc smiled. "Yes, *made-moiselle*, he meant it. But I do not blame M. Kramer. I too have a sister. I will send a car to, discretely, pass the castle. To do more now would waste resources and perhaps violate your sister's rights to privacy."

"And if you don't see her?"

"She may not want to be seen. Have patience. If, in forty-eight hours, she does not appear, I will do everything I can to locate her."

Returning to the street was like jumping into a pool. The breeze had intensified with the approaching storm and the darkness seemed to swallow them. It was just as well as both needed cooling off.

"God," Brandy said. "I can't believe he pulled a gun on you."

"He's a cop. I'm surprised it took him so long."

Brandy took his arm and, as they started away, wondered if she was offering comfort or looking for it. It didn't matter. Ray tensed at her touch and, when enough time elapsed for both to avoid embarrassment, she let go.

"Maybe they're right," Ray said. "My sister isn't exactly an angel."

"What's that mean? Must she be before they take an interest?"

"Easy. I'm on your side."

"I don't have a side. I'm worried about Vicki."

"I am too, damn." Ray forced a smile. "If she doesn't drag herself in by morning, we'll rent a car and find her ourselves." She nodded, agreeing to his unspoken truce. In the distance came the first roll of thunder. Ray stared at the sky. "We'd better get back to the hotel. We're going to get drenched."

Seven

The rusted bars of the castle gate were cold in Vicki's hands. They towered over her, solid as Gibraltar... locked. Beyond there was nothing to see. Night had fallen and country dark covered all. Vicki lay her head, her hair a confusion of dirt and blood, against the bars and closed her eyes. Vicki hoped she had a concussion. The way she felt, if it wasn't that, it could only be something worse.

Vicki wasn't a decision maker; never had been. Decisions brought consequences which, as a rule, she detested. Both were better left to others. How then to decide what to do with her mind scrambled like an egg?

She staggered back to a courtyard she had to have passed to reach the gate (with no memory of having done so). All she knew was her head throbbed. She felt sick and dizzy. All she could do was stare at the ruins and wonder how she'd gotten there.

It was going to rain... *chats... et chiens*.

That was it! Vicki laughed sadly. She'd looked it up in a translation book earlier that day, or a month ago, or a year ago... It was going to rain... cats and dogs; *chats et chiens*. Her brain still worked – kind of. Vicki began to cry again.

Through her tears she saw that, with neither door nor roof, the castle wouldn't serve as a shelter. She needed shelter. And, Vicki realized, she needed to lie down.

Across the courtyard stood an old chapel with, thank God, a roof. She weaved toward it, stumbled up the steps, and against the door. A hasp and padlock frightened her at first but neither were in place. Grateful, but hurting, Vicki slipped inside.

She leaned heavily against the door shutting out the wind. Alone in the silence, her head swam. "Hello?" It was silly, she knew. There was nobody. "Hello?" Arms outstretched, she moved through the darkness. Vicki wasn't a churchgoer and didn't know one room from another. What she knew was it was dark and empty.

Two stained-glass windows were all that remained in a row near the ceiling along the far wall. The rest were boarded over. It didn't matter. The light was gone. Vicki's head battled her reason. Her pain crossed swords with her confusion, traded punches with her dizziness as she moved. "Help me," she cried out. The only answer was an echo.

She stumbled up three steps and came in contact with a flat surface - solid beneath her hands. A flash of lightning, rainbow tinted by the stained-glass, startled Vicki. She was standing at the altar beneath a huge crucified Christ. She laid her head on a big book, a Bible she imagined, and whispered, "Help me," to whoever heard prayers. "Please, help me." Then, sick and frightened, Vicki slid to the floor. She curled into a ball, closed her eyes and cried as a sea of dizziness lapped over her.

Socrates was a bundle of nerves. Loitering tourists and falling stones had left him behind time. On a night like this, with work yet to do there in the stable, that was nowhere to be. A storm in these hills was nothing to take lightly and the castle after nightfall was no place for a superstitious man.

By lamplight, Socrates mucked the soiled straw from Zorion's stall. Despite his haste, he whistled something (Verdi, perhaps, he didn't know) as if he had all the time in the world. It kept his mind off of the wafting ammonia. Then, with fresh bedding in place, he

led Zorion in as the clouds rumbled over-
head.

"I have no sugar, no apples," Socrates
said, patting the beast, "no way to thank
you for today's hard work. I am sorry, old
friend. And I am sorry for tomorrow, which
promises more of the same. Some day, Zorion, I would like to make it up to you."
Socrates bid his mule good night as he slid
the gate home. He carried the lamp out and
the stable, and his mule, fell into darkness.
As he secured the door, Socrates realized he
had been right, at least his knee and feet
were right, a storm was coming.

The caretaker used the chapel to store
tools and materials and secured the building with a padlock. He was already past,
watching the storm, when he realized he'd
forgotten to lock it. He hurried back.

Socrates had never heard of Vicki Kramer.
He had no notion she'd been attacked on
the property. He had no clue, as he started
home again, that he had just locked the unconscious young woman inside the chapel.

———+———

Socrates passed the chapel cemetery and
headed across the eastern field unable to
shake the unease which had been growing

on him all evening. It only intensified as he neared the Templar burial ground.

His wife, Annabella, a religious woman, was terrified of this graveyard. He'd tried for years to calm her fears, assuring her there was nothing left; the dusty bones of ancient Crusaders, a few weathered markers, a rusted fence. She called it The Devil's Bed, the unholy resting place of Satan's servants. She warned him away. Socrates, while not a man of God, was superstitious and, more to the point, knew better than to disobey his wife. He routinely passed the cemetery in a wide arc, eyes averted, whistling or humming as the mood struck, until he reached the timber separating him from his home. Tonight his nerves precluded a tune and his agitation had him all but running for the trees.

The thunderstorm that had threatened all evening was nearly upon him. A bank of fog had settled on the ground. Strange that a fog should appear with a storm. *Bein*, Annabella's Lord worked in mysterious ways.

Socrates was grateful to see his cottage as he left the timber. A weight lifted from his shoulders as he passed safely through his gate. Though he didn't know why, this was one night he would be glad to put behind him. Then he heard a sound that sent a chill up his spine.

He stared to the west, to the timber and the Templar cemetery, to the castle and the storm, and caught his breath. Was it his imagination? Was it the wind? Or was he hearing the tolling of bells?

———†———

Socrates entered the cottage and was accosted by his wife.

Annabella was country stock, muscular yet feminine, small on top, wide at the hips. She was attractive, without beauty, and had a deadly wit but rarely smiled. She popped from the kitchen, wet hands strangling her apron, declared, "You're late," and disappeared like a cuckoo clock figurine.

"My boots?" Socrates barked.

"I washed them," she called from the kitchen. "You don't need your boots."

"I need them. Minotte is hungry."

"*En vérité.* You don't need them. Minotte is not hungry."

"Minotte is always hungry," he said, feeling abused.

Socrates, by his own admission, was a man battered by life. An estate caretaker in his native Portugal, he immigrated to Paradis with hopes and dreams. He met and married Annabella. They had a lovely daughter each called 'my Marthe' and a troublesome son each called 'your Luis'. With his life's savings, Socrates planted a vineyard in anticipation of owning one of the great French wineries. Of course, the land was wrong and disease destroyed the grapevines. Annabella, ever an optimist, convinced Socrates to try again.

After hearing 'she beat thirteen dogs and two other pigs in her last hunt', he bought Minotte, an eight-year-old champion pig truffle hunter. He purchased a membership in, and proudly wore the medal of, the *Confrérie de la Truffe Noire* (the Brotherhood of the Black Truffle). Of course, the land was as wrong for truffles as it had been for grapes. Annabela resigned herself. Socrates was a good man, but there would always be an 'of course'.

So, a lifetime later, Anibal Socrates was a caretaker again. Of course, he was. He was a man battered by life.

"I've already fed Minotte."

"Why would you feed Minotte?" Socrates asked, feeling slighted.

"You were not here. I fed her."

"Why didn't Luis feed her? Where is your lazy son?"

"What difference your son? Minotte is fed! I was beginning to wonder if you were coming home." Annabella popped from the kitchen again and saw the distress on his face. "Anibal. . . what's the matter?"

"Strange." Socrates removed his hat and coat, ran his hand through his thinning hair. "As I came through the gate, I could have sworn. . . I heard the bells ringing."

"The bells? What bells?

"The chapel bells."

Annoyance twisted her lips. "Have you been drinking?"

"Of course I have not been drinking!"

"Of course."

She disappeared again and Socrates felt foolish. He returned to the door, summoned his courage and pulled it open. Leaves skittered in on a gusting wind and he tightened his grip on the door. The night sky rolled with black-green clouds. He blinked as he stared into the storm, listening. "Can you hear anything?" A bolt of lightning flashed and thunder cracked. "Annabella, can you hear anything?"

"*Oui*," she called from her kitchen. "I hear a storm. Close the door before we blow away. Get washed for supper."

Eight

The storm brewed violently; the wind, thunder and lightning acting as winds, percussion and pageantry for a nightmarish opera. And in the distance, evidence Socrates was correct; somber chapel bells were ringing.

The fog swirled through the ruins of Castle Freedom, over its grounds, and into the Templar graveyard. It enveloped the sarcophagi, settled over the flat tombs, and turned dirt, moss and decay to a clammy slime on the cut stone.

There arose a grating sound. The stone lid of the blood-stained sarcophagus began slowly to slide open. Though it took some time, a gap of several inches opened. A skeletal hand, gray and decayed, slid through the breach from within. It flexed and took hold of the covering. It pushed slowly gaining space. A second hand appeared. They tugged and, as lightning flashed, the covering slid free, fell at an angle to the tomb and thudded on the ground.

Beneath the rolling black and green clouds, the lightning struck again, laying bare the face and form of the mummy within the tomb. His eyes snapped open revealing two flaming red orbs in what was virtually a skull; parched skin stretched over the orbital bones, sunken cheeks bracketing two black holes – all that remained of the nose. A long pepper and salt beard hung limp, matted with dirt beneath a grinning set of teeth, stained with Vicki's blood, in gumless jaws.

The seven hundred-year-old mummy gasped, sucking in a chest full of air. The Templar breathed fitfully, a hideous chorus of occlusion, that slowly settled to regular respirations. The knight sat up in his grave. He grabbed the edges of the sarcophagus, stood unsteadily, and stepped over and out of the tomb. The Templar lost his balance and fell to his knees with the crunch of ancient bone and the sing-song chink of rusted metal. He pushed himself up from the weeds and stood beside the grave.

The knight's knee-length hauberk of chain mail showed, at his head and arms, beneath the white mantle of his Order, burned, rotted by time, filthy from the grave. A leather belt sagged at his waist bearing a sheathed sword on his left hip and a dagger on his right. Over all, reaching to his feet, he wore a sleeveless, hooded white surcoat emblazoned with a red cross; the Templar arms.

Tall and thin, the mummy cocked his head staring through the flashes of lightning at the lid of the tomb crooked against the grave. He studied the inscribed threats and accusations. Then his red eyes crossed the name chiseled there: Francois de Raiis.

Yes, that was... who he was – long ago.

From a distance, beneath the building storm, carried faintly on the wind, came a familiar sound. He rose to his full height and cocked his head, listening. His sense of hearing, it seemed, was amazingly acute for he clearly heard – a woman crying. It was a sound he remembered and relished.

The Templar knight started away, fumbling at first, then gaining composure. He found the gate, petrified with rust, and yanked it open. Then he shambled from the cemetery and was swallowed by the fog.

———†———

Vicki awoke in pain, screaming from a nightmare, her cheeks stained, nose running, head throbbing - to what sounded like church bells. Alone in the dark, she struggled up using the altar for support. A lightning strike flooded the chapel with a rainbow burst of light. As it faded, Vicki eased herself around a waist-high wooden rail, down the sanctuary steps, to the floor.

Shuffling more than walking, using the rail for balance, she moved past the sanctuary, straining her eyes and listening to the reverberations as her shoes sanded the stone floor. She reached a doorway, fumbled a lighter from her pocket and flicked it to life. The soft light displayed a long hallway with intermittent closed doors and an alcove with stairs heading up. Beyond the lighter's range the hall disappeared into nothingness. She burned her thumb and the light went out.

Her head rang on a downbeat to the bells. She fought nausea as her stomach rolled with the thunder. She sucked her aching thumb. "Is anyone here?" Only her echo.

"I'm hurt!" Vicki screamed with what strength she could muster. She held the sides of her head and began to cry again. "Please, please! I'm hurt!" Again the echo.

It faded leaving only the wind, the bells, and the darkness.

Beneath the lightning strikes and rolls of thunder, the leather soles of the Templar's boots snicked on the stones as he strode into the courtyard. His hooded cloak danced on the wind like a malevolent spirit.

The knight halted as the chapel bells ceased their ringing.

He cocked his head to listen. Faintly he heard the voice again. Still crying, but speaking now as well. The first human voice he had heard in seven hundred years. A female voice, crying, "Please, please! I'm hurt!"

———————

Vicki's pleas received no reply. Only echoes.

And the wind. And the bells. She thought she might go mad from the bells. Until the ringing stopped. Then she realized how wrong she'd been. While they were ringing, even had it been the Devil pulling the rope, it felt as if someone were there. Now, in the silence, with only the wind and the darkness, Vicki felt truly alone.

She'd strained her eyes and felt her way across the chapel back to the door, she thought, through which she'd entered. But she must have been mistaken for it was locked from the outside. Vicki leaned on the door, crying again, and now did nothing to stem the tide. She wanted her brother, Ray. She wanted her best friend, Brandy. She was frightened, alone and in pain. If anyone had reason to cry surely she did.

Images flashed in his brain, jarring, quick, loud. A descent into hell. A preceding death. An earlier life. Battle. Blood. A woman's tears. A memory. Memories. Once, in life, tears had meant something; happiness, tenderness. Later those same tears spelled pain and sorrow. Then came the great awakening, after which a woman's tears were nothing more than a part of things dark and delicious. Dark and oh, so... delicious, Francois de Raiis thought, as rain began lightly to fall.

The Templar drew his dagger and followed the caterwauling across the courtyard to the chapel.

Vicki wiped the tears from her eyes. Enough was enough.

She was locked in. That was bad but it could have been worse. She had other concerns, like not dying from her head injury and, as she could hear the rain, and was grateful being dry, finding a way to stay warm as well. Then getting real sleep until help arrived. No, Vicki decided, as she fought for mental clarity, she wouldn't entertain any other thought. Help would arrive in the morning.

She flicked her lighter, throwing dancing shadows across the walls. She was in a chapel vestibule; shouldn't there be candles somewhere about?

She found a mirror, placed it on a small table against the wall and brushed away the dust. Her reflection startled, bloodshot and swollen eyes, tear-streaked cheeks, hair matted with dirt and gore. She looked as bad as she felt.

Then came a metallic scrape at the door. And again!

She realized someone was trying the latch. "Hello," she shouted. "Help me!" The lighter went out as Vicki stumbled to the door. "I'm locked in. Please help me!" A breathless beat passed. Vicki heard it again - metal on metal. Somebody was fiddling with the lock; metal on wood as the hasp was wrenched free.

"Oh, God. Thank God!"

She struggled with the latch from her side. She yanked the door open, falling back to the floor with the effort. Breathless, Vicki looked up. Lightning flashed - turning her rescuer into a silhouette.

"Thank God," Vicki shouted despite being blinded.

Thunder rolled. The darkness returned. Vicki lifted her lighter as she tried to rise. She struck the flint. The flame revealed her rescuer, the bearded, hooded, hideous walking corpse of a Templar knight. Vicki screamed, dropped the lighter and plunged the vestibule back into darkness.

The Templar raised his dagger and, without ceremony, drove it down and into Vicki's right breast. In one mingled sound, she screamed in horror, grunted in pain and gasped for breath. The knight tugged, extracting the blade, and watched with pleasure as she fell back to the floor.

The cold rain fell as the Templar returned to his ancient burial site with Vicki in his arms. She was still alive. By design, the knight had thrust his dagger through her right lung, collapsing it and disabling her. She had another - for all the good it would do her.

Inside the cemetery, the mummy dropped Vicki. She groaned on the ground at his feet. The knight ignored her. He stared across the plot at the six graves between his sarcophagus and the other; Francois de Raiis' six most loyal knights, executed with him, fellow worshippers of the dark One.

Raiis advanced to the grave nearest his own. He read the name and remembered the faithful Geoffrey de Charney. Charney had been the able student of the Order's Grand Master when they'd met. What a delicious pleasure it had been leading him astray,

77

corrupting his faith, and bringing him to the altar of the Unholy. Charney, faithful to their dark lord and to him at the terrible end, had earned a new beginning.

Raiis grabbed the lid of Charney's tomb in his boney fingers and, with unnatural strength, threw it off - revealing the mummified knight within. He moved to the next grave, that of Henri Ethelbert, and tossed the lid open with the scrape of stone and a scurry of spiders. The Templar leader broke the ancient seal on the next and shoved the shrieking lid away, exposing the dried corpse of their chaplain, Benoit Lambert. Then he attended the remaining in-ground tombs, those of his last three executed disciples. The stone lids cried out as he shoved each aside and the remains of Louis Godenot, Jules Lefebvre, and Gaston Morel stared sightlessly up into the rain.

Raiis backed into the other raised sarcophagus; the only tomb in the cemetery free of the inscribed curses. The Templar stared at the engraved name with furious red eyes then turned away leaving the tomb sealed.

Vicki cried out when the mummy lifted her again but was unable to offer any resistance. He carried her to the first tomb, held her over the opened grave and, ignoring her scream, ripped her throat open with his teeth. Her blood spilled onto the mummified corpse. The Templar attended each of the tombs alike; splashing Vicki's blood on the faces and into the mouths of the long-dead knights. He reached the eighth, the unopened sarcophagus, and again ignored it. Then he dumped Vicki's body on the ground.

Francois de Raiis, his rotted cloak flying in the wind, watched the opened graves as the thunder rolled, the lightning struck, and the rain fell. And listened as, spurred by evil, the chapel bells at Castle Freedom began to toll again.

Socrates yanked the cottage door open and stared out into the rain. He stepped into the wind and scanned the dark. He saw nothing; but he heard it. "There! The bells!" he called into his house. "Do you hear them now?" His eyes were wide with a triumph that out-weighed his fear. "Drinking, *hein*? I did not imagine it! The bells are ringing!"

Socrates disappeared into the cottage.

A moment later, carrying shotgun and coat, his hat askew, he reemerged into the wind and rain. He stared west, listening between gusts and thunder crashes, to the ominous peels riding the waves of the storm. He threw on his coat.

"Anibal!"

His wife and daughter were in the doorway watching Socrates with fear in their eyes. Annabella tore herself from Marthe and ran to her husband. Desperately, she grabbed his coat, bringing him around to face her. "Anibal, you can't go up there!"

"I must. It is my job."

She grabbed his cheeks, wiped the rain from his brow, pleading in genuine terror, "There is... something... evil up there."

"Oh, silly." He kissed one of her chore-worn hands. "You're going to catch cold in the rain." She showed no sign of returning to the cottage and his smile faded. "There are trouble makers up there. I won't have trouble."

"Don't go alone. At least take Luis with you."

His eyes darkened. He shook his head. "I haven't seen your lazy son all night. I won't look for him now."

He started through the gate. Marthe joined her mother; braced her in the wind. "We'll pray for you," Annabella called out. He seemed not to hear her and she repeated it shouting against the storm. "We'll pray for you!"

Socrates smiled and waved. He pointed to the dark woods and the castle beyond with his shotgun, shouting, "Pray for them!" He laughed and disappeared into the stormy darkness. His laughter floated on the air like a ghost. Then it too was gone.

———

The chapel bells rang eerily in the distance. The lightning flashed, the rain fell around Francois de Raiis. The resurrected Templar watched as the corpses of his knights jerked, heaved and flexed their way back to life - awakened by Vicki's blood.

The first was surreal in underarmor, haubergen *maille*, white mantle, a hooded surcoat and, emblazened across his chest, the red cross that was the Templar coat of arms. He stretched from Louis Godenot's grave and wobbled like a marionette. Then he lifted a helmet from his filthy tomb and, risking comic absurdity, donned it over his mail coif like a gentleman stepping out.

The others followed, each emaciated like Raiis and Godenot, gray, rotted flesh over skeletal frames with shining red eyes gleaming from grinning skull-like heads, wearing, to varying degrees, the uniform of their Order; with and without underarmor, with and without mail, with and without helms, but all with the Templars' mandatory mantle, cross and full-length surcoat. But, as theirs was a bastardization of life, so their uniforms were a bastardization of the glory of the Order. Each was burned, rotted, covered in the dirt and decay of seven centuries in the grave.

Benoit Lambert, the only knight in a brown mantle, had in life been their chaplain and was responsible for their spiritual well-being. Death, and this unearthly return to life, had not changed that. His face still splashed in Vicki's rejuvenating blood, Lambert lifted his clawed hands and began to pray – albeit not to God.

"*Diabolus, meus Senior.*" His atrophied vocal chords, restored by Black Magic, produced a frightening gurgle. "*Quod three everto in Hierarchies' of Abyssus. Lucifer, Diabolus, quisnam to order totus. Beelzebub, procer of seraphim, quisnam tempero men per superbia. Leviathan, quisnam tempero men per heresies quod sins repugnant unto fides. Sonneillon, procer of cado cherubin, quisnam tempero men per odium obviam suum hostilis. Tribuo nos vox. Plumbum nos in victoria super nostrum hostilis.*"

As motion returned to their corpses, each Templar left his grave and fell into ranks before their resurrector. Raiis, beaming with evil pride, his boney hand caressing the hilt of his sword, nodded his approval and started out of the ancient cemetery.

On his heels, Lambert began a low pitched, ritualistic chant that the knights, in unison, joined in singing as they followed in horrific parade.

"Laus Lucifer, unde totus bona flow.
Laus Him totus creatura hic in Terra.
Laus Him supremus minions of Abyssus.
Ut is eram secundum cado, est iam quod umquam vadum exsisto,
universitas saecula saeculorum.
Laus Him. Laus Him."

They disappeared into the storm leaving behind seven empty graves, one undisturbed tomb and, in the weeds beside it, the bloodless body of Vicki Kramer.

Socrates wasn't certain. With the wind bending the trees, whistling through the timber, repeatedly slamming the shutter on his barn's loft (behind) and howling through the fissures in the castle ruins (ahead), with wet leaves flying in autumn's take on a blizzard, with the rain falling and the thunder rolling... how could he be certain?

But now, on top of the bells, Socrates thought he heard singing!

He took Annabella's arc, passed the unhallowed graveyard away to the south, humming, eyes averted, and continued to the castle. This, no doubt, protected his soul. But it prevented his seeing the Templar cemetery had been disturbed... and from realizing that all of the graves, save one, were now empty.

Normally, the Annabella-inspired dread fell away once past the cemetery. The walk across the open field usually charmed; the flowers, tall grasses, and wildlife, leading to the serenity of the old cemetery, the apse and pitched roof of the chapel, the bell tower beyond and, in the distance, the remains of the keep against the morning sky. Normally, approaching the castle from his cottage was a comfort. But not now.

There was the storm. And being near the castle at night was unpleasant. But he'd been wet and windblown before. He'd been on the grounds in the dark as well. No. It was the vandals and their foolishness that was making him uneasy. What were they doing and why? Even under the rain he could hear bells - and that made no sense. And he could still hear them singing, or was it chanting, louder now. None of it made any sense. Socrates gripped his shotgun tightly as he passed the cemetery, rounded the chapel and entered the courtyard.

Then, as if someone had thrown a switch, everything ceased. The chanting, the bells, even the rain stopped. Only the wind remained; white noise adding presence to the sudden otherworldly silence.

Ten

Socrates scanned the courtyard, from the drive that vanished into darkness on its way to the main gate, past the castle ruin, across the ghost-like blur of out-buildings, to the chapel on his right.

"What the hell?" he muttered.

The chapel door stood open. Of all the property on the castle grounds, it was the last door that should have been bothered by the wind. It was new, designed to look old, with a good latch. And he remembered clearly having backtracked to lock it. He pointed his shotgun at the door and ordered whoever was inside to come out. There followed neither stirring nor reply. He shouted again and, switching from French to Portuguese, a third time.

The caretaker cautiously climbed the three short steps and approached the door. He peered into the darkness and called again, but now his fear was audible. Sensing something at his feet, Socrates crouched to examine the threshold. "Mother of God!" He jumped back. Congealing there, inside the door, was a pool of blood.

Then the chanting started.

Socrates moved back into the courtyard. The sound was in front of him, then behind, then all around. Socrates crossed himself and squeezed the shotgun with white bloodless hands.

The chanting grew louder. A tall figure emerged from the shadows in a dirty white hooded wrap. He shrugged the cloak open, revealing a soiled tunic with a red cross, a thick leather belt and what looked to be a sword. His skeletal left hand rested on the hilt. His right drew back the stiff linen hood.

The caretaker gasped. The Templar knight (that's how he was dressed), the thing before him, had the face of a skull with stretched gray skin, a ragged beard, and eyes blazing with hellfire from deep sockets.

There was another flash of lightning, another roll of thunder. The demonic chanting continued and Socrates' heart raced. A snick of leather and metal on stone forced him around. A second moldering knight emerged from the shadows. And then they came, one by one, from the shadows. Four, no five, more Templars – chanting in Latin – as they surrounded him. Socrates gasped; his mind reeling.

Then logic took over. Surely what he was seeing was not real. The legends were rubbish. There was no such thing as – the living dead. His fear became anger as he realized they were making a fool of him. There were no ghosts. But there were delinquents. "Who the hell are you?" he demanded.

In answer, the first Templar drew his sword.

Those who knew Socrates would agree that was a mistake. His face flushed with rage. He leveled his shotgun and fired.

The blast hit the knight in the chest. Dust spattered into the air while shrapnel of corroded mail links bounced on the courtyard stones. The front of the knight's tunic was peppered with holes. The Templar casually surveyed the damage.

The others, quieted by the attack, stared – then started chanting again.

The caretaker's anger was gone. He trembled. From behind came a strange noise. Then his eyes flared wide – with shock – as a dagger penetrated the nape of his neck. The handle guard sank to his hair line while the blade passed through his throat; the tip showing beneath his elevated chin. He made an effort to scream but failed. Choking on blood, and the weapon, Socrates dropped to his knees.

The chanting Templar horde descended upon Socrates. He struggled uselessly as they bit into his flesh and drank his blood.

———✝———

Mules, unfairly reputed to be stubborn, were actually intelligent creatures that refused to be put in harm's way. Zorion was feeling abandoned; in danger. The storm startled him and he moved unsteadily in his stall. Then came the chants, the screams, a shot, carried on the wind. Whether or not he recognized them, Zorion feared them, and cried; a whinny growing to a desperate hee-haw.

A bolt of lightning struck near the stable. The explosion terrified Zorion. He kicked, blasting wooden slats from his stall. The whimpering cries of the mule were carried on the swirling winds.

In the courtyard the Templars heard them. Raiis lifted himself from Socrates' corpse, his mouth and chin bathed in blood, and located the new sound. He started for the stable and his knights followed.

The Templars approached, forced the south door and poured into the stable. What happened next only God and the Devil knew. It may have been so evil even the Deity turned away, leaving Satan the only witness.

A long metallic scrape was repeated seven times as the dark knights drew their swords. Zorion cried, terrified whinnies, whimpering hee-haws, and kicked his stall. Then the stable went silent while the chapel bells again began tolling.

The fog churned round the building. The deep throated chanting of the Templars began anew. What happened then was unbelievable and absolutely impossible. Yet, it happened all the same. The chants faded beneath a series of nerve-rending demonic screams that just as suddenly evolved into the whinnying of horses. And the Templars rode out.

The living mummy of Francois de Raiis led the way. He ducked as he burst through the fog and cleared the threshold mounted on a saddled horse. The animal was real - bone, blood, sinew, snorting, whinnying on the move. At the same time it was dead - with dried skin stretched over atrophied yet magically flexing muscle. A four-legged creature in the image of a steed somehow called up from the deepest pits of hell. A machination of unchecked evil. Like its rider, the horse was suited in worn and rusted armor, blanketed and hooded in rotted linen and leather moldering from the grave, and fitted with the ancient accoutrement of war.

Their leader cleared the doorway. Their chaplain followed immediately behind. Lambert too sat aboard an undead mount. He carried the standard of their Order, a golden cross atop a long wooden staff, depending through the crook of his arm along the side of his horse. It glinted as the lightning flashed.

The others trailed their leaders in rank, each aboard a hellish, mummified mount, weighed down with the armaments used by that knight in life. A pistol crossbow and quiver of bolts hung from Charney's saddle while, over his shoulder, the knight carried a compound bow of wood, bone and sinew. An assorted cache of daggers were tied to Ethelbert's saddle and he wore one on each hip matching his long sword. They continued to pour from the stable, through the swirling fog, like water through a burst dam. Godenot emerged clutching a halberd spear. The living mummy of Lefebvre, spiked maces on his saddle, raised his arm as he cleared the door and cut a swath through the fog with a black iron flail. Morel brought up the rear hoisting a battle hammer aloft as if threatening the heavens. Free of the stable, the knights reined their mounts in around their leader.

Raiis steadied his horse, if it could be called that, and cocked his head to listen. On the wind he heard the comical sound of women – praying. What could be more blessed, or delicious, then the destruction of God's children in prayer!

Raiss spurred his mount, rode away from the stable and across the courtyard. The others gouged theirs and followed. They rounded the chapel and passed its cemetery. Across the field, the horses found their stride and thundered like the wind. As they rode, the sky, which until that evil moment had only been teasing, split open and poured rain in a cold deluge.

The bloodthirsty Templars rode past their own tombs and into the dark timber.

Annabella Socrates was terribly frightened. Her husband was gone. Luis, their son, was... Heaven knew where. She and Marthe were alone; praying for Anibal's safe return.

Marthe ploddingly repeated her mother's prayer, rolling her rosary beads between bored fingers and wishing she were upstairs listening to music. "Glory be to the Father, and to the Son and to the Holy Ghost. As it was in the beginning, is now, and ever shall be, world without end. Amen."

The rain drubbed, harder now, on the cottage roof. The thunder rolled in the distance. Then came a new sound; the stamp of approaching. . .

"Horses!" Marthe exclaimed. She tried to rise but her mother grabbed her. Annabella pointed at her prayer book. "Hail Mary, full of grace, the Lord is with thee."

It wasn't fair ignoring horses. How often anymore did you get to see horses?

"Blessed art thou among women, and blessed is the fruit of thy womb, Jesus. Holy Mary, Mother of God, pray for us sinners, now and at the hour of our death. Amen."

"Mother, aren't we going to see to the riders?" She could clearly hear the horses had come to a stop outside. Their riders were, no doubt, dismounting at that very moment. "They're here! Mother?"

Annabella looked up with terror in her eyes.

Eleven

Luis Socrates awoke with a start.

He bolted up, struggling for cognition, his mind afumble. A moment elapsed before he was fully in touch with his surroundings. Happily, he found everything as it should be. He was in the hay loft of the old barn; his home away from home. The loose shutter on the loft door was banging and the assault on the tin roof told him the rain had come in buckets. He was wondering what awakened him when Luis heard... something. Horses? And... something more. Chanting?

Luis lifted his little worn black book, his constant companion, his Shakespeare, from the hay where it'd fallen and slid it into his back pocket. He climbed from his loft bed, took hold of the bale rope, and swung out over the floor of the barn. Luis hung there, allowing the rope to quiet in the ancient block, then shimmied down. He eased the barn door ajar and found he was right.

A group of horses stood outside their small yard fence. What sorry looking animals they were; gray and skeletal, wrapped in rotted blankets, hoods and (he doubted his own eyes) heavy with armor and weaponry. He'd been right about the chanting too. Luis heard it now, even louder, somewhere out of view.

He hurried to a window on the other side of the barn, scrubbed the cobwebs away with his sleeve and, keeping low, peered out. Luis wondered if he was still asleep and having a nightmare. Armed knights, wearing red crosses, their faces as rotted as their cloaks, were gathered at the cottage door. Templars. The word came quickly; its meaning more slowly. *"Mon Dieu,"* Luis whispered breathlessly. Their front stoop was thick with chanting, mold-covered Templar knights!

Though his parents never spoke of them, or their legendary curse, he'd seen their whispered reactions to the subject all his life. His crazy father, caretaker of the Templars' ruined castle, averting his eyes like a child whenever he passed their graves. His mother crossing herself and showing the evil eye at their mention. The very name of the Order forbidden in a house that lived off of them. A hysteria. A hypocrisy. A bogey story.

Now a nightmare... come to life.

"Our Father, who art in heaven, hallowed be thy name. Thy kingdom come. Thy will be done..."

Something heavy slammed against the cottage door above the latch. The metal was rent, the jamb splintered and cracked. The wood shuddered as the frame gave way and the door exploded inward.

From her knees before the hearth, Annabella refused to look. She tightened the grip on her rosary and on Marthe's arm. Marthe couldn't help but look. She stared in disbelief at the armored corpses flooding the doorway and cried aloud from the pain of her mother's hold. Terrified, Annabella could think of nothing but prayer. "On earth as it is in heaven. Give us this day our daily bread."

The Templars ceased their chanting. Rain-soaked and stinking of the grave, they moved into the cottage intent on their own sustenance.

Marthe pulled free of her mother and backed away screaming.

Annabella clamped her eyes shut and gripped her rosary so tightly her fingers turned white. She prayed, as quickly as she was able, spitting out the 'Our Father' as if reaching the end was the key to their survival. "And forgive us our trespasses, as we forgive those who trespass against us."

Marthe, neither looking for forgiveness nor handing it out, ran for the stairs screaming. One of the Templar mummies broke from the group after her.

Annabella, eyes pinched, tears streaming, realized she was not going to win the race. Still, she forced the words, "And lead us not into temptation, but deliver us from. . ." Evil, the last word of the prayer, became a horrified scream and, in turn, a tortured groan as a knight shoved his sword through her back.

Marthe reached the top of the stairs, and could see her bedroom door, when the decayed hand of the Templar seized her ankle. He yanked her to the floor and dragged her, bouncing and screaming, back down to rejoin the horror show. Marthe kicked, screamed and, when the Templar grabbed her hair, dug her nails into the dead flesh of his hand. The knight drew the hammer from his belt and, as he'd often done throughout the Crusades, brought it down with all his might. Marthe's scream was silenced.

The Templars, like suckling pigs, swarmed Annabella. Ignoring her cries, they stabbed her, ripped at her clothes and began viciously biting her.

At the foot of the stairs, the lone Templar did the same. He fell on Marthe, unconscious but breathing, and sank his teeth into her throat. A fountain of blood arced and the Templar sated his thirst.

Luis watched the Templars bust in. He heard the screams of his mother and sister. Yet he'd been too terrified to move. Now he forced himself, on wobbling legs, to slip from the barn and quietly move past the open front door to a window at the side of the cottage. He peered through and was stricken with horror.

The Templars had his mother on the floor before the fire. They were biting her, stabbing her, drinking her blood. He saw his sister's feet at the foot of the stairs and the boots of one of the knights. One of those on his mother left that horde, drew a blade, and joined the knight killing Marthe. The screams subsided, replaced by the sounds of the living corpses feeding in grotesque satisfaction. Luis inhaled to stave off being sick.

One of the Templars suddenly raised his head, blood dripping from his mouth into his matted beard. Luis froze. The Templar rose to his feet, wiped the blood from his lips and licked his boney fingers. He cocked his head; listening.

The others joined him revealing Annabella on the floor. Her partially naked body was torn and smeared with blood. Her sightless eyes stared; her mouth was locked in a silent scream.

Luis gasped. He saw the Templars react and realized he'd been heard. Only then did it dawn how quickly, loudly he was breathing. He shuddered and held his breath.

The bloody knights stood still; waiting – listening.

Luis held his breath until he thought he would explode. And, as he stood in terror, wondering what to do, despite the storm, he heard the rapid beating of his own heart. He peered through the window again. . . and that same heart nearly stopped. The Templar leader was staring at him.

The knight pointed dried phalanges through the window at Luis. The others followed his hand. One in the group opened blood drenched lips and croaked an alarm. The last two, still-feasting, abandoned Marthe. They rose, dripping blood, and added their stares of hatred and lust.

Luis couldn't swallow, couldn't breathe. With a strength of will he didn't know he possessed, he forced himself to move. He pushed away from the window and ran.

The Templars, spattered with blood, poured from the cottage. They mounted up and, lit by flashes of lightning, spurred their horses into motion. Two knights, reeling with delight from Marthe's virgin blood, were last to their horses and last to disappear into the timber after the terrified Luis.

The rain fell in a downpour; blasted by lightning and thunder.

Luis raced through the timber; twisting, leaping over fallen limbs. Fern leaves and briars bit his ankles, low hanging branches scratched his face and hands as if he were running a gauntlet. His tennis shoes grew heavy with mud. His clothes grabbed, clung to him, weighted by the freezing rain. He panted for breath, overheating at the core, while his arms and legs turned to gooseflesh from cold and fear. Behind, he heard the whinnying screams, the heavy hoof beats, the snapping foliage as the knights on their horses raced through the timber.

The off-trail brush was thick, tough going, and he stopped to catch his breath. A lightning strike and, through the icy silver darts of rain, he saw one of the Templars closing. Luis screamed. The monster drew a weapon, something like a hammer, and spurred his mount.

Luis, running, looked back again as the lightning flashed through the trees. The Templar was upon him, his horse – as dead as its rider – kicking up water. Luis dove from his path as the knight swung the heavy iron hammer; pick out. Despite the raging downpour, the slosh of mud and wet leaves, the snapping dead fall beneath his feet, Luis heard with crystal clarity the whistle and swoosh as the hammer narrowly missed his head. He hit the wet ground face first.

He lifted his face to breathe and blinked through a mask of dripping mud. The Templar, trying to recover from the swing and readjust in his saddle, dropped his reins. The horse, unguided, raced headlong toward a massive fallen branch jutting from the ground at the base of a grizzled tree. The horse jumped. The Templar came undone in the saddle. Propelled up and forward with terrific velocity, the hurtling knight met the end of a low-hanging branch. The Templar howled as the limb tore spear-like through him, his cloak and mantle, hauberk and gambeson, dried flesh and ancient bone, and jutted from his back. The knight was transfixed on the branch. A puff of dust escaped the wound and was quickly knocked down by the rain. His riderless horse disappeared whinnying into the blackness of the soaked timber.

Luis scraped his eyes with muddier fingers and watched in horror as the impaled knight kicked. He let his hammer fall with a splash to the swamped floor of the timber and, using both hands, wriggled in vain to free himself from the branch.

Luis sat, momentarily stunned, up to his hips in mud and up to his chest in wet undergrowth and downfall. The rain fell, even through the thick trees, in sheets. It ran down his matted hair in rivers. He scrubbed his hands on his pants then ran one over his eyes, like a wiper blade, tossing off the excess water. Again he found himself staring at the knight; hypnotized by the grotesque sight.

It... he... was still alive (what passed for life), flailing and writhing on the tree limb. He... it... screamed, hatred and frustration meeting in a voice roiling up from the depths of a hell Luis never imagined existed. But the rain, coming even harder, muted it and the frequent eruptions of thunder drowned it out altogether.

Or was it thunder? It continued; deep, booming. Luis was suddenly shaken from his trance. Though thunder still highlighted the storm, he realized now that was not what he was hearing. It was hoof beats.

Twelve

The other Templars were still in the timber, on horseback, searching for him.

With a great splash of water Luis jumped to his feet and, in the dark and rain, ran. Around trees, through soggy leaves, over fallen limbs, through mud, in the torrential downpour, he ran. He cleared the timber and raced, as fast as his sodden feet would carry him, past the Templar burial ground and into the field beyond. Behind him, Luis heard the Templar riders break through the trees in pursuit. Ahead lay the chapel and castle grounds. He fought for breath and ran.

With his mother and sister dead, and his father missing, the panicked Luis could think of nowhere else to go. It may have been the knights' ancient stronghold, but he'd been raised there. He crossed the open field, through the rain and lightning flashes, saw the cemetery and chapel, and knew the castle was right ahead. He neared the graveyard and began to feel a sense of relief. Then he made the mistake of looking back.

One of the Templars, a spiked ball twirling murderously above his head, was in front and gaining on him. Luis yelled, cut right – as the mounted knight was upon him – and raced into the chapel cemetery.

The Templar's horse reached the boundary of the hallowed ground, whinnied in horror, and planted its hooves in the spongy ground. The animal lowered its head, as the knight flew from his saddle, then veered away wanting nothing to do with the graveyard.

Luis dove between grave stones to avoid the hurtling Templar. He slid, rolled through a puddle and came to his feet as the knight smacked a marker head on. Luis watched, aghast but unable to tear his eyes away. And the words flooded into his head:

> Now it is the time of night
> that the graves all gaping wide,
> every one lets forth his sprite,
> in the church-ways paths to glide. . . .

Luis doubted this was the sprite his beloved Shakespeare had in mind.

No sooner did the Templar's body splash to a stop in the 'church-way path' than it began undulating like bacon on a griddle. The knight came off the ground, its mouth spread as wide as the dead flesh allowed. What passed for a scream in the realm of the hellish creature blasted the night.

Luis was suddenly the farthest thing from its mind. The knight dove for the high grass outside of the cemetery as if trying to escape a pool of acid. The screaming ceased when it landed back in the field and smoke billowed from beneath its chain mail as the mummy rolled on the wet ground.

The other Templars had arrived and rode the perimeter of the cemetery. They made no attempt to enter. They reined in their horses, and fought to stay in their saddles, as the nervous animals reared trying to throw them off.

Luis huddled beneath a monument, a whispering winged angel holding a cross, and watched the circling horses and their damned riders through the rain. He had to get out of there. Luis left the angel and serpentined through the tombstones, eyes darting from one knight to another, as he made his way toward the chapel. The Templars couldn't get near. That, Luis hoped, would give him time. He reached the far end, burst from the graveyard, and ran for the castle.

The Templars, forced to skirt the cemetery, kicked ancient spurs into the atrophied haunches of their mounts and took off after him.

Exhausted, terrified and weighed down by soaked clothes, Luis stumbled into the flooded courtyard where the rain, thudding on the wet ground, turned to high-pitched snaps as it hit the stones. He slipped and slid on his face throwing up a huge wave. Blinded by freezing water, near drowned, Luis struggled back to his feet. Beneath him, blood fanned out across the water like paint splashed in a pool – and he couldn't understand why. Until he saw the mutilated body of his father. Luis screamed, and kept screaming until he thought his mind had snapped.

Then he saw the knights ride into the courtyard and, with a herculean effort, got control of himself. He ran across the courtyard in the raging storm as the mounted demons gained on him. He reached the wall of the castle ruin, backed against the wet stone and, with nowhere to go, watched as the Templars dismounted. They started toward him with raised weapons. Luis moved down the wall, his eyes trained on the advancing mummies. The faster he backed away, the faster the undead knights came on.

All the troubles of a short and misspent life, the regrets, the pains, and the accumulated horrors of this one night raced toward him and all Luis could do was scream.

Thirteen

It was unfortunate that, on such a bright morning, Brandy's thoughts should be so trained upon darkness. She awoke to discover her future sister-in-law still missing. Which may or may not have led to an early argument (all right, it was a fight) with Ray. He'd already spent the night on the couch so she felt justified discounting it. A fight was inevitable. Either way, when they started their search for Vicki later that morning, darkness hung over both.

Brandy wasn't at all surprised to find that 'dark' was the only word to describe Marcel Fournier. You could use others. Short, thin, muscular, curled black hair, olive skin, a groomed mustache... None of it mattered. Fournier was dark. And in questioning the tour business owner, Brandy and Ray gained nothing but a feeling of dread.

"Already I have told you," Fournier growled, "the guide he is off today." He fell back into his chair, thumped his shoes on the desk and resumed hurling darts at a cork board on the office wall. "I cannot help you."

"Is there anyone who can?" Brandy asked. "Please."

Fournier tossed his last dart onto the desk. He laughed showing a gap in his teeth. Then he sighed and, without warning, shouted, "Loup!"

Red curtains hung in a doorway behind Fournier. Half a minute passed, before the man Brandy facetiously knew as 'Don Juan' parted them and stepped out. The two spoke, without his acknowledging the Americans, then Fournier said, "This is Loup Wimund. He was at the castle yesterday."

Brandy wanted to say, 'Yeah... he was a jerk.' What she said was, "We're looking for a girl missing from the tour yesterday."

He murmured something. Fournier growled and pointed at the Americans. Loup looked up and said, "There were many women."

"This was an American," Ray said. "Vicki Kramer, my sister." He gave a description but the Frenchman seemed uninterested.

"She was with me," Brandy added, to jog his memory.

"I know nothing of her or what happened to her. If I saw her, I do not remember."

"Don't you count your passengers, for God's sake?"

"This was not a children's outing, *monsieur*. We offer a travel tour for adults. They are for themselves responsible."

"That's it? That's all you can tell us?"

"I cannot tell what I do not know. I do not know this woman." Loup looked to Fournier. His boss shrugged and Loup disappeared into the back room.

He pulled the curtain closed shutting out the obnoxious foreigners. Who the hell did they think they were? What happened to the blonde bitch... Before Loup could finish the thought the back door opened and Eve Molyneux stuck in her pretty little face. Eve was the red-haired beauty scowling at Felix on yesterday's tour. No surprise; she was his girl. Which made her a stupid whore in Loup's eyes. She was candy, no doubt, but dedicated to a lesser man. Her loss. Loup had no time for her.

"Is Felix here?" she asked, trying to enter.

Loup blocked the door. "He is busy." Her 'look to kill' only amused him.

Eve had every reason to be upset. This Fournier... She'd told Felix she'd had enough. He had agreed. He would quit Marcel Fournier, his ridiculous castle tour and, far worse, his other business. He would leave it behind for her. They would be married. They would leave Paradis together. He had promised. Yet here they were still. Eve loved Felix Bussey madly... and was mad as hell he had not kept his promise.

"Can... I... help you?" Loup asked, dripping sleaze.

"I do not find you funny," she said, disgusted.

"I was not being funny."

"That is funnier still."

The office curtains flew open; Brandy and Ray stared in. Fournier stood behind them, looking amused. Loup glared, Eve reddened with embarrassment. Fournier asked, "You are satisfied, *n'est-ce pas*?"

"I'm sorry," Brandy told the girl. "I thought you were someone else." Fournier reached past her and closed the curtain, leaving Loup and Eve alone once more.

Bored with it all, Loup growled at Eve, "Felix is busy. If you want nothing else, I have work."

Arguing with Loup Wimund was a waste of time. And negotiating with him a game for fools. Eve was no fool. "Will you tell Felix I was here?"

"I have already forgotten you."

Eve stomped out while Loup laughed.

The front of the shop was quiet. Fournier's curtain was in place and Loup was finally free from prying eyes. He pushed on the wall, on the far side of the room, opening a concealed door to a flight of stairs. He closed the panel behind him and started down.

In this secret basement, Felix was busy packing kilos into plastic-lined cardboard boxes. Atop these solid pillows of white powder he poured loose coffee grounds. He looked up at Loup's approach. "What is going on?"

"None of your fucking business. Just finish."

Felix bit his tongue.

Brandy and Ray walked sullenly away from Fournier's tour shop. They passed Rousseau's tattoo parlor with Brandy showing no interest and Ray breaking his neck to look the other way. (His mother had not raised an idiot). Neither knew Jerome was watching them. Nor that, once they'd passed, he started dialing his telephone.

Ray, fitted in the driver's seat of his rented *Deux Chevaux* like a Shriner in a parade car, maneuvered jauntily across the countryside. The shiny gray tuna can had four tin doors in a body big enough for two. The sole mirror, on the driver's side, was so close Ray had to bury his chin in his chest to use it. Brandy insisted the car was cute.

They passed the small dock at the edge of the village, where recreational boats hired by the hour, and followed the road past cyclists and pedestrians heading into the countryside for - whatever. Ray didn't ride bikes without motors and he didn't walk. They crossed the canal that wound through the vineyards and wooded foothills. Then they climbed into the Languedoc mountains; a region of natural monuments, grottoes and, higher up, dolmens and standing stones dating to prehistoric times.

Brandy flipped her window up on its hinges and breathed in the crisp morning air. She'd read the region enjoyed 300 days of sunshine a year. The previous night's storm had been a rarity. Lucky them. She kept it to herself.

They scooted past a walnut orchard where a farmer shook a tree with a rope tied to his tractor. A boy with a burlap satchel scurried beneath collecting the fallen nuts. Walnut mills, where oils were extracted, were a booming business here. She'd read that too. Brandy considered mentioning it; but didn't.

Despite her racing thoughts, when Brandy finally spoke, what came out was, "This is all my fault." Then her eyes misted over.

Ray wanted to reach over; to touch her. His brain begged him to comfort her. His hand wouldn't move. And he couldn't think of anything to say.

"If we don't find Vicki. I don't know what I'll do."

"We'll find her," Ray said. "Don't worry." He drove on, staring ahead, stoically hiding his own worries.

Fourteen

Stone and dirt roads, half of them ancient cart paths, cut through the countryside dotted with trees and blanketed, between fertile fields, with ferns so lush and tall the car periodically vanished beneath them.

The ruins of Castle Freedom soon came into view on the ridge. And, after several switchback maneuvers across the face of the climb Ray and Brandy found the unmarked road leading there. They passed a sign reading *Propriété privée*; with its warning that *Trespassers seront poursuivis*. Though neither read French, they shared a knowing look and drove on in violation of the law.

Once across the castle's drawbridge, it appeared their search was ended. A chained gate barred their passage. Ray pried himself from the vehicle to examine the situation; then reported the obvious. "It's locked."

He breathed in a barrel of air. He studied the wall, as it disappeared in an arc on either side, surprised by how little of the grounds he could see. He thought of Vicki and felt his fear rising. He shook the gate bars, as if he were a prisoner, and exhaled his frustration. "Well, what do we do now?"

He felt Brandy's hands on his shoulders. Suddenly, she was aboard him – piggy back. She pinched his waist with her knees, grabbed the bars above his head, and pulled herself up to stand on Ray's shoulders.

"I take it," Ray said, her boots biting his collarbones, "we're climbing over?"

"Hands!"

He lifted his palms. Brandy stood on them and Ray shoved her to the top of the fence. She flipped over and lowered herself to the gravel on the castle side. Truth be told, they'd done this before. Ray checked the drawbridge and road, confirmed they were alone (as if it mattered now), and followed Brandy over.

They started up the curved drive and, despite the gorgeous autumn, felt a pall descend as they entered the courtyard. The morning was crisp, the sun brilliant, the birds sang yet something hung in the air. Ray headed for the castle while Brandy milled in the courtyard. She shouted for Vicki.

No answer came.

Brandy was about to call again when she spied something on the ground near the chapel. She started that way but, the nearer she drew, the more she slowed her step.

Brandy did not know Anibal Socrates. Meeting the caretaker hadn't been part of Fournier's offering. And, arguing with the driver, she'd paid no attention to the man locking the gate at their departure. So, as she stared at the object in the courtyard, Brandy did not know who she saw. But she clearly recognized what she saw.

"Ray-y-y-y," she sputtered. "Raymond!"

"What is it? What's the matter?"

Ray ran to Brandy. Then he saw it too. They took hold of each other, without reservation, staring together at the washed out stain of congealed blood and the mutilated corpse lying at its center.

The *Gendarmerie* arrived in a two color parade. Blue lights flashing atop blue and white vehicles. Blue and white plastic tape protecting the scene, where scientists in white coveralls and blue gloves and soldiers in blue uniforms with white gunbelts went about their work.

Colonel Blanc, wearing a kepi with a flaming grenade badge, was his usual charming self; stabbing Brandy and Ray with his eyes as he bounced back and forth between them. "You knew this fellow?" he demanded, pointing at the thing inside the barricade that once was the caretaker.

"No. We didn't know him."

"Yet, you came to see him?"

"I told you," Ray said, an angry flush rising. "We came up here to find my sister. We found this instead."

"You came last night?"

"No," Brandy chimed in. "This morning. Just before we called you."

Blanc glared at the Americans.

So intently he failed to hear someone – something – moving, inside one of the few remaining windows in the wall of the castle, above and behind him. So intently he failed to notice the shadow of someone - something - looking down upon them.

"How long have you known M. Fournier?"

"Who?"

That's where the conversation ended.

Another of the *Gendarmerie's* cars rounded the bend from the gate and onto the courtyard. A young soldier jumped out and hurried to Blanc. Pallid, obviously alarmed, he took the Colonel aside and whispered into his ear.

Brandy and Ray watched as Blanc's lips tightened to a thin line. He asked several questions and, receiving the answers, began to lose color as well. A nod sent the soldier away. Blanc pulled at his jacket, straightening wrinkles that didn't exist, and turned back to the Americans. "You will wait here, please." It wasn't a question.

Blanc returned to his own car, signaling his driver. The lanky gendarme, whose name tag read 'Delvit', jumped behind the wheel and, in a flashing blur of blue and white, they were gone.

———

As at the castle, tape now cordoned off the Socrates' cottage. Excepting Lieutenant Colonel Petit, one gendarme, and one lone scientist (they were spread thin) scurrying between van and house, and Minotte the truffler, squealing with hunger and nudging the filthy bed in her sty, nothing else moved or made a sound. Nothing else on the farm had been left alive.

Pierre Dupont arrived at the scene as he arrived anywhere; in a chauffeured limousine and in a huff. Life was a bother as far as the aged regional magistrate was concerned and he held that against everyone. Regardless of a crime's jurisdiction, all investigations in France ultimately fell under the authority of the magistrate. The system had few supporters among the Paradis residents, among the *Gendarmerie*, or among criminal suspects. Dupont, however, liked it fine. Dupont was corpulent, red faced and mean. He handled all of his duties by doling out verbal hell while stroking his great gray mustache with corresponding fervor.

Petit, at the cottage door, snapped to attention as the magistrate entered the yard, saluted, and moved aside the threshold to give him access. The magistrate got one foot inside the cottage and froze. He saw the front rooms splashed in maroon. He saw the mother and daughter hacked and thrown down like forgotten puppets. The blood drained from Dupont's face as if his throat had been slit. He spun on his heels, grabbed the door frame, and pushed himself out and down the stone path toward the gate.

Petit was caught off guard by the magistrate's rapid retreat. It appeared the judge would faint and the Lieutenant Colonel grabbed his arm. Dupont shouted, yanked free and ran to vomit over the fence. Petit returned to attention – facing away.

It was some minutes before Dupont recovered sufficiently to tamp his fouled lips with his pocket kerchief, adjust his vest and re-trace his steps to the soldier.

"That is the wife and daughter?"

"Yes, your Excellency. We are certain it is."

"Anibal?" he asked, nervously tugging his mustache. "Where is Anibal Socrates?"

"Dead also, your Excellency," Petit said, "at the castle."

Dupont swallowed hard. "And the boy?"

"He is missing. There has been no sign of him."

"Is he dead, do you think? Or has Luis Socrates killed again?"

"Are you asking me, sir."

"No, no, no! Where is Colonel Blanc?" The judge regained his attitude with his strength. "Where is he for God's sake? I am talking to you now! Why is Blanc not here?"

"The Colonel is in the timber, magis-trate, between here and the castle. They have found. . . " Petit searched for the words. "They have found. . . something else."

———

It's my own fault, Colonel Blanc thought, I should not have asked.

He'd been standing over the caretaker when he'd learned of two more bodies, Socrates' wife and daughter, found muti-lated in their cottage. Three sickening murders; two horrendous crime scenes. Then one of his soldiers reported a third scene, which he ridiculously described as 'strange'.

"After this," Blanc demanded, "what in God's name, could possibly be strange?"

Now as they stood in the timber, between the castle and the cottage, shielding their eyes against the morning sun and staring up at a particular tree branch, Blanc had his answer. It was strange. He was sorry he had asked.

"Is that a suit of armor?"

"It. . . looks like armor." Unwilling to commit himself, the soldier, Tristan Maigny, called for a ladder.

Blanc concentrated on what looked like a scabbard, hanging from a leather belt, midway down the length of the linen and chain mail. "That is a sword is it not?"

"*Oui*, Colonel. It. . . appears to be a sword."

Blanc scanned the timber, heavy with wet dead fall, pungent with decaying leaves, cloying with mossy trees. He wondered at the temerity of whomever had been in these woods the previous night. The storm must have been terrifying. Even in the light of day, something ominous hung in the air.

Maigny crouched on the timber floor directly beneath the impaled suit. He donned blue latex gloves and carefully began digging in the mud.

"What is it?"

Maigny lifted a mud-caked implement. "It's a hammer. It's heavy; feels like iron. Looks like a rock hammer."

Another soldier, with the requested ladder, butted in. "An iron rock hammer?"

"I don't say it is. It looks like one." He pointed. "That is a pick."

"*Oui*. For big rocks."

"It would take big rocks to swing it." Both laughed.

"Are you finished?" Blanc asked. "Have you had your laugh? Get back to work."

Maigny saluted his superior and slipped the hammer, mud and all, into a bag. Fulke (the other soldier) sank the ladder into the mud and leaned the top against the tree limb beside the curious evidence. He tapped a rung. "Here you are, Colonel."

Blanc looked at the soldier as if he were a moron and said, "I will be bereaved if you fall."

Recognizing an order when he heard one, Fulke climbed. At the top, he lifted the garment and found it to be exactly what it appeared; underarmor, chain mail, a moldy mantel, a leather belt and sword, and a burned and rotted cloak – all transfixed on the branch as if the wearer (a knight?) had been impaled. But there was no wearer. Perplexed, Fulke stared down at his superior. "It is; it's a suit of armor."

A photographer, newly arrived and standing near the Colonel, shot a picture of the suit in Fulke's hands.

"Collect everything," Blanc said, his mind in a whirl. "Carefully."

Fifteen

The nightmare had only started for Brandy and Ray. All morning they'd been held a stone's throw from the caretaker's body, questioned as if they were criminals and, despite the sunshine, kept completely in the dark.

Now, apparently, they'd been summoned. They were escorted across the eastern field to the unhallowed grave-site of the executed Templars and there made to wait again – without explanation. A female soldier, who'd brought them, stood between Brandy and Ray outside the fence. A second gendarme, a young man, stood inside behind the raised tomb at the opposite end. Neither spoke; just stared with unreadable eyes.

Brandy felt disconnected as if she were having an out-of-body experience. She stole a glance at Ray. He, too, looked remote. Poor Ray. He'd convinced himself there was a logical reason for Vicki's absence and tried to convince Brandy of the same. Then he'd bottled his fears while trying to reassure hers. They'd approached the castle that morning in dread, but not even in their nightmares had either expected what they found.

And, still, there was no sign of Vicki.

Colonel Blanc and his shadow, Petit, finally arrived on foot from the timber. Wearing haggard faces, they entered the cemetery without acknowledging the Americans. In no mood to be ignored further, Brandy and Ray launched a barrage of questions over the fence. What's going on? Why are we being held? Where is Vicki?

Blanc raised his hand, said, "Wait there, *s'il vous plaît*," to silence them, and headed for the gendarme behind the sarcophagus.

En route, Petit paused, directing the Colonel's attention to one of the ground level graves. Brandy stared. Excepting the soldiers, she assumed the graveyard looked as before. Now she saw that wasn't the case. The grave to which Petit pointed was open. The lid, etched with the name Gaston Morel (which meant nothing her), was pushed aside. The grave was empty.

"The source of the knight's uniform?" Petit asked.

The Colonel did not reply but continued to the waiting soldier. He nodded and the gendarme bent out of view. He came up with the corner of an olive drab tarp in his hand. It covered, Brandy saw now, something in the grass at his feet. Her view was blocked but the officers got an eyeful.

"*Mère de Dieu*," escaped under Petit's breath.

Blanc said nothing; merely swallowed. The Colonel motioned for Ray through the gate. Brandy tried to follow but Blanc called out, "Not you, *mademoiselle*." He pointed at Ray. "Just you, please."

The lady soldier prevented Brandy's progress. Ray mouthed, 'It's okay' (though his expression suggested it wasn't), and entered the cemetery. He crossed to the officers and the tarp.

Blanc said simply, "Prepare yourself." Then he nodded and the gendarme lifted the tarpaulin again.

Nothing could have prepared Ray for what lay beneath. His beautiful 'big' sister bled white and discarded like trash. He stared, trying to wrap his brain around the horror, then he gasped - unable to get a breath. Ray felt himself pitching forward.

Blanc and Petit steadied the big American and eased him to his knees; aware the whole time of his girl screaming behind them. The gendarme left his officers and joined his colleague at the gate. It took both to keep Brandy back.

The Colonel asked, "Your sister?" When Ray didn't reply, he asked again, "M. Kramer. It is your sister, M. Victoria?"

"Yeah," Ray managed through tears. "Yes. It's Vicki." He reached for her.

Blanc grabbed his arm. "Do not touch her, *merci.*"

An overgrown cart path wound its way across the rocky field south of the cemetery; the closest thing to a road. Upon it, one of the *Gendarmerie's* cars now came bouncing to a stop. The driver opened the passenger's door and Dorian Durand, the police surgeon, looking grouchy and exhausted, climbed out. He rubbed his eyes, donned a paper coverall, grabbed his kit and started toward them.

Ray had rejoined Brandy outside the fence. They stood, crying together, but grieving separately. Each wanted to console the other but didn't know how.

Inside the burial plot. Durand paused, as Petit had before him, and raised his brow. Blanc followed his stare to the open grave.

"I'm no use if they're already buried," Durand said. The doctor was rarely at his best in public. This morning was no exception.

If he was amused, Blanc didn't let it show. He considered telling the doctor he was usually of damned little use but decided, with the Americans present, to save it for later. He merely pointed to the tarp and said, "There."

Durand took several steps before something else caught his eye. He paused again with a quizzical look on his face. "That's funny."

Irritated, Blanc barked, "What is funny?"

The doctor pointed to another grave and said, "It's inverted." Blanc stared but clearly didn't understand. Durand stepped closer and pointed directly at the carved writing. "The inscription," he said, "it's inverted."

Blanc nodded. He saw the writing but failed to see the significance. He had work to do and so did the doctor. Not bothering to hide his annoyance, he passed Durand, leaving him to that work. As he headed out of the cemetery, Blanc shouted for Petit to follow with the Americans.

Even in her grief, Brandy *had* seen significance in Durand's find. He was right. The lid's inscription was inverted. Though Felix, the tour guide, had rushed them along yesterday, she'd taken in all she could of the cemetery. And there was no doubt. Someone had lifted the cover off the grave, turned it and set it back going the opposite direction.

The interrogation room of Paradis' *Gendarmerie* station reflected Brandy's and Ray's misery. The couple sat on folding chairs at a scarred wooden table surrounded by four empty, dirty yellow walls. Or were they faded brown? Only God knew for sure and He wasn't there. In His place, Colonel Blanc circled like a hungry lion.

"Why are you in France?"

"For the fourth time," Brandy said. "I'm researching my Master's Degree. Ray and Vicki came with. . . to keep me company and sneak in a vacation."

"Why were you at Castle Freedom?"

"This is ridiculous," Ray shouted. "My sister is dead. She's the victim. Brandy's been over this. We've been over this."

"And we must, unfortunately, go over it again. How long have you known Marcel Founier?"

"You asked that before. . ."

"And you did not answer."

"The way I remember it, we were interrupted."

"And your answer now?"

"We don't know Fournier."

"And yet, you were seen, how do you say it, 'hanging around' his shop."

"Seen?"

"*Oui, monsieur.* Seen. On more than one occasion."

"By whom?"

"*Quel?*"

"Who saw us? Who reported us?"

"And what were we supposedly doing?" Brandy demanded.

"None of this matters, *mademoiselle.* You have been seen with the scofflaw."

Brandy and Ray stared incredulously at each other.

"Do you know Luis Socrates?"

"No. Who is that?"

"You've never met him?"

"Is he French?" Ray barked, coming out of his seat. "Because, if he is, we've already said, we don't know any of you sons of bitches!"

"His entire family was slaughtered last night. That was his father you found at the castle. His mother and sister were murdered in their home." Ray sat again. The Colonel continued, "Luis was nowhere to be found. So we are concerned about his well-being. And, as he is himself a released killer, we are interested in his whereabouts."

"A killer on the loose? Mass murders? Grave robbers? What kind of country are you running here?" Ray saw Blanc tense and laughed humorlessly. "Forget it; doesn't matter. We didn't do anything."

On guard at the door, Petit laughed too. "Maybe it *was* the Templars."

Blanc gouged the Lieutenant with his eyes and barked, "Get out."

Eduoard Petit had been a gendarme for sixteen years and the Colonel's friend for twice that long. When Blanc yelled, you were wise to respond.

He pulled the interview room door closed regretting the remark and nursing a scowl. He was immediately accosted by a local newspaper reporter loitering at the counter. Petit's scowl deepened.

As looks went, Aimee Laurent was just about right; tall without lankiness, curved without voluptuousness, fair without being blonde. 'Awkward... but pretty' her admirers agreed. But... she attacked her day with ceaseless energy and good humor; just what the gendarme officer didn't need at the moment.

"Lieutenant Colonel Petit." Aimee leaned with her notepad and pen. "What can you tell me of the events at Castle Freedom?"

"Absolutely nothing."

"Oh, Lieutenant Colonel, that is not the way. The bodies... how many?"

"No comment, M. Laurent."

She tilted her head, letting a lock fall over one eye, and clucked her tongue. "Come, Petit, you must say something?"

He lit a cigarette and blew smoke to the ceiling. "Just between us?"

Aimee studied Petit. He was not a man with whom one makes deals. But she needed a story. "For a start. *Oui.* Just between us."

Petit took another drag; exhaled. "I suspect," he said, leaning to whisper in her ear, "that you have a lovely body. Further investigation will be necessary."

Aimee clicked her ballpoint, fighting the temptation to jab it in his eye.

The door to the interrogation room came open, saving Petit's vision, and the reporter watched as the Colonel led a young couple out. "Go back to your hotel and stay there," he told them, sounding near exhaustion. "You will hear from me."

The big tattooed man appeared hesitant to leave. But Blanc was unwavering. Finally the man, and the small woman who accompanied him, allowed themselves to be ushered out the door. Aimee was all eyes.

Laurent's interest did not go unnoticed by the Colonel. In a low voice, he told Petit, "Get me the file on Marcel Fournier." Then he entered his office without acknowledging the reporter.

"Colonel. . ." Aimee called out.

"I do not hear you. I do not see you." Blanc closed the door.

Aimee twisted her lips. Then her frown became a smile and she hurried from the station.

Sixteen

On their first visit it had been too dark to see the police station. Now, in the light of day, Brandy saw it for what it was, a gray building on a gray cobblestone side street. A perfect home for Colonel Blanc with his missing empathy and AWOL sense of justice.

Ray just got their rental unlocked as an excited female shout got their attention. "Hello. Excuse me. *Voyons.* You know someone killed last night at the castle?"

They took in the tall drink of Perrier who'd kicked them both without lifting a foot. "What the hell kind of question is that?" Ray demanded.

The girl seemed genuinely confused. "I'm sorry?"

Brandy squeezed Ray's arm to halt a rise in temperature. She took in the woman who'd addressed them in accented, but impressive, English. "We just passed inside," Brandy said. "Who are you?"

"Aimee Laurent. I am with the *Presse Regionale*. I write for *Le Courrier Paradis*; the local paper."

Ray pulled open his car door. "We don't have anything to say to a reporter."

"If I offend you, I am sorry," Aimee said, afraid she'd ruined her chance. "But if you expect help from this *Gendarmerie* you are wasting your time." The American shut the door again and leaned on the car. He was listening now. "I could be a friend. You need a friend here."

Brandy frowned. She wasn't the jealous type but she knew Ray. She stepped between them and their proposed friendship. "So, Aimee, what is it you want?"

"The same as you... to discover what happened at the castle."

Ray wanted nothing to do with a reporter – or anyone. He intended to return to their hotel room and pass out. And did just that. Brandy, on the other hand, needed human contact and accepted Aimee's invitation to walk, talk and lunch at a local café.

Paradis during the day, Brandy found, was a lively village featuring everything from the quaint to the modern; butcher, baker, candlestick maker, and a massive central park all within minutes of each other. There was an open air market where locals sold fresh produce and wines (with samples for tasting), a pub called The Cave featuring ales and wines (with samples for tasting), council fêtes with music, dancing, fireworks and wines (with samples for tasting).

Two and three story stone buildings, stores on the ground floor and residences above, made up the downtown. Brightly colored umbrellas formed an inviting gauntlet leading pedestrians to a courtyard filled with colorful foods and colorful vendors. Tourists in search of souvenirs, picnickers preparing for the country and hungry villagers were drawn in and surrounded by arts, crafts, fresh-bottled fruits, vegetables, and a cornucopia of foods from *foie gras* and goat's milk cheese to prune tarts and truffles.

At the far end of the market, the eastern boundary of the village, the charming *Le Marché du Café* was gracious with its outdoor eating space. White wrought-iron tables and chairs filled a wide patio, surrounded by manicured trees and connected by criss-crossing tile sidewalks. There, with the warm afternoon sun and the cold autumn breeze clashing, the women convened their meeting.

Brandy didn't feel as if she could eat a bite but, when Aimee insisted, felt even less like arguing. She ordered something 'to keep up her strength'. Meanwhile, the reporter asked questions. She kept it conversational, displaying neither notebook nor pen, committing whatever she got, to memory.

Brandy told all she knew of the events at the castle, which wasn't much. Then asked, "How did you know anything happened at all?"

"This is not America. When sirens sound in Paradis, and every gendarme is called to duty, something important has happened. I followed them. I could not get in but I got close enough to hear some things. It is terrible."

"It is terrible," Brandy said sullenly.

"Yes. I am sorry. For you and your fiancé. And for the Socrates family."

"I've been thinking so much about Vicki, I'd forgotten them. A whole family."

"Not all. The son, Luis, was not found."

"The Colonel asked about him. We didn't know who he was talking about. This Luis; he's a murderer?"

"No." Aimee waved the silly idea away. "He was charged with manslaughter. His girl... what was her name? Micheline... was run down and killed by a drink driver. The driver showed no remorse and escaped justice on a. . . technicality. Outside the court, he even laughed. Luis Socrates beat him on the courthouse steps."

"Beat him to death?"

"Badly. He died from his injuries and Luis went to prison. I know it is not right. The knight in shining armor is gone. But does not every woman want a lover who will protect and defend her life? Or, if need be, revenge its loss?"

Despite her usual practical leanings, Brandy found herself appreciating Aimee's romantic version of how life ought to be.

"His trial," Aimee added, "was the biggest thing to happen. Crime here is small. To write about, there is none except, of course, drugs. That is what I assumed the soldiers were for this morning."

Aimee dropped that bomb so casually it knocked Brandy for a loop. "Drugs?"

"It is the only crime here to merit headlines."

What, Brandy wondered, had drugs to do with sleepy little Paradis? Then Aimee's meaning hit home. Brandy's mouth fell open. "What do drugs have to do with Vicki's murder? She had nothing to do with drugs."

Aimee smiled politely but said nothing.

"All right. I can't know," Brandy admitted. "But I don't believe it. Vicki wasn't just my sister-to-be, she was my best friend, and she didn't do drugs. Even if she did, what would that have to do with her murder? Were these Socrates people into drugs?"

"I don't know. As I said, Luis' girl and his conviction for what happened to her killer were the first criminal death here in years; and that was over five years ago. These new murders are the only thing of importance the *Gendarmerie* are investigating. Before I left their station, Colonel Blanc asked for Marcel Fournier's file. That means drugs."

The waiter delivered their meal and Brandy, grateful for the reporter's presence, smiled and let Aimee do the talking. Her gratitude was short-lived.

Aimee had suggested she order *Bourride*. Now, as she stared into the bowl, she discovered it was vegetables in wine with scrambled monkfish. Aimee meant well. But a sleepless night, and a devastating morning, was no lead-in to fish soup. An earlier headache and dizziness returned. Brandy pushed her bowl away and inhaled deeply.

Despite her discomfort, something Aimee said resonated. "Did you say Fournier? The tour bus guy?"

"*Oui.*" Aimee shoveled in a spoonful of *Rouille de seiche*; a stew made with squid.

Like Brandy, she hadn't eaten all morning. Unlike Brandy, she was ravenous. "Tours to the castle. That is his business, eh, legitimate. But you do not earn Fournier's style of life selling tours and trinkets. So the gendarme suspect drugs."

"Petit said something else," Brandy said. "Something about the Templars."

"The Templars?"

"He may have been joking, I don't know, but he suggested the Templars were responsible for these deaths. Other than the knights buried at the castle, are there still Templars? Do you know what he was talking about?"

Two women at a nearby table, one round and red, the other lean and pale, overheard them and ogled - stricken.

"*Avez-vous entendu?*" the pale stick whispered. The middle of her comment was inaudible, but it ended in an excited, "... *des Templiers?*"

The other answered, "*Mère de Dieu!*," and raised an arm, sausage fingers pointed to the ceiling, fear in her fierce eyes. Then she told her companion. "*Nous allons.*"

The stick dropped her sandwich. They gathered their things; the thin one without looking up, the other staring. They hurried around the tables and trees and were gone.

"That," Brandy said, "was freaky."

"Freaky?" the reporter asked.

"Mmm. Was it something I said?"

"Mmm," Aimee nodded. "The Templars."

"Colonel Blanc wasn't happy when his Lieutenant said it either." Brandy screwed up her lips. "What gives? What have the Templars to do with anything?"

Aimee, celebrating the waiter's return, hadn't heard her questions. She *oohed* and *aahed* as he set a plate before them. Brandy studied the small black pyramid he'd delivered wondering what the excitement was about.

"It is a weakness." Aimee cut the pyramid's shell, scooped out a creamy glob and spread it on hard bread. "*Valençay*; goat cheese. I adore it. Nutty. Delicate."

Brandy poked the covering. "What's that?"

"Salted charcoal ash," Aimee said, licking her lips. "A protection. The goat's milk is not pasteurized."

Aimee pointed for her to dig in, but Brandy's stomach, coupled with the fear of losing a finger to the ravenous reporter's knife, gave her pause. "We were talking about the Templars."

"*Oui*. I don't know. For many it is nonsense. For others. . . there are many superstitions here." She considered for a moment then brightened. "Perhaps you should talk to Father Trevelyan." She weighed the idea. "I think so. Father Trevelyan. He's. . . "

Brandy groaned. "Ray won't go. He's not Catholic. He's not religious at all."

"No, no, no." Aimee swept the objection away. "I do not suggest his religion. I suggest him. He is the priest at Saint Thomas Church here, but he... knows the history. . .

"A historian?"

"*Oui. Merci.*" She touched Brandy's arm gratefully. "A historian. He knows of the Templars all there is to know."

"I can hear Ray now, 'I don't give a damn about their local ghost stories.'" She considered a moment – and decided. "He'll get over it."

"I will arrange an interview," Aimee said, then hopefully added, "If you do not object that I should accompany?"

Seventeen

While others dined, the police surgeon starved. Dorian Durand had been performing autopsies all day; four, from what was presumably one crime. Remarkable in Paradis. Not that they were medically difficult. All the victims were so badly lacerated, bludgeoned and torn, he could safely list any cause of death – from blunt force trauma to myocardial infarction - without fear of contradiction.

What commanded extra time was the American girl's reassembly. Vicki Kramer was the only one of the four Durand had taken care to put back together. There was no point with the others. Excepting Socrates' missing son, who the *Gendarmerie* suspected, there were no living relatives to impress with a fancy reconstruction. The American, on the other hand, had family.

Her throat was no work of art when he finished, but it looked like a throat again. A funeral director back in the States would make it pretty. What remained of her vital organs after Durand dissected, collected, weighed, examined and catalogued his samples, were placed in one plastic bag and returned to her abdominal cavity (everything in its place). He threaded a formidable curved needle with brown, twine-like coronal suture and stitched the chest and abdomen closed.

With a few harmless bumps Durand wrestled Vicki's corpse from his exam table onto a wheeled cart. The neck support slipped and her once attractive noggin hit the cart with a thump. "Poor thing," Durand said, as he wheeled her to the refrigerated wall. "They're lucky they're dead when they get to me."

He transferred her to a temporary resting place, an extended tray, this time with a tad more grace, then covered Vicki's corpse with a sheet. Durand rolled the tray in, secured the numbered door, and removed his gloves with a rubbery snap.

It had been one hell of a day. As he entered his office, Durand wiped the fatigue from his eyes – and lowered his hands to find it wasn't over. Colonel Blanc was pitched back in his chair, hands behind his head, his boots atop Durand's desk blotter.

"Comfortable?"

"I was an hour ago," Blanc said. "Now I just want to go home."

The whiskey bottle Durand kept secreted in a lower drawer stood beside the Colonel's feet. He'd obviously gone a-hunting. The surgeon felt his ire rising – and squelched it. Butting heads with Blanc was an exercise in futility. Why bother? Durand smiled and reached for the bottle. "Drink, Colonel?" The bottle was nearly empty. The surgeon returned it to the desk and eyed Blanc vacantly. Still, he kept his tongue.

"I helped myself." There was no apology and no further explanation. "The autopsies; what took so long?"

"I had four bodies."

"You sit on your ass six months a year. What did you find?"

"I won't have toxicology back for weeks."

"I know that. I'm not asking for toxicology. I'm not asking for inquest findings. And I'm not that bitch Laurent looking for a story. You've been a surgeon for thirty years and you've had these bodies for five hours. Tell me what you know."

"Tell us both, *monsieur le doctor*."

Blanc looked past Durand with a scowl. It disappeared, and he jumped to his feet, as the magistrate came through the door.

Judge Dupont flicked his mustache in annoyance as he took in the doctor, the gendarme, and the near empty bottle. He dressed Blanc down with the hammer drills he called eyes, then mentally erased him, and aimed the fierce orbs at Durand. "Yes?"

The doctor sanded his eyes again. "I was about to say, magistrate, that all four are homicides; all with multiple lacerations, punctures, blunt trauma..."

"The murder weapon?"

"Weapons, your Excellency, plural. Multiple double-edged blades; swords, actually. Perhaps more than one."

"How many?" Blanc asked.

The magistrate checked Blanc peripherally, but let the question stand.

The doctor threw his hands into the air with a frustrated exclamation. "Two or three. Several knives, also doubled-edged. A square blunt instrument and a pointed blunt instrument."

"We found a heavy hammer with a pick end?"

Durand shrugged. "I have yet to see the collected evidence. I find it interesting... most of the wounds were not immediately lethal." The magistrate and Colonel traded questioning looks. "They were tortured; their killers more interested in the victims' bleeding than in their dying."

"Why?"

"Not my department."

"Guess," the magistrate ordered.

"Sadistic mania? Ritual? I haven't a clue, your Excellency."

"That's incredible," the Colonel said with a disbelieving air.

"No. That was the credible part." Durand offered the last of the whiskey to the magistrate. Dupont twisted his lips in disgust, his mustache in impatience. Durand drank the dregs, exhaled the fumes and said, "All of the victims. . . were bitten."

"Bitten? What do you mean bitten?"

"They're covered in bite marks. The American girl was bitten once; a ripping wound in the throat. The others - all over. And no, I don't know how many. It will take a forensic dentist and much study. But the bites go completely through the sub-dermal layers of skin – deep into the flesh."

"Are these sex murders?" the judge demanded.

"No. The American girl, eh, has some suggestive bruising, but there was no penetration. The torn clothing. . . Perhaps there was an attempted molestation that was not consummated for some reason."

"Her attacker was interrupted?" the Colonel offered.

"If rape was a motive!" Durand shrugged. "Neither of the other women showed any indications."

"If it wasn't sexual," the Colonel asked. "Why were they bitten?"

"The blood of all four of the victims has gone missing."

"For God's sake," the judge erupted. "The blood of the mother and daughter is splashed from one end of their cottage to the other. I saw it."

"With all respect, magistrate, it isn't. The scene was horrid, no doubt, but the blood spilled does not equal what ought to be there. The bodies were drained but the blood is missing."

Dupont tugged on his mustache. "If your feet are rested, Colonel," the magistrate said, "perhaps you'll find these murderers before they strike again?"

Eighteen

The reds of sunset bleeding into dark offered a stark background to the imposing St. Thomas Church. Brandy and Ray stared in silence. The yellowed stone, stained-glass, angular roofs, towering spires and circumambient wrought-iron drew one and repelled the other. She stood in awe of the power of God and he man's power to manipulate.

Ray turned from the looming edifice to the lady reporter who'd brought them and said, "I just don't see the point in this?"

"We're not even through the door!" Brandy turned to Aimee. "See? I told you."

"Told her what?" He bounced back to the reporter. "Look, I don't mean to be rude. We appreciate your help, but. . . "

"I appreciate you," Brandy cut in. "He doesn't appreciate anything."

"I stand corrected. You appreciate her."
Ray returned to Aimee. "My only interest is
in who killed my sister. And, no, I don't give
a damn about your local ghost stories."

It was a strange match. They were spar-
ring - by hitting her. "Neither do I. You
have questions without answers, *monsieur*,"
Aimee said. "I have similar questions.
Should we not seek these answers elusive?"

Brandy took Aimee by the arm. "Forget
him." She tossed her hair and reshouldered
her carpet bag. "We'll go."

"I didn't say I wouldn't go! I'm here." The
girls were already moving. By the time he
finished his sigh, Ray had to hurry to catch
up.

Inside the heavy oak doors, Aimee and
Brandy dipped their fingers into the font
and crossed themselves. Ray merely crossed
his eyes. Aimee nodded through the open
double-doors, directing their attention
across the decorated length of the church,
to the priest, Father Clive Trevelyan.

He was handing candy to a boy and girl at
the front of the sanctuary. The altar servers,
Brandy supposed, giggled and disappeared
through a door in the aisle. The priest snuck
a sweetie for himself as he watched them
go. He turned to see he'd been caught.
Trevelyan coughed the candy into a hand-
kerchief as he started their direction.

From the vestibule, the new arrivals saw three different things. Aimee saw a priest very like the Father in her own church in Paris which she'd left long ago and now visited rarely. Ray saw a black costume, stiff at the shoulders, tapering to a belly (beer, he assumed), tied at the waist; with buttons from the starched dog collar to the flowing hem near the floor. The square hat with pom-poms was precious. The uniform of the trade, Ray guessed, but he wouldn't be caught dead. Brandy looked beneath the clerical accoutrement, the biretta, the cassock. She saw a tall, aging man with a nervous step, a dark gray widow's peak, silver tufts at each temple, wild eyebrows and wire glasses that enlarged already big brown eyes and made him look like a barn owl. Trevelyan's voice, as he greeted them in French, disappointed. Brandy'd expected authority or wisdom, but again got nerves. They met, as a group, in the center aisle. Aimee introduced her small group, then asked if he spoke English.

Trevelyan, at first unsure, finally blurted, "Yes." More thought brought an amendment. "I speak English. And French. And Spanish. Italian, German, Portuguese. And just enough Tagalog to get into trouble in the Philippines." Then, fearing he'd been indiscreet, tacked on, "but not enough, I'm afraid, to get out."

It was, Brandy thought, like watching an old lady park a car; indecision in motion. She couldn't help but laugh. The rest, including Trevelyan, joined her. He had, in one sentence, toppled the wall between the mortals and the imposing Roman Catholic Church. Just that quickly, with a familiarity nearing goofiness, Trevelyan had gone from Father to father. Brandy liked him.

"These are the visitors of whom I spoke on the phone," Aimee said.

"The Americans. Yes, I thought so."

"Does it show?" Brandy asked.

"Not at all. Er, It's simply that. . . well, ah, only tourists walk the square at this time of the evening."

"Why's that?"

"Because, er, the setting sun causes the shadow of the, eh, castle to fall upon the square." The priest stared with menace. Dressed as he was, surrounded by the ancient iconography of the church, it had a disquieting effect. He waited a beat, then chuckled lightly. "It doesn't really, of course."

"What's that?" Brandy asked, her mouth suddenly dry.

"The, eh, shadow of the cursed castle. It doesn't really fall on the square. It doesn't come within miles of it. Oh, but that's the local superstition."

Brandy and Ray traded looks; Ray's a deadpan suggesting he'd like to slap someone, Brandy's a plea that it not be the priest.

"Eh, how can I help you? A matter of faith?"

"No, no, no, Father. Not faith," Aimee said, taking the lead. "It is more, we believe, a matter of. . . a hobby of yours."

"Really?" Trevelyan looked the church over and shook his head. "Oh, this is too formal a setting to discuss hobbies. Er, come with me."

He led them out and down a long hall.

"You're not French?" Brandy asked as they walked.

"Heavens no. British. Transplanted, oh, so long ago, even I barely remember."

He followed up with several favorable comments about the south of France, then apologized to his native Britain if he'd iterated there had been anything wrong with it. Trevelyan, apparently, liked both and disliked neither, yet seemed neither happy nor unhappy. He simply was. Sad, Brandy thought. The poor man was either without romance or awash in it, she didn't know which. Perhaps that's why he found satisfaction in studying long dead religious sects?

They passed to a connected porch. The sun was gone but, above the tree tops, its final ribbon of red streaked the sky. Trevelyan searched his pockets. "Now, eh, what hobby of mine interests you?"

"The Templars."

The priest paused in genuine surprise. "Oh. You are tourists." He produced a key and resumed his step.

"Why do you say that?" Ray asked, speaking for the first time.

They reached the end of the hall. Father Trevelyan opened a door and, as he waved them in, said, "There are few in Paradis, er, courageous enough to express a curiosity, ah, even if they have one, concerning the Templar Knights."

Brandy, Ray and Aimee filed past him into the study and Trevelyan pulled the door closed. He removed his biretta, struck a match and lit an oil lamp on his desk. A golden glow flooded the room. "Please," he said, gesturing.

Brandy and Ray took chairs near the desk, and Aimee found a seat on a book-laden couch, in a room more museum than study. The walls and floor overflowed with framed paintings, weapons, religious artifacts, ancient armor, a suit of white linen (emblazoned with a Maltese cross), chain mail - and even a church bell, its cast bronze glistening, as the centerpiece of a wooden cabinet behind his desk.

"Er, now then, the Templars." Trevelyan said, his elbows finding the desk, his fingertips finding each other. "I confess, ah, I'm not certain where to begin. I know neither what you know nor what you're looking for."

Brandy didn't need to be asked twice. "Well, Father," she said, "I'm here writing a thesis on burial practices and would have liked to pick your brain regarding the Templars. We see you're an expert. Of course, that's changed now. Aimee, I mean, Miss Laurent...."

"Aimee is fine," the reporter said.

Brandy smiled. "Aimee, I assume, told you about Ray's sister?"

"She did, yes. Er, I'm very sorry. Your sister... Ah, are you Catholic, Ray?"

"No."

His tone required no follow-up. "What can I do for you?"

"We need help," Brandy blurted out. She apologized, laid her hand on Ray, then the dam broke. "I'm Catholic, Father, but that isn't why we're here. In the last twenty-four hours, we've gone from being tourists, to losing our sister, to being questioned about

161

drug dealers, to practically being accused of murder. We've had guns pulled on us, been interrogated," Brandy paused for breath. "This morning, an officer suggested that, if we weren't responsible, maybe the Templars were."

"The Templars?"

"That's what he said."

The priest shook his head. "The Templar Knights, and their Order, er, have been dead for seven hundred years."

"We don't know from dead," Ray said. "All we know is they were brought up in a discussion about my sister's death."

"And every time we mention them," Brandy added excitedly, "or their castle, people whisper and cross themselves. I chased a couple right out of a café. And they were saluting us as if we were Nazis."

She could see the wheels turning in the priest's head. His eyebrow kicked up a fuss and he laughed loudly. Once he regained himself, he said, "Forgive me, please. That is not a Nazi salute. It is called the, er, *mano fica*. You double together the fingers and insert the thumb between the fore and middle digit." He demonstrated. "It is an ancient guard against the evil eye."

"The evil eye?" Ray frowned and crossed his muscled arms.

"Would it be fair, Mr. Kramer, to say you're, eh, not a believer?"

"I've never done the whole God thing."

"Are you superstitious?"

"It's all horsesh..." Ray caught himself or, more accurately, caught Brandy's eye and put on the brakes.

Trevelyan smiled. "For hundreds of years sailors refused to carry a woman on board or even to set sail on a Friday. There are ten thousand superstitions."

"People don't think like that anymore."

"Don't they? I would be willing to wager your mother, certainly your Grandmother, when she spilled salt, gathered a pinch and threw it over her left shoulder. What actor, today, will utter 'Macbeth' inside a theater? And don't you, situation permitting, go round rather than walk beneath a ladder? Or hesitate when a black cat crosses your path? Or fret when you break a mirror?"

"What's that got to do with the Templars?"

"To discuss the Templars," Trevelyan said, rising, "it will be necessary to alter your perceptions. This is not the States. And, here, it is not the twenty-first century."

Through a window, on the far side of the study, the last of the sun's light faded like dying embers behind the hills. Darkness overtook the corners of the room and only the lamp prevented its settling over all. The priest lifted the window and a cool autumn breeze followed him back to his desk.

"Paradis is not the City of Lights. It is a lonely village." Trevelyan's nervous vocal ticks disappeared as he entered his area of expertise. "Unlike Paris, when the sun sets here, it isn't replaced by electric lights. There's little music and no revelry. With the exception of a few candles and a few prayers it is quiet and dark." He slowly turned the valve on the oil lamp. The glow dimmed, the shadows grew. "Imagine what actual darkness and real silence are like." He closed the valve. The lamp went out. "The darkness is all encompassing. The silence gives way to a symphony. But who or what are the musicians?" The night-sounds, the chirps, calls and cries of nocturnal creatures, the flapping of night wings washed in through the open window.

Trevelyan struck a match, starkly underscoring his face with shadow and startling his guests. "What is that old poem? Something about... corpses riding beasts; corpses wandering graveyards. I'm sorry, ah, my memory fails me. All but the last stanza; that I remember." And he recited in a deep and resonant voice:

> *"Creatures God had never planned,*
> *Creatures never taught to die."*

164

Surrounded by the symbols of the church, the remnants of religious war, lit by the doubtful flicker of a single match, the priest appeared to have a ghost story to tell. His visitors looked nervously from one to the other.

"This, you must understand, is the land you've come to, a breeding ground for age-old superstitions." He relit the lamp, chasing the gloom back to the corners and the fear from their hearts.

"All of us here in Paradis have heard the 'bogie stories' concerning the Templar knights. Of their Black Masses, their blood sacrifices, their curses and threats of revenge from the grave. With the ruins of their castle in the mountains above, the locals are inundated with it from childhood."

"But it is just a legend," Brandy asked. "Right?"

The priest shrugged. "All legends are based, in part, on fact. The Templars are no exception. They traveled broadly throughout the known world. They met and lived with many peoples; believers, non-believers. It seems likely, to make in-roads, some non-Christian rites were assimilated into their Masses."

Trevelyan crossed the room to a large painting.

It was a handsome portrait of a knight in a flowing white cloak, brown tunic, and *chausses* (armor leggings) with a sword in his powerful right hand. He had a head of untamed hair, perhaps cut before a campfire with his own dagger, and a mustache and goatee that added to his darkly sinister aura. He bore a likeness to the Russian monk Rasputin, but 'madness' was far from Brandy's mind. The bold knight stared defiantly over his shoulder. He was every woman's dream; white knight and black knight in one. Brandy was drawn. Framed in gold, the portrait featured a plaque bearing the knight's name, the year '1136' and, in French, 'Grand Master of the Knights of the Temple'.

"This is Hugh de Payens," Trevelyan said, "a deeply religious man; and the father of the Templar knights."

He seemed to be looking past the portrait. To another century, Brandy wondered? Maybe he was a romantic after all.

"In the twelfth century," Trevelyan continued, "Crusaders captured Jerusalem from the Moslems. But it was a strange victory. For, after the Christians fought their way in and took their prize, they were trapped, completely surrounded by their enemies."

The priest drew several ponderous volumes from an overloaded bookcase.

"Then, in 1188, Payens, with eight of his closest friends, began the Order of the Poor Knights of Christ and the Temple of Solomon; what we have come to know as the Knights Templar. They dedicated their lives to seeing Christians safely in and out of the Holy Land through hostile territory."

Trevelyan thumbed one of the books. He turned it on the desk, showing his guests a picture of a hand-painted disc decorated with two Templar knights, bearing white shields with red crosses, riding together aboard a single horse. The image was encircled by a Maltese cross and a phrase in Latin.

"Sig-il-lum. . . " Brandy stuttered, giving it a try.

"*Sigillum Militum Xpisti*," Father Trevelyan said. "The seal of the soldiers of Christ."

"Why only one horse?"

"It's symbolic of the Order's early poverty."

He stared at the photo, lost in thought. "Many knights, afire with religious fervor, joined. They organized and rapidly grew in number. Payens became the first Grand Master of the Knights of the Temple and, for years, he and his men were regarded as Holy. They were monks but also excellent soldiers. Templar fortifications sprang up in England, Spain, Portugal, here in France. They became the main support for Christians in the Holy Land. The church showered privileges on them. Wealthy nobles who did not join gave the knights property and money. Ironically, the members took a vow of poverty while the Order grew rich. They became bankers, even loaning money to kings, and this wealth would eventually cause their downfall."

Trevelyan opened the other book, leafed through several pages and sadly said, "I'm going to tell you an awful story."

Nineteen

"For one and a quarter centuries the Templars held a position of power and respect throughout Europe and the world; with the Church and the King. But that came to an end on 13 October, 1307. It began with a long, desperate ride south from Paris for Jacques de Molay," Trevelyan said, "the last man to hold the title of Grand Master of the Templar Knights."

The priest's passion carried his listeners with him – seven centuries into the past.

Molay was a contradiction as he rode. In appearance, he was a resplendent Father Christmas; a bald dome wreathed in long white hair, dark eyes in a red, breathless face behind a great gray beard and mustache. In costume, he was a shining knight;

a white tunic emblazoned with a black cross over a hauberk of chain mail, a white cloak with a matching black cross and a gray over-cloak pinned with gold at his throat. In manner, he was intimidation on horseback; one hand on the reins, the other gripping a brown leather belt from which depended a dagger on his right and, on his left, a scabbard holding his black banded, golden handled sword of the Savior. A racing contradiction, with the heart and soul of a Saint and the boiling temper of a demon.

Molay was a heartbroken man spurred on by angry determination. The fields, the hills, the miles faded behind. His mount climbed the rocky Languedoc countryside. The keep of the *Château de la liberté* appeared in the distance and, finally, towered above. There had been rumblings of decadence and evil among members of their secret Order for years; rumors of witchcraft, human sacrifices and Black Masses at the Paradis stronghold. Jacques de Molay, a godly man, would end this nonsense for good.

"Lower the bridge," Molay called, riding the edge of the castle's dry moat. His call went unanswered and he had to rein in his horse. The animal cantered, panting, in need of rest. Molay steadied him. "Lower the bridge!"

A single silver helmet finally appeared in the gate tower window. The guard stuttered fearfully, "I'm s-sorry, m'lord. I c-c-can not."

"*Comment*. What do you mean, you can not?" Molay stood in the stirrups, a trick for a big man, steadying his mount. "Do you not recognize me?"

Even at that distance, the air was redolent of terror. "M-my master has o-ordered no one. . . be given entrance. . . during services."

"Services!" Molay hollered in disgust. Molay had to steady the animal again. "I am your master! You serve my Order! And I command you in the name of our Savior, and in the name of his Holiness the Pope, lower the bridge. . . and give me entrance!"

Another moment elapsed. Then with a grating of gears, the shifting of timbers and the resonance of ropes stretched to their limit, the windlass was set into operation. The drawbridge dropped into place across the dry moat. The Grand Master spurred his mount and crossed the bridge.

Molay rode into the courtyard, dismounted and strode angrily up the steps to the chapel. He inhaled to steel himself and pushed the door open. The squealing hinges echoed as he barged through the vestibule. He pulled up short in the nave, alone. The chapel was empty. "What in the name of God is going on here?"

A squire, holding the reins of Molay's wandering horse, looked up shaking when he saw the chapel door open.

"Where is Francois de Raiis?" Molay demanded, descending the steps. Raiis, a name once respected and now feared, was the knight in charge of Castle Freedom.

"Conducting services, Master," the boy said. "He has ordered. . . "

Molay stuck his dagger in the lad's face. He shook with anger but, breathing deeply, stayed his hand. Squires were not members of the Order; they were outsiders hired by contract. Whatever was happening here was not this boy's fault. Molay reminded himself but his patience was wearing thin. "I will not hear his rite called a service again," he said through clenched teeth. "Where is Francois de Raiis?"

A moment later, Jacques de Molay burst into the foyer of Castle Freedom. His entrance startled two chaplains and a sergeant talking by the keep staircase. The sergeant left the others and rushed forward. Drawn from the lower strata of society, the sergeants were the Order's working class, performing the menial tasks of life in service of the knights. As he closed the distance to the Grand Master, the sergeant threw up a hand, calling, "*Arrêtez-vous, s'il vous plaît!*"

Molay drew his sword and, without breaking stride, swung mightily. With a sickening thwack, the sergeant's head somersaulted off his shoulders. His corpse stood for an instant, a macabre fountain spurting blood, then crumpled. Its brown mantle settled in the crimson pool on the floor and its black tunic, bearing the red cross, floated over it like a pall. Without a glance at the mortified chaplains, Molay strode across the foyer toward the curved staircase to the dungeon. The Grand Master descended and, at the base of the stairs, forced one of the thick doors open.

Molay stared - stunned.

Benoit Lambert, Castle Freedom's senior chaplain, was an ordained priest entrusted with the spiritual needs of the resident Templars. And who better? Benoit literally meant 'blessed'. He stood on the far side of the dungeon in flickering torchlight, beneath a brilliantly colored, Ankh-emblazoned pall, before a makeshift altar. But nothing about the scene was blessed by any heavenly deity.

Francois de Raiis stood at Lambert's side with blood dripping from his lips down the front of his mantle.

Five knights, their backs to Molay, stood in a semi-circle before their leaders. Two gulped hungrily from gold chalices as blood ran down their chins. Then, their teeth and tongues coated in blood, they passed the vessels to the knights beside them.

Lambert raised his hands and prayed, "Lord Satan, we thank thee for accepting this pathetic sacrifice and, in your mercy returning unto us, this, your key to immortality. Oh, Lord of Flies, Ah-mon."

The knights, spewing blood, called back the blasphemous, "Ah mon."

And then, on the opposite side of the dungeon, Molay saw the sacrifice of which Lambert had spoken. A young woman, in a horrid parody of the crucifixion, was tied on a large inverted cross. Her clothing was ripped away. She was mutilated, dead.

Jacques de Molay gasped. "In the name of God!"

Raiis saw the Grand Master in the door. "Dare I welcome you, old friend?"

"Welcome me? Welcome me!"

"I thought not." Raiis wiped the blood from his chin with his cloak - smearing it. Then he spoke with resignation. "You have no place here, Molay."

Molay was aghast. His lips trembled but nothing succeeded. What could be said?

Raiis stepped down. His knights, their raiment splashed in the peasant girl's blood, formed a line behind their master and their makeshift sanctuary.

Sanctuary, dear God! Molay's mind reeled. There was no sanctity here; nothing sacred. "Blasphemers," Molay sputtered, finding his voice. "Idolators."

Still carrying the sword with which he'd killed the sergeant, Molay advanced on the cruciform and cut the leather bindings holding the girl. He eased her body to the floor. He bent to her, his tunic marred by her blood, crossed himself and whispered the beginnings of an "Our Father." Suddenly aware of his jeopardy, he stood facing the dark knights.

"Murderers!" he shrieked – and ran at them.

Startled and off guard, Raiis, Lambert and his knights scattered. Molay swung his sword at the altar knocking the chalices away. Blood flew and soaked his tunic. He shoved the altar over. He cut the pall down and threw it to the floor. He turned on the knights – his eyes shot with anger.

Then, for the first time, Molay saw his student and friend, Geoffrey de Charney, among the blasphemers with drying blood splashed down his chin. "Charney!" he

cried. He passed his hand over his disbelieving eyes. "I've... been... blind."

"You are blind, Molay," Raiis said with a
cruel laugh. "Blinded your whole life by the
pitiable biddings of an aging Pope and his
dead god. Open your eyes! Know the sweet-
ness of perversion!"

Molay, shaking with anger, lifted his
sword toward Raiis. "Knights of the Order,
godly men, are being arrested across Europe. You've brought this upon us!"

Shouts arose in the stairway beyond the
chamber; the clash of swords, running feet.
The doorway to the chamber was suddenly
filled with armed and armored men, the soldiers of the King.

The Templar knights pulled their swords
and looked to Raiis in questioning fear. Raiis
raised his hand, staying theirs, and turned
defiantly to the soldiers. Molay, soaked in
blood like the blasphemers, stood wide-eyed
in shock.

The leader of the soldiers, shaking at the
sight before him, closed his eyes and inhaled deeply. Steady again, he stepped hesitantly forward. He identified himself, drew
out a parchment, and read, "Jacques de Molay, in the name of King Philip IV of France,
I arrest you and your Knights of the Temple. The charge is heresy, practicing Black
Magic and worshipping the devil."

Twenty

"The Templars were arrested. All of them; including Molay." Trevelyan said. He stood behind his desk, running his hand across the surface of the bell, staring seven hundred years into the past.

Brandy studied the priest. She understood grief, God knew, but for someone simply relating history the Father's sorrow seemed almost ludicrous. Still, she said nothing as he resumed his story.

"It was a terrible day. One hundred and forty Templars across Europe, many here in France, were arrested for consorting with the devil." He sat. "Because the Templars had always been so secretive many believed the charges. Others owed them money and knew, if the Order was disbanded, they would not have to repay their debts. They supported the authorities."

"On 14 March, 1310, a trial was begun in Paris. The Articles of accusation were read and each knight found himself facing 127 charges. Pierre de Bologna and Renaud de Provins appeared for the defense. Under the false impression their clients might receive justice, they went before the trial commission to secure their rights. They demanded full disclosure of gathered evidence. They demanded witnesses be banned from discussing the case. They demanded the proceedings be kept secret until put before the Pope."

"In answer, the Archbishop of Sens, disbanded the commission, took over the trial as sole judge, and burned fifty-four Templars at the stake. Then he summoned Pierre and Renaud. You will not be surprised to hear the lawyers failed to appear. They were caught trying to escape Paris and were made to confess to heresy. There would be no justice. The Templars would be found guilty."

Including the knights of Castle Freedom.

The Archbishop sat at the bench surrounded by the empty seats that once held the commission. The Templars were led before him in chains. One of his Cardinals, acting as clerk, intoned in a reedy voice, "Francois de Raiis, you stand accused of heresy and practicing the Black Arts." Then he read the charges, a stomach churning list of ungodly acts, and passed the indictment to the judge.

The Archbishop looked over his crooked spectacles. "How do you plead?"

Too far away to spit, Raiis merely laughed and said, "To hell with you."

With the same disregard for the judge's authority each of Raiis' knights pled the same. All were found guilty. All sentenced to death.

"Because of his exalted position, Jacques de Molay was tried separately," Trevelyan said. "With no evidence he was involved in any Black Rites, no evidence of heresy, he was finally accused of participating in secret ceremonies. (The Templars held their initiations privately and at night.) This allowed the court to intimate guilt for 'unspoken evils'. It was the only charge ever levied at him."

"Molay was questioned, and by that I mean tortured, until he confessed. With that confession, the Grand Master convicted all of the Templars. He was forced to repeat it before the University of Paris. And, a month later, ordered to confess again before a Cardinal sent by the Pope. This was the last disgrace. Molay refused and recanted. And so, despite never having been charged with heresy, he was returned to his cell, the same as that of Raiis and his knights, to await trial as a relapsed heretic."

"I don't understand," Brandy said. "This all happened in Paris?"

Trevelyan blinked behind his magnifying glasses. "Ah, eh, oh, you're referring to Fournier's tour. Eh, Sorry, you've been, what's the American phrase. . . sold a load of goods. Though the setting is real, eh, I mean, er, Castle Freedom is an actual Templar stronghold, the tour is fright and fiction. The knights were arrested here, but they were imprisoned and tried in Paris."

"And the executions?" It was the first time she'd spoken since their introductions and Aimee caught the priest off guard.

"Eh, er, yes," Trevelyan said, still blinking like an owl. "On 19 March, 1314, following seven years of brutal imprisonment, Molay, Raiis and his six knights were brought from the dungeons to the eastern side of the *Ile de la Cite*, before the people and the cathedral of *Notre Dame de Paris* for execution."

"The cathedral, begun one hundred and fifty years before, was still under construction. But the western facade, the main entrance, had been completed and the grand twin towers rose triumphantly above the city square. A dais, upon which the heretics would be executed, was erected at the foot of the church steps, before the massive doors;

the portals of the Virgin, the Last Judgment, and St. Anne."

———†———

The clerk stepped forward, waved for the silence of the excited onlookers, and inquired, "Jacques de Molay, Grand Master of this disgraced Order, you stand before the King, the Church, the court and the people as a convicted heretic; already dead and damned in the sight of God. His Holiness, Pope Clement V, through his representative, the Archbishop of Sens, offers you a last chance at redemption. Will you now, publicly, renounce Satan and confess your iniquities?"

Molay couldn't do it. No one was more aware he was going to die than he, but he could not repeat the lies he'd been made to utter under torture. He could not confess to blasphemies he hadn't committed. He had proudly worn the Templar arms; the symbol of their dedication to martyrdom. Could he fail that dedication now?

"My only sin," Molay said, "was lying. . . to save myself from torture. The Order of the Knights of the Temple, with the exception of these men, is innocent."

The crowd, hundreds strong, jeered.

"I have served the Lord faithfully."

Their derision escalated; boos and cat-calls.

"I have carried the sword of the Savior. . . "

The executioner, known only as Fasset and only for his icy demeanor, knocked Molay to his knees. He would have hit him again, but the Templar called out to the Archbishop. He begged that his hands be retied, before him, that he might pray, and that he be secured to the stake facing the Cathedral.

The Archbishop conceded. Molay's request was honored. Then Fasset brought forward a lighted torch.

The end had come. All Molay could do was stare at the flickering light and cry out, "I will hope in the resurrection."

"I will hope in the resurrection?" Brandy repeated, unable to hide her disappointment. "That was the evil curse?"

"Oh, er, ah, no. According to legend, and mind you it's only apocryphal, it was Francois de Raiis who leveled the Templar curse."

As the Grand Master claimed salvation, Raiis screamed at Molay:

"Shut up, you damnable coward."

The Archbishop signaled Fasset and the executioner approached the condemned Raiis.

"The Pope and the King will pay for their conspiracy," the Templar screamed, spittle flying from his lips. "By year's end, Clement and Philip will meet each other in death!"

"With you!" Fasset shouted, drawing laughter from the crowd.

"No!" Raiis stared wildly at the executioner. "We will not die. We will return from the grave to have our vengeance on all of you. We will kill all of you!" Then he laughed maniacally.

It was a disturbing cacophony; a concert of insane human noise. In the crowd, some cheered, some wailed, and some went about their business selling refreshments, cutting purses, disciplining children, shouting, jeering, or passing their own judgments in whispered conferences.

On the dais, Raiis continued his insane laughter, his knights cursed the crowd, and Molay recited the Lord's Prayer aloud. The fagots beneath the stakes were set ablaze. Cries went up from the condemned Templars.

"I will hope in the resurrection," Molay screamed.

Raiis laughed. Then, he too, was overcome by flames and smoke. Like the others, he died screaming.

Twenty One

Blanc wanted to scream.

Interrogation was normally the Colonel's cup of tea. The duty he excelled at but got to do so infrequently. Finally the opportunity had come. He'd jumped in with both feet, pressing, pouncing, friendly one minute, fierce the next. So far, it had come to nothing. He'd been at it all morning and Marcel Fournier, day-time tour company executive, suspected night-time drug dealer and subject of the inquiry, sat unruffled and uninterested. Blanc wanted to scream.

The Colonel could no longer sit opposite that smarmy grin. He paced the room and, rather than ask questions, threw them like darts. Blanc had lost control of his temper and the conversation.

Fournier blew a smoke ring into the air. "Let me understand," he said, with amusement. "Your theory is I committed murder to keep people away from the castle; the castle to which my business takes people on tours. Is that right?"

"What is right, *monsieur*, is that your real business has nothing to do with giving tours. Everybody in the district knows it. You're a drug dealer, a thief and a liar."

"And yet my mother loves me."

"She's a whore," Petit chimed in.

Fournier lunged. Blanc caught him and forced him back. "Sit down."

Until then the Lieutenant Colonel, as was his custom, had been silently guarding the door. But he was growing tired of this criminal insulting his commander and friend.

"Can you or your pet," Fournier crooked his thumb at Petit, "prove anything, Colonel?" He lit another cigarette. "Or are you merely tossing grenades in the water to see what floats to the surface?"

"When did you last see Luis Socrates?"

"Never heard of him."

"That is, frankly, not believable. His father was your caretaker at the castle."

"It's good to have a father."

"He doesn't anymore. His father's dead!"

Fournier blew another smoke ring. "Nothing lasts forever."

———————

186

Brandy couldn't wait another second.

Ray was on her all through breakfast, for which she had no stomach, to put everything out of her mind. But she didn't want it out of her mind. She wanted answers. Ray hadn't any and, in the end, hadn't any patience either.

By mid-morning he complained he wasn't going to spend the day with a pacing lion. And he left; just left. To do whatever... in a strange country. He had no bike, no beer and no Brandy. The thought gave her a moment's satisfaction, followed by a realization he could easily buy a close approximation to all three. Just then, she didn't care whether he did or not. Vicki was back on her mind.

Brandy had the hotel room to herself. But morning begrudgingly turned into afternoon and impatience evolved into frustration. Eventually, she couldn't wait anymore. Not another second. As she had heard nothing from the police, Brandy decided it was time the police heard from her.

She entered Paradis' *Gendarmerie* station with questions, determination and, thanks to her dear old, beer-sated dad, attitude. She plunked down her massive handbag, and was about to address the weary but wary-looking soldier behind the counter, when the Interview Room door came open.

Three expressions paraded out; Lieutenant Colonel Petit's frown, Colonel Blanc's scowl and, in-between, looking like the winner, Fournier's gap-toothed grin.

Blanc spotted the American girl immediately and, as quickly, noted the recognition in her eyes when she saw the drug dealer (and suspected murderer).

Fournier stretched as if at the end of a long drive. He rounded the counter and tipped his hand to Blanc. "*Merci,* Colonel. I've had a wonderful time." He wasn't convincing but didn't seem to care. He passed Brandy as if she weren't there.

No sooner had he gone then Blanc, without disguising his accusatory tone, demanded of Brandy, "You do know Marcel Fournier?"

"We've met. Did he have something to do with Vicki's death?"

"How did you meet?"

"What does it matter?"

"We're investigating four murders, *mademoiselle.* Your relationship with a known drug dealer, who owns the site of the murders, is part of that investigation."

"I don't have a relationship with him. When Vicki went missing, we asked him and his partner what they knew."

"His partner?" Blanc sputtered a laugh. Her association with Fournier was innocent, obviously. Ignorant, but innocent. "If you mean Loup Wimund... He isn't smart enough to be anybody's partner. That, how would you say, degenerate... We are looking at him. Leave him to us."

"What do you mean 'degenerate'? And what do you mean 'you're looking at him'? What do you think happened?"

"We have the situation under control. Now, please, stay out of it." He waved her to the door and vanished into his office.

———+———

Brandy Petracus was not a crier. She could cry, and sometimes did, but she wasn't a crier. That said, when she stepped from the *Gendarmerie* station it took all she had not to burst into tears.

Ray had a full plate, but was being an ass. The Colonel had his duty which, apparently, included keeping secrets. Everyone had their point of view, but what about Vicki? And what about her? She stood, grinding her teeth, her right hand clenched on her ever-present bag, her left balled in a white-knuckled fist. She wanted to hit something, someone. She wanted to scream. She wanted to cry. And, at that moment, all of the elements necessary for cataclysm came together.

In the distance, Brandy saw Ray, heading her direction.

At the curb, Fournier sat behind the wheel of a deep blue, idling BMW talking with someone hunched in his driver's window. Then Fournier pulled away - leaving Loup Wimund behind in the street.

Brandy stared. What had Colonel Blanc said? Loup was a degenerate. They were looking at him. And there he was. "Hey," Brandy said. "You're Loup Wimund. I want to talk to you." Loup backed away. "Hey," Brandy shouted. "Wait!"

Still coming, Ray saw Brandy – and heard her yell. Then he saw Loup backing away from her in the street. He didn't know what the hell was happening but picked up his pace.

The little American woman was still coming, still yelling, and Loup continued to back away. Then, down the street, he saw the big one, her boyfriend, coming fast.

"You!" Ray shouted. "Wimund!"

Loup turned and bolted.

On the far side of the block, Ray took chase. Brandy threw down her purse and did the same. Loup was in the lead with Brandy on his heels screaming. They crossed the square, in front of Ray, headed for Jacques Chambon.

After a life of angering people, collecting taxes for the *Trésor Public*, Chambon retired. He built a park, then bought a horse and cart. Now he spent his days cheering people; giving children rides around his park. Chambon, and his faithful horse, Auguste, were at their usual corner when Loup, Brandy and Ray raced past in a screaming parade and entered *Le Parc Chambon du Paradis*.

Built at Chambon's personal expense, on a nearby meadow, the park and gardens grew to nearly twenty acres before the village annexed it. Now it was Paradis' biggest tourist attraction. Picnic tables and vending machines dotted the play area between swings, slides, manual carousels and, new that summer, an air-filled trampoline shaped like a castle. In the gardens, musicians played (for the adults) up and down the sculptured paths and over the tiny bridges and streams, while painted clowns frolicked (for the children). At the little menagerie farm peacocks strutted, cocks crowed, chickens pecked, and lambs and horses roamed while visitors saw they were never hungry. These were all cared for by Eloise, Chambon's wife, whose *Veterinary Clinique* bordered the park on the main street side.

For older children, and the more adventurous adults, there was the *Histoire Labyrinthe*; a maze of ten foot high hedges created by Chambon, his wife, and the village school. The maze featured twelve locked doors within its twists and turns. Each door bore a question whose solution unlocked it and allowed the answerer deeper access to the maze and the doors beyond. To reach the end, the player needed a working knowledge of French and of the day's selected subject. (Changed daily). Those deficient in history or French could 'piggy back' through with others. Or they could cheat with an answer card available at the admission booth.

It was that same booth that Loup ran by now with a screaming Brandy, and further behind an angry Ray, in hot pursuit.

A bench sat, against the hedge making up the outer wall, at the entrance to the maze. Loup saw it and, without slowing, leapt. He stepped on the back of the bench and jumped for the top of the hedge. He cleared it, ugly, and busted twigs and leaves flew in his wake. The woman in the ticket booth shouted.

Brandy, on Loup's heels like a doberman, vaulted the bench as well and cleared the hedge cleanly. Now the ticket lady was screaming.

Twenty Two

Ray, running behind Brandy (and way behind Loup), saw the ticket lady screaming. He cringed, imagining the trouble they were looking at, and pulled up panting at the maze booth. The ticket woman started shouting at him. Ray grabbed his wallet, pulling out money to calm her and pay for their tickets. The woman continued to scream; a cocktail of French, English and something that was neither. She pointed at the top of the hedge, claiming damages. Ray saw none.

He balked when she demanded payment for Loup's ticket. Then, afraid he'd never get away, relented and threw down enough for all three, promising he'd take it out of Loup's ass with interest. Ray grabbed a 'cheat' card from the booth and turned to the labyrinth that had swallowed his fiancé.

Several young people who'd just breached the first door were ahead of him. He slipped past them and into the maze shouting for Brandy. Behind him, the youngsters shouted derision. Behind them, the booth lady, still mad about her hedge, shouted for the authorities.

Trapped in the maze and sweating like hell Loup feverishly read the door's question. He'd been a rotten history student - until the day he was thrown out of school. But, today, luck was with him. The subject was Napoleon; and what idiot didn't know the name of the little general's woman? He tapped in the answer, heard the click of success and bolted through. Over his shoulder, Loup saw the crazy American whore round the corner. She was fast and he just shut the door in her face.

Brandy pounded the door and fought the tears welling in her eyes. She didn't have time to cry but, God, when she got back to the hotel. . . Now, as she stared at the puzzle, she needed to think.

Nom de l'amour de Napoléon.

"L'amour," Brandy whispered. "L'amour." Her French was awful; almost non-existent. But this she'd heard. She knew. Then it dawned. Love! Napoleon's love was. . . Josephine!

From somewhere near, she heard Ray shout, as she entered *Josephine* into the pad. "Here!" she screamed. "I'm over here!" The lock clicked, the door opened and she hurried through. The chase was on again.

For Ray, it had ground to a halt. "Fuck!" Staring at another dead end, he clamped his teeth and reversed direction. Left. Forward. Right. "Brandy?" he shouted, coming upon another door. He scanned the cheater card, matched the door number with the answer (printed, thank Christ, in French *and* English) and opened the lock. Ray stepped through and followed the hedge further into the maze.

Loup's progress had slowed. He'd been two doors ahead of the American bitch and thought himself home free. The thought was premature. He had the advantage of speaking and reading French (two different talents), but his ignorance of history was screwing him. Who'd have thought his teachers would ever be right? He read the next question and yelped. How in hell was he supposed to know to what island Napoleon had been exiled?

Ray was getting mad. He heard Brandy, barely, and yelled again. "Where are you?"

"For heaven's sake, Ray... what's the point of telling you forty times? I'm right behind him, but I can't read French."

"What door..." He tried to catch his breath. "What door are you at?"

"Something about Egypt! What? Nine. I'm at door nine! What's the difference?"

Ray checked the card and shouted, "The Rosetta Stone." Behind him, other paying guests were getting angry. Apparently they didn't want the answers and were letting him know. Fuck 'em. "The answer to door nine is the Rosetta Stone!"

Shouting was the name of the game in Chambon Park; particularly in and around the *Histoire Labyrinthe*. The children were shouting. The admissions woman was shouting. The maze occupants were shouting. Lieutenant Colonel Petit joined in; shouting to his gendarmes as they arrived at the maze. He received a brief account, and a master key to the doors, then led four soldiers into the labyrinth to pursue the law breakers.

Brandy dialed in the answer, door nine clicked, and she was through. She ran the alleys, back-tracked for dead ends, and arrived at door ten. The next question, in French, was Greek to her. "Ten, Ray," Brandy shouted. "Can you hear me? I'm at door ten."

"What did you say?"

"What the heck do you think I said?"

Brandy breathed deeply. It wasn't Ray's fault. She couldn't have gotten this far if it hadn't been for him. He was on her side and she loved him. He'd been through a lot. It wasn't Ray she was angry with; it was Loup. "Listen, for God's sake! Door ten!" Ray would understand.

Somewhere to the right, behind, or was it in front, angry voices shouted. All through the maze, tourists were getting mad. That was their problem. Somewhere ahead, Brandy heard Loup scratching at a door like a dog. He was her problem.

Ray ran his finger down the card. "Elba!" he shouted. The people behind him were screaming like hell. They hadn't, it seemed, wanted the answer to door ten either. Oh, well. "He was exiled to the island of Elba!"

Somewhere Loup heard the big American screaming, but he wasn't listening and didn't care. He had problems of his own, "Damn it," as he beat on door eleven. He'd pulled 'Elba' out of his ass at door ten. But here he was at eleven and how the hell was he supposed to know where Napoleon died? He entered a guess. Nothing. What the hell? Didn't all Frenchmen die in bed?

He heard the door behind open. And, though he couldn't see her, Loup knew he soon would. "Leave me alone!" he screamed, beating on door eleven again.

Brandy rounded the corner, shouting, "Don't go any further!"

Out of places to run, Loup screamed, "I'll kill you, you little...

The hedge beside him exploded in and Ray, screaming like a maniac, flew through. Leaves and branches shot across the maze, into the air, and rained down as he rolled ass over tea kettle.

Chaos ensued. Ray, prone on the ground, yelled. Brandy, still running, shouted. Loup, trapped, screamed like a little girl. Brandy leapt over her prostrate boyfriend. Ray saw her hurdle over. Loup, with nowhere to go, ducked. Brandy came down on top of Loup and tackled him to the ground. Arms and legs flew as they tumbled.

"I want to talk to you!"

"Get off... bitch!"

Brandy gouged her nails into his fleshy cheeks. "You know what happened to Ray's sister. You're going to tell me... or I'm going to scratch your eyes out."

"I...," Loup said, fighting for breath, through clenched teeth, "am telling you nothing."

Ray, scratched from stem to stern, his hair and clothing peppered in leaves and sticks, made it to his feet. He saw Brandy atop the Frenchman and, in a misguided show of compassion, grabbed ahold of her. She wasn't having any of it and added a six inch forearm scratch to Ray's already impressive collection. Ray let go.

Brandy turned back to Loup and punched him in the face. The soft tissue around his left eye blushed and began to swell. "You think I'm kidding you," she yelled. "You saw Vicki?" Loup didn't answer and Brandy punched him again. . . and again.

Ray, painfully sorry he'd gotten between a dog and her meat, hovered, dabbed at the blood on his aching arm, and left Brandy to him.

"All right!" Loup screamed. His left eye was temporarily closed for business. His nose had an admirable crimson flow. "*Oui. Oui,* I saw her."

"What happened to her?" Brandy demanded, claws poised over Loup's eyes.

"I do not know," he cried. Blood and terror muted his voice. He spit out the blood; the terror remained. "I did not kill her."

Now Ray was angry. He clenched a fist and stepped toward them, yelling, "You son of a bitch!" ready to join Brandy in the assault.

"*Arrêtez-vous!*" The insistent command came from behind. Ray's French wasn't worth a damn either, but the tone made it obvious the speaker meant business.

"*Arrêtez-vous! Monsieur. . . Mademoiselle.*"
Then, calming, the speaker switched to a
slow, over-enunciated English. "Let him go!"

Ray looked over his shoulder and down
the length of the hedge aisle. He saw Petit with grim seriousness on his face and
his pistol, for the second time, pointed at
him. Most people, finding themselves the
target of a *Gendarmerie* handgun, would
have been mortified. Ray was merely disappointed at the interruption. Lifting his
eyes from Petit, and his gun, Ray took in
the panting soldiers filling the maze behind
him. They, in turn, took in Ray and his
foliage adornments, Loup howling on the
ground, and the American girl straddling
him.

Ray tapped Brandy on the shoulder. She
looked back in annoyance then, past Ray, to
the new arrivals. Brandy saw the situation
for what it was and let Loup's shirt slip from
her fingers. Ray helped her off of him.

Loup sat up and leaned against door
eleven to catch his breath. Then he laughed;
the blood from his nose coloring his front
teeth.

Ray pointed at the door and laughed
himself. "Saint Helena, you stupid bastard.
Napoleon died at Saint Helena." He tossed
the answer card to the grass at Loup's feet.

Loup chuckled again, soundlessly. Then he stood, leaned toward Ray and whispered, "Your sister had nice tits."

Ray spun, busted him in his already bleeding nose, and jumped on him as he fell. The soldiers scrambled down the aisle. They tugged Brandy out of the mêlée and pulled Ray off Loup, whose face gushed crimson like a running tap.

As an impartial agent of the law, Petit ordered everyone into handcuffs.

Twenty Three

Despite the cool autumn day, it was cloistered in the *Gendarmerie* interrogation room. But the heat, intended for the Americans' discomfort, was a double-edged sword. Steam was rising off the Colonel's collar as well.

"For the last time," Blanc screamed, "we have no *evidence* Loup Wimund did anything at all."

"He raped her, for God's sake!" Brandy said.

"*Sacré.*" Blanc threw his hands into the air. "Your sister was not raped."

Ray was equally exasperated; unable to hide it and out of ways to express it. Brandy expressed it for him. "If it were your sister, Colonel," she said, "you wouldn't make the distinction. This Loup... he tried to rape her. He admitted he..."

"No, no, no," Blanc screamed. "His so-called admission is useless."

"So called?" Brandy came out of her chair. "Ray heard him." She pointed at Petit, hovering as usual. "He heard it, if he was paying attention. I got Loup to admit..."

"Sit down." Blanc clenched – head to toe. The veins in his eyes shot full of blood. "Sit down!"

Brandy sat. Blanc leaned across the table.

"Who do you think you are, *hein*? You have no authority here. *En vérité*, you are not even citizens. You elicited information from Loup while... how would you say, *mademoiselle*, beating from him the hell. That does not count even in your country." He paced away drawing breath. "As far as Loup Wimund is concerned, we are looking at him, but so far we have only evidence you, both of you, violated his rights. You assaulted him. We have his complaint, your admission, and four gendarmes as witnesses." He grunted. "Not to mention the damage to the *Histoire Labyrinthe*, *n'est-ce pas?*"

"You're making us the bad guys?" Brandy asked incredulously.

"We are investigating people of interest."

"Including us – apparently."

"We do not know you, *mademoiselle*. We are looking into you." He jabbed a finger at

Ray. "But we have read M. Kramer's criminal record."

Brandy's mouth fell open. Ray's did not.

"Ahh, M. Kramer, I see, shows no surprise. He knows we will check; knows how things are. *Mademoiselle* is surprised a violent record follows one. Or surprised, perhaps, only that we can read?" Blanc snapped his fingers.

Petit drew a folder from under his arm and handed it to his superior.

"*Eh bien*, let us see." Blanc opened the file and flipped through the report. "Public intoxication. Assault. Robbery. Ahh, of course, a weapon's charge. Everyone in America is a cowboy, *n'est-ce pas?*"

"I was young and stupid," Ray said. He'd been dabbing his cuts and scratches with gauze. Now he leaned back in his chair; defiant. He caught Brandy's stare and dropped his eyes to the floor. His face reddened. "I was young and very stupid. Read the dates, Colonel. I haven't done anything like it in years!"

"The time, they must tell it differently in your country," Blanc said, taking the moral high ground. "By my count, your last assault was committed, *en passant*, under forty minutes ago."

"I meant... besides this time."

"*Comme ça?* M. Kramer, this time counts. You do not get... what is it you say in the golf... *voyons*... a McGuffin?" Blanc sneered. Petit laughed.

"Mulligan," Brandy said.

The laughter stopped. Both turned back to the American girl. "*Quel?*"

"It's a Mulligan; a free shot, another bite at the apple. A McGuffin is..." Brandy noted Blanc's scowl and, more importantly, the twist in Ray's lip. Apparently, he didn't think she was helping. "Never mind."

In appreciation, Ray jumped back in the barrel. "Are you going to charge us?"

Blanc stared at the American, trying to figure him out, then turned to Petit and barked, "*Sortez!*"

The Lieutenant Colonel's eyebrows pitched a tent. He thought better of it and left without a word, pulling the door closed behind him.

Blanc sighed. He grabbed his head on either side and twisted. His neck cracked like dried twigs. A chill ran up Brandy's spine. The Colonel wagged his head, pleased with the results. "No, M. Petracus, M. Kramer, I am not going to charge you." He pushed on his lower back eliciting another horrendous crack. Then he sat opposite Brandy and Ray and crossed his arms on the table before him. He stared and, finally, wearily said, "Loup Wimund is a worm. I have no doubt he richly deserved all he got. But you can not, you will not, take the law into your hands again. Not here. Or you will see the inside of my district prison."

"So what happens now?"

"Let us do our job, *monsieur*," Blanc said.

"And, in the meantime, Loup goes free?"

"*Parfaitement.*" Blanc held up his hands pleading. "Rape was not your sister's problem. She was, *pardonnez-moi*, viciously stabbed and left to bleed. Those are not Loup's methods. He steals candy from children. He has no stomach for killing."

Blanc rose from his chair. "We look still for Luis Socrates. As the only survivor of his family, he is of interest. We are questioning others as well." He gestured to the door. "You can go. But I urge you to keep in mind there are many victims and, perhaps, as many motives. If Loup Wimund killed your sister, or took part in her death, he did not act alone. You will leave him be. And you will leave us alone. We will solve these murders... without you."

Twenty Four

Menderez Chitichia had reasons for leaving Turkey and, more pointedly, leaving behind the Istanbul authorities. He'd speak of his birthplace but never of why he left. France was now his home. That he was perfectly content with his third shift position at the solitary Paradis District Mortuary should have indicated, to anyone who cared, his desire to exist under the radar. The best thing about life in Paradis was... nobody cared.

Chitichia, thin, brown and asthmatic, peered through the door's wired window at the hall, leading to the offices, laboratory and gloomy pathology room beyond, and the starkly lit reception area with the second shift attendant, Pierre Vayssie, at his desk. Vayssie was a pig; too fat, too loud, too leering (when he wasn't eating). Now, of course, he was eating. He cringed as his colleague shoved half a liver sausage sandwich into his mouth. Not ready to face him, but already late, Chitichia pushed into the morgue.

"It's about time, *mon ami*," Vayssie said, the sandwich hanging from his mouth. Disgusted, Chitichia nevertheless amused himself knowing that, while it looked like Vayssie had a tongue made of rye, he most certainly did not have a wry tongue. Not one to cast pearls before swine, he did not share his quip.

As Vayssie yanked his jacket from the back of the chair, a glob of mayonnaise fell onto the open pages of their log book. "*Sacré*," he exclaimed. Then he shrugged on his jacket as he shrugged off the mess.

At the door, he turned and said, "Take a look in number four. Despite the suture and being kept frozen for three days, she is... *tré magnifique*." Thankfully, the liverwurst prevented a whistle.

"You make me sick. She is dead!"

"So is my wife." Vayssie laughed his head off. "*Merci.* I will be here all week."

In the freezer room, Chitichia checked the paperwork, looked to ensure he was alone, and opened cubicle number four. He slid the metal tray from the wall and pulled back the sheet. Vicki Kramer lay naked; awkward stitches closing the autopsy incisions.

Chitichia, his mouth free of chewed liver-wurst, whistled in appreciation.

"Forgive me, *Leydim*, but that pig Vayssie was right. You were beautiful."

A buzzer sounded. Chitichia jumped. Then he laughed, realizing it was merely a delivery. "Do not move," he said, recovering the body.

Chitichia opened the side door to find Soliveres, the old paramedic, waiting. He had a round head beneath a flat gray haircut and a round belly beneath a strained gray uniform. The head was renowned for the beer it took in; the belly for the beer it held. Soliveres passed Chitichia guiding a body bag on a wheeled stretcher. It was pushed from the other end by a young man that the morgue attendant did not know. "One of these is yours," Soliveres said. "The other one is my new partner, Aldric."

Aldric was little more than a boy, tall, slight, spectacled, with as much acne as he had face.

"I get the one on the cot?"

"Take your pick. Both are useless to me." Soliveres laughed. The boy's smile fought embarrassment and pimples to get to the surface. Chitichia felt for him. (Or would have had he cared). On second thought, he didn't.

"My last partner couldn't take it. Not a job for the faint of heart, eh, Aldric?"

Chitichia moved to shut the door and, only then, realized they were accompanied by a gendarme. The soldier, Leon Pomeroy, with whom he had worked often, and partied more often, was sandy-haired, sunny, and when under the influence, eager to confess – in detail – that his best military memories had been made on leave. Chitichia apologized. Pomeroy smiled, chirped, "Suicide," and handed the orderly a report.

Chitichia admitted the body then led the parade, footsteps echoing, wheels squeaking, down the hall. Through the swinging doors, in pathology, the orderly opened a compartment, rolled out an empty tray and offered the medics good luck.

Soliveres and Aldric transferred the body.

Chitichia, meanwhile, pretending to laugh at one of Pomeroy's jokes, failed to notice a crumpled sheet lying on the floor. He also failed to notice the number four tray, upon which Vicki's body had been lying, was now empty.

The orderly secured the suicide behind its door and ushered the ambulance crew and the jovial gendarme out. He bid the medics good night, assured Pomeroy they'd drink again soon, secured the door and went back to pathology. Only then did he see his problem. Chitichia stared in silence at the empty tray. Then he felt his chest tighten, heard his breathing turn to labored pants, and realized he was hyperventilating. An asthma attack seemed on the horizon.

The phone rang. Chitichia jumped nearly out of his skin.

At the front desk, struggling for breath, trying to collect his thoughts, Chitichia wouldn't have believed his night could get worse. Then he answered the phone... "Paradis Mort... *Oui*, Colonel. *Oui*, Colonel Blanc. A body? Victoria Kramer." The orderly's world fell apart. He repeated the name, stalling. "Victoria Kramer?"

On the other end of the line, Blanc damned his hesitation which didn't help his nerves or his asthma. Chitichia stuttered and finally confessed. "I am sorry, Colonel. But, you see... I can not find the body. It was there, in its place, a moment ago, but now she's... *Oui. Oui*, Colonel. As you say."

The orderly couldn't hang up fast enough. He stared at the phone, as if unable to place its function, praying it did not ring again. Chitichia's lungs felt like bricks. He dug out his inhaler, fired a blast into his mouth and held the medicine in – deeply.

"Do not touch anything," he said, repeating Blanc's last command, as he stared dumbfounded at the empty freezer tray. "She is gone. What is there to touch?"

His asthma attack was worsening and he gasped to catch his breath. The rales and rhonchus made his exhalations sound like the roar of a lion. Yet, despite the noise he was making, Chitichia thought he heard something else – in an empty morgue. The hair stood on the back of his neck and, though he didn't know why, Chitichia looked straight up.

Vicki was on the ceiling - above his head.

She hung upside down her fingers and toes gripping the tiles like a spider. With a gurgle, she rotated her head and stared hungrily down on him. Then she shrieked, let loose, and dropped on the startled orderly. Chitichia had no time to react. Vicki sank her teeth into the flesh of his smooth brown throat. A pain, unlike anything he'd ever experienced, shot suddenly through his body. All he could do was shout to God.

Again and again, she ripped into the morgue attendant's throat as she rode him to the tiled floor. She lapped the dark oozing blood until Chitichia lost consciousness. Then she gouged deeply, tore an artery, and relished the spurt. Vicki drank the crimson flow as if it were mother's milk and she a starving infant.

Chitichia's asthmatic alveoli, bronchioles, and bronchus slammed shut with finality. His screams ended and too his breathing. Gorging herself, Vicki drank the orderly dead, the hungry sounds of her feast mixed with hisses and moans. Then, bathed in and sated with Chitichia's blood, she fell away to the floor.

Vicki caught her breath and, renewed, skittered up the wall and across the ceiling. She opened a window and crawled out into the night. She paused in the shadows outside, clinging to the side of the building, while a couple passed below. When they'd gone, Vicki leapt to the ground and, naked, vanished into the dark.

In the District Mortuary, Menderez Chitichia lay dead; his throat torn, his body drained. The worst thing about his life there in Paradis was. . . nobody cared.

Twenty Five

Brandy was in pain. Father Trevelyan heard it when she called and could see it now, ironically, by what he couldn't see. The feisty American girl was wrapped in a long winter coat, though the autumn air was only just too cool for shirt sleeves, wore a wide-brimmed hat, and hid the windows to her soul with dark glasses. Ray, it was obvious, hurt as badly. With his open indifference to the church, his mere presence spoke volumes.

The priest suggested neutral ground; the church being a too formal reminder of their troubles, and their hotel room a too vacant reminder of the same. An admission that neither she nor Ray had eaten settled it. Trevelyan insisted they had to eat. So, at a café small enough to soothe Ray's dislike for crowds, in a corner secluded enough for Trevelyan to encourage talk, and dark enough for Brandy to expose her reddened eyes, they met for a meal.

Ray had scallops. The priest had skate. Brandy bore the tides of her uneasy stomach, watching both and thinking, good God, more fish! She pushed a cheese soufflé and green salad around on her own plate and wished she were hungry.

Though more attuned to the spiritual, Trevelyan soon realized the couple were hurting in body as well. Brandy took her chair sporting stiff limbs and a decided limp. Ray, in comparison, looked as if he should have been in hospital. Each movement brought a gasp, each bite a moan. He was lacerated and scratched from head to foot, had a bruised hand and, when pressed, admitted to a swollen knee. With no way around it, the pair confessed their afternoon adventure in the park.

The priest listened with alternating expressions of amusement and dread but added only, "Our, eh, er, choices are sometimes costly."

"In more ways than one," Ray said with a grunt. "The Colonel made it plain I'll be billed for the damage." He glared at Brandy.

"Don't look at me. I didn't ask for your help. And I didn't tell you to jump through the hedges."

"You asked for my help. . . repeatedly."

"Well, I didn't ask you to jump through the hedges. Besides... I broke a nail."

Neither the poor humor, nor the poorly disguised aggression, hid the fact both were hurting. Trevelyan, as much as he wanted to avoid confrontation, addressed it head on. "It, eh, isn't your fault, Brandy."

Their table froze while life went on normally around them. Brandy looked down. Ray looked away. The priest was about to apologize and retreat, when he heard himself reiterating, "Vicki's death isn't your fault."

"She was just in the wrong place at the wrong time, is that it?"

"If I said so, you'd claim that was your doing as well."

"Wasn't it?"

"You're strong, Brandy, but, er, not enough to shoulder responsibility for the free will choices of others. Blaming yourself would be the definition of hubris. Who, ah, after all, do you think you are?"

"You act like I'm trying to take credit for something."

"That's what your subconscious is doing. Taking credit or, if you will, blame. And handing out blame for perceived wrongs. There's no short-cut to understanding, no magic to instantly heal the hurt. I'm not a pop psychologist. But there is one fact you must believe – before all else. Vicki's death was not your fault."

She nodded.

"And it's not Ray's fault either."

Brandy nodded again, noncommittally.

"I had a brush with the same feelings this morning," Trevelyan said.

"How's that?"

"I was visited by the gendarmes, your Colonel Blanc."

"He isn't ours!"

"Hell no!" Ray added; expecting and receiving a 'don't swear in front of the priest' look from Brandy. "Hell no," he repeated. "What'd he want with you?"

"The same thing you did, I'm afraid. He wanted to know about the Templars. That's one of the reasons I, fleetingly, toyed with the idea you two had gotten me into something. I apologize. Turns out I alone was responsible for his curiosity."

"I don't understand." Brandy said.

"I don't either. He interrogated me thoroughly about the knights, the castle; then asked about my collection; the relics, armor, weapons. Wanted to know if any, several in particular, were missing. Wanted to know my whereabouts during the murders. It was quite disturbing. He made some rather insane insinuations."

Ray traded looks with Brandy. "You're a suspect?"

"Er, ah, well, eh, he didn't say as much. But I, er, confess to having felt like one. Hence my rather foolish thought to blame you. A cup of tea cleared my head."

They returned to their meal at the urging of the priest; a man both had underestimated. Ray remained distant and melancholy, unable Trevelyan imagined, to shake the image of his sister. Brandy was more eager to leave it behind, at least for the moment. He led her, at length, back to the subject of her studies. Trevelyan learned that, not only had the castle tour provided a gateway for their troubles, but had also washed-out in its intended purpose of informing her thesis. She felt shallow, she said, beefing about it now.

"Nonsense," Trevelyan told her. "Historically, Fournier's tour is a sham and you have every right to be disappointed. The Templar history is fascinating and could be helpful to you. Now more than ever you must fulfill your purpose."

"They were burned," Ray said, tired of the whole thing. "What more is there to the Templars?"

"Backstory. Isn't that right, Father?"

"Er, ah, well," Trevelyan said, "there is that, yes. And, of course, their death and burial; exactly what you're writing about."

Brandy smiled for the first time in days. Ray lifted his good hand in surrender.

"Jacques de Molay was completely heartbroken by the horrors he'd found at Castle Freedom," the priest said, chasing the fact with a bite of fish and steamed potatoes. "Francois de Raiis was once his close friend. Geoffrey de Charney, another of those arrested, a student and friend. And Molay found himself double-crossed by King Philip."

"Double-crossed?" Ray slowly lifted another bite.

His *scallops gratinéed* were staring at Brandy from a white clam shell-shaped plate. Her stomach objected and she set down her fork. The men didn't notice.

"Oh, er, yes. Molay was godfather to one of Philip's children. Oh, and don't think the Grand Master was executed because Philip believed him guilty of heresy. There wasn't a more pious man in all of Europe, including the Pope, and the king knew it."

"Then why have his friend killed?"

"Greed," Trevelyan said.

"Money is the root of all evil," Ray said flatly.

"An oft misquoted bible verse. The problem isn't money, it's greed. First Timothy 6:10. For *the love of money* is the root of all evils; it is through this craving that some have wandered away from the faith and pierced their hearts with many pangs." He saw Ray's smirk. "You think I'm foolish. Perhaps I am. But I, er, couldn't be more serious. The Kingdom was heavily in debt. In July of 1306, Philip confiscated the assets of every Jew in France and expelled them from the country. But it wasn't enough. He was still deeply in debt, much of that owed to the Templars; and they were vastly wealthy. Philip knew if the Order were dissolved most of their wealth would go to him. In the fall of 1307, to eliminate that debt and claim their wealth, he ordered their arrests for heresy. These were charges, incidentally, Philip had used on enemies before the Templars."

"If he'd done it before, fraudulently, why didn't the church step in? They were Christian knights, weren't they?"

"Whatever Templar wealth didn't go to the king went to the church."

"There's a big surprise," Ray said, without any. "The church was in on it."

"Not at first. Pope Clement tried to intercede. He openly expressed his indignation at his knights' arrests. He insisted on trials."

"That was big of him."

"You, er, ah, don't understand, Ray. The king didn't want trials. He wanted the Order dissolved, period. He ordered the burning of those first Templars, through the Archbishop, to prevent trials. In February, 1308, to slow the king, Clement suspended the work of the inquisitors and would not relent until Philip agreed to trials."

"It's simple human nature that the Templars inspired rumors. Their secret meetings, particularly those whispered of as initiations into the Order, caused both romantic notions and fears. The Chinon Parchment, found recently in the Archives of the Vatican, proves Clement actually absolved Jacques de Molay in August of 1308. The Pope wanted to know what the Templars were doing in secret. And, not wanting to delay the trials he'd fought for, sent three of his cardinals to the Templar leaders. They reported they did not believe the Templars had committed any sins, that they should be granted absolution and be allowed to receive the sacraments again. They were absolved by the Pope. But King Philip had his own agenda and, despite the Pope's proclamation of innocence, the Templars were returned to prison."

"And, in the end, the church made money off of the Templars?"

"Eh, yes. The king wanted it. Both he and the church would benefit financially from it. And, since only the Pope could declare the Order dissolved. . . Well, for want of a better phrase, it was a match made in heaven."

"Speaking of heaven, Father," Brandy said, taking up the dessert menu. "As a transplanted local, have you any suggestions for - what do you Brits call them?

"Oh, ah, afters. Sweets. The *Tarte fine aux Pommes* is excellent," he said lustily. "Thinly sliced apples in a delicate pie." He made a *yummy* noise, drawing looks from other tables. Trevelyan didn't notice. Without looking at the menu (his eyes had glazed over), he began worshipping the restaurant's idols of sugar and fruit. "The baked *Crème* caramel custard; nothing like it, I assure you. Oh, then there's the *Poire Belle-Héléne*." He kissed his fingertips and scattered it to the air. "Pear, chocolate, ice cream."

Brandy remembered the first time she'd seen the priest (giving candy to the altar servers) and, suddenly, realized they'd stumbled upon the chink in his armor. Outside of his passions for the Church and the Templars, it seemed, Father Trevelyan was a sugar addict. Brandy and Ray laughed. Trevelyan was on a roll.

"*Profiteroles au Chocolat*," the priest said. He bit his lower lip and rolled his eyes toward the heaven in the top of his head. ". . . *the* French dessert; a *choux* pastry and vanilla ice cream covered in hot chocolate sauce!"

"Stop!" Brandy cried, holding up a palm. "I feel a diabetic coma coming on! That last one sounds good." She set down her menu. "How about you, Father?"

Trevelyan smiled warmly. . . and shook his head. "No. Nothing for me."

"After that build up, you're not having any dessert! If Ray did that, I'd kill him."

Trevelyan stared, blushing. Ray offered no help; he simply shrugged and nodded. "Oh, eh, p-please, forgive me," the priest stuttered. "I would love to. . . I do love it so. Unfortunately my vocation provides little opportunity for exercise. I'm not getting any younger. And I have been rather over-doing the candy lately. Ray can have mine."

Brandy's lips twisted into a frown. "Ray doesn't do chocolate."

"What?" Trevelyan turned on Ray. "There's something wrong with you."

Brandy burst out laughing. The waiter came to Ray's rescue. "If I might offer a suggestion, *monsieur*. The *Gratin de Fruits rouges*. . . is a. . . Morello cherries, raspber-

226

ries; in a cooked cream and sugar gratin sauce... ohhh."

"Sold," Ray said, sending him away. "Now, if you two don't mind, can we get back to our discussion?"

Trevelyan looked grim. "Forgive me. Where were we?"

"You've been defending the Templars but weren't they guilty? Weren't they caught in the act?"

"Yes. Raiis and his six knights were, as you say, caught. They deserved their punishment. But in all my years of study, Ray, I've found no evidence their practices ever spread beyond Castle Freedom."

"How did the Templars get back here," Brandy asked, "if they were executed in Paris?"

"Normally the remains, the ashes and bone left after the fire, were dumped into the Seine. But here, to send a message, Philip ordered the fires extinguished the moment the Templars were dead and their bodies returned to Paradis for public burial. The Pope, happy to have the matter out of his hands, made no argument."

"Upon their arrival, my predecessor, and we are talking seven hundred years ago, refused their burial in the chapel cemetery. Likewise, he revolted against those wanting them buried in the crypt. He insisted they had no kinship with the blessed."

"Are you all right?" Brandy's interruption startled Trevelyan. Ray's look startled him more. The big man was 'green round the gills'. He waved them off.

Brandy put the moment down to stress, exhaustion, and bad café lighting and returned her attention to the priest. "So that's why the Templar cemetery?"

"Ah, yes. The king ordered them buried and, eh, so they were; interred in unhallowed ground in the wood beyond the castle. A much larger wood, at the time, and they were buried deep within it."

From a silver tray the waiter delivered Brandy's ice cream and chocolate pastry. She *oohed* and grabbed her spoon. Trevelyan *aahed* and relished her dessert by proxy. Ray wasn't feeling well. He shook his head at the new interruption, and the renewed antics of the sugar fiends, as the waiter set down his bowl.

"*Monsieur...*"

Ray stared into the thick sea of heavy cream and caramelized sugar brimming with warm chopped cherries and raspberries... all bleeding shades of red into the... grass beside the ancient sarcophagus... Ray gasped, unable to catch his breath, and unable to look away from the chunks... a swirling pool of crimson... chopped chunks and deep red... Vicki!

His head spinning, Ray fell into his afters.

Twenty Six

Ray buzzed their tin rental to a stop beneath the hotel's car port. He shook his head in disgust as it idled like a gerbil on a wheel. God, he missed his muscle car. And, God, he missed his bike. Brandy hid her amusement behind a mock look of fear. "I don't think this car has ever gone that fast," she said. "And you're still not happy."

"I'm sorry if I embarrassed you."

"You didn't embarrass me. The berries up your nose were fun."

Ray didn't laugh. She couldn't cheer him and was too tired to convince him. She climbed out. "Are you all right?"

"Yeah. I just needed some air." Ray patted what passed for a dashboard. "I'll put the skateboard on a shelf and be up in a few minutes."

He drove off leaving Brandy at the curb. She thought of Ray; something she'd done a lot lately, then admitted she was too tired for that as well. She needed a drink and she needed her bed.

Because people don't watch the sky without a specific reason, Brandy wearily entered the *Le Alexandre* without looking up. Had she done, she would have seen Vicki's naked corpse; first, clinging to the ivory stucco between the second and third stories, then skittering, in fits and starts, up the side of the building like a spider.

The name Alexandre meant 'protector of men'. That sounded good, in theory, but Brandy was about to discover the hotel's name offered female guests no protection whatsoever.

She entered their fifth floor room (it was the tallest structure in Paradis), dropped her bag o' plenty and jacket inside the door and made a bee-line to the bar. Too exhausted to go around, but keen on the bottle's whereabouts, Brandy reached over. She dropped on a stool, poured a shot and lifted the glass. Then she saw Ray's pillow and blanket folded on the couch. As if the horror of Vicki's murder were not enough; why was the rest of her world falling apart? What were she and Ray to do? How had things come to this? What had happened since that first wonderful night? She was just starting post-graduate work on her Master's, when she met Ray Kramer and melted like butter.

It was late September. A local garage band, The Prince of Space, was vibrating the windows of the I-90, a biker bar (in the last days of biker bars) on the western outreaches of Madison. Dragged there by a friend, she had no experience with bikers. She'd been waiting forever to buy a drink and couldn't see the bar for the people (and the tall hunk blocking her view). She was enjoying his butt in jeans, and giggling at the ponytail under his Harley bandana, when he blinded her with his smile.

It was now or never. "Have you seen a bartender?"

He took in her wave of brunette hair, big hazel eyes, and the biggest purse he'd ever seen. His eyes said, 'Nice.' He said, "Not only have I seen one, I actually ordered. I'll be out of your way in a flash."

"Could you order for me?"

His delicious smile widened. "My pleasure."

"You're that easy to please, huh?" She smiled back - and meant it. "A gin-and-tonic. And a vodka and cranberry."

"Thirsty?"

His tone hinted he was asking something else entirely. Normally, she'd mind. This time she didn't. "I'm with a lady friend."

"In that case, please, tell me the gin's for you?"

"It is. Why?"

"My sister drinks vodka and cranberry." He made a face and shivered. "There's something sick about trying to make liquor good for you."

She laughed, pushed a twenty into his hand, and told him her name. He shouted back his own (twice; over the noise). She pointed a general direction and, moving to the beat, disappeared back into the sea of bodies.

Minutes later, performing a three-drink juggling act, Ray snaked through the crowd. He spotted the little brunette in a corner booth with her companion. Ray made the table, circled to set down the drinks and, seeing her friend's face, groaned, "Oh, God hates me!"

Vicki looked up, incredulously asked Brandy, "Is this the cute guy?", then horse-laughed.

Brandy studied them. "Do you two know each other?"

"No!" they both said.

"Remember my vodka drinking sister?" He chucked a thumb at Vicki.

"You're telling strangers I drink? What'd you say, you little twerp?"

"Can you believe that?" Ray asked, as he scooted into the booth beside Brandy. She made room, but not much. "I'm nine inches taller, outweigh her by eighty pounds, still I'm a little twerp."

Their first dates came out of a book (if there are steamy romances about bikers). They were lovers on their first night. Then Ray told her he loved her. Normally, she'd have run for the hills but – this was different. She told him she was happy they were together and made love with him again. The months raced by. They rode the countryside and open roads on his bike, they walked in the parks, went to concerts, movies. She'd even forced him into a museum. They ate in nice restaurants. They drank in dive bars. They spent a lot of time in bed. Then came a welcomed engagement ring.

But all good things. . . Brandy's post graduate work suffered and she was warned her Master's was in jeopardy. She wanted, intended to get, her degree and told Ray so. He said he wanted what she wanted. But, as their time was impacted, was not a good sport. And, as her studies progressed, seemed less accepting with each passing day. It created a rift and, concentrating on her thesis as she was, mending it wasn't Brandy's priority. She'd decided a trip to Europe would help with her work and hoped it would help with her life. She'd invited Vicki, her best friend, and though it wasn't part of her original plan, Ray wound up invited as well.

Now Ray's pillow and blanket waited on the couch. It occurred she ought to stash them because, really, avoiding a subject was one way to solve it, right? Or she could just tell Ray to sleep in bed. To heck with it. Brandy was sick of pretending things were okay. She left them there, drank the shot, and poured another.

The room was nice; nothing special. One of many, in the median price range, in the only hotel in Paradis. It had a balcony with a charming view of the village, a comfortable mattress on the (lonely) bed, a couch and chairs that held their weight and, most importantly, the wet bar conveniently stocked with a variety of wet. Brandy had paid more for less and stayed in worse. It was what they could afford. It - and a smaller room for Vicki across the hall.

Poor Vicki. How she'd complained when she first saw her room.

Brandy knew Vicki like she knew herself. Her future sister-in-law dreamt of where they'd stay and, in her dreams, she'd felt the silk sheets, inhaled the freshly arranged flowers, tasted the complimentary chocolates in the 'Louis XIII' apartment of the

Château de la Treyne. She'd hoped for a room over the gardens – with a spectacular view of a winding river. Poor Vicki.

Brandy held her drink without drinking. Her study in death had brought them halfway around the world – and killed Vicki. Tears welled and ran down both cheeks.

She heard Ray at the door. Quickly, she wiped away the tears and checked her face in the mirror behind the bar. It was as good as it would get; good enough, at least, to deny she'd been crying. Not that he'd ask. She stared at the door, waiting, but it didn't open. Then she heard the sound again and realized it hadn't come from the door.

The sound, a rap and scratch, had come from the sliding doors to the balcony across the room. Brandy set her drink down, went to the doors and stared out. Here and there throughout the tiny village yellow lights glowed softly but, for the most part, she saw what Father Trevelyan described – limitless darkness. She returned to the bar thinking seriously now of getting drunk.

There wasn't, of course, any ice. God, what do Europeans have against ice! She wasn't in the mood for the tone, the looks, she'd get if she asked for it. Oh, well, here's to gin with no rocks. She drank. She inhaled. She poured another shot – and

237

spilled it when the tapping started again on the balcony glass.

The mirror behind the bar reflected the room. She saw the doors, the empty balcony, and the fear in her own face. There was nothing else. She felt foolish.

"Brandy?"

The voice was harsh, grating and muffled as if it came from outside. Then a new sound; fingernails skating on the glass. Still there was nothing to be seen in the mirror. Brandy turned, knocking the bottle over with a crash, to stare out the doors.

A movement, or suggestion of movement, in the corner of her eye startled her. But, staring, she saw nothing. Brandy, perhaps without reason, was frightened. A second look confirmed there was nothing there. Still her anxiety grew. She continued to examine the glass and, finally, saw something – in the upper right portion of the window. But what? She stared to give it a face; then realized that's exactly what she was seeing. A face, upside down, and hanging down from above the sliding glass doors. Her golden hair (Brandy was certain it was a girl) draped like a curtain as she peered in. Then she extended a thin arm and tapped the glass recreating the noise from a moment before. Brandy stood mesmerized as the girl climbed down onto the glass, like a fly on a television screen, maneuvered upright and jumped from the window onto the balcony.

She was naked, gray as sculptor's clay, and prominently displayed the results of a bizarre surgery. She bore an incision that started at each shoulder, met between her breasts and descended as one cut to her navel in a 'Y'. The bloodless wound was stitched together; pinches of flesh haphazardly sutured with thick brown twine.

The girl laid her gray fingertips on the window and stared through the glass, twisting her head mechanically like the animatronic presidents at Disneyland. Her eyes were shining black marbles in a sea of yellow – at once horrifying and captivating.

For no earthly reason, and against all logic, Brandy found herself drawn to the door and to the gray-as-death thing on the other side. She reached for the handle and for the lock beneath. Only then did it dawn, a faint glimmer in the dark, what – who – this thing was. "Vicki?" Brandy said weakly. "My God. Vicki, it can't be you. You're. . . "

"Help me!" the thing said in a voice dredged up from the pits of hell.

Brandy snapped the lock off, then turned back to see the mirror behind the bar still reflected only her image. There was nothing on the balcony.

Vicki turned the handle, forced the door and pushed a hand through to hold it. While Brandy, her fear growing, held it closed as best she could - unsure whether to struggle with her friend or not.

"Vicki... you're in the morgue."

"They treated me so badly there. You don't know."

Now she recognized it, Vicki's voice, but different; filtered, gurgling over rocks like a waterfall, choked with smoke, angry. Tears streamed down Brandy's stunned and dis-believing face. And, as if on cue, thick, glob-ular tears slimed their way down Vicki's ashen face as if in unholy parody of her own.

"I'm so cold," the Vicki thing said. "I'm so hungry."

Brandy, struggling to escape the drown-ing pull of the deep black and yellow eyes, backed away from the door. It swung wide and Vicki entered; her arms raised to em-brace. The room was suddenly rife with the antiseptic odor of alcohol and an acrid un-dercurrent of spoiled meat. Brandy felt her stomach knot.

Yet the shining black eyes were drawing her in.

Vicki took hold of her and, though she nearly drowned in revulsion, Brandy felt powerless to withdraw. Vicki's hands were as icy as the grave. The stench of rotted meat flooded her nostrils. Vicki kissed Brandy on the lips and disgust overwhelmed her. It was evil, horrid, empty; no affection, nor even warmth, merely a parody of a human act. Still Brandy felt powerless to resist.

Vicki gripped Brandy's chin in her cold hand and forced her head to the side. Brandy heard an ecstatic intake of breath. She heard Vicki's mouth open, heard her hiss hungrily and imagined her wetting her lips with her bloated blue tongue. Vicki bared her teeth and inched toward the rapidly pulsing vein in Brandy's exposed throat.

"Victoria!"

The Vicki thing snapped around at the sound of Ray's voice. Again the strange rotation of her head as if trying to recall the big man in the hall door. Ray stood, horror trading place with disbelief, trading place with horror, on his face. Vicki released Brandy, smiled pleasantly, and stretched her gray arms toward him.

Ray stared, as Brandy had, captivated by the eyes. His sister had always had such lovely green eyes. These were not Vicki's eyes. They were sickly yellow with deep black pools... Pools that dragged you down. Eyes full of fear, hate and hunger.

Ray jumped, startled to find Vicki had crossed the room, without seeming to move, and was, even now, cupping his face with her icy hands. "I missed you," she gurgled. Her mouth opened as her face disappeared below his line of vision.

"I command you!"

The Vicki thing looked up angrily.

Behind Ray, inside the door, stood a priest Vicki did not know. She gave the man of God a fleeting glance, then ignored him, and returned her attention to Ray.

"I command you," Father Trevelyan shouted again. He stepped forward and pushed his hand between their faces. "Unclean spirit. . . "

The next instant was nothing short of explosive.

Vicki saw something in the priest's hand, thrust in her face, and then recognized it – a crucifix. The crucified Christ. She shrieked and was propelled back from Ray.

"Whoever you are, along with all your minions now attacking this servant of God," Trevelyan stepped around Ray, "By the mysteries of the incarnation, passion, resurrection and ascension of our Lord Jesus Christ, by the descent of the Holy Spirit, by the coming of our Lord for judgment, tell me by some sign your name, and the day and hour of your departure."

The Vicki thing swore as she screamed and, as if struck, flew backwards. Her naked body struck the wall with thunderous force. A stitch broke on her incision, a slight gap appeared in her chest and the bag holding her organs was partially visible beneath.

Even Trevelyan began to tremble now. He breathed deeply and steadied the crucifix with both hands. "Depart transgressor," he commanded. "Depart, seducer, full of lies and cunning, foe of virtue, persecutor of the innocent."

Vicki cried out, shielding her burning eyes and trying to climb the wall to get away from the priest and the hated object in his hands.

His momentary panic behind him, Trevelyan drew a vial of holy water from his pocket. "Give place, abominable creature," he ordered. "Give way, you monster, give way to Christ. He has cast you forth into the outer darkness, where everlasting ruin awaits you and your abettors."

Trevelyan shook the vial throwing holy water on Vicki in the shape of a cross. "In the name of the Father, the Son and the Holy Spirit." The splashes hit her like acid. She clawed at her burning flesh; screaming. Then, incredibly, she burst into flames.

"Vicki." Horrified, Ray started forward.

Trevelyan grabbed him. "It's not Vicki," the priest said. "That is not Vicki!"

"What are you talking about?"

The creature stopped screaming and dropped to the floor in a flaming heap. The curtain over the door had caught fire, the charred paint on the wall peeled, and the carpet around the body was catching.

"Look at her!" Trevelyan said. "That is not your sister, Ray. Your sister is dead and whatever killed her caused this to happen."

Ray's fight vanished as he fell into shock. Trevelyan eased him from the heat, then threw open the balcony doors, coughing as black smoke rolled from the ceiling. Somewhere a fire alarm screamed. Then Brandy was there spraying the wall and curtain with the small extinguisher kept behind the bar. She extinguished the fire on the wall but stopped short of the thing on the floor.

The priest nodded in agreement. "Let it burn."

Twenty Seven

The Colonel, his knees locked, held a hand-kerchief over his nose with a shaking hand and stared through the hotel room door. Inside, a smoke-ejecting fan, two firefighters, and two medics worked over the burned thing on the floor. In twenty-three years, Blanc had never seen anything like it. It was turning into one hell of a night.

It started with that foreign idiot at the morgue telling him the American girl's body was missing and then, apparently, just walking away from his work. Followed by a frantic call from the *Le Alexandre* staff reporting a hell-raising assault on their fifth floor. Now this. Good Christ – what was this?

His call to Durand, that lazy son of a bitch, was a waste of time. The surgeon insisted he'd already declared the Kramer woman dead, autopsied her and delivered his findings. She was out of his hands and no longer his responsibility. Return her to her family, Durand yelled, slamming down the phone.

As he watched the workers collect Vicki Kramer's remains, for the second time, the Colonel realized he couldn't blame the doctor. Nor could he just return a burned corpse to the family and wash his hands of it. Especially this family. Something inexplicable was happening. He wanted answers.

Blanc tucked away his handkerchief and entered the room opposite the horror. The American couple and the local priest, of all people, waited there. Yes, something inexplicable was going on. Blanc closed the door on the activity across the hall.

The Americans sat on a sofa looking exhausted. The priest, on the edge of a chair, jangled a cup and saucer. Unable to halt his tremor he soon gave up on the tea.

Blanc cleared his throat. "There was a report of a disturbance in your room. I was already en route, when that call came, to deliver the news that your sister's body was missing. I arrive... and am appalled to find you disposing of evidence."

"Disposing..." Brandy stared aghast through red eyes. "Evidence of what?"

"Come, are we children?"

"We told you what happened."

"Your story is nonsense!"

"See here," Trevelyan said, rising.

Blanc ignored the priest and kept his glare on the Americans. To his surprise, even in their grief, they returned the look unflinchingly. He reconsidered his approach. "For some reason, someone or some group is trying to make us believe the Templar curse. That the Templar knights have... from the dead been resurrected. *Monsieur, Mademoiselle*, I ask, is it you?"

Ray stood with the priest. "How in the hell can we be suspects?"

"We found four bodies at the castle, your sister among them. You and your fiancé were at the castle. The property is owned by Marcel Fournier; a known criminal. You were both seen at Fournier's. We found a Templar's armor and weapons, weapons used in the killings in the timber. Again, you were nearby. And you are now keeping company with a man who collects Templar relics."

"Are you making it official, Colonel?" Father Trevelyan asked. "Are you accusing me of murder?"

"Someone committed these murders, vandalized the Templar cemetery, and left these ancient trinkets to scare others away from the castle."

"I've never heard such horseshit," Ray said.

The Colonel carved a hole in Ray with his eyes. "You are this close to being arrested, *monsieur*."

Brandy looked up incredulously. "On what charge?"

Blanc pointed at the door and, by proxy, at Vicki's body in the next room. "Murder," he said. "What else?"

"First me; now them? Colonel!" Trevelyan, out of character, was actually laughing at the officer. "Ray murdered his sister? Brandy murdered her friend? A woman your medical examiner pronounced dead two days ago?"

"I could certainly charge them with body snatching."

"When did they do this? They have been with me all the evening."

"Watch yourself, Trevelyan."

"You're claiming he stole a body you would have released to his custody probably tomorrow morning?"

The Colonel jerked the door open. Across the hall, in the room still gray with smoke, an ashen Soliveres and a pimpled Aldric (trying not to breath) lifted Vicki's scorched remains to the open body bag on their cot.

"When we are done," Aldric said, unaware they were being observed, "I quit."

"Coward." Soliveres spoke without conviction then inhaled not to be sick.

Brandy jumped up, crying out. Ray swore. Heads spun in the burn room and the medics nearly dropped the body. Blanc ignored them all. He pointed across the hall and shouted at the priest, "There... is the body of his sister!"

"*Ayez du sens, l'homme,*" The priest shouted back, arms akimbo. "You're suggesting they stole it, brought it here and set it afire in their living room? For heaven's sake, make sense!"

Brandy buried her head in Ray's chest.

Blanc waved the workers back to their task. Then he turned to the priest, his cheeks purple, his shock of white hair bringing out the dog. He poked a finger in Trevelyan's face. "Your influence," he said, through clenched teeth. "... and that of the Church, only go so far. As I have to you clearly indicated, you are, with your American friends, 'persons of interest' in this case. I warn you to understand that."

Blanc turned abruptly and stormed out.

"I'm sorry we got you into this."

They'd stepped across the hall, Brandy, Ray and Father Trevelyan, and were taking in the scarred, blackened mess that had been their hotel room. Brandy, rescuing her purse, jacket and little else, felt overwhelmed.

"Things happen for a reason, Brandy," the priest said. "God got me into this."

"Don't blame God." Ray lifted his melted pillow and blanket (now one polyester sculpture), choked on the smell, and threw them down again. He turned a suspicious eye on the priest. "The last time we saw you, outside a little café, you turned down a ride in favor of a walk in the night air. Don't take this wrong but. . . why are you here?"

"Ah, er, eh, I followed you." The fidgeting Father was back. Trevelyan picked his crucifix up from the floor and his holy water from a soaked and battered end table. He pocketed the crucifix and was about to do the same with the vial. "I, eh, was concerned. So, er, I followed you."

"It's a good thing you did," Brandy said, giving Ray the evil eye. She pointed at the vial. "And it's a good thing you had that."

"I, eh, had an American cousin who used to read comics, eh, comic books. They lived in Wyoming in the States and my Aunt drove him sixty miles to the nearest town to buy them. When he'd finished with them, my Aunt sent them to me in England."

Trevelyan stared past the couple, through the smoked window, no longer seeing them or the lights of the village. He saw a little boy, himself as a child, running the green rolling hills of Cornwall. He closed his eyes for a sweet moment then shook off the reverie. "When I was growing up," he said, quietly, "I always wanted to be a super hero."

He turned the vial in his hands, silver cap and shaker top, round cut crystal with a cross etched on either side, now nearly empty.

"Super heroes derive their abilities from a higher power. And they carry the most incredible toys. I guess the priesthood was as close as I was ever going to come."

Trevelyan escorted them back across the hall to what had been Vicki's room. He was about to bid them good night when Brandy asked, "Why did this happen? Why is any of this happening?"

"I don't know," the priest said helplessly. "I'm sorry."

"None of it makes any god damned sense." Ray's explosion came from nowhere. Then he stood there - spent.

"No, Ray. Believe me, you're wrong. You see, there are no contradictions. Had we all the facts, I am certain everything would make sense. Even if the facts seem, on the

251

surface, unbelievable. Within their framework they will make sense."

"I don't get it. I'm a simple guy. . . Hell, I don't even know what to call you. Priest? Father? I'm not a Catholic. I'm not. . . "

"You're my friend, Ray," Trevelyan said. "Call me Clive. It's my name."

Ray nodded. "I'm a damned simple guy. . . Clive. I work hard - in the real world. I'm not a religious man. I don't even believe in God. But I'm not one of those morons who turns atheism into a religion either. You can believe what you want just leave me out of it. I like bikes, beer, tattoos. I love Brandy and I love. . . I loved my sister. After Mom died, Vicki and I only had each other."

Ray looked at the door separating them from. . . that room. The room where the unbelievable had become real. Where the remains of. . . that thing. . . had called him brother and attacked his fiancé. The room where. . . something. . . (the power of God?) had caused that evil creature to go up, screaming, in flames.

Ray started to shake. "I admit I'm not all that bright. But I just don't get it."

"You're looking for rationale where it may not exist. I said the facts will make sense. . . within their framework."

"You've lost me."

"It's simple," the priest said. "You weigh two hundred pounds here. If I ask you to float on the air my request makes no sense. In a spacecraft, in space, you're virtually weightless. You float regardless of whether or not I ask it of you. In fact, you must be tied down to prevent it. You haven't changed. What's changed is the framework in which you exist."

Ray nodded. But what one had to do with the other he had no clue.

"We're dealing with the supernatural," the priest said. "But we don't know the rules. We don't have the facts to make it rational. Without those facts, the unexplained cannot be explained."

"Then we need those facts," Brandy said. She took Ray's hand and held it to her face. "We need to go up to the castle."

"What!" Trevelyan grimaced. "That is a remarkably bad idea."

"You said we need to do some fact finding."

"I said there were facts to be found. I didn't say they ought to be found and I certainly did not suggest you two find them."

"I want an explanation. If one exists, I think, it will be found at the castle."

"Brandy, you have both suffered enough. Please, go back to America."

"I can't do that." She turned to Ray and, happily, found him nodding support. "We can't do that. We're going to go right on suffering until we have some answers."

Trevelyan saw the determination in Brandy's eyes. Then he saw the loyalty in Ray's. The biker moved to the small bar in this room and poured drinks for Brandy and him. Then he waved the bottle, silently offering one to Clive. The priest nodded and watched Ray pour the third.

Brandy downed the shot, was startled to find it was whiskey, and felt the heat burst in her chest. She took a breath then looked to Trevelyan with renewed determination... and not a little hope. "You know more about the Templars, more about that place than anyone, Father. Will you come with us?"

"I came to France," the priest said quietly, "a long time ago – to hide. I thought, eh, no, that's a lie, I always told myself, I joined the priesthood to help people. I'm afraid, all along, the truth was I wanted to protect myself... from everything." His eyes began to tear and he told himself it was the whiskey. "For the longest time, I've felt the Lord pulling me, scolding me really, to stop hiding. Clive Trevelyan, he's been saying, I created a big world. Go and see it. And really be of use."

The priest lapsed into silence for the longest time. Brandy and Ray waited and, finally, with a strong voice and no hint of hesitation, Trevelyan said, "Yes. I will go with you to the castle."

Ray poured another round and, together, they drank their drinks - late into the night and early into the morning.

11 - The Dead of the Legend

One

Marcel Fournier was dead on his feet. His sleeplessness had been further aggravated by – of all things in quaint little Paradis – sirens. Sirens in the middle of the night as if they were in Paris. The long night crawled into a long morning.

Fournier had just poured himself a cup of coffee and was headed for his desk when the curtain to the back room came open. He scowled at Loup. His underling looked like hell. His eye was a swollen mess, his nose a purple abomination, his lower lip pulped meat. And a woman was responsible. Pathetic. "Is everything ready?"

Loup nodded. Apparently, it hurt to talk. Pathetic.

"Be sure. I do not want any mistakes. The shipment tonight is going to make..." Fournier stopped abruptly, his cup halfway to his lips, his thought half expressed...

staring through the front window. He could not believe his eyes.

There they were, across the street, marching on his shop like gun fighters in one of their westerns; the mean little American bitch (with her huge purse), the big American (with the dead sister) and, of all things, a priest (and what did that bastard want?). "Do you see this?"

Loup joined his boss at the window. He too wondered if he could believe his eye. "These *Americains* are crazy." The usual nastiness in Loup's voice, Fournier noted, had been replaced by disbelief - and fear.

The trio stopped out front. A discussion followed which, to Fournier and Loup, played like a bizarre pantomime. The woman was soon angered by something the big man said. Her reply sent his arms into the air. The priest, true to form in Fournier's opinion, added nothing. Whatever their debate they, apparently, came to an agreement. The couple left the priest, headed in.

Fournier returned to his desk and shuffled papers as the bell over the door sounded. When it ceased, without looking up, he said, "No tours today."

"We didn't come for a tour." The big man re-introduced himself, re-introduced the woman, then added, "We need your help."

Fournier looked up. His face, usually a threat, was now a question mark. "My help?" He dropped the papers he wasn't reading. "You and your little bitch beat one of my men." He pointed to the pulped and purple Loup. "You interfere with my business. You come here as agents of the *Gendarmerie*. And you ask for my help?"

"Your man left my sister alone at the castle. He may or may not have had a direct hand in her death, but he certainly contributed. He deserved worse than he got and you'd have done the same. As for your business, we don't know anything about it and don't want to. As for the *Gendarmerie*, they're half convinced we're helping you and neither of us give a damn what they think. We're here for personal reasons, nothing else."

"The priest?" Fournier asked nodding toward the window. "What has that worthless bastard to do with this?"

Geez, and Brandy thought he had issues with the church! "We asked for his help," Ray said. "He agreed."

"Now we're asking for yours," Brandy added.

Fournier stared, amazed, annoyed and impressed by the Americans' temerity; if not their tenacity. He considered offering them a drink and then, with equal sincerity, considered shooting them both. It was an odd sensation not knowing whether to laugh or explode. Without consciously choosing, he went with the former – and roared.

"You... you are crazy, *mon ami*. You are both crazy. You do not know when to be afraid. But I like you because you are crazy." He slapped his desk, decided. He was as good as any damned priest. "So... what is it you want? How is it I can help you?"

"We're going back to the castle this afternoon; the two of us and Father Trevelyan. We intend to retrace my sister's steps and find out what happened to her."

"The castle is mine. I own it. I have not given you permission to go there."

An icy moment passed. "You're right," Brandy said, breaking the tension. "You're right, Mr. Fournier. We would really like to return to your castle and retrace Vicki's steps, if we're able. We request your permission."

She looked Fournier in the eyes, confidently but without defiance.

"And if I agree?"

Ray jabbed a thumb in Loup's direction without taking his eyes off the boss. "In that case... we'll need him. He was there."

Loup looked like a cornered animal. Bruised and beaten he flashed hatred at Brandy and Ray as their 'request' sank in.

Then he looked to Fournier displaying cowardice with his working eye.

For the first time in a long time, Fournier actually felt something for Loup – pity. He laughed again, a joyless exhalation, and shooed the Americans toward the door. "*Aller à l'enfer.*"

Neither Brandy nor Ray needed any translation. 'Go to hell' was pretty much 'Go to hell' in any language. But they needed Loup's help and Brandy was not willing to give up. "If you give it some thought, Mr. Fournier, you'll find it's in your best interest."

He eyed Brandy, allowed himself a base hunger, then turned it off. She wouldn't be worth the trouble. "How – my interest?"

"I was at the *Gendarmerie* station when you were questioned. They have already hauled you in because of what happened at the castle; perhaps because of what Loup did. They will again until they solve these murders. Is he worth that hassle?"

Loup pulled a gun on Brandy. "Like Fournier said, you can go to hell."

What followed startled and impressed the drug dealer; the combination of instinct and training only a leader of men can appreciate. The American, big as he was, jumped, snapped a kick to Loup's hand that sent the gun into the air. He landed, pivoted then kicked him on the sternum. Loup crashed, backwards, ass over tea kettle. To finish the trick, Ray caught the gun as it came back down. He offered Fournier the gun butt first.

The drug dealer took it shaking his head. "I like you, *mon ami*. But you are more than crazy. You are suicidal."

"What if it were your sister?"

Fournier considered the question. He studied Loup, rising from the floor and dabbing his aches with his fingertips; his chest, his eye, his lip, and now his ass. Pathetic. Fournier turned back and nodded. "Take him."

Loup opened his mouth, but nothing came out, making him look like a landed trout. He tried again and his question arrived full of air and incredulity. "What?!"

"You're going with them."

"Why should I?"

"For the same reason you do everything. Because I say so. This whole thing is bad for my business. It draws attention to me. I do not like attention."

"Can't you just get rid of them?" It wasn't a question. It was a plea.

Fournier looked from the biker and his woman to their companion in the street. He shook his head. "Killing two Americans and a priest would also draw attention. You'll go

264

and help them any way you can." He turned to Brandy and Ray. "For my assistance, my crazy American friends, I am never going to see either of you again."

They asked to leave at four, as if it were the last tour of the day, and Fournier consented. For his part, he turned over the keys to the castle gate (the grounds had just been released by the police) and assured them Loup would be among them. The deal was struck and Brandy and Ray left Fournier's Tour of Terror for the last time.

"Crazy," Fournier said, watching them go. "These Americans are crazy."

———†———

Brandy and Ray traded sighs of relief as they rejoined Father Trevelyan outside. It hadn't gone smoothly, but it had gone and that was what was important. Both nodded - giving him the good news. He sighed too.

It was then the trio heard a tisking like a chattering squirrel and turned to see Felix, Brandy's original tour guide, vying for their attention from the corner of the building. He pointed at Ray and whispered, "*Monsieur. Monsieur.*"

As Ray and Brandy drew near, they saw Eve, Felix's red-haired girl, there behind him.

Felix was having difficulty. He opened his mouth but nothing came out. He reset his lips and tried again. The second attempt was better; dry but audible. "I. . . I was listening, behind the curtain, from the back room. If Fournier knew he would kill me."

Ray shrugged. Their presence was no secret. "Listening for what?"

"When you go to the castle," Felix said, "I want to go with you."

You would have thought he'd kicked Brandy. "You didn't care the other day," she shouted, startling the others. "Why do you care now?"

"Easy."

"Well, he didn't."

Felix looked nervously from Brandy to Eve, then back to Ray. He took Ray by the arm and led him away. "Eve, my girl, she is angry with me. She often is. I can not blame her. She does not want me working for Fournier. She is a good girl. She says doing right is more important than money. I have never found that to be true."

Ray smiled but stifled it. Felix was painfully serious.

"I am not a bad person. But not being bad, Eve says, is not the same as being good. I have cheated people but I have never hurt anyone - really hurt them. I had nothing to do with your sister. But people will talk. I know if we are called murderers I will never get out of here. . . and I will lose Eve."

"Brandy believes you know more than you've said."

"I do not. But I feel responsible. I would like to come with you. I will answer as I am able and help you discover what happened to your sister."

"What have the Templars to do with this?"

"Nothing! What could they possibly have to do with this? The Templars are nothing but eight old graves and a legend. I do not believe in the Templar ghosts. I have been selling them to tourists for too long."

Ray turned and looked to Brandy. "You thought he knew something before."

Brandy nodded. But before she could speak she was interrupted by an unmistakable voice.

"Felix." Fournier stood in his shop doorway. "Felix, let us talk. . . alone."

Despite Eve's obvious disapproval, and the others' concern, Felix disappeared around the rear of the building with his drug dealing boss.

They followed a stone path to the rear fenced-in yard with Fournier leaning, almost threateningly, on the young man's shoulder. "You are a good boy, Felix. You are stupid but you are a good boy. I have treated you like my own son."

"I must be done, Fournier... for Eve. I must go." If Felix didn't know better, he'd swear he saw real pain in Fournier's eyes. He couldn't let it matter now. "I must go. But I would like to help these Americans before I do. I owe them."

"Never do anything for anyone else."

"I owe Eve."

He laughed. "Especially a woman." He ran his hand across his lower lip and stared hard at the young man. "You would leave me now? Today?"

"I should have left before now."

"This is gratitude?"

"I am grateful. But I feel I have no choice."

"If you leave me now, you are done. You don't come back."

"Unless you kill me I'm leaving."

What a morning it was turning out to be. What a very strange morning. "Go." Fournier almost spit the word. "But do not come back. When you are broke, and you will be broke, remember the bank is closed to you and your little bitch."

Felix nodded slowly. In his mind's eye, the only safety net he'd ever known was cut to ribbons. And he held the scissors. The image vanished when he saw a cold steel gun pointed at his chin. Fournier cocked it – with mist in his eyes.

"If you were anyone else, knowing what you know, I would shoot you now. Take your last tour of the castle. Help these crazy Americans. But know this... if you say anything to anyone about my business, or tonight's shipment, you will wish the Templar knights *had* come back from the grave and gotten hold of you." He patted Felix's cheek then slid the gun back into the small of his back.

On the opposite side of the fence, unknown to either of them, Jerome Rousseau sat silently rubbing down a boiled animal skull, his own ears pricked like a predatory creature, breathlessly listening to every word spoken. When Fournier and his man ended their discussion and left the yard, Jerome quietly crept back into his tattoo parlor. He had a phone call to make.

————

"It is settled," Felix told Brandy as Eve took his hand. "We will go with you."

A blue Peugeot, its toy horn blaring, raced up and stopped beside them. A tin can with two doors, Ray noted, while Brandy thought, 'How cute'. Their favorite reporter was at the wheel.

"Are you all right?" Aimee shouted as she jumped out. "I was to cover a story on a fire last night at the *Le Alexandre*. They wouldn't let me in. The fire department insisted I talk to the police. The police would say nothing. I find from someone in the kitchen the fire was in your room. Were you hurt?"

"No," Brandy assured her, "We're all right."

"What happened? What caused the fire?"

"You wouldn't believe it," Ray said stiffly.

For the first time, Aimee examined the suspicious looking group; Brandy and Ray, Father Trevelyan, the tour guide Felix and his girlfriend and, in the doorway, Fournier watching all with an expression that kept changing. Her reporter's senses were tingling. "What is going on? What am I missing?"

The group traded looks in silence. Finally, the priest said, "We're, eh, ah, organizing an expedition."

Fournier sniggered.

"We're going back to the castle," Ray explained. He turned to the group. "We'll go at four."

"I'm going too!" Aimee said.

"Christ, we're going to need a bus."

Fournier laughed uproariously. Then he drew a set of keys from his pocket and dangled them. "That fat bastard Blanc has released my property but disallowed my tours until further notice. For now I'm out of the business." Fournier threw the keys to Felix. "Consider it my last contribution to the ghost hunters."

He turned and, laughing again, entered his shop.

Two

Shortly after four, the gray battleship that was Fournier's tour bus, still displaying its *Tour de Terreur* banners, arrived at the castle. Ray pulled down the police warning tape and opened Fournier's padlock. Then, with Felix at the helm, the bus revved through the castle gate, groaned beneath the arch and sagged to a stop near the courtyard.

"All ashore," Ray said. He turned back to see he'd only confused the passengers; particularly Eve and Aimee. Apparently they were still in France. Ray shooed them to the door. "Everybody out."

The group piled from the bus, pulling hats and sunglasses into place or, in the case of Trevelyan, squinting against the late afternoon sun. Everyone, that is, except Loup. He stretched across a rear seat, arms folded, legs crossed, eyes closed. He was an island unto himself, above and outside the loathsome Americans who'd forced him there.

Ray stood over him frowning. "Do you need a special invitation?"

Loup condescended to open his working eye, was unimpressed with what he saw, and closed it again.

When Ray told him to get up, Loup ignored him. When Ray jerked him from the seat and propelled him down the aisle, Loup regained his balance, straightened his collar and locked his jaw in defiance. And when Ray shoved him off the bus into the crowd, he finally ran out of attitude. "All right, my rough American friend," Loup sneered. With a plaster strip across his nose and a purple mound where his left eye ought to have been he failed miserably at looking tough but didn't let that stop him trying.

Ray looked the group up and down. Aimee had a backpack, Brandy had her purse, Trevelyan had a large black shoulder satchel containing God only knew what, Felix had Eve, and Loup had his bruises; all ready to begin.

"Well," Loup demanded, "what now?"

Brandy and Ray shared a look; amazed such a loathsome creature could show so much contempt for others. "We reconstruct what happened the other evening."

"This is stupid. Would it not make more sense to let the police. . . ?"

"Nothing makes sense," Ray yelled cutting him off. "We're not waiting for the police. We are going to recreate the tour from that day as closely as we're able. Which means Brandy, Felix, *and you* are going to tell us everything you remember and everything you did." He stuck his finger in Loup's face. "And, if you know what's good for you, you'll do everything you can to help. And you won't leave anything out."

It was the definition of 'unheard of' for a quiet country village; Lieutenant Colonel Petit and six gendarmes loaded rounds into rifles, ratcheted shells into shot guns, and secured their sidearms outside of their station. As each weapon was checked, it was loaded through the door on the passenger side of a blue van (red and white stripes and *Gendarmerie* emblazoned on each door). All down the line the soldiers prepared, it seemed, not for an arrest but a battle.

The deep blue sky, streaked with flames of red-orange as the sun sank, threw long shadows on the ground. Jerome Rousseau stood in one, at the corner of the building, watching the gendarmes and looking as if he'd rather be anywhere else.

Then Colonel Blanc broke from the station descending the steps at a clip. Petit shouted the unit to attention and the soldiers fell in. Blanc liked what he saw. It was good to be king. "Are you ready, Lieutenant Colonel?"

"*Oui*, Colonel."

Chest out, gut nearly sucked in, Blanc paced before the unit. "Men. . . " (Five men, one woman, but it was the military), "we have that bastard!" He waved a fist in the air. "We have him! Fournier has a shipment, no doubt cocaine, coming in tonight. And we are going to receive it for him. We will catch them red-handed."

"A raid on Fournier's shop?" one of the soldiers blurted out.

"No, no," Petit shouted, glaring at the soldier. 'No' to it being Fournier's shop and 'No' to speaking in the ranks. The Lieutenant Colonel mentally put him on report.

"Not his shop, you idiot," Blanc said. "Fournier is bringing his drugs in to the castle. All of this nonsense, these murders, have been in preparation of this delivery. They are using the legend of the Templar ghosts to frighten people from the castle. I have sources and will bet my life on it. Tonight we collect the evidence. We arrest the killers with blood on their hands. And we stop a shipment of hard drugs."

"The men have been instructed to hold their fire unless. . . "

"At the slightest provocation," Blanc said, interrupting his junior officer. "And there will be one. We will be forced to shoot Fournier to death."

Eyes darted. A lip or two thinned under pressure. One eyebrow momentarily arched. All quickly returned to front and center. Good, Blanc thought, very good. "Move them out, Lieutenant Colonel."

The soldiers loaded into the van. Petit took the trailing car with Andre Fulke as his driver. Blanc scanned the block, as he headed for the lead car, and spotted Jerome at the edge of the building. "You're late," he shouted. "What are you waiting? You will ride with me."

Jerome stepped nervously over. "Bloody hell, this has nothing to do with me."

"You are forgetting to whom you are talking, you little rat!"

Jerome swallowed hard and the word "psycho" did the wave across his throat.

"You are my eyes and ears in Paradis, my tattooed friend," Blanc said. "In particular when it comes to Fournier. I would not dream of going to the castle without you; for I would be deaf and blind."

"If he sees me he'll have me killed."

"He need not see you. Get in." After a pause, he added, "Or I will kill you."

Jerome sighed heavily. He and Blanc climbed in. The driver, Maurice Delvit, pulled the car away.

As they turned onto the main drag, and into an aggravating bottleneck of tourist vehicles, Blanc ordered Delvit to turn on their emergency lights. The van and trail car followed suit. Flickering swaths of blue cut through the rising dusk as their vehicles moved through the village.

"I still don't know why I'm here," Jerome complained, slumped in the rear seat.

"I already told you," Blanc said. "And, if I were you, I would pray my information was correct. If you are wasting our time, M. Rousseau, you will be sorry."

Jerome slid still lower.

"Once we have reached the edge of the village," the Colonel told Delvit, "turn the lights out. We shall make at the castle the stealthy surprise."

Several of Fournier's men carried cardboard boxes, all boldly (and bogusly) labeled *Coffee*, to a truck parked beside his unlit building. Furnier quietly hurried them up from the cellar, through the wall panel, the back room and outside, reminding them in

278

no uncertain terms to protect his merchandise as they worked.

"*Ne perdez pas de temps. Dépêchez-vous*," he said. "*Et soyez prudent.*"

He'd counted on Felix. . . No matter. Soon they would be on their way.

Then he saw the parade of blue lights coming toward his shop. He launched the box in his arms into the truck and slammed the tail gate.

He stuck his head inside the back door and gave away his age, shouting, "*Le marechaussee!*" It was the name by which the *Gendarmerie* had been known when Fournier was a kid and he spit it out as if it were spoiled food. He waved his arms at his workers. "Drop them," he shouted in a whisper. "Drop the boxes! Hide!"

His men did as instructed; following the boxes to the floor. When they were out of sight, Fournier went to the floor too – sliding the back door closed with his foot. Then he held his breath. Fournier saw the reflection of flashing blue lights through the windows against the darkening walls. And then. . . all was gloom again. He raised his head but saw and heard nothing. He stood quickly and quietly and peaked out a side window to see the flickering blue lights of the *Gendarmerie* disappearing in the distance. They had raced by, without slowing, and continued on headed out of the village.

Only then did Fournier realize he was still holding his breath. He exhaled forcefully, inhaled deeply and tried to still his racing heart. His men closed in around him watching after the police.

Finally, the disbelieving Fournier asked aloud, "Where are they going?"

The soldiers, packed into their tactical van, knew where they were headed. What they didn't know was what they would find when they got there. They silently traded smiles; looking forward to the fun.

The Colonel's car, and the vehicles behind, followed the trail of Fournier's bus out of the village, across the canal and, into the rocky hills that led to Castle Freedom. They were halfway up the mountain face, a quarter-mile from their destination, when Blanc ordered the vehicles to the side of the thin country road. He did not want to surprise Fournier too early. They would wait there and give the drug dealer all the rope he needed to hang himself. Then they would drop on him and his men and catch them breaking the law.

It wouldn't be long. The sun was nearly gone and soon the darkness would be upon them.

———†———

The sun set in a glorious explosion of blood red that ran away into the black horizon and was replaced by a shining full moon. Its blue light lit the stage and threw eerie shadows like glass shards across the rocky Languedoc hills, the ruined castle, the lonely chapel, the stark field, and the unhallowed cemetery at the edge of the timber.

In that forgotten graveyard, what had, the previous night, been an elaborate rite of bloodletting was, this night, simplicity itself, as the sleeping Templar mummies awoke in their tombs. The creatures again pried free and shoved clear the stone lids covering them and, driven by the powers of hell, began to climb from their graves in a swirling fog.

Francois de Raiis, the leader of the living dead knights, stood beside his sarcophagus. Benoit Lambert, their chaplain, shambled over and joined him. He lifted their golden cross in skeletal claws and began to chant a mantra of evil.

*"Diabolus, meus Senior, quod three ev-
erto in Hierarchies' of Abyssus. . ."*

The other tombs disgorged their horrors.
The thing that once was Henri Ethelbert,
glistening daggers on his belt, slithered from
his resting place and joined in the chant.

An unsteady Louis Godenot used his halberd throwing spear as a crutch and pushed
himself to his feet. His rusted chain mail
jangled and scratched against the stone as
he stepped from his grave.

Jules Lefebvre, his teeth clacking - in
pain and anticipated pleasure - in his skull-
like face, fought eagerly to again escape the
grave. In the name of the Devil, in the cause
of vengeance and, hopefully, in a torrent of
blood, he looked forward to putting his flail
and mace to work.

Free again, Geoffrey de Charney stuck
his long-dead talons back into his tomb
and withdrew his crossbow. As he stood,
the last resting place of Gaston Morel (destroyed the previous night) fell under his
red gaze. He didn't mourn. He didn't care.
He just paused, briefly, and stared at the
vacant tomb. Charney kicked the cracked
lid, already yawning, and toppled it into the
empty grave. Then he turned and took up
Lambert's chant.

From somewhere in the distance came a series of hair-raising sounds, like the shrieks of damned spirits carried on the wind, that settled quickly into the cries of whinnying horses. The Templar knights, still chanting, shambled from the cemetery and disappeared into the fog.

Three

Brandy and Ray stood side by side in the courtyard chilled by the night and alarmed by a settling fog. Had the dark of the previous night fallen over Castle Freedom now they'd have been in hot water. Worse, Brandy thought with amusement; pea soup. Instead, they were given a gift in the form of a shining full moon. Why not, Brandy wondered. Nights of unparalleled darkness, moons too full to be believed. It was, as Father Trevelyan said, a land of ancient legends, mystery and superstition.

Still not everyone was pleased.

"This is ridiculous." Loup planted his feet and crossed his arms with no intention of taking another step. "We have been over it."

The rest of the group stared in disgust and weariness. They'd gained little by their experiment but, with their jackets pulled tight, were still willing to try. All but one.

"We're going over it again." Ray said. "Felix, have you a flashlight in the bus?"

"I do not know. I have never used the bus at night." Glad to escape the argument, Felix and Eve headed for the bus. Ready for a break, Father Trevelyan set down his satchel, called, "I'll help look," and followed after the young lovers. Aimee, ever the reporter, remained wishing Loup would just get on with it.

Tired of the argument, Ray bottled his frustration and creeping desperation, turned to Brandy and calmly asked, "Where to next?"

Brandy looked intently about the moonlit courtyard, closed her eyes to concentrate and finally shook her head. "I don't remember, Ray."

"Honey, you need to try."

"Don't you think I'm trying?"

For the hundredth time Ray assured her it wasn't her fault but Brandy wasn't listening. It was and she knew it. Her mind was off to the races. Had she been paying attention, had she not left the castle without Vicki, had it not been for her thesis, had they not been there in the first place, they wouldn't have given a damn about the castle or the Templars and Vicki wouldn't be dead.

Ray lowered his head to hers and wrapped his arms around her. "I'm sorry," he whispered. "I'm sorry."

She leaned into Ray, giving him the weight of her shoulders, but painfully aware he couldn't lift the weight off of them; the weight of the world.

Felix, Eve and the priest returned carrying one flashlight that, for reasons unknown, worked sporadically and one rusted gas lantern, the condition of which had yet to be determined.

"This is stupid," Loup complained. "We can't go on with such equipment. We can't go on in the dark. What do we gain?"

Still holding Brandy, Ray said, "We're going on by matchlight if we have to. Where to next, Felix?"

"As I told you, I gave the execution speech here," Felix spread his arms reliving the invitation his charges observe the courtyard. "Everything was without event as always. We went to the chapel. Then. . . we went to the cemetery."

"By the chapel?" Ray pointed.

"No. Well, yes, but not that one. I told you, I was referring to the one beyond."

"I can't keep it straight," Ray shouted, throwing up his hands. "Give it to me again. What's holy and what's not."

"This near graveyard is the chapel cemetery. It is holy ground." Felix pointed into the dark and the fog in the direction of the distant timber. "We went to the Templar cemetery, the burial plot at the edge of the timber, in unhallowed ground."

Ray nodded and turned on Loup. "And you?"

Loup hesitated choosing his words carefully. "This is where the girl and I first began talking."

"And then. . . "

"What do you want me to say? We talked for a moment or two. Then she left."

"That's what you said before, but it's not what you said in the park." Ray was growing angry.

"This one hit me," Loup whined, pointing at Brandy. "I was giving you the tough. . . the hard time. . . I told you before, your sister left me here. She followed everyone else. I did not go to the Templar plot. Why should I? I have seen it a thousand times. I did not see your sister after. What happened to her I do not know."

"You are lying."

Eve said it - taking everyone by surprise. She stepped forward with the same light in her eye, the same twist to her lip, Brandy remembered from the tour that afternoon. The red-head looked at Loup with fire in her eyes and repeated, "You're lying. I saw you at the Templar cemetery. You were with the American girl."

Ray moved in on Loup with blood in his eyes. "Do you think this is a game? Do you? What happened at the cemetery?"

"Nothing. We..."

"You... what?"

"We... just... We had..."

"You just had... what?" Ray grabbed Loup by his shirt front.

"*Sexe*," Loup screamed, throwing a hand up to protect his wounded face. "*Elle a voulu le sexe!* She wanted it! I gave her what she wanted." He fell back and only Ray's grip kept him from hitting the cobblestones.

"Get up, you son of a bitch!" Ray dangled Loup as if he were a puppet, his free hand clenched to strike. "You're still lying! You're going to tell us what happened or, I swear to God, you're not going home alive."

The Frenchman struggled, shouting, "Leave me alone."

"Wait a minute, Ray," Brandy said, interrupting. "Ray. Be quiet."

Ray scowled at her. "Didn't you hear what he just..."

"Raymond, be quiet! I'm sorry, Ray, I know, but listen! Be quiet and listen!"

Ray released Loup. The group went silent and strained their ears.

"Listen. . . to what?" Loup asked with a sneer. He pulled at his clothes trying to reclaim his dignity.

One by one they heard it; a rhythmic tattoo, heavy on the ground, growing nearer. Another joined it. And another. And. . .

"Horses!" Brandy said. "Riders!"

"*Épatant*," Loup said, the sarcasm slurring his voice. "We are in the country. You hear horses in the country."

"At night?" Aimee said. "Who rides at night?"

Brandy shushed them. Hoofbeats; approaching, slowing. Then somewhere in the dark, the horses were reined up. A whinnying followed here to the right, a breathy snort there on the left, a stamp of the ground over there. Their party was surrounded. Then came a new sound; a rising choral chant from the darkness.

"Laus Lucifer, unde totus bona flow."

"What the hell is that?" Ray asked. A shiver shook his frame; a feeling his grandmother always described as, 'A ghost passing through you.'

"Laus Him totus creatura hic in Terra."

"It sounds like. . . singing. . . " Aimee said.

"No," Trevelyan snapped. The priest closed his eyes.

"Laus Him supremus minions of Abyssus."

"It isn't singing. It's chanting. It's a doxology. They're chanting. . . in Latin." The chorus grew in volume and strength. It drew nearer.

"Ut is eram secundum cado, est iam quod umquam vadum exsisto, universitas saecula saeculorum."

"What are they saying?" Brandy asked. Father Trevelyan held his hand up, silencing her and listening intently.

"Laus Him. Laus Him."

Even in the limited light Brandy saw the color drain from his face. He shook his head in confusion and dismay. "It's blasphemy. . . "

Four

A mounted shape suddenly appeared from the dark to the south. The horse's hooves thudded the ground as it rounded the corner of the chapel. They hit the stones of the courtyard and the thud became a *clip-clop* as if someone were shaking a bag of bones. The horse reared, pawed the air, snorted a cloud and whinnied. They could just make out the rider in the blue moonlight. He wore a hooded cape, a soiled white mantle, chain armor and a sword. His bearded face, with eyes like burning red lanterns, had the dried gray features of a corpse. The vision was all the more horrible because, in the darkness, the evil chanting continued unabated.

"Laus Lucifer, unde totus bona flow."
"Laus Him totus creatura hic in Terra."

293

Aimee, Eve and Loup screamed. Felix shouted. Ray swore an oath and Trevelyan called upon God. Brandy simply gasped and stared as another rider appeared from the shadows to the north. All could see, as he moved in the moonlight, he too looked like a mummy. He clopped across the courtyard and reined up at the right hand of the first.

"Laus Him supremus minions of Abyssus."

Two more riders appeared behind him. "My God!" Eve shrieked. Then, again, two more to the south.

"Ut is eram secundum cado, est iam quod umquam vadum exsisto, universitas saecula saeculorum."

One of the last, Brandy saw, was cloaked differently. He wore a black (maybe brown; it was hard to tell in the gloom) hooded cloak and carried a long wooden staff at his side adorned with a gold cross that glinted in the moonlight.

"Laus Him. Laus Him."

The group from Paradis had moved into a knot. Aimee swallowed and whispered,

"We're surrounded." Loup, his working eye wide with exploding panic, turned a circle within theirs as if to verify the reporter's assertion - or perhaps looking for room to run. What to Brandy had once felt like a large courtyard, shrunk significantly with the addition of six riders. She and Ray, independently, scanned them back and forth.

Felix took hold of Eve, cocked his head toward the priest, and called out, "Who are they?"

Breathlessly, Trevelyan said, "They're. . . Templar knights."

"Nuh-ahh," Ray said in disgust. While Brandy, in spite of her fear, shook her head at his brilliant addition to the conversation. But Ray wasn't through. "Nice duds," he shouted. "Is it Halloween already, you French fucks!"

"What's the matter with you?" Brandy barked.

"Me?" Ray cried. "What's the matter with them?"

The riders' grinning skulls stared back with hellish red eyes. Then the first rider drew his sword.

"I don't think those are costumes," Brandy said. "Let's get to the castle." She looked around and, though no one spoke, most in the group nodded. Loup was already backing toward the ruins behind them.

Trevelyan was concentrating on the two knights to the left; particularly the one carrying the cross. He was appalled by the blasphemy of the Christian symbol in the fiend's hands yet couldn't look away. Brandy saw his obsessed glare and grabbed his sleeve. "Father? Father Trevelyan?" He seemed not to hear. "Father!"

"Y-Yes-s," he said. His voice cracked. He licked his dried lips. "Y-Yes. I'm sorry." His brilliant eyes found their focus. "Yes, Brandy, everybody, we'd better go."

Felix, standing behind Eve, his hands on her shoulders, started backwards at Trevelyan's suggestion. He quickly discovered that fear had frozen his girl in place. With no time, he dragged her along.

The first Templar, the leader of the hellish group, waved his hand. The knight in the dark cloak sauntered his horse in a loop to his right. Another living mummy followed after. They clopped to a halt on the left side of Brandy's group blocking the courtyard to the north and escape to the castle. The Templars dismounted. The first set the standard on the stones, as if planting a flag, and held the gold cross triumphantly above them. The second drew something from his saddle; a black object of considerable weight. He extended his arm and let one end drop – a spiked iron ball swinging from a chain.

"He has a mace," Felix whispered.

"It's not a mace," the priest said. "It's a flail."

"*Merci*," Felix said, glaring at the crazy priest.

The leader waved the other clawed hand. Two more Templars spurred their horses and moved, in an opposing arc, cutting off escape to the entrance and the drawbridge. They too dismounted. One stung the air with hissing metal as he drew daggers from the scabbards on his belt. The other brandished some sort of spear.

"Ray," Brandy whispered. "We better get out of here."

She heard a strange metallic click and, as she turned to the leader, saw the knight to his right notching a little arrow into a crossbow. As if that were a cue, all of the knights began slowly to creep forward.

"The chapel," Ray whispered. Then again, but this time shouting, "The chapel! Everyone. . . run for it!"

And they did – with the exception of Loup. Terrified, the pathetic rapist froze in place so, when the others broke and ran, Aimee slammed into him. The Templar fired his crossbow with a startling twang and the bolt, like a bullet, passed between Aimee and Loup as they fell. The arrow sparked as it struck the courtyard stones then skipped

away to bounce off the castle steps. Loup
untangled himself from the reporter. He got
his feet beneath him and used Aimee for
leverage to push himself up. She screamed
in outrage. He ignored her cry and ran for
the chapel.

"Come back, you bastard!" Brandy
screamed. She'd witnessed the appalling
cowardice and ran to Aimee. "Are you all
right?"

The reporter, despite her angry tears, said
she was and let Brandy help her to her feet.
Both joined the others – running.

The Templar knights broke ranks and
took chase. Eve, somehow separated from
Felix and still on the castle side of the courtyard, found herself confronted by the dark
cloaked Templar. He waved the cross and
stared with blazing red eyes.

Loup was running toward the Templar
reloading his crossbow. Brandy thought, for
a second, he'd found his courage and might
take the monster on. Nothing could have
been further from the truth. The Templar
was simply between him and his intended
hiding place. Loup skirted around him, took
the steps in one bound, and grabbed the
chapel's heavy front door. Despite his panic,
Loup quickly opened it and disappeared inside. The door banged shut behind him –
leaving the others to the demonic knights.

The Templar leader had Aimee's arm. She screamed and beat his moldy tunic with her free hand. The ancient knight looked unconcerned, almost unaware, of the pummeling as he pulled her toward him. Unable to use his sword at such close quarters the mummy threw it down with a clang. Then he grabbed the screaming reporter with both grizzled hands.

Ray appeared and took hold of the knight. The Templar threw Aimee away and turned on Ray. He lunged; both fell and rolled on the ground. The mummy fought atop Ray and moved in, mouth opened wide. It took a second for the big American to realize the damned thing was trying to bite him. He grabbed the creature's wiry beard using every ounce of strength to yank him back.

By then Father Trevelyan had Aimee on her feet. Though aching, she assured him she was unhurt and Trevelyan gently pushed her toward the chapel. He turned back to the fray and saw Ray in jeopardy. The priest inhaled to gird himself and grabbed the Templar's molded cloak. Trevelyan pulled with all his might. The knight, in spite of Ray's hold on his dry beard, turned screaming, teeth bared, glaring hatred at the priest.

"Dear God! Oh, Dear Lord!" Trevelyan released the living corpse and retreated. The Templar snapped like a vicious dog. Beneath them, Ray took advantage of the diversion and kicked the Templar off.

———

Another knight swung his heavy flail in a great arc; the spiked ball whistling. The blow missed but drove Felix back and to the ground. The monster threw the weapon down and grabbed Eve. His glowing eyes bored into the soft pink flesh of her throat as he drew the red-head, screaming, toward his open mouth.

Recovering on the stones at their feet, Felix laid his hand on a stray crossbow arrow. The tour guide grabbed it, jumped to his feet, and hurled himself at the Templar. Felix rammed the metal bolt into the creature's back. The knight bucked and released the girl. Eve fell to the ground. The Templar swung, howling at Felix, struggling to reach the object impaled in his back. Felix, with both hands and more effort than he'd have guessed necessary, lifted the discarded flail and swung it.

The spiked ball struck the mummy solidly in the chest. His mail and soft underarmor took the blow with a metallic chink and puff of dust; still it knocked the undead creature onto his back and drove the impaled crossbow bolt completely into the Templar's body. Felix lifted the flail to deliver another blow – unaware the knight in the dark cloak was behind him.

Seven hundred years since, Benoit Lambert rode at the right hand of Francois de Raiis and, as Christ's intercessor, at the right hand of God. He carried the golden cross standard as a symbol of devotion to their holy mission. Now he dropped the same wooden pole over Felix, a gnarled hand on either side of his head, and yanked it back against his throat; choking him. Felix dropped the flail and grabbed the pole. As they struggled the standard snapped in half. The upper portion, baring the cross, clattered to the courtyard stones while the Templar adjusted quickly and continued to strangle Felix with the lower half.

Eve had risen to her knees and was crawling away when she froze in terror. The knight Felix had knocked down was back on his feet and standing over her. With fury in his red eyes, he tore his own rotted mantle and pulled it aside, exposing the gray stretched skin on his chest. He clawed into the dried and rotted flesh and tore it open. He howled, a hair-raising sound, grabbed something inside his chest and pulled it out. Triumphantly, the Templar held up the crossbow bolt. He threw it down and, again, grabbed the screaming Eve. The knight sank his teeth into her throat.

Felix was all but unconscious. The dark cloaked Templar released him and let him fall. Then he bent over Felix, lifted him in his boney grip, and drew him to his mouth.

Brandy, on the run, scooped the broken standard from the ground, turned the golden cross in her hands and rammed the snapped end of the pole through the knight's back. The wooden shaft passed through what once had been the chaplain's beating heart and burst from his chest and tunic in the front. The Templar roared and released Felix. He stood – impaled - with the wooden shaft protruding from his chest and the Templar cross jutting behind.

Brandy shook Felix awake. Then, with his help, she grabbed the rotted cloak of the Templar biting Eve. They pulled him away; the red-head's blood pouring from his mouth, running down his lips and chin. They threw the Templar onto his back, scooped up Felix's girl and dragged her toward the chapel.

The dark cloaked Templar struggled to his feet. He angrily hissed at the shaft protruding from his chest and fought, with little success, to reach the cross sticking from his back.

With Eve on his shoulder, Felix tripped on the chapel steps, falling. Brandy, on her other side, had no option but to fall with them.

"Father!" she screamed to Trevelyan – behind.

The priest, satchel in one hand, flashlight in the other, came to their rescue. He lifted Felix and Brandy, they lifted Eve. Beyond them, Trevelyan saw Ray coming from the courtyard with the Templars' leader, sword raised, fast after him. "Ray, behind you!" the priest shouted. He threw the American the torch.

Ray caught the flashlight, turned and blocked a strike as the Templar brought his sword down mightily. The flashlight rang like a bell. The blow sent a vibration zinging up Ray's arm and the force spun him. As he came round, Ray drove the obscenely dented light across the knight's skull with a boney crack.

Aimee was suddenly there, holding the chapel door open. Brandy and Trevelyan, dragging Eve, raced past the reporter. Ray hoisted Felix up the steps and pushed him safely over the threshold. He waved Aimee in, followed her, and helped shove

the chapel door closed against the headlong
rush of the dark knights.

Five

They were seven breathless, terrified people in the dark.

Ray heard the latch fall into place and felt for it making sure. Still holding the dented flashlight, he leaned back, bracing the door and letting it brace him. Among the group he heard crying, gasps for breath, incomprehensible bits of French, a whimper of pain and a whispered prayer. Outside, he heard the somber, blasphemous chanting of the Templar knights.

"She needs to lie down."

Ray's flashlight, miraculously operable, stabbed the darkness with a horizontal shaft of light. "Dear me!" Trevelyan howled, trying to cover his eyes with his free hand while still holding up his share of Eve. Ray apologized for blinding the priest, aimed the light up and cast the vestibule, overstuffed as a midtown elevator, in a gray gloom.

Trevelyan nodded at Eve and repeated, "She needs room to lie down." Brandy agreed and pointed into the dark chapel. The injured girl merely moaned.

Then Aimee startled them all, screaming, "What are you...?"

She pointed past Brandy into the chapel. There in a pool of moonlight filtered through two stained-glass windows in the high south wall was the figure of a man. Ray shown the flashlight past them. As their eyes adjusted each breathed a sigh of relief. It was Loup standing alone in the dark.

"You frightened us," Aimee complained.

Loup made no reaction.

"Felix," Brandy called, passing Eve to him. "Here, help Father." With a hand on each, she guided Trevelyan and Felix from the vestibule into the chapel. Her goal was a place to lay Eve down and the going was slow. The darkness along the sides of the chapel was all encompassing; Eve's pained moans and the labored breathing of those carrying her only added to the eeriness.

To the left of the door, along the western wall, they found a table all agreed would serve as a bed. Felix rolled his coat into a pillow and they laid Eve down.

"We need light."

On the day she lost Vicki, Brandy had stood not ten feet from that spot on a chapel tour so unsatisfying she'd committed little of it to memory. She closed her eyes now to concentrate. They'd entered the vestibule and filed into the back of the chapel. Ropes, like the cattle lines in a bank, prevented their forward progress. Thus corralled, they listened to another of Felix's by-rote speeches (mercifully short). When it ended, they were ushered back out again. Any half-hearted book on the subject, Brandy remembered thinking, would have shown as much and told more without the expense of a trip to France.

No matter, the trip down memory lane helped; there were candles. She found the rope line, pulled it out of the way, and crossed the expanse toward the front of the chapel. She passed Loup still frozen and trembling in the moonlight, found and pulled down a second set of ropes, and reached the altar. There in the dark, she located one of several candelabra. She dug a lighter from her bag and lit the candles. A yellow glow pushed back the gloom.

Brandy pocketed a handful of unlit candles and returned, delivering some to Felix and the Father. No sooner was their corner lit than they heard shouting in the vestibule. In her zeal to help with Eve, Brandy had forgotten Ray.

She found him and Aimee, in the dark, bracing the door. The Templars, still chanting, were bearing down, banging and pushing to get in. Brandy's candle threw stark shadows that revealed empty brackets on the door's inside frame. There was a locking bar somewhere. She found it in a tiny closet and a delighted Ray helped her slide it home securing the door, at least for the moment, from the onslaught.

Ray's body ached before. Now he flexed his hands just trying to get the blood... He paused as a thought suddenly occurred. "We had better..."

"...check the building," Brandy said, finishing his sentence. She retrieved her light from the table and offered her last unlit candle to Ray. He passed, opting for his cockeyed flashlight. "For looking round corners," he explained.

She headed back into the chapel, calling, "Spread out! Check the building."

Her candelabrum flickered by the distant altar. A tiny pool of light glowed in the corner where Felix and the priest tended to Eve. Brandy's candle gave her and Aimee light. Beyond these the chapel lay in darkness.

"Brandy," Aimee stammered, trembling. "I am afraid of the dark."

"I know how you feel." Brandy said. "Tell you what, later on you and I will be girls, okay? We'll just sit and we'll cry. But right now we have to get the building secure before those things find another way in."

She lit her last unclaimed candle, shoved it into Aimee's hands and started for Eve's corner. Aimee hurried after her.

Ray shook his head. He understood Brandy but felt for Aimee. The chanting and thumping grew louder outside as the Templars hammered and hacked. Ray returned his attention to the entrance, ran the flashlight across the inside of the barred door - hoping it would hold.

The bite was high on Eve's shoulder and, thankfully, had missed the major veins and arteries. That said, a sizable chunk of flesh had been avulsed and her bleeding to death remained a possibility. Not to mention the risk of God only knew what kinds of infectious diseases. Felix tamped the wound with a pocket handkerchief, under Father Trevelyan's supportive gaze, as Brandy and Aimee passed.

"That needs to be cleaned, Felix," Brandy said. She handed him a plastic First Aid kit from her bag.

"*Oui...*" He fumbled opening the kit and the priest relieved him of it. Felix, near panic, was having difficulty arranging his thoughts.

"Have you any water?"

"There is a kitchen, I think," Trevelyan put in. "Felix, we need water for Eve. There is a kitchen here? Or water?"

"*Oui.* Yes." He pointed to the north wall. Brandy's candle revealed a door – and more darkness. She led Aimee through.

It was an ambulatory hallway that, in candlelight, had the cramped feel of a tunnel. Aimee's frozen grip was alarming and Brandy felt her tremble as they made their way through the gloom. They passed a door on the left, an alcove with stairs heading up and, beyond that, a second door. At the end of the hall stood a final black and gaping doorway.

"That should be the kitchen," Brandy said. "See if you can find water? And secure any windows or doors that aren't secure. I'm going to make sure of these rooms."

There was terror in the reporter's eyes. Brandy squeezed her hand, nodded and turned back down the hall. Aimee lifted her candle and crept toward the open doorway.

Felix packed a new bandage over the already blood-soaked one at Eve's throat and, crying softly, whispered that he loved her. Trevelyan turned away to catch his breath. He saw Brandy and Aimee's candlelit shadows dancing on the walls of the ambulatory hall and reaching into the chapel through a door by the sanctuary. The priest's gooseflesh popped as, in the glow, he also saw a figure by the altar.

A second glance showed it was Loup. He'd finally moved and now sat on the sanctuary steps, like a cathedral gargoyle, hugging his knees to his chest and rocking rhythmically. The girls passed the door, their light vanished down the hall with them, and Loup was again swallowed by darkness.

Trevelyan was no friend of Fournier's chief henchman. Still, at that moment, Loup was a lone soul and despite his personal feelings the priest felt his duty. Eve was in good hands. He had an obligation to the others.

"If you're all right, Felix," Trevelyan said, "I'm going to see where I can help."

—————⟶—————

"Mr. Wimund?" The priest stood by the sanctuary steps, candle in hand, looking down on the unresponsive Loup; still sitting, gently rocking, in a world of his own. "Loup?"

Nothing. Trevelyan hesitated; feeling he'd failed. But he'd given it his best. For the moment, there was nothing further to be done.

The sound of hammering took Trevelyan into the ambulatory and to an open door across the hall. In the room, crowded with tools and building materials, Brandy worked by candlelight securing the only window with a sheet of plywood.

"My heavens," Trevelyan exclaimed. "Let me help you!"

"I've got it," Brandy assured him. "If you'd like to help," she pointed with the hammer. "Aimee's down the hall somewhere. Make sure she's..."

A tremendous bang sounded. Brandy and Trevelyan jumped. Somewhere in the dark, Aimee screamed.

Six

Moments earlier, Aimee found the dirty little kitchen Felix spoke of at the end of the ambulatory. It was small, her candle lit all but its corners, and rustic but not as old as the chapel. It had evidently been added on.

To her right, cupboards, a worn countertop, and cabinets filled the far wall. A large window occupied the one opposite the door. Aimee checked and found its wooden shutters secure. An island rose off-center from the floor; a small counter with an inset metal tub built under a hand operated well pump. Its prominent, but odd, position suggested the kitchen may have been built around it. Odd or not, Aimee hoped the old thing worked. She was looking for a vessel to carry water when a thunderous bang scared the living hell out of her.

As she spun, her candle snuffed, plunging the kitchen into gloom. A faint sliver of light like the blade of a knife stole in from the ambulatory. By it, through the rope of smoke climbing from her extinct candle, Aimee saw a blur of motion in the far corner.

One of the doors in the upper kitchen cabinet had burst open. The hinges were snapped and the door blown across the room. With a shout, a man in shadow jumped (fell?) from his hiding place inside the cabinet. He landed on his feet - and growled.

Aimee screamed.

The man crouched, claws flexing, swaying on the balls of his feet, staring. Aimee stared back; breathless and unmoving. They faced off for what seemed an eternity. As the time elapsed, Aimee's fear began to melt beneath a comical impatience. What kind of monster was this? She was about to ask when a yellow-white glow arose and Father Trevelyan appeared in the door. "Aimee!" His candle revealed the strange man was handsome, young and no stranger at all.

"You are. . . " Aimee stiffened the tremor in her voice. "You are Luis Socrates."

Recognition dawned on the priest's face as well.

"Who are you?" Luis asked in French. "How do you know me?"

She answered, also in their native language, and added, "I covered your trial... and your conviction."

A commotion at the door announced Brandy's arrival, and soon after, Ray's. They pushed in behind the priest, Brandy's fear spurring her curiosity, Ray's spurring his anger. "What in hell...?" Ray began, trying to catch his breath. Brandy cut him off with a tug on his arm, "What's going on?" She saw something in the gloom at her feet and picked it up without taking her eye off the stranger.

Ray, irked by Brandy's abridgement, demanded, "Who the hell are you?"

Luis drew himself to his full height, several inches shorter than Ray, and met his stare. Clearly he had no intention of answering the question as posed.

"His name is Luis Socrates," Aimee said.

"Luis Socrates! He's the one Blanc was..."

"Ray," Brandy said, "that can wait."

"Stop interrupting me! What do you mean it can wait?"

"He's obviously human. We have bigger fish to fry right now."

"She is right," Aimee said. "The Templars must concern us now."

"Fine," Ray said, turning. "If he cuts our throats, I'm blaming you." He angrily disappeared through the kitchen door.

Brandy held out a little worn black book. "This was on the floor," she told Luis. "Is it yours?"

"I do not think he speaks English," Aimee said.

Luis looked curiously at the reporter. Then he smiled. He repeated the smile to Brandy and nodded as he slid the book, his beloved Shakespeare, into his back pocket.

Aimee found a pail in the island tub, jacked the rust from the old plumbing, with Luis' assistance, and collected Felix's water. Then she and Luis followed Trevelyan back into the chapel.

Brandy lagged behind. She flicked her lighter and searched the lower cabinet drawers. She found plenty of grime, an assortment of junk and, to her delight, a butcher's knife. She slid it into her boundless purse, reconsidered, and instead concealed it in her belt with the handle in the small of her back. Ray wasn't, after all, stupid. And Luis, despite his nice smile, was still suspected of murder. Better safe than sorry. Brandy left and the kitchen was dark again.

A semblance of order was initiated. The kitchen was quiet, Felix had water for Eve, and the others were making sure of the chapel. The banging, scratching and chanting outside, while still a harbinger of danger, had become a sort of white noise. Though fear and dread remained they began to find panic too exhausting an emotion to maintain. One by one, with the exception of Loup, a strange calm settled over them.

Father Trevelyan followed Aimee as she slipped into the work room and began digging among the tools.

"We should find weapons in here, *n'est-ce pas?*"

"Is that what we're doing?" Trevelyan asked. "Looking for weapons?"

Aimee grunted a response and lifted a monstrous wrecking bar; literally a threat fashioned from iron. Trevelyan, wide-eyed, gulped comically. He found the nearest tool box and selected a large screwdriver for himself.

"That... little thing," Aimee said, shaming him, "is your weapon of choice?"

"You must forgive me, my dear," the priest said. "Forty years in the church makes you either a full-time bludgeoner or takes all the bludgeoning out of you. There's no middle ground. I'm afraid I've nothing but a stab or two left in me." He awkwardly flourished the screwdriver as proof. "Besides, silly me, it may work as a tool."

Utterly disappointed, Aimee walked out with her wrecking bar. The priest, an expert at disappointments, smiled weakly. He took a last look around and, confident the room was secure, followed after her.

Now armed, the reporter and priest passed the alcove and found Brandy checking the lone window in the second room off the ambulatory. It was an office, empty, save for stray clutter in the corners, eerily lit by her candle on the floor by the door.

"Do you need a hand?" Aimee asked.

Behind Brandy the shutter slats exploded in. Brandy screamed as the razor sharp tip of a halberd punched through the window missing her head by a fraction of an inch.

Aimee and Trevelyan fell back, alarmed, then were startled again as Ray ran into the room behind them. Hearing Brandy's scream, and with no time to search, he'd grabbed the nearest 'weapon' he could find, a heavy iron candelabrum, and hefted it now as he charged. He saw the priest and the reporter back on their heels and followed their gaze to Brandy.

His fiancé was hunched beside a shattered window with glass at her feet and a spear rammed through the broken shutters. The tip bounced, the shutters splintered, as the weapon was maneuvered from outside. "Look out!" Ray yelled.

A skeletal hand shot through the opening. It grabbed Brandy at her shoulder and clutched her blouse. She shouted in surprise and disgust and tried to pull away.

"Hold still!" Ray barked.

He stormed forward and, drawing the candelabrum up and over his shoulder like an axe, chopped at the Templar's wrist. The parchment skin tore, the radial and ulna bones snapped like twigs and the disembodied hand fell to the floor. Outside the window a hellish shriek erupted.

It was a fair guess this situation had never arisen before. It's also a fair guess that most freed from such a menace would run like hell. Not Brandy. She searched the floor, calmly asking, "Where is it?"

They followed her eyes down. The hand was gone.

Brandy scanned the shadows for the boney claw, finding instead splintered wood, glass shards, shoe prints in the layers of dust and dirt. Aimee joined her in looking. Ray shook his disbelieving head and stepped back with Trevelyan. Together they watched the women.

Aimee gasped. She tugged at Brandy's sleeve and excitedly whispered, "There! In the corner."

The gray tips of the fore and middle fingers were barely touched by a ray of moonlight through the window's smashed wood slats. Straining her eyes, Aimee could just make out the lifeless silhouette of the boney claw and a thin rivulet of liquid *whatever* trailing from the severed wrist. As she drew near, to better see the horrid thing, the hand hopped onto its fingertips and 'ran' at her.

Aimee screamed, jumped up and backward, all but bowling over Brandy who'd grabbed her candle and was returning. Still the reporter kept her eye on the damnable thing moving along the floor. She tried to stomp it as it passed, but missed, and like a grotesque spider from the eighth level of hell, the hand scurried away. It skittered across the hardwood on ticking phalanges and shot between the priest and Ray at the door. Trevelyan screamed, "Dear God!" Ray simply screamed. The hand vanished into the ambulatory and the dark chapel beyond.

In a flush of anger and embarrassment, Aimee got around the bewildered Brandy and took chase. Brandy recovered, and raced from the room on her heels, calling for the others to help as she passed.

"Not a chance!" Ray shouted, as another of Grandma's ghosts went through him. "I don't touch small living things... especially when they're dead!"

Trevelyan, unable to secure the window, ushered Ray from the room and secured the door instead.

——————

"It's over here," Brandy screamed. Ray and Trevelyan returned to the nave to see the hunt for the Templar hand was on in earnest. "It went over here."

Aimee darted after Brandy. Both hit the floor, on hands and knees, searching. Ray watched the commotion, through the gloom, until he couldn't stand it anymore. "Leave it alone," he yelled in exasperation. "What's it going to do; give us the finger?"

Something grabbed Ray and he all but had a heart attack. He spun around loading a fist but, before throwing it, recognized Felix in the candlelight. The tour guide had both hands up. "I am sorry, Ray," he said.

"Jesus! You scared hell out of me! Where'd you come from?"

"Eve is asleep. What is going on?" He watched as Brandy and Aimee squealed at each other. "What are they looking for?"

"A disembodied hand."

Felix jumped as Trevelyan appeared from the dark.

"It's on the loose," the priest continued, "crawling under its own power. They are looking for it." He disappeared back into the shadows.

Ray saw the startled Felix staring wide-eyed after Trevelyan. "Are you all right?"

"A priest ought not do that; come and go from the dark so." Felix swallowed air. "This is like... *le cinema fantastique*."

Ray breathed deep, air in, frustration out, trying to slow his heart rate.

Somewhere in the dark, Brandy yelled, "You aren't going to believe this when you see it!"

"I saw *le film de terreur*," Felix said, caught up in the excitement. "There was a hand... with no body. It crawled and gave people... the strangle."

"Felix!" Aimee hollered. "Shut up!"

Felix's English, it occurred to Brandy, was less clear now than on the tour. Obviously, his speeches were by rote. No wonder he seemed bored delivering them.

"Where did it go? Where is the hand now?"

"It's gone."

322

Eyes darted everywhere about the chapel; from one deep shadow to another.

"Are you done playing?" Ray shouted. "Yes? No? Maybe? Is the building secured? Do we know? Or are we just going to see who gets grabbed next?"

Seven

They'd made a good work of securing the chapel. All that remained, according to Felix, was the second floor viewing area; accessible by the stairway in the ambulatory. This gallery in the north wall offered a bird's eye view of the chapel and opened, through a door in the wall, to an exterior balcony overlooking the courtyard, stable and countryside to the north.

This door had a hasp and padlock already in place. When Ray borrowed Trevelyan's screwdriver, and slid it in the lock, Brandy came unglued. "What are you doing?"

"We're blind here," Ray explained. "The balcony will give us a vantage point to watch those things."

"Yes. . . and give them an entry point. I've got the place secure and you want to open a hole in it?"

"If the hasp is intact, we can use the balcony and still secure it."

"Do you want to risk that? Think about Vicki."

"What are you. . . ? What about Vicki?"

"She reached our balcony at the hotel. Five stories in the air." He stared vacantly. "How did she get there, Ray? Did she climb? Did she fly?"

"Fly?"

"She got up to our balcony somehow."

"Jesus, Brandy, don't get crazy. It was her apartment too. She had a key. Or she could have dropped down from the roof. Or climbed from a neighbor's balcony."

"She was buck naked. She didn't come through the neighbor's room or the lobby. So how did she. . ."

"Nobody saw anyone climb the sheer side of a building and, sure as hell, nobody saw her fly. Besides, you can't compare them. These things *may* have killed Vicki, turned her into whatever the hell she became, but they're not the same. They're seven hundred years old, for Christ's sake, and weighed down with armor. They aren't going to be climbing any buildings – or flying. And if they can. . . we'll put the hasp back on."

Ray wrenched down on the screwdriver and ended the debate. And, whether the Templars could fly or not, the padlock did.

Ray opened the door, smiled at Brandy and said, "See, no monsters." Then he stepped into the cool night air.

Brandy, Trevelyan and Aimee hesitantly followed Ray onto the balcony. There wasn't much to it; six feet wide, fourteen feet long, with three pillars, extensions of an outside wooden rail, rising up to support a wooden roof.

Thwack. "Geez!" An arrow hit the eave with a startling crack, and lodged there, just above Ray's head.

A Templar, bathed in moonlight in the courtyard below, shrieked. He nocked a second arrow into a long bow and raised the weapon. Three more knights, two on horseback, rounded the chapel to join him as he drew on the bow.

"Watch out!"

The arrow ricocheted off the chapel wall. Fear rushed them all back inside.

And now the Templars (at least one) were at the balcony door.

There was no need for new panic. They were already, intermittently and in varying numbers, at the other door and windows. It was just another straw. Trevelyan's screwdriver, slipped through the hasp loop as a makeshift lock, bounced and rattled. The door shuttered but held. Swords and daggers it seemed, while lethal, made poor tools for prying and chopping wood.

This door too had brackets on the inside for security (no doubt, compliments of Luis' late father) and Trevelyan was sent in search of a batten to fit between them. Ray, meanwhile, sat sentry on the gallery floor watching the screwdriver dance and wondering when Brandy was going to say, 'I told you so'.

Brandy stood at the gallery rail; listening to the door rattle and biting her tongue.

The wait became intolerable and Ray struck preemptively. "It doesn't make you right."

"I didn't say a word."

"Anybody can climb onto a second story balcony."

"Even seven hundred-year-old knights?"

"It doesn't mean a thing. And doesn't prove a thing about Vicki."

Brandy watched the others move in and out of pools of light below. Loup was still rocking on the altar steps. The Father interrupted his search for a crossbar to check on Felix and Eve then vanished again. Luis stepped from the vestibule and shouted in French. Then Aimee appeared from beneath the gallery and shouted back.

When they met in the shadows between, Brandy called down, "What's going on?"

"Nothing. Luis says they are still. . . bashing. . . the front door but it is holding. It is the same in the tool room. The window is secure." She traded words with Luis, then added, "For the moment."

The balcony door rattled again, emphasizing their 'momentary' safety, as the Templar thumped away.

Brandy'd had it. Needing to change the subject or go mad, she said, "They make a cute couple."

"What?" Ray asked, looking up.

"I said they make a cute couple."

"I heard you. I meant, what are you talking about?"

"Aimee and Luis. They're cute together."

He shook his head. "Don't you think it's strange his appearing from nowhere?"

"What do you mean strange?"

"Strange. He just drops out of a cupboard?"

"He didn't just drop out of a cupboard. He was hiding."

"You say it like I'm nuts. It isn't strange, hiding in a cupboard?"

"If you haven't noticed, Ray, we're all hiding. Those things outside inspire it."

"I'm concerned about who or what we've let in with us. What the -"

"I, eh, didn't plan to eavesdrop." Father Trevelyan, on the stair landing, panting and red-faced, wrestled a heavy wooden chair up the second flight. Brandy and Ray relieved him of his burden and lifted it into the gallery.

"A bar will, eh, have to be cut for the door," the priest said, fighting for breath. "There are, er, ample materials. I'm just not much, ah, with a saw," He pointed at the chair. "Perhaps, eh, this Deacon's chair would serve, oh, for now. I wouldn't think of such an abomination. But it was in the work room therefore, I assume, was taken out of service. I am normally opposed, I must tell you, to the irreverent use of God's property."

Ray fought the urge to salute. Instead, with Trevelyan's help, he tipped the heavy chair and jammed its high back beneath the knob on the balcony door. Then he yanked the screwdriver from the hasp. The Templar was still rapping but the rattling stopped.

"Bless me," Trevelyan said. "Wonderful." He brushed the dust from his clerical suit. "Ah, Ray, er, on the other, eh, subject. I'm sorry to eavesdrop, eh, and I, ah, don't mean to cast aspersions, but you insisted Loup come with us. And you invited Felix, who is also a known criminal. You've surrounded us, ah, forgive me, with those who've proven they're, eh, not above villainy."

"And you have a police record," Brandy added.

"Thank you for that up-date."

"Uh, to suggest....," Trevelyan said, reclaiming their attention, "that, er, Luis carries more guilt or needs sharper scrutiny than the others seems rather, uh, incoherent."

"I didn't expect we'd be under siege together."

"My point is, concern is good, excessive concern is unfruitful. Before the night is out we may need each other... more than we know."

"All right. But, out of simple concern, what can you tell us about him?"

"Very little, I'm afraid."

"You've been the parish priest here his whole life."

"Yes, but Luis was not a churchgoer. I know..." pain played across the priest's weary face. "I knew... his mother and sister. Both were devout parishioners. Neither Luis nor his father ever were." He chose his words carefully. "Anibal Socrates was a larger than life character with no use for religion. He was friendly but never receptive. It was very much... what do you say in the States?... like father like son."

"Is that a criticism of the father or the son?"

The voice was Aimee's, the words belonged to Luis, as they appeared side by side on the stairs.

Trevelyan was mortified. "I, eh, ah, meant no criticism at all, I assure you."

Aimee relayed the message, then passed on Luis' reply, "He says his father was not religious, but was superstitious. Both require belief in that which cannot be seen." She came onto the gallery, while Luis stayed leaning on the banister, and told Ray, "And, he says, if you want to know about him, or his family, you need only ask."

"All right. I will," Ray said, without Clive's embarrassment. He proceeded to do just that; questioning Luis, through Aimee, hard and fast. And, with a distrust honed in prison, Luis answered openly but carefully.

Aimee enjoyed translating. It offered a chance to contribute without the need for strength or grace. What she didn't enjoy was Ray's hostile tone. Inexplicably, she felt an attraction to Luis and a desire to protect him. She took it upon herself to soften the American's more severe inquiries and, conversely, to favorably embellish Luis' more caustic replies. Aimee Laurent, peacemaker.

Her editorial license, undetected by either Brandy or Ray, was not lost on the multilingual priest. He said nothing, but Trevelyan knew what she was doing and, at intervals, said so with his eyes. Still he let the questioning go on.

"His father was the sole caretaker here?"

"*Oui.* Yes. For years," Aimee said. "This was his playground as he grew up."

"Not much of a playground," Brandy said distastefully.

"You're not a little boy," Aimee said for Luis. "It was a wonderful place to play."

She didn't understand his French, but Brandy recognized the nostalgia in Luis' voice; the joy, the pain. As he told his story, Luis was alive with emotion. She envied him the feelings. Right now, she envied any feeling.

Ray continued to hurl his questions. "If his story is true..." Feeling ridiculous yelling at Aimee, he turned to Luis. "If *your* story is true, you know this place as well as the authorities."

Aimee translated. Luis laughed.

"He knows it better than anyone alive."

"It would appear," Trevelyan said, "you know it better than the dead."

Silence. Stares. The priest reddened again.

Luis filled the void (with Aimee's help). "The dead know I am here. But there have been changes since the Templars were in residence."

Discussing the Templars in an historic setting was one thing. Admitting, and accepting, the reality of bloodthirsty resurrected knights laying siege to a building they occupied was quite another. Stranger still was hearing someone speak with conviction as to what the dead *know*. Brandy shivered involuntarily.

"They know I'm here," Luis repeated, "but they can not find me."

"How long has he been here?" Brandy asked. Now she was doing it; talking to Aimee instead of Luis. "I'm sorry. How long have you been here?"

Again the language exchange.

"He's been secreted here since the murders; hiding. He watched you, both of you," she said, pointing to Brandy and Ray, "the morning after. From the keep, he watched you. . . " Aimee laughed, then nodded agreement and passed it on. "He says he watched you with that gendarme ass, Blanc."

"He doesn't have a very high opinion of you either," Ray said.

"Of what difference is Blanc's opinion?"

"He says you're a murderer."

"He is a liar."

"He misrepresented the facts, Luis," Trevelyan said, "but you did go to prison for taking a man's life."

The gallery grew deadly silent; save for the Templar scratching at the door.

Aimee did not translate the priest's comment. "The Inquisition," she said hurtfully, "is done." But she was not. She reiterated Luis' justification; his girl's death and what followed. "I was there. I reported on his trial. I believed him; and still do."

Whether or not he understood, Luis watched, with admiration and a budding infatuation, as Aimee pled his case. It had been a long time since anyone had taken his side. He couldn't help but appreciate the young woman.

"Still the police are looking for you," Ray said. "Why didn't you show yourself to the authorities? Why haven't you shown yourself before now?"

Unimpressed with Ray's tone, Luis spoke quietly to Aimee. "The authorities suspect Luis of murdering his family. The ability to listen is not among Blanc's virtues. And Luis has no alibi. No doubt, they suspect him of killing the girl as well."

"My sister?" Ray barked. "Are you responsible?"

Now Aimee was angry. "I won't ask him that."

"Ask him," Ray demanded.

"*Êtes-vous?*"

"No," Luis said plainly.

"Why should I believe him?"

Luis' smiled at the big American. Bad tempers were nothing to him. The prisons were full of men issuing threats and throwing tantrums. He answered and Aimee passed it on: "He says, it makes no difference. Believe him or no, he could not care less. His mother and sister were killed by Templar knights. He was helpless to defend them; could only watch these monsters drink their blood – like the vampyre. His father died in the courtyard and, again, the Templars were responsible. They even killed his father's mule. If your sister died here, *monsieur*, by violence, she died at the hands of the Templars."

"It's just strange he showed up out of nowhere."

"For God's sake, Ray," Brandy screamed. "He didn't. He was hiding!"

"Who hides in a cupboard?"

"A little boy on a playground," Trevelyan said. "Just what he said he was."

The Templar on the balcony groaned and renewed his efforts. *Chip. Chip. Chip.* Luis pointed and spoke again. "If you do not believe him," Aimee said. "He invites you to open the door."

Before Ray could respond to Luis' invitation they were interrupted by Felix's scream from below.

Like a startled herd, they abandoned the gallery on the run; Luis, Brandy, Aimee, Ray and, on their heels, Father Trevelyan. Their uproar, as they descended the two short flights, shook the gallery, vibrated the floor, and made so much noise... none of them heard the scratch of the legs or the thud of its high back as the Deacon's chair slipped from the door and fell away.

Eight

They arrived running from the gallery, alarmed, with many questions, and found Felix holding a candle at the west end of the ambulatory. Behind him, undetected in their earlier search, illuminated now in the soft yellow glow, was another padlocked door.

"Where the hell'd that come from?" Ray shouted.

Brandy shook her head at her fiancé's latest display of subtlety and, as she turned, was nearly skewered. He still had Trevelyan's screwdriver and was brandishing it like a weapon. "What are you doing?"

"I thought he was in trouble. We all thought he was in trouble."

Felix signaled for quiet then, in explanation, pointed around the corner at Eve.

"You're the one that screamed."

"Ray!" Brandy returned her attention to the tour guide. "What's going on Felix?"

"I'm sorry," Felix said. He pointed at the door.

"That's just the bell tower," Trevelyan said. "The ringers' chamber, actually, and stairs, and the bell chamber above."

"Yes, but I heard something," Felix said. "Inside the tower."

Ray lifted the screwdriver and stepped toward the door.

"Ray! What are you doing?" Brandy grabbed his arm. "You opened the gallery door, wasn't that enough? We're trying to secure the place, you're turning it into Swiss cheese. Stop while you're ahead."

"Until we know what's in the building, we're not secure."

"Father just said it's the bell tower. That means it's open at the top. By definition it's not secure. So it's better locked. I let the gallery go; I'm not budging here. If you break that lock. . ."

Suddenly they heard Felix's 'noise' behind the door. A scratch, a skitter, on the stairs, perhaps on the wall. Something *was* in the bell tower.

It wasn't a competition; they were in this together. Brandy knew that. She also knew it felt nice to be right. She enjoyed watching Ray walk away with an unused tool in his hand.

She got an even better feeling a short while later when Felix wished aloud for something to sustain Eve. Brandy had taken a lot of crap from Ray, more than she cared to admit, about her purse. Now she had her revenge. No sooner had the tour guide made his desire known than Brandy opened her bag o' plenty – and disgorged breath mints, chewing gum, three candy bars, two granola snacks, a sleeve of crackers, a tin of water packed tuna (with a key chain can opener) and a pack of bouillon cubes.

Using an altar chalice (Trevelyan bristled) and a candle, Brandy soon had hot chicken broth for Felix's injured love.

Father Trevelyan contributed to the kitty. He dug out his cassock, removed a mound of candy from its pockets, and carefully stored the vestment back in his satchel. Then he handed the treasure over, confessing, "They don't normally come with pockets. I had several sewn in. Between you and me, I don't travel well without sugar."

Brandy promised his secret was safe with her.

Getting into the spirit, Aimee produced one of the ash-covered pyramids of cheese she so adored. (She'd stopped at the café that afternoon, but had yet to take it from her backpack). Coupled with Brandy's tuna and crackers, the feast was on.

Luis disappeared, to an inconspicuous box amid many in his father's work room, and returned with a bottle of red wine. It was already opened but no one complained.

Truth be told, Ray complained. But not about its being open. Merely that they were drinking at all. He thought it better they remain mentally sharp – and was roundly jeered for his concern. "There are eight of us," Brandy said, chewing a cracker daubed with *Valençay*, "and one bottle of wine three-quarters full."

"I, er, ah, applaud your positive attitude, Brandy," the Father said. "Some, er, cynics would have called the bottle one-quarter empty."

Brandy, Aimee and the priest were suddenly laughing.

"And we don't want no cynics round here," Brandy said, pausing her study of the bottle's label to eyeball her fiancé over the top of her glasses.

"Do not worry, Ray," Aimee said. "We shall not get drunk."

"Yeah, stop being a poop." Under the circumstances, Brandy was enjoying herself. Laughing, she looked around the candlelit chapel as if for the first time. "Speaking of poop," she said. "Where are the pews?"

Even Ray was laughing now; though partially from embarrassment.

"There are no pews," Trevelyan said. "In the 13th century, the nave was wide open. Worshippers stood through the service." With Catholic superiority, he added, "Fixed pews were a 16th century Protestant, eh, er, innovation."

"The nave?"

He spread his hands indicating the width and length of the open chapel. "The central approach to the High Altar from the vestibule to the chancel. Nave is the original Latin; the base word for Navy." The priest pointed to the ceiling which rose to a sharp vault above their heads. "Shaped like the upended keel of a ship."

Their candles, through rising ropes of smoke, threw flickers of gold light and stark shadow against the gloomy ceiling. A shaft of colored moonlight stole through the two stained-glass windows in the otherwise boarded-over row in the south wall. And, oddly, a shaft of moonlight no one noticed before crossed the ceiling from the north.

Aimee screamed.

Above the gallery, clinging upside down to the ceiling, hung one of the Templars. On hand and knee, his rotted cloak dangling like a banner, his head spun backwards, he stared down at them with blazing red eyes. Even in shadow, Brandy knew it was the monster that had grabbed her through the office window. The creature's right hand was missing, amputated above the wrist by Ray's candelabrum. He hissed, then like a spider skittered across the ceiling.

Felix, in the far corner, blew out his candle and plunged himself and Eve into darkness. Then he stood watch; over Eve. . . and the thing on the ceiling. Loup, oblivious, merely rocked on the sanctuary steps near the south wall. The others abandoned their meal and ran. Perhaps instinctively, they wound up in a knot behind the High Altar.

Above, the creature came on like a demon. He reached the transept in the ceiling, marking the boundary between the nave and the sanctuary, then stopped as if he'd hit a wall of glass. He glared down at them, bunched beneath the altar crucifix, hissed again angrier than before, and crawled back into the shadows. There, partially hidden by the thick beam at the height of the vault, he hesitated. Then the knight saw Loup and was off and crawling again across the ceiling and down the wall.

Father Trevelyan bolted down the sanctuary steps. He reached Loup at the same moment the creature did. The priest grabbed him and, surprising even himself, threw Loup backwards. Ray caught the blackguard and, unceremoniously, shoved him again onto his butt on the sanctuary floor.

The Templar, red eyes blazing, was livid.

Trevelyan, like a sheriff in an American western, drew a crucifix from his jacket pocket and held it up. The icon glinted in the candle light. The knight shook his helmed head and screamed as if he'd been poked in the eyes.

Then, in a further defiance of the laws of physics, the knight scuttled, upside down and backwards, back up the wall. Trevelyan held the crucifix aloft – driving the monster. The knight crossed the ceiling and Trevelyan hurried across the nave after him. The Templar crawled into the gallery; apparently from where he'd come.

Trevelyan ran for the ambulatory and, showing no sign of his age, took the stairs two at a time. He reached the gallery to find the Deacon's chair pushed aside and the balcony door gaping. The Templar clung above the door.

His wall-walking trick was something to see up close. The priest couldn't help but gawk. The creature hung there like a fly;

only the toes of his boots and the fingers of his left hand making contact. The knight's anger was also something to see; a hatred brewed in hell. But there was something else the Father recognized – desperate fear.

Terrified himself, but resolved, Trevelyan raised the crucifix. The creature howled, dropped to his feet in the door way and, shrieking, was propelled back through the door and onto the balcony.

Trevelyan didn't waver. He followed the mummy out.

The knight, flailing left claw and right stump to protect his eyes from the image of the crucified Christ, continued his retreat. He scrambled for the rail.

Trevelyan advanced as the Templar, still screaming, stepped from the rail to the roof. The knight missed his footing and fell to the courtyard. He hit the stones with a sickening *thwack* and the clank of metal as his helm bounced away. A fluid, more black than red, spurted from his head. Yet he climbed back to his feet.

Trevelyan retreated to the gallery. He slammed the door, busting the jamb, and sagged against it. Shaking violently, he dropped the crucifix beside him.

Brandy, with Ray behind, raced up the stairs. She ran to the priest, got his assurance he was unhurt, then turned on

Ray with menace. "Quote," she said acidly. "They can't climb buildings. Unquote."

Ray knew when to keep his mouth shut. He knew when Brandy was right.

Nine

Everybody had "their space" in the chapel; museum tableau in pools of flickering light surrounded by stark shadow. Felix at Eve's bedside; in candlelight when she was awake, in the dark when she slept. Aimee and Luis encamped mid-way down the nave, their backs against the wall with the vestibule, ambulatory door to the bell tower, and gallery all in view. Father Trevelyan in the gallery, crucifix in hand, watching and listening at the broken balcony door; God's sentinel. When Brandy or Ray relieved him, the priest floated down the stairs like a character in a gothic novel to pray at the High Altar or rest upon its steps.

Loup, free from his catalepsy since the Templar's attack, avoided these pools and their occupants and roamed the patches of darkness between like a nocturnal predator.

When they weren't standing in for the Father, Brandy and Ray moved relentlessly about, candles in hand, making sure of the building, cheerleading and looking for cheer. On one changing of the guard, Brandy pointed at the gallery door and asked the priest:

"Why did that work? The crucifix?"

In their camp, Luis heard the question. He said something that Aimee hesitated in repeating. He nodded his insistence and she shouted up, "Luis says, they cannot abide that which is Holy."

Ray grunted derision.

Luis heard that too but couldn't have cared. His girl was dead, his family was dead, and now he was facing death. He had real problems and the doubting American was not one of them. He had information that might help and would offer it to any who would listen. Through Aimee, he tried again:

"They can not abide the graveyard."

Ray leaned over the gallery rail. "What does he mean by that?"

"One of the Templars, chasing him, fell from his horse into the cemetery. It was, he says, as if he fell into acid, as if he were on fire. He could not crawl out fast enough."

"In the cemetery?" Trevelyan asked, joining Ray and Brandy at the rail.

"Here, outside the chapel. When he crawled out he stopped burning."

"The others?" Trevelyan asked. "Were they there? How did they react?"

Through Aimee, Luis said, "The others rode the perimeter. They were angry and frustrated but they did not enter."

"Perhaps they couldn't," Trevelyan said thinking aloud. "Perhaps they couldn't."

"What do you mean?" Brandy asked.

"Huh, er, ah, haven't you ever gone to the movies, for heaven's sake? Luis is right. They can not abide holiness. That's why the crucifix worked."

"That's stupid!" Ray shouted. "They're wearing crosses!"

Trevelyan was appalled. Brandy would have been, but. . .

"He is right," she told the priest. "I ran a shaft of wood through the one in the brown cloak. He was wearing a crucifix – and the pole had one on it!"

"That isn't a crucifix," Trevelyan said. "It's a cross."

"What?"

"You're using the terms interchangeably and they're not the same. Ray is right; they are wearing crosses. It is, or was, the symbol of their religious Order. The shaft of their standard, the stick you stabbed the Templar with, was topped with that symbol. But it's a cross; not a crucifix."

"What's the difference? I mean, I know one has Jesus on it but, what's the difference for the Templars?"

"The difference, I think, is the blood," Trevelyan said, mulling the mystery as he examined his crucifix. "A cross is two intersecting lines; nothing more. A crucifix features the martyred Lord. If this truly is a battle of good and evil then the crucifix is the blood of Christ. It is the symbol of sacrifice for absolute good. They cannot abide it."

"What about the one you just chased? If they can't abide good how was it able to enter the chapel in the first place?"

"Oh, eh, there's nothing necessarily good about a chapel or a church."

"Isn't it the house of God?"

"Eh, yes, but, er, it isn't the church that's holy. It's the sanctuary."

Trevelyan pointed to this 'holy' area and, for the first time, Brandy really looked at the sanctuary, from the steps and rails at its approach to the apse (the half-dome wall) at its rear. It featured the High Altar, a table at the apse wall, smaller credence tables on either side and, hanging above, an ornate and intimidating crucifix. The area was adorned in the expected accoutrement; red and white faded palls (hanging like curtains), liturgy books, hymnals and a massive Bible, gold chalices, and candles (alone and clustered in wrought-iron, tree-like candelabra). It looked wrong. As if a movie crew, without knowledge of the church, had been called in to dress a set. Still it felt right. Behind the banners, the unevenly faded wall and empty niches hinted at the icons, paintings, and sculptures displayed there when real worship took place. As the Templar must have, Brandy felt God was there.

"To put it simply," Trevelyan said. "The evil creature couldn't come into the holy part of the chapel. He entered the nave, which is not sanctified. It's for the laity."

"The unwashed?" Ray asked.

"In a way, they were. On weekdays the nave served as a marketplace and, probably, smelled of animal dung and urine. Certain evenings it would have been used for political meetings."

Ray snorted a laugh. "When it smelled of human dung and urine."

Trevelyan lifted his hands in surrender. He tried not to be judgmental, outside of the confessional, and wasn't by nature political. "Instead of the unwashed, shall we agree on the *non-clergy*? For centuries, churches and chapels, this one included, were built sanctuary first. They could worship immediately and finish the church as they were able."

"Why not just get it done?"

"With unstable government, lack of funds, poor weather, difficulty getting building materials, and the lethality of those materials, it took years to complete the work. Money and war kept this chapel from being finished; which is why it has so many design styles. Cathedrals, like Notre Dame, took centuries. It wasn't unusual for the construction to be completed by grandchildren, even great grandchildren, of its designers."

"But I've strayed," Trevelyan said. "My point was... the sanctuary is the only blessed part of the chapel. And we all saw the reaction of that creature when he reached its boundary."

Brandy stared at the ceiling vault, then back to the sanctuary, thinking. Suddenly her eyes lit up. She raced from the rail down the stairs. Ray shouted and, when she didn't reply, followed after her.

She stopped in the middle of the nave and turned to Ray. "They're wearing away at this building. The balcony makes us vulnerable. We can't baby-sit one door all night. We need to secure it or we can't keep these things out. It's only a matter of time." She pointed at the crucifix over the altar. "That's what we need."

Ray looked from the sanctuary, to Brandy, to the rail above where a grim Father Trevelyan stood.

"No." Trevelyan spoke with quiet authority. "You cannot take apart the altar."

"You're guarding a hole in our fort," Brandy said, pointing, "that was secure until *somebody* broke the lock."

"That's enough," Ray whispered defensively.

Brandy ignored him. "We've got to keep those things out, Father. You just showed us how."

"It's. . . sacrilege!" Trevelyan screamed, leaning over the gallery rail. It was a startling image, the black suit, the white collar, the crucifix in his hand, and the explosion of fire and brimstone. "It's blasphemy!"

"Father, don't you understand. . . "

"It's blasphemy! Do you understand that! Can you understand that? There are some things you cannot do!"

Excepting Eve, everyone was watching the pair; even Loup. Aimee looked on in amazement. It was the Landlord and Mimi from La Bohème, Mephistopheles and Gretchen from Faust. "It's like an opera," she whispered to Luis. "Like an epic novel."

Luis nodded but said nothing.

"Do you want to die?" Brandy shouted at the priest.

"Some things are worth dying for," he said. The ice in his voice melted, replaced by a plea for understanding. "Or worth dying to prevent. Some things are more sacred than life!" He kissed the crucifix and disappeared from the rail.

Ray saw Brandy's exasperation. "I'm sorry," he whispered. "I should have taken you to Paris."

"It isn't your fault. The trip was my party, remember."

"Yes, but I should have made you. I should have insisted on lights and romance before letting you chase the dead."

"Letting me..." Brandy paused. What gave offense also offered illumination. She turned to Ray, hazel eyes alight. "That's it," she said. "Paris."

"Yeah, Paris. I said I'm sorry."

"No! Paris! The catacombs. The catacombs of Paris." Ray shook his head – bewildered. Brandy pulled free and called up to the gallery. "Father! You said this chapel had a crypt?"

Trevelyan reappeared at the rail. "That is the public view of it," he answered with trepidation. "Yes."

"The public view? I didn't think it made any sense. What you meant was the chapel has an ossuary, right?"

The priest tensed. Even at that distance, Brandy could see he was chewing his bottom lip. "Yes," he admitted finally. "That is what I meant. Why?"

"You know why. The ossuary will have the iconography we need. And it won't be a desecration of the sanctuary."

The battle was on again, and raged for ten minutes, back and forth, without respite. Trevelyan took the moral high ground, citing his standing with the Almighty, and closed the debate. Which merely opened the flood gate. Brandy denied it to him and demanded to be heard. The others stayed well out of the fight which so intensified the priest abandoned his post and came to the nave to wage it.

By request, and under duress, Luis took the priest's place in the gallery. He would rather have watched the clash. Truth be told, he would rather have been back in his hay loft with his little worn book of Shakespeare.

That notion passed like a mist. The estate, his home, belonged to Fournier. The drug dealer had cut Felix off and, certainly, Luis could expect the same. There was no loft, cottage, or family. There was nothing left and nothing would ever be the same.

Luis was shaken from the sad thought by a strange sound, and stranger feeling, coming from the balcony. He swallowed hard and edged forward, crucifix in hand, to the door. Carefully, he cracked it, to take a peek. A flash, a glint reflecting off metal in the moonlight, caught his attention. One of the Templars had hold of the balcony rail and was pulling himself up and over.

Ten

Luis flashed the crucifix through the door. The knight growled, let go of the rail and dropped back to the courtyard. A second Templar, on the roof, leaned over the eave at just that instant and gave himself an eyeful. The mummy howled in pain and retreated.

Luis slammed the door and put his weight against it. Suddenly he appreciated the argument raging below. And he was on Brandy's side.

"You cannot do this," Trevelyan cried again. "You cannot desecrate the resting place of the dead."

"And you can't have it both ways, Father," Brandy replied. "We can't lock the balcony door. We're all going to end up among the dead."

"Why can't you understand. . . ?"

"When is the last time you were in the ossuary?"

"What has that to do with anything?"

"When?" Brandy demanded.

"I've only been once. Thirty years ago."

"And when was the last time it was used?"

"It's not used anymore. Not since I came to Saint Thomas. But I don't see. . . "

"You do see," she barked, cutting the priest off. "I have respect for the dead. But you're practicing religious grandstanding. If you want to be martyred, have at it, but you can include me out. Now, are you going to tell me where the entrance to the ossuary is or should Ray hold you down while I rip the chapel apart?"

Ray scowled at Brandy. Then he turned it on the priest, giving Trevelyan his most threatening *I'm about to hold down a priest* look; whatever the hell that was.

"Er, oh, I'm no match for you, Ray," the priest said. "Physically, I'm, eh, no match for anybody. I wasn't an athlete when I was a young man, let alone now. But, if I don't stand my ground, I don't stand for anything."

Looks were exchanged between the three as Trevelyan waited to be man-handled. The seconds ticked by, filled with silence - and the endless scratching of the Templars. Ray's scowl eased to a frown but he didn't move. The sad, grateful priest said, "I am going to relieve Luis. Do what you think is best."

Trevelyan walked wearily from the room.

"You are wasting your time!"

Brandy and Ray, Luis and Aimee, traded looks. They looked to the corner to see Felix engrossed in Eve's care. They looked to the gallery's empty rail and knew the priest was guarding his door. Then they looked, as one, to Loup who'd come out of his funk with a vengeance. He was laughing at them, shouting at the top of his lungs. "Pray! Fight to stay alive. You are already dead. As dead as those walking corpses outside."

"Thanks, Loup," Brandy said. "Feel free to go back into your coma."

He wandered away, amused, as if he knew a secret they didn't know.

Brandy had been arguing with Ray when the rapist climbed from the mental cellar in which he'd been cowering and dumped his hysteria atop their already palpable gloom. With Loup gone, she returned to Ray and their fight. He'd failed to back her in her confrontation with Father Trevelyan and she wanted to know why.

"I really wanted to," Ray said, the sarcasm dripping, "but I wasn't sure of the best way

361

to hold down a priest. I mean, do you grab the collar? Kick him in the nuts? Or just bulldoze him?"

"I'm trying to save us," she insisted.

"And I'm sure everyone's grateful, Brandy. Who elected you Savior?"

"I meant I was just trying to do what I could."

"Yes. But for you that means demanding everyone else do what you want."

"Why didn't you just say you agreed with Father Trevelyan? That you thought searching the ossuary was a bad idea?"

"Who said I did? I don't even know what the hell you're talking about!" Ray paced away, took a deep breath and returned. "I don't know what's right or wrong, Brandy. I assumed it was a good idea because it was yours. I find you're usually right. That said, I don't want to hold a priest down while you rip his church apart."

"This isn't his church."

"You're avoiding the point. I object to strong-arming a friend. Get me a priest I don't know; I'll kick his ass."

"It never fails. Straight to the smart mouth."

"Oh, give me a fucking break!"

"Followed immediately by the foul mouth. The train's on time."

Luis shouted something at Aimee.

Brandy and Ray, surprised by the outburst and annoyed at the interruption, stared daggers. Ray beat Brandy to it, "What did he say?"

"He said, the ossuary, it is under the apse."

"What's that mean in English?"

"I have no idea," Aimee said with a shrug.

"I know what it means," Brandy told Ray. Then she pointed at Luis. "How does he know where it is? While we're at it, how does he know what we're talking about?"

Aimee wondered too and translated their curiosity. His answer left the reporter feeling so foolish she apologized to Luis before passing it on. He smiled his acceptance.

"He did not know what you were talking about," Aimee told them. "When Father Trevelyan relieved him, he told Luis why he was upset, and that he felt badly for having had words with you. As to knowing this. . . ossuary. He says nobody ever listens to him. He already told you, he knows the castle inside and out."

Brandy felt foolish herself but didn't allow it to interfere with the smile she cast at Luis. Neither did she, or Ray, allow it to slow them when Luis said, "*Venir. Je vais vous montrer*," and waved for them to follow. They weren't positive, but it looked and sounded like, Come on. I'll show you.

The trap door was secreted beneath the sanctuary floor. Its hinges groaned, dust danced in their candlelight, as Ray lifted and threw it, teeming with spiders, webs and worse open on the floor. Ray groaned, coughed and swore.

Luis leaned against the altar watching with amusement but little sympathy. He was well familiar with the door and what lay beneath. Besides, Ray and Brandy had gotten exactly what they'd asked for. *C'est comme ça.*

Ray aimed the dented flashlight into the hole. "No way!" Brandy started for the trap. "You're not going down there?"

"Yes, dear. We are."

"I'm not going down there."

"Yes. You are."

Brandy stepped through the opening. Wispy spiders' webs clung, their builders scurried, and cold subterranean air enveloped her as she disappeared through - out of earshot of Ray's grumbling.

She reached the stone floor and moved away from the mold encrusted ladder making space. Ray followed, ducking and grumbling. He barely fit beneath the low ceiling, and webwork filled the headroom. Then his flashlight blinked out. "Nice."

Only the open trap prevented their being plunged into darkness. Brandy produced a candle and made short work of lighting it.

"God bless the Girl Scouts," Ray said.

"And you thought all we did was sell cookies."

Ray peered into the darkness beyond the glow of her candle. "What is this?"

"It's an ossuary."

"Yeah, that I got. What is an ossuary?"

"It's the final resting place for the dead of Paradis."

Brandy passed her candle back and forth, shifting eerie shadows across hundreds of grinning human skulls. The light floated over ovoid caps, dashed against jutting mandibles, skipped over stacked craniums, and insinuated itself deep into the rounded orbits of uncountable empty eye sockets staring from the walls. Dead and buried, decayed and forgotten, resurrected, interred here... and forgotten again. Row upon row, layered to the convex ceiling. And spread beneath, the length and width of the floor, the dismantled remains of their skeletons. Layer upon endless layer; scapulas, clavicles, femurs, fibulas, ribs and on, sticks of dull ivory with rotted stains of black riding on a bed of vertebrae, metatarsals, and metacarpals sifted by time and scattered like gravel. An organized chaos of human bones.

"Graves are temporary in France," Brandy said. "Burial space is scarce. Bodies are buried in rented plots. After a finite numbers of years the skeletons are removed. The graves are made available for the newly dead. The long dead are moved to an ossuary; a permanent mass tomb. In Paris they're called the Catacombs."

Candles, melted to their sconces, unused in ages, were situated at intervals about the chamber. Small crucifixes hung from each; others lay intermingled among the remains. And, against the far wall, its painted eyes triumphant in suffering, hung a four-foot-high, faded, crucified Christ. "That's what we're after," Brandy said pointing.

"Eh. . . After?"

"We need it. We're taking it upstairs."

Beneath the skulls, the scattered human remains rose three feet off the floor. The only avenue to the crucifix, Ray saw, was up and over the bones. "I'm not walking on dead people."

"There aren't any people here, Ray. There's nothing but bones."

"Bones are people too."

Brandy sighed, her shoulders sank. A second later, she hitched them back, fixed her mouth in grim determination and started over the piled remains.

"Brandy!"

It sounded like she was walking on gravel. The bones shifted, bowed, settled; some smaller, older or more fragile snapped, cracked, and some disintegrated. She lost her balance, teetered and grabbed a skull cap atop the pile to stay upright. Ray swore and went after her. The pile shifted and settled again. *Crunch. Snap.* A thin skull here, a rib cage there, turned to powder beneath his weight. Thicker bones, the more recently dead, stood the test and held him up.

"Brandy, I can't do this."

"Yes, you can."

"You can. I can't!"

"Stop being a baby! We don't have all night."

"Would a baby walk over a room full of bones?"

"They would. . . if you put them in a room full of bones." Brandy held her candle to his face. "You can do anything, Ray. Look at the gun thing you did with Loup."

"What gun thing?"

"When you kicked the gun from his hand and caught it. That was more than cool; it was impressive. It was hard. How many people could do that?"

Ray teetered on the undulating remains. "I pulled that out of my ass."

"Perfect. Because we're pulling this out too." Brandy reached the crucifix, set down her candle, and took hold. She shook the icon. "Give me a hand."

Ray reached his fiancé. They steadied each other and together pulled the crucifix down. Slowly, awkwardly, to the sound of snapping bone, they carried it back to the foot of the stairs. On the way, Brandy paused repeatedly to swipe the little crucifixes dotting the chamber. As they neared the ladder, she pocketed what must have been her sixth one. Ray laughed. "What are you doing now?"

"It can't hurt," was all she said.

Ray balanced their prize while she retrieved her candle. During her absence, he noticed another small crucifix near at hand and, though he didn't know why, and would deny it if asked, Ray stuck it in his pocket.

Brandy was back quickly. She hurried up the stairs with the candle letting the ossuary fall back into gloom. From above, she told Ray to lift the crucifix to her. He did as instructed jockeying the icon through the trap in the floor.

Eleven

Consumed with Eve's care, Felix was oblivious to the activity in the chapel. Loup restlessly roamed the nave listening to the Templars hammer at the walls, windows, and doors. Aimee and Luis, waiting by the altar, cheered as Brandy and Ray raised the crucifix through the floor from below. Trevelyan watched frowning from the gallery rail.

The Americans rested the religious icon, upright at Brandy's insistence, and brushed away the dust and spiders webs they'd carried up with them. Ray dropped the trap door closed, shuddered and declared, "Never, ever, ever, under any circumstances will I go down there again!"

"*Eh bien*," Loup said, watching from the dark ambulatory doorway. "At least not while you're alive, *hein*?"

After a brief flirtation with mental illness, it seemed, the old Loup was back. Ray welcomed him with an extended middle finger.

"An interesting paradox," Loup said. "How often, M. Kramer, do you think that gesture has been made from there... by a man carrying the crucified Christ?"

Ray didn't bother to answer. He and Brandy carried the crucifix down the sanctuary steps, past Loup and his big mouth, and out of the nave. Luis followed, in case they needed help, while Aimee stayed to check on Felix and Eve.

Brandy and Ray climbed the ambulatory stairs, with Luis trailing, and Loup babbling in the ambulatory like a Greek chorus, "What is good, M. Kramer? What is evil? Who is good and who is evil? Shall we leave it up to you?"

Trevelyan was unhappy with Brandy and Ray following their 'robbery' of the ossuary. But it was useless to hold a grudge and his duty to seek understanding. Once they'd raised the cruciform into the chapel, it would have been a poor Christian who'd let them wrestle it up the steps alone. He left his post at the balcony door to lend a hand.

Together they got the crucifix to the gallery and prepared to put it in place. Luis listened at the door, heard nothing and, at a nod from Ray, opened it. The balcony was empty. Father Trevelyan backed out first holding the foot of the icon. Brandy and Ray followed with the head. Luis, as ordered, closed the door behind them.

As the priest neared the rail, Brandy shouted, "Behind you!" Another of the Templar mummies was climbing onto the balcony.

There was no time to raise the icon before the monster, red eyes glaring, came over and at the priest. Trevelyan yanked his cruciform from his pocket and jammed it in the Templar's face. The creature howled and dove over the rail.

His hair-raising shrieks were nothing compared to those that erupted from the courtyard, a moment later, when the trio lifted the crucifix into place. They secured it to the middle roof support while the blood drinkers screamed, backed or rode away, and hissed their hatred. Ray climbed on the rail to tie off the top of the crucifix. He worked quickly and was nearly finished when a knight none of them saw reached for him from above. Ray ducked, lost his footing, and slipped off the rail. Brandy and Trevelyan screamed as Ray caught the rail in the notch of his elbow and stopped his fall. Then he screamed too.

The monsters in the courtyard wanted Ray. Their bloodlust urged them forward. Their pain and fear of the big crucifix kept them back. The knight on the roof wanted Ray too. But the big man was below his reach and the same crucifix stood between them.

Brandy reached for Ray. The Templar on the roof reached for her.

Trevelyan lifted his crucifix and scorched the knight; chasing him back out of sight while Brandy helped her fiancé. Confident the monster was gone the priest gave Brandy a hand. They tugged Ray over the rail and all three spilled onto the balcony floor.

"Thank you," Ray told Brandy, trying to catch his breath.

"Thank you," Brandy told Trevelyan, catching hers.

"Thank God," the priest said.

Frightened by the tumult, Luis stole a look out and gaped at the sight of the American couple and the priest in a pile. He said nothing but stepped onto the balcony and peered into the courtyard. Brandy had been right. The big Jesus on the cross was too much for them. Unable to look at it or approach the balcony, the knights were abandoning the courtyard on the north side of the chapel. "*Épatant*," Luis exclaimed.

Trevelyan, back on his feet, agreed it was amazing. His smile matched Luis'. Brandy's matched his. Ray, despite his mounting aches, would have joined them – but for the scream.

It scared the living hell out of Loup.

No, not those *things* outside. Yes, they were unbelievable; their picking and scratching frightening, their groans and chants mind-numbing. But the place was secure and you got used to the noise. It was the scream. Felix's sick little red-head had, without warning, unleashed a heart-rending scream. It scared the living hell out of Loup.

And here came the heroes... the tattooed American biker, the mean brunette and the convict, tripping over themselves from the gallery, down the stairs and into the nave with the priest following like a poodle. Amusing. Upon arrival, they found utter chaos.

The clumsy reporter (with the nice ass) and the worthless fool were scrambling around the chapel making the devil's own racket. Aimee was searching the floor on her knees. Felix was on his feet struggling to use a candelabrum as a weapon. In the corner, Eve was up, leaning on an elbow, looking gray as a ghost and crying her eyes out.

"What's going on?" Brandy demanded, only to get more yelling. "English," she pleaded. "Tell us. . . in English."

"The hand!" Aimee yelled. "It has returned!"

"What the hell are you talking about?" Ray barked.

"The Templar's hand," Felix shouted, throwing the candelabrum down with a violent clatter. "The hand you chopped off. It is still here. It ran out of the dark. . . like a rat. It ran over top of Eve while she was resting. It is here - somewhere."

Great, Ray thought, shaking his head. Just great.

Luis jumped to his knees and joined Aimee searching. Felix returned to comfort Eve. Brandy and Father Trevelyan looked a question at each other, shrugged and started searching too. They didn't have to look long.

Luis and Aimee were in front of the sanctuary steps, young Socrates on one side, the reporter on the other. Aimee momentarily set down her candle and - the hand burst from the shadows. It scurried at her with two boney metacarpals raised like daggers. Aimee squealed.

Brandy, standing nearby, pulled the butcher's knife from the small of her back, leaned and threw it – over Aimee's shoulder. The knife pinned the hand to the floor like a bug in a science project. The boney phalanges clicked and pushed trying to pull loose. A crowd gathered to watch it struggle.

"That's fucking incredible," Ray said.

"It's an incredible story," Aimee said. "If I write it, nobody will believe it."

The melancholy priest added, "I pray we will survive it."

"Look!" They followed Luis' gaze.

The impaled hand spasmed violently and sank unmoving against the floor. Then, as they watched, the horrid thing was overtaken by decay. The parched skin disintegrated and fell to rot, leaving a moss-green pool of muck in its place – with the upright butcher's knife stabbing the floor at its center.

The amputated hand had frightened Eve but, thankfully, hadn't hurt her. The young woman was desperately ill from the first Templar attack. She fell back, afire with fever, soaking in her own sweat.

Father Trevelyan joined Felix at her side. The wounds on Eve's shoulder and throat had gone septic. The hellish monsters, parading as Crusading knights, were filthy and only God knew what bacteria they carried. They stood in silence for some time. Then the dam burst and the tears cascaded freely down Felix's cheeks. "Father, she's so sick. She's...."

Trevelyan laid a hand on his shoulder.

"Pray for her. Please, pray for her."

Trevelyan removed his vestments from his satchel and pulled them on; the white linen alb and the bell-shaped chasuble. He dug out a pocket flask, a tin box, a crystal vial, and a small bottle (wine, the Host, holy water, and blessed oil). These he laid at the foot of the table.

The priest kissed his stole. "Grant me, Our Father, I beg you, on the last day, the garment of immortality forfeited by our sinful first parents." He draped the scarf around his neck and bent to Eve.

Trevelyan crossed himself and laid his hands on her head. "At sunset, all who had people sick brought them to him. He laid his hands on each and cured them." Trevelyan prayed over the oil then poured the sign of the Cross on Eve's forehead. "Through this holy anointing may the Lord, in his love and mercy, help you with the grace of the Holy

Spirit. Amen." He anointed her palms. "May the Lord who frees you from sin save you and raise you up. Amen."

Eve was asleep and, for the moment, her agonized moaning silenced. Trevelyan replaced the bottle of oil. "Have faith, Felix. Have hope."

"She is so very sick, Father."

"In Hebrew," the priest said, gripping his shoulder. "Eve's name would be *Chavah*. It means *to breathe*; *to live*. Surely, her name demands you have hope."

Watching the accelerated decay of the Templar's amputated hand had been too much for the group. One by one, they turned pale and turned away; only to face Eve's crisis. The sole exception was the reporter. To give Felix and Eve some privacy, and in an odd moment of practicality, Aimee approached the putrid mess that was the demon claw, took a deep breath, and yanked the blade from the floor. Unwilling to walk away from a perfectly good knife, Aimee headed for the kitchen.

Loup watched her. The others had gone; Felix back to Eve, Brandy and Ray back to the gallery, the priest and the convict about their business. No one was paying the slightest attention to him. Loup slipped into the hall - and followed the reporter.

Twelve

Using the kitchen's well hydrant was getting easier as the night progressed. Aimee worked the pump for nearly ten minutes to get clear water for Eve. Now, the rust and debris vanished in under five. In no time at all Brandy's knife was clean and ready for the next Templar. She jacked the pump handle again, rinsing the tub, when she heard:

"You have many talents."

Aimee recognized the leering voice and looked up with loathing to see Loup posed in the kitchen door. He'd have been more impressive without the black eye, but not much. "What does that mean?"

He rubbed his chest. "I like the way you pump that."

Aimee released the handle and yawned. "Tell me, *monsieur*, assuming this were the time for such nonsense, which it clearly is not, does such a pathetic and impotent line work on the women you know?"

"You would be surprised what works, *mon cher*."

"You will be surprised how fast the other men come to my assistance."

Loup made a sound of derision and waved the idea away as if it were a gnat. "They are playing with the dead; while I am playing with you."

Aimee pointed the business end of the dripping butcher's knife at Loup's eyes.

"*C'est comme ça*," he said with a laugh. "The little stenographer barks."

"You are confused, *monsieur*. I bite. And I am no stenographer. I am a reporter."

Loup raised his hands, in mock surrender, studying the girl and noting again her awkwardness. He smiled, inched forward - and then lunged. She managed a shout as Loup seized her, grabbed the knife, and covered her mouth. "Forgive me!" he whispered. "I cannot resist a lady reporter... who bites."

A guttural cry, a peripheral flash, and a thunderous bang interrupted Loup as a tool box flew through the door and slammed against the wall disgorging its contents. Tools, hardware, dust and debris rained down like an exploded firework. Luis followed after, airborne from the door, hurtling at Loup. He landed on his back and the would-be rapist had no option but to let the reporter go.

Though he'd lost hold of Aimee, Loup outweighed Luis and failed to go down. Luis held on riding him like the Duke of Gloucester's hump. Loup tried to pull him off and Luis sank his teeth into the knife wielder's hand. The blade clattered to the floor. Loup howled. Then he swore, threw Luis off, and turned on him with murder in his eyes.

From the floor, Luis kicked with both feet, caught Loup in the gut and drove him back against the shuddered window. The shaken Loup shouted, "You little bastard." It was all he had time to shout.

With a bang, the shatter of glass, and the crack of breaking wood, a spiked iron ball exploded from outside through the window. Wood shards, glass and splinters flew. Before anyone could react, the flail disappeared back outside and a razor sharp halberd shot through the broken slats - and into Loup's back. The would-be rapist, wide-eyed with disbelief, raised his hands – pleading. He groaned as the spear pierced his right lung from behind and grunted as it burst from his chest (above his pocket) with a spurt of blood.

Luis, rising, lurched back as the crimson arc splashed his face. Aimee screamed.

Behind Loup, through the window, both saw flashes of grinning skeletal faces, clawed hands, the rotted mantles and red crosses of two of the Templar knights. One held the other end of the halberd shaft. He pulled on it, yanking Loup backward like a speared fish. The second Templar wrapped the flail's chain around his neck, jerked him off his feet, and dragged Loup out the window.

It took only a second. Luis almost laughed. Not that he'd seen anything funny but because it was surreal. Loup was there, ready to kill. Then there was only the barely scuffed bottoms of his new shoes. Then he was gone. The Templars dragged him, screaming, into the dark. Luis knew, as sure as he knew his own name, he would never forget the sight of the bottoms of Loup's shoes.

"Again with the kitchen!" Ray shouted as he ran through the doorway. He pulled up panting to see tools spread from one end of the room to the other, and Aimee and Luis hurriedly boarding the window back up. Something had broken in. Brandy and Father Trevelyan arrived on Ray's heels. All three gaped while Luis and Aimee hammered away.

"Well?" Ray asked. "What in the hell is going on in here?"

Only when Aimee turned did the others see how frightened she was. "The Templars," she said breathlessly, "they grabbed Loup!" Luis confirmed it with a nod.

"Loup?"

All three realized there was no Loup. Suddenly, the broken window held a whole new reality.

Luis said something to Aimee, apparently amusing himself, and finished with a laugh. Aimee frowned and shook her head.

"Luis!" Trevelyan snapped. Appalled, the priest walked out.

"What's that about?" Ray asked.

Aimee twisted her lips; less than eager to repeat the comment. "He said the Templars did for us a favor. They took out the rubbish."

———†———

In the days of old, the *Gendarmerie* were the mounted divisions of the French military; their cavalry. It was fitting then their modern counterpart should arrive over the hill in the nick of time. Colonel Blanc's car led the procession, followed by the van carrying their Tactical Team, with Lieutenant Colonel Petit's car bringing up the rear. They extinguished their headlights as they crossed the drawbridge and, beneath the full moon, curved around to the courtyard. Blanc's driver parked beside Fournier's dilapidated bus. The van fell in beside and Petit's vehicle beside it. All three vehicles were shut off and fell into silence.

Blanc stared, expressionless, through the windshield. His driver, Maurice Delvit, whispered under his breath in disbelief, "What the hell is going on?"

Men, four that Blanc saw, milled about the courtyard. They were dressed in the cloaks, tunics and armor of Templar knights or, more accurately, what Templars might look like following a fire and several centuries moldering in the grave. Though details were elusive in the blue-white moonlight, they appeared to have weapons and several rode armored horses.

"Have you ever seen the like?" Blanc's question was rhetorical. Delvit had never ventured thirty miles from Paradis. He'd seen nothing, anywhere, until now. "I knew Marcel Fournier was crazy but I would never have credited him with an imagination."

"I do not understand, Colonel," Delvit said. "What has this to do with drugs?"

"Idiot! What do you think? Do you believe in ghosts? This is a show to scare away interlopers. These are, how would our American friends put it, scarecrows."

Screams, a demonic shriek and human shouts of pain and terror split the night.

"*Mon Dieu!*" Delvit started in his seat. Blanc remained expressionless but dissected the gloom with his eyes.

Around the distant side of the chapel two more figures emerged from the darkness and entered the courtyard. They too were dressed as knights. They walked abreast carrying weapons in their outside hands and dragging a man on his knees between them.

Blanc ordered Delvit to turn the car's exterior light on and, over his radio, ordered the others to do the same. Three spots illuminated the ruined castle's entrance, the chapel, and the courtyard in a white glow. Blanc squinted, straining to see, and nodded as he identified the man on his knees. "I knew it. That is Loup Wimund." The front of Loup's shirt had a gaping hole and was stained by blood; black in the moonlight.

The Colonel hefted himself from the passenger seat with a chip on his shoulder and a satisfied grin on his face. Behind Blanc, his gendarmes piled out of their van. They fell in, drew their weapons, and slipped their safety catches 'OFF' down the line.

Within a few minutes the soldiers' names would no longer matter to anyone but the mason hired to carve their grave markers. Still, to complete the record, they were:

Antoine Beauvais, six and a half feet, two hundred, thirty pounds of imposing muscle whose uniform, kepi to boots, was special ordered. His name meant *beautiful* and he was gorilla ugly.

Bernard Sigismund, a barely passable marksman, but formidable at hand-to-hand.

Leon Pomeroy, smiling now from nerves, who had the previous night without knowing visited his drinking buddy, Chitichia, at the morgue... for the very last time.

Tristan Maigny, who, marooned on an island, would survive comfortably with nothing more than a regulation manual and an iron to press his uniform.

And Aurore Vasser. The *Gendarmerie* were as modern as any military. That said, staffing shortages left Vasser the only female in the Paradis unit. The others considered Aurore their little sister. Until this moment she had been well guarded.

Petit and Andre Fulke left their car to round out the unit.

"What is happening?"

Blanc followed the voice to see Jerome peeking up from his back seat like a bird in a nest. "Stay down and keep quiet, you idiot. Unless you want Fournier to see you."

As Delvit came round to stand beside the Colonel, they heard Loup weakly calling for help. Blanc scowled. He had no love for Loup. Even so, the filthy scoundrel Fournier would pay for the humiliation he was doling out.

The Templar who looked to be in charge (Fournier himself?), stepped in front of the wounded Loup. The other knights watched him as hounds would their master. He pointed a boney finger at the soldiers.

One of his knights drew two daggers from his belt.

Thirteen

The daggers glinted keenly in the spotlights. Even at that distance the weight of the elegant weapons, gripped in the knight's gauntlets, was unmistakable. Unquestionably the weapons were real.

And so, Blanc thought, was their implied threat. He had had enough.

"We are the *Gendarmerie*! You will let that man go and surrender your weapons. Marcel Fournier, you are under arrest. You are, all of you, under arrest."

As if Blanc had said the magic word the knight threw one of his daggers.

It lodged in Delvit's chest. He shouted in pain, spun reaching for the protruding handle, and was hit from behind by a second blade.

In the car, peeking against orders, Jerome saw the assault through the side window. He saw the driver fall into Blanc's arms.

Jerome squealed and dropped down again on the floor.

"Get them!" The Colonel screamed as he lowered Delvit carefully to the ground.

"Open fire!" Petit shouted to his squad.

Blanc had no time to aid Delvit further. He let his driver go, drew his sidearm and stood. Then all hell broke loose as he and his soldiers opened fire. Bullets ripped past and through the staggered line of Templars. The knights in reply released Loup and brought their weapons to bear on the *Gendarmerie*.

Freed, Loup crawled away, forced himself up and staggered into the darkness. The dark cloaked Templar saw him. He sheathed his sword, mounted his horse and turned the animal to follow.

"Stop him!" Blanc shouted, pointing at the Templar chaplain. "He's getting away!"

Big Antoine Beauvais unloaded his weapon into the knight's back. His cloak bucked and dust clouds erupted. Peppered with bullet holes, he stayed in the saddle and rode - uninjured. When shooting him proved fruitless, Beauvais shot the Templar's horse. That had no effect either and the beast rode on.

Across the courtyard, for the gendarmes and Templars scattered as they fought, the soldiers were discovering their bullets had no effect on their targets. Obviously, Blanc thought, Fournier's men were wearing body armor. But, *sacré*, what armor!

Several more men, or knights, if that's what they were, climbed aboard their horses. Not to escape, but to fight.

Leon Pomeroy, wide-eyed, couldn't swallow or even breathe. A one-handed Templar rode at him with the reins to his horse clamped in his teeth, his right stump flogging the air, and a spear clutched above his helmet in his left hand. Pomeroy stood courageously shooting the damned thing. He held his ground longer than most would have but finally had enough. He quit his position and ran like hell for their vehicles. The one-handed Templar bore down at full stride and hurled his halberd. The javelin impaled Pomeroy from behind. His rifle flew. So did the gendarme; driven forward, up, and onto Blanc's vehicle. Pomeroy smacked the windshield with his head, cracked both, and came to rest sprawled across the hood, the halberd jutting skyward, staring into the car with unseeing eyes.

The one-armed knight rode on between the vehicles; the hooves of his horse leaving the clatter of the courtyard for the soft ground in the dark beyond.

Andre Fulke, Petit's driver, ran to the car. He laid a hand on Pomeroy and quickly determined he was dead. Before he could retreat, Fulke saw the Templar returning; riding from the dark at full gallop. He passed the van and leapt from his saddle taking the soldier down. There was no fight. Despite having only one hand, the knight pinned Fulke to the ground, jerked his head to the side and, with a hair-raising growl, ripped the gendarme's throat out with his teeth.

The archer, back aboard his mount, towered over the gendarme's little sister, Aurore Vasser. The Templar grabbed her by the hair. He slapped the rifle from her hands and hauled her up onto his saddle before him. Vasser kept her wits despite her disgust at the knight's touch. She drew her sidearm, jammed the barrel under the mummy's chin and pulled the trigger.

Vasser was so disconcerted by the deafening report, the blinding muzzle flash, she didn't see the explosion of the Templar's hood or the top of the creature's head blown through the hole. But her vision quickly cleared, her hearing quickly returned. The Templar glared down at her - and laughed in her face.

Tristan Maigny appeared below the Templar's horse. He fired his weapon, at point blank range, into the mummy holding Vasser. Nine shots into the monster's chest. The Templar, with Vasser still struggling, turned his pistol crossbow. He fired it and sent Maigny reeling to the ground. Before the gasping soldier could rise, the Templar who'd started the battle with two well-placed daggers fell on him, tore into Maigny's throat with his teeth and began to feast.

The archer was laughing again. Vasser, her courage exhausted, could only scream. And she did. . . even after he bit into her throat.

It went on for several minutes more; the gunfire, the *snicks*, *clangs*, *clinks*, and *thunks* of ancient weaponry being employed, the horrified, disbelieving screams, the hellish laughs, the whinnying of horses, the thunder of hooves upon stone.

Petit and Sigismund tried to put down the Templars' leader - to their everlasting regret.

Gasping, oozing blood like tap water, Delvit pulled himself up onto his hands and knees. He was crawling; to where and for what even he didn't know. Despite the two daggers in him, one in his chest and one in his back, he was alive and his brain was ordering him to move. Beneath him, the gray, black and white stones of the courtyard were cold, uneven. . . and, as he moved, speckled with crimson. Amid the cries and the chaos, Delvit paused and raised his head. In the long shadows cast by the full moon, he saw a Templar knight walking purposely toward him dangling a spiked ball on a chain. It swung to and fro with his stride like a clock's pendulum. Delvit's time was up.

Blanc, as spent as his empty gun, looked in terror on six of his soldiers and friends dead or dying at the hands of these hellish monsters. He'd been so very wrong about Fournier. Then he saw his seventh soldier, big, ugly Antoine Beauvais, backed against the cold stone wall and surrounded by, *Dieu dans le ciel*, real resurrected Templars moving steadily in on him near the entrance to the castle ruin.

Beauvais screamed for Blanc's help.

Blanc holstered his gun with a trembling hand and ran in the opposite direction.

"Colonel!" Beauvais screamed as the Templars set on him.

Blanc tripped and hurtled headlong up the chapel steps toward the severely hacked door. He turned his head and avoided breaking his neck but took the full force of the impact with his shoulder. Adrenaline kept him from feeling what, if he lived, would be a bruise from neck to hand. "*Ouvrez la porte!*" He screamed, banging the door with his only working fist. "*Ouvrez la porte!*"

The door came open. Blanc rolled across the threshold and into the vestibule. The door was quickly shut behind him.

Blanc, a quivering mess on the floor, held his shoulder with a shaking hand and cried, "This cannot be happening! It cannot be happening!"

Ray slid the batten back into its brackets to secure the door. He looked at the blubbering mass that once was a *Gendarmerie* Colonel and shook his head in disgust. "Isn't it about time you got over that?"

Alone on the floor of the Colonel's car, Jerome talked quietly to himself. Even he didn't know why; perhaps to pass the time, maybe to avoid going out of his mind, or perhaps because he had already gone crazy. "What's so bloody terrible about the establishment? Can you tell me that, Jerome? What are you going to do with your life? Go into bleeding civil service, son. Listen to your old dad." Jerome adjusted, searching for room that didn't exist.

"Why, in God's name, do you want to go back to Paradis? See the world! Let someone else pay for it. Never go home unless you're called. Then you know you're wanted. Stay in England. And stop with the bleeding tattoos! You'd think you had a self-esteem issue, for heaven's sake. For heaven's bleeding sake."

Jerome looked up from his hiding spot.

At the front of the car – to see a soldier, sprawled unmoving on the bonnet, dead eyes staring blankly in through the cracked windscreen. It was Pomeroy and his days chasing women on the Riviera were over. Then to the side - to see a Templar staring through the passenger's window. The knight's red eyes deep in his grinning skull seemed almost to burn. Then to the other side – to see what, at first, looked to be a reflection. It was not. The mirror image was a second Templar.

The tattoo artist began singing in the high, whispered voice of a child, repeating a song his mother sang, a thousand years ago and a million miles away.

"Forgive me. Forgive me. I know not what to say."

One of the knights lifted a heavy mace, reared back and struck the passenger's side rear window with a dull thwack. The tempered glass splintered to a smoky spider's web. Several spikes from the ball's head poked menacingly through the glass. Amazingly, the window held.

"Father never showed me. Mother never told me."

The other hit the driver's side window with the butt of his crossbow. The glass bounced with the blows. Once. Twice. Three times was a charm. That window, too, cracked into one large spider's web.

"*My parents never showed me what it means to pray.*"

The mace and crossbow were driven home again. *Thwack. Thump.* The passenger's side window shattered and the mace was withdrawn. The driver's side followed with a rain of glass shards and the crossbow was pulled back.

Jerome Rousseau had nowhere to go. "I'm a hemophiliac!" he screamed.

From both sides of the car, through the shattered windows, the claw-like hands of the Templars reached for him.

Fourteen

From somewhere outside the chapel they heard a final tortured scream. Then all fell silent. The Templars were feasting.

Blanc, their new arrival, wandered from the vestibule into the nave teetering on the edge of sanity. His lips trembled and he babbled, "How? I do not... Why? Do you... "

"We don't have any answers," Ray said sharply. "Besides, it doesn't matter. They're out there and we're trapped." He walked away making it clear the gendarme officer could keep whatever authority he thought he held.

Blanc followed after the big American. "But what do they want?"

"Revenge," Ray said, taking the stairs to the gallery two at a time. "If you believe Clive, eh, Father Trevelyan. Human blood, our blood, to pay for their executions."

The gallery door stood open and Ray took it to the balcony; protected now by Brandy's ossuary crucifix. Blanc followed like a child. Trevelyan, at the rail, stared silently out over the courtyard. He too had heard that final scream and was praying for the soul involved. He paid no mind when Ray and the Colonel joined him.

The shadowy forms of the Templars appeared sporadically, in the distance, in and out of the moonlit courtyard, now littered as far as the eye could see with the bodies of dead soldiers. Drawn by the warm-blooded humans on the balcony, they guarded their eyes and hissed their hunger. Ray stared, wondering what he could do about them.

Blanc gripped the railing, steadying himself as he fought to steady his nerves, and followed Ray's gaze. A light shown in his eyes and the Colonel shouted, "Fire! We could burn them! Fire took care of your sister."

Ray's mouth fell open in disbelief. The muscles in his face tightened and he stared daggers at the despicable military man. "You sons-of-bitches already burned them, seven hundred years ago, for all the good it did."

"It wasn't the fire. . . " Trevelyan said quietly.

"What did you say?" Blanc demanded.

"It wasn't the fire that burned Vicki. It was the hand of God." Trevelyan kissed his crucifix.

Ray looked from Trevelyan, to Blanc, and back again. He'd already reached the conclusion the Colonel had lost his mind. Now he wondered about the priest as well.

A new scream arose in the courtyard. Ray, Trevelyan and Blanc watched as a Templar rode in from the shadows. It was the dark cloaked chaplain, carrying his ornate cross on its half-staff (since Brandy broke it) in his up-raised hand. He was dragging someone on the ground behind him.

His captive screamed again and turned his face into the moonlight. It was Loup; the rope on his wrists stretched to the knight's saddle. The Templar pulled him to the center of the courtyard and let him fall. The chaplain rode around him and, when Loup tried to rise, kicked him back to his knees. The standard bearer dismounted, lifted the cross with skeletal hands, and called out to the others. Again he started their Latin chant. The other knights joined in, and moved in, gathering around the terrified Loup.

Trevelyan stared, appalled and captivated at the same time. It looked to be some black religious rite and the dark cloaked one was obviously their minister – if Satan sanctioned ministers.

Blanc, staring too, suddenly looked hard to the left of the knights' circle.

Ray couldn't help but follow his gaze. "What is it?"

"Something. . . moved."

Ray stared. He saw the gathered Templars, their sacrifice, the courtyard bathed in moonlight and shadow, and the scattered remains of the soldiers. "What moved?"

As if in answer, the corpse of Lieutenant Colonel Petit sat up.

There wasn't any doubt in Blanc's mind. He'd seen the massacre with his own eyes. His entire compliment of soldiers were killed; Petit among them. But the devil was playing tricks, for those same shell-shocked eyes now watched in horror as Petit lifted himself to his feet and began shambling around.

The chanting, that damnable Templar chanting, led by the knight in the dark cloak, continued. To the sounds of this evil song, one by one, the rest of his gendarmes came back to life. Fired by something from the pits of hell their neurotransmitters traveled again, their dead eyes opened, their stilled muscles flexed. Each in their turn sat up, or lifted themselves to stand up and, horribly wounded, soaked in their own blood, walked again. Blanc, his mouth agape, stared in disbelieving horror. Beside him, Father Trevelyan crossed himself with a shaking hand and muttered, "God in heaven."

No longer alive, but not quite dead, Andre Fulke, Petit's driver, arose. Antoine Beauvais, now ugly in a way nobody could ever have imagined, followed. He leapt up with a snarl and landed in a crouch. Across the courtyard, Bernard Sigismund stood from a pool of his own blood. In life, Sigismund was a happy man. No longer happy or sad, he gazed now, hungrily, through piercing yellow eyes that suddenly saw in the dark. Maurice Delvit, the Colonel's driver, wobbled before finding his balance. The daggers that led to his death were still in position; one in front, one in back. He yanked the blade from his chest with a sucking sound and dropped it clattering to the ground. Several attempts at the dagger in his back failed and the once proud soldier, now a stumbling thing like the rest, soon gave up trying. The others followed in time, Tristan Maigny, and their 'little sister', Aurore Vasser. Seven new vampires risen from the dead.

Only Pomeroy escaped this walking damnation. Killed instantaneously by a flying halberd, and left atop the hood of Blanc's car, Leon was untouched by the vile infection manipulating the others. Sometimes it was good to just be dead.

The undead gendarme soldiers, some energetically and others in stumbling fits, moved in around their Templar masters. The Templars likewise encircled their chaplain; a gathering of the minions of hell. The chapel bells started ringing again.

Then, like an electric shock, something occurred to Trevelyan that hadn't before. With it came a flood of fear and disbelief. He grabbed the balcony rail, to curb his swoon, and stared up at the chapel's tower. "It's. . . It's. . . " He caught his breath and released it in a whisper. "It's not possible."

"We've spent the whole night surrounded by the living dead," Ray said angrily. "Why don't we get over whether or not it's possible?"

Trevelyan turned on Ray. "I'm not talking about the Templars!" He pointed to the balcony roof and, by implication, to the tower above. "I'm talking about the bells. They can't be ringing. It's not possible."

"Of course they're ringing." Ray hesitated, listening. "We can all hear them."

"The castle grounds were vandalized ten years ago. The perpetrators were caught and convicted and, how would you say, given a slap on the arm. They got into the chapel and into the tower. They tore the bells out, threw them down, broke them. The *Gendarmerie* allowed me to take one following the trial. It sits in my study; been there for nearly a decade."

Ray nodded, remembering the bell behind the priest's desk.

"They cannot be ringing," Trevelyan said. "There are no bells in the tower."

And yet the somber rhythmic tolling of the chapel bells continued.

———┼———

Madness. . .

Father Clive Trevelyan had never given it much thought. He had, of course, heard parishioners over the years confess to feeling they were "going crazy" but that wasn't the same as crossing the boundary into insanity. He'd spent his entire adult life pontificating on the subject of religion. But only in the last few days had he discovered true evil; the murders of the Socrates family and the death of the American girl, her return from the dead and her necessary but awful immolation, the courtyard below teeming with resurrected Templars and undead gendarmes. Still, in all that, he'd given no thought to madness. Then the missing tower bells rang. Trevelyan was traumatically affected. Now the priest feared he'd lost touch with reality; that he was going mad.

But his companions heard them too. *They heard!* What power governed them, the priest didn't know, but the bells were real. Which meant he was not insane.

It also meant the Templars were real.

If his marbles were all there, Trevelyan wondered, what about his companions; particularly Blanc? The priest was considering whether or not the agitated Colonel could take the situation much longer, when he got his answer. Blanc suddenly screamed – a long insane bleat. Then he pulled his pistol from its holster, reloaded it (ignoring their questions), and started firing.

The gunshots were deafening. The muzzle flashes blinded.

Several blasts ripped through the Templars' bodies. The result was laughable; a hole blasted through the rotted fabric, a puff of dust and dried flesh, a dull look as the creature realized he'd been hit, then the inevitable red-eyed glare from the completely unharmed knight.

An undead soldier, once Bernard Sigismund, took a bullet to the chest. The impact knocked him down. A moment later he made it back to his feet showing little effect. A second shot struck him in the head. He dropped over... dead again.

Trevelyan and Ray both watched in bizarre fascination.

Another shot barked and hit the thing that once was Petit just above his right eye. The walking corpse wobbled, rotated his hands in a failed fight for balance, and toppled into an unmoving heap.

Trevelyan turned away; the fleeting fascination gone.

Blanc fell forward, aghast and struggling to breathe, and would have plummeted to the cold stones had it not been for the rail. He let himself slide to the floor. "He... He was..." he spluttered, crying. "He was best man at my wedding."

Ray and Trevelyan looked from the heap in the courtyard that once was Petit to the heap on the balcony that once was a Colonel. There was nothing to be done. Neither could find any compassion. Ray felt only anger, Trevelyan overwhelming despair.

"Why are they coming back...? Rising?" Ray fought to get it out. "It took Vicki days..."

Trevelyan hesitated having already considered the question. He knew he had no choice. "Forgive me, Ray," the priest said. "Your sister was. . . badly mutilated. It took a day for the police surgeon to perform the autopsy and. . . put her back together. . . "

Ray felt the tears and looked away. His eyes fell on Blanc, still on the balcony floor, dumping spent cartridges from his weapon. He dropped them, tinkling and useless, and wound up with a live bullet in his shaking fingers.

"One round left," Blanc whispered as he slid it back into the chamber. A rivulet of spittle trickled from the corner of his mouth. He seemed not to notice.

"You're wasting your time," Ray said, turning away in disgust. "What are you going to do with one bullet?"

A thundering report followed.

Fifteen

Ray closed his eyes knowing what had happened. He steeled himself and opened them again. The crumpled body of the gendarme Colonel lay on its side on the cold floor. Blood gushed from his mouth and a pool grew beneath his head.

Another scream demanded their attention at the balcony doorway. Aimee, shaking and crying, stared at Blanc's corpse. It was clear she'd seen the whole thing. "*C'est fini*. We are all going to die!" Aimee screamed. "There's no hope." Babbling and crying, the girl disappeared back into the chapel. Though they knew they should, neither Trevelyan nor Ray followed her. Both were too exhausted; too numb.

Ray began to shake as well. He fell to his knees at the Colonel's feet, threw his clenched fists into the air and screamed,

"You coward! We needed you!" His voice trailed to a whisper. "We needed you. . . ."

Again the priest found himself thinking of madness. He put his hand on Ray's shoulder. "Do not fear, for I am with you. Do not be afraid, for I am your God. I will strengthen and guide you. I will uphold you with my righteous right hand."

"Words, Clive," Ray said, crying. "Just words."

"Good words. True words, Ray. Only believe them."

The noise was driving Brandy crazy. The screams. The gunshots. The bells. The shrieking, skittering and infernal scratching of the vampires trying to get in, the insufferable pleas to the demon world through the infuriating chanting of the Templars and their constant whacking away at the timbers of the chapel, the deafening sound of her own relentless thoughts. It was all too much.

Then, on the balcony, Aimee screaming. Now, on the steps, what must be Aimee running. Brandy stood in the doorway to the ambulatory hallway fighting the fear rising within her.

Luis ran past her to the bottom of the stairs and met Aimee as she reached the ground floor. She was in hysterics. He grabbed her face and tried calming her, telling her, Brandy imagined, that he was there with her. He pushed her head to his shoulder and cooed to her in their native language.

Aimee cried in a jumbled mix of French and English, "*C'est fini.* We are all going to die! There's no hope. We're never going to get out of here. *C'est fini.*"

Brandy turned away, angry and unsure why. She was horrified as well, but Aimee's public display of those fears rubbed her the wrong way. She was tired.

Behind her, Brandy heard splintering wood. She turned from the hysterics in the chapel to look the hallway up and down. Though it was painted with the warm glow of candlelight from the nave doorways and the kitchen, at the far end, the hall seemed suddenly longer, darker and colder. But there was nothing to see.

Then she heard it. The clawing, the scuttling, something making uninvited entrance. Brandy opened the work room door and saw nothing. Then localized the sound to the office locked earlier by Father Trevelyan. The room where the Templar had grabbed her. Brandy stepped to the door;

saw the hasp lock firmly in place. Then someone banged from the inside. The door vibrated. Something had crawled in and was fighting to get through.

The banging stopped. Brandy stared, wide-eyed.

A hand exploded through the door. With a tremendous crack, the wood panel flew past, missing Brandy's head by an inch, and slammed against the hallway wall. The talons flexed, reaching for her, clawing at her face, while the creature's other hand grabbed at the hole for leverage. The vampire wanted in.

Through the jagged hole in the door, Brandy saw a yellow-green eye with a wide black pupil deep enough to fall into. Then it was gone, replaced by the flash of a screaming, blood red tongue. She was mesmerized.

"Brandy!"

Luis and Aimee were in the ambulatory and he was calling her. Brandy shook herself out of it, knowing Luis didn't need two hysterical women on his hands. She felt for one of the ossuary cruciforms in her pocket, drew it out and stuck it in the grasping hand of the vampire. Hell erupted.

There came a shriek of pain as if she'd handed the monster something molten. It dropped the crucifix, smoke curling up in gray puffs between its fingers. The air stunk of putrid burning flesh. The hand disappeared back through the door.

Brandy fitted the crucifix neatly into the hole and looked past it into the office. The vampire, one of the transformed gendarmes, leaned with his back against the broken window shrieking and spitting hatred back at her. It clawed madly as if the air were full of acid and like some awful spider skittered backwards out the window. Its scream followed it back out into the dark.

To Brandy's surprise, the others were there. Aimee was still crying in Luis' arms, everyone else merely looked stunned. Father Trevelyan had all he could do to simply stand upright. Ray, flexed, fists clenched, ready to offer his physical strength, but unable to lend any emotional consolation.

Brandy, despite Luis' reluctance, took over comforting Aimee; admitting, to herself at least, that she needed the contact as much as the reporter did.

Luis floated alone into the work room and peered out through a crack in the plywood. He watched the blood drenched Templars while he moved from one foot to another, vibrating with pent up energy, but unable to discharge it in any practical manner.

Brandy led Aimee, still crying uncontrollably, into the nave. Her eyes fell on a lit candelabrum and she stared, listening to

413

Aimee, "It is over. There is no hope. No hope." Aimee's voice seemed to fade while Brandy continued to stare at the candle. There was something about the flame. . .

"There is no hope!" someone said, far away.

The flame. . . searing red, yellow and orange. . . crackling with rising heat. . .

The heat of the flames fanned by a sudden gust of wind was so intense Fasset, the executioner, had to turn away. It was a hell of a night, he thought, for the death sentences to be carried out. Eight men, tied to stakes here and now, beneath the shadow of Notre Dame. Seven of them already alight. Drowning in sweat from the heat, squinting against the brilliant orange, red and yellow fingers of flame, breathing through his mouth to stave off the odor of charred flesh and carrying a torch on top of it, the executioner looked beyond the row of dying convicts to the glorious cathedral still under construction. A monument to God, a thing of beauty, towering over this sacrifice of Satan's beloved. And on a night like this; with the gusting wind. It would be a hell of a thing, Fasset thought, to burn these miserable bastards to death and burn the new church down before they've even finished building it. *Eh bien*, it was not his problem.

With his torch, he moved to the last of the convicted; Jacques de Molay, the Grand Master of this Order of the Devil. Fasset looked to the Archbishop of Sens, hoping he'd receive the signal soon. *Sacré*, the heat was incredible. The noise, too, was incredible. The crackling of the fire, the gusts of wind, the shouts, cheers and jeers of the crowd looking on, and the screams of the condemned roasting like pigs beside him.

Officially they were Geoffrey de Charney, Henri Ethelbert, Louis Godenot, Jules Lefebvre, Gaston Morel; knights Templar all, Benoit Lambert; their chaplain, Francois de Raiis; commander of the *Château de la liberté*, and Molay; their Master. Their names meant nothing to the executioner. They were the condemned. He, Fasset, was being paid to make them the dead.

The Archbishop nodded, thank God, and the sweating executioner put his torch to the last pile of fagots, the last Templar. Like the others, in this wind, it erupted in flame around the prisoner's feet. Fasset backed away and descended from the platform. The crowd shouted; having the time of their lives. Behind him, at the stake, Molay was screaming. Nothing unusual about that. But he wasn't just vocalizing searing pain. He was still forming sentences, trying it seemed, to deliver a final message to the world.

Why not, Fasset thought. What the hell do I care!

"I will hope in the resurrection," Jacques de Molay screamed as he died. "I will hope in the resurrection."

———┼———

Brandy ushered Aimee to Trevelyan. He cleared a chair for the reporter and took her off her hands. Then the American girl was gone.

She hurried away to the front of the sanctuary looking for something. She circled round the altar slowly, almost reverently, staring at one of the decorated palls hanging above the communion table at the apse.

"Brandy?"

It wasn't reverence exactly. She ignored Ray. . . and jumped atop the table.

"Brandy!"

She grabbed the cloth banner and, holding her breath, yanked it down. Her guess was right as a cloud of dust erupted. What she hadn't anticipated was the storm cloud from Ray.

"Geez! What are you doing?" Ray wasn't a churchgoer. But damn. . . He also wasn't thinking of swimming laps in the baptismal font.

He was worried about his fiancé - body and mind. When he voiced his concern, Brandy gave him the hand to silence him. She rolled the ceremonial curtain into a manageable wad and jumped from the table, nearly landing on him. Then she hurried away with her prize across the nave.

Ray watched her go, following but no longer chasing. His shouts as she disappeared into the vestibule diminished to a quiet, "Brandy?" Then came a tumultuous smash and a splintering of wood and he was shouting again. "Brandy!"

Ray got an eyeful when he found her. The small table that lived near the holy water font was overturned and lying in pieces on the floor. Brandy crouched over it breaking off one of its legs.

"What the hell are you doing?"

Brandy pointed at the barred door. The chanting of the Templars, the incessant scratching and banging of their vampire off-spring continued unabated. "We can't keep holding them off. And we can't just sit here – waiting to die."

"Okay. So. . . what are you doing?"

She wore a look Ray hadn't seen in a long time, one he'd seen frequently back when she confided in him; sincerity. "I am. . . hoping. . . in the resurrection."

Brandy set the table leg on the floor, unrolled the banner she'd liberated from the sanctuary apse, and began tearing it into strips. She paid Ray no further mind but went about her business. She wrapped the torn fabric about the end of a table leg and tied it securely making a crude but serviceable torch.

"Where are you going?"

"I will hope in the resurrection."

"What does that mean?"

Brandy didn't answer. The candlelight glinted off something in the dark corner. It caught her attention and she picked it up. It was a lighter; Vicki's lighter. She tossed it to Ray then grabbed the batten on the chapel's front door, apparently, intending to open it.

Ray laid a hand gently but firmly on her shoulder. "Brandy, what are you doing?"

She turned with fire in her eyes. "Let go of me!"

"What are you doing?"

"Father Trevelyan was right. This is about good and evil."

"Okay," Ray said, nodding. "I'm with you so far."

"Don't try to stop me. I have to do this."

"I'm not trying to stop you."

Brandy looked deep into Ray's eyes. "What did you say?"

"I'm not trying to stop you. I just want to know what you're thinking."

"What I should have thought a long time ago," Brandy said, looking far away. "There is another grave in the Templar cemetery."

Sixteen

Ray talked Brandy out of it.

Not the idea; not in a million years. She would go through with her plan and he knew it. But he talked her out of the rush which, in his opinion, was the part that was going to kill her. It had been no small feat. He circumvented her anger, fear and stubbornness by appealing to her intelligence... and her vanity. It's one thing to be smart, another to be told you're smart. Regardless of her determination, Ray knew, an intelligent woman could appreciate the courtyard was no place for anyone to be... alone.

"I think I know what you're doing," he said, "and I think you're right."

Brandy reacted as if she'd been slapped. Then the tension drained from her body; her defenses melted. She stared uneasily into his brown eyes watchful for deception.

"Yes," Ray nodded, "I believe you're right. But that doesn't change the fact that the courtyard is no place to be alone. I'm not saying you can't do it alone. You've proved you can do anything you put your mind to. But maybe. . . you could use some help."

Brandy nodded slowly.

"You'll let me come with you?"

She nodded again, relieved, almost happy.

"Great." Ray laughed and shook his head. "This is. . . absolutely insane."

"I thought you said you believed me?"

"I do. . . and I'm with you. That doesn't make it sane."

She conceded his point and her smile returned.

"So," Ray said, "what do we tell everyone?"

"Can we tell them the truth?"

"We can tell Clive the truth."

"The others?"

Ray shook his head. "They might believe us. But they'd never let us go. Not without an argument."

"So what do we tell them?"

"The best kind of lie; one with a big chunk of truth in it."

Father Trevelyan was back on the balcony keeping watch on the courtyard; what Ray

422

indelicately referred to as 'standing ghoul watch'. Though the Templar archer was still firing arrows it was, the priest admitted, a safer task with the ossuary crucifix in place. Thank heaven for it, for Brandy, and for the others.

Thank God too for the caretaker's workroom and all of its collected equipment. Including the tarp now covering the body of Colonel Blanc. It had been dragged into the corner and the tarp laid over. Trevelyan was in the opposite corner as far away as possible from the dead officer. Could anyone blame him?

Brandy and Ray seemed nervous when they joined him.

Brandy jumped when something on the roof hissed at her. It was one of the gendarme vampires crouched at the eave, ten feet away, where it couldn't see the crucifix head on. "I didn't see that there!" she said, her hand on her heart. The monster blindly reached for them with his yellow eyes averted.

"I'm sorry," the priest said. "I should have mentioned. He's been there since I came up." He closed his eyes and shuddered, wishing it away. Of course it remained, hungrily leaning over the eave. Trevelyan laid a hand on the big crucifix. "It's alarming how quickly I've taken God's protective power for granted."

"That's a cue," Brandy said, "if I've ever heard one." Ray nodded his agreement.

"I'm sorry?" the priest asked.

They spilled their guts, explained as best they could Brandy's revelation, and what they intended to do about it. "As far as everyone else is concerned," she said, "we're just going for help. That's the easiest explanation. And it isn't untrue."

"Have you a plan?"

"Not one that makes sense. Just... get to the cemetery."

Tears appeared in Trevelyan's eyes. "That is what I imagined you would say. It's mad. Even if it weren't, can you possibly cover that great distance without being caught?"

"Your guess is as good as ours," Ray said.

Brandy scowled. "You're having second thoughts?"

"I'm not. I'm with you."

"You don't sound like it."

"Why? Because I don't believe this?" He pointed to the courtyard. "I don't know what the hell these things are or why they're out there. Okay, they're there. That doesn't mean I believe in magic."

"Then why go?"

"Because I believe in you."

Her eyes teared too and glinted in the moonlight.

"That doesn't mean I wouldn't like an advantage if we could get it." Ray stared down on the dead and the living dead. Then a light went on behind his eyes. "Do you think," Ray said, pointing to the tarp covering Blanc's corpse, "that he has the keys to one of the cars?"

Trevelyan shook his head. "He probably had a driver."

"We'll never know," Ray said, clapping his hands, "until we check."

"Do you want me to do it?" Brandy asked.

Yes, Ray thought, hell yes! But he said, "I'll do it."

Attending the occasional funeral was no preparation for searching a corpse. Particularly when it's smoky gray eyes, on either side of a large caliber gunshot wound, stared at you all the while. Thankfully, it didn't take long. And, of course, Clive had been right; there were no keys. Blanc apparently had a driver.

"What about the others?" Ray wondered aloud.

Brandy pointed at the hissing, gyrating thing on the roof. "With our luck," she said, "they're in his pocket." Then she took in the creatures below. "Or one of theirs."

"May as well be on the moon," Trevelyan lamented.

"We need a ride," Ray complained. One of the police vehicles would have been perfect. But that seemed out of the question. The bus was an albatross. It might make the trip, but not fast enough. Ray tried to think. But the thousand sounds that made up their night were also making it difficult; the banging, scratching and hissing, the shrieks, the sporatic chanting.

Then Ray heard another sound... and it got him thinking.

Before they could initiate Brandy's plan they needed to ensure those left behind would be safe. Which meant a reassessment of the chapel's condition; and more hammering and sawing. The doors to the bell tower and office were toe-nailed to reinforce them. The windows to the work room and kitchen given another covering of plywood. Brandy laid several of the small ossuary cruciforms in accessible places.

Then they explained their plan to the others...

Only to find that 'we're going for help' was an excuse not to be believed. Aimee asked if they really thought they'd make it to the village alive. And if so, what help were they hoping for? All of the local gendarmes were dead – or worse. Luis asked if they planned to lead the Templars to the village. Brandy and Ray looked to Trevelyan for support, but he merely shrugged as if he'd known all along neither would buy the lie.

So... they explained their actual intention. Then the argument truly started. And raged for some while with no one changing their point of view.

"You can not go out there," Aimee exclaimed.

Brandy waved her objection away for the third time. She appreciated Aimee's concern. But, with her mind made up, the reporter's pleas were falling on deaf ears. Brandy had bigger worries.

"Father," she said hesitantly, "can you give us... some sort of blessing. I'm not asking for a miracle or a guarantee... just something to take with us on our way?"

Luis suggested something – and Trevelyan and Aimee reacted in horror. The priest answered brusquely. Though the words were unintelligible, the meaning was clear; he'd told Luis not to be ridiculous.

"What was that?" Ray asked.

"It doesn't matter. He's young. He says things."

"What did he say?"

"He suggested I give you the Last Rites!"

"Hell, no!" Ray said flatly and slapped Luis with his eyes.

"I certainly didn't mean the Last Rites!" Brandy added angrily.

"I know. It's all right." Trevelyan laid a hand on Brandy's shoulder and offered a reassuring smile. "We don't even call it that anymore. It's the Anointing of the Sick. You both look healthy to me."

Brandy returned the smile. "Just a simple blessing," she said. "Something to send us on our way. . . and hopefully bring us back."

"I've been thinking about that," Trevelyan said. "It occurred that I could do better. I think I can provide you with a weapon."

———×———

The small kitchen was full to bursting as the group of besieged humans reconvened. They watched as the unarmed pacifist priest donned his liturgical vestments with the ironic intention of presenting Brandy and Ray with a weapon. He kissed his stole and draped it about his neck. Then he placed an empty bucket in the sink tub and, working the pump handle, filled it with water.

"I appreciate the thought, Clive," Ray said without sounding appreciative. "But I'm not sure throwing water on them will be enough. I mean, what the hell, unless we poke them in the eyes and scream 'Nyuk, Nyuk' what's the point?"

"Ray," Trevelyan said. "I'm consecrating water for you."

"Huh? What's that?"

The priest looked up with a guilty satisfaction. This having the upper hand, he thought, could become addicting. Anyway, at least he had the American's attention.

Ray looked a question at Brandy who also was smiling and had apparently caught what he'd missed. "Holy water, Ray," she said. "He's making holy water."

"You can make holy water?" Ray was dumbfounded.

Trevelyan fluttered his eyebrows above his glasses, tapped the tip of his nose, and returned to his task, saying, "The water already exits, Ray. God blesses it through me. Where did you think it came from?"

"I never thought about it."

Luis, who had a knack for making himself invisible when it suited, chose suddenly to make his presence known. He shouted.

Aimee translated: "He says none of us are thinking."

"What does he mean?"

Luis told her as he crossed to the cabinets in the far corner. He grabbed the handles of the upper, right side cupboard doors.

"He says, to save room at home and, more probably, to keep from reminding himself of his failure, his father stored them here."

"Stored what?" Brandy asked - as Luis jerked the doors open.

Brandy was reminded of a novel she'd read in childhood, *The Invisible Man*, as she stared into the cupboard at the real-life embodiment H.G. Wells' Thousand and One bottles. Green bottles, brown bottles, white bottles, large bottles, small bottles, fat bottles with short necks, slim bottles with tall necks, and on and on. The cupboard was stocked top to bottom with empty glass wine bottles.

Luis pulled a dust-covered cloth from a tall square 'something' occupying the shadows in the corner nearest the door. Brandy saw it earlier, assumed it was an appliance, and ignored it. It was, in fact, more bottles, stacks, in even more varieties. And on the floor beside them, boxes of unused corks.

Luis spoke again, directing Trevelyan's attention from the cupboard to the boxes and back again. The priest laughed. "Luis says, if I am going to make holy water, I may as well make enough for everyone."

Seventeen

Not long after, Brandy screamed, "I don't wear dresses!"

With the priest providing the blessed water, and Luis providing the bottles, a discussion followed as to the best method for getting their holy weapons in the field.

"I've got that covered." Brandy disappeared and returned a moment later waving her outsized shoulder bag.

"You're taking your purse with you?"

Ray found the priest's naiveté amusing. "What she means, Clive, is she refuses to leave it behind. They're two different things."

"Yes and?" Brandy asked.

"And, dear, it's a good start. But your bag isn't going to be enough. Assuming these things really work. We'll need as many as we can carry."

An impromptu brainstorming session produced a number of suggestions ranging from the impractical to the silly. When Luis wished aloud they both had *de nombreuses poches*, 'many pockets' according to Aimee, a light shown in Ray's eyes, memories of a misspent youth played in his head, and he announced that Socrates had brilliantly given them the answer. He took them to the caretaker's work room where, in no time at all, Brandy made it known that Luis' brilliant idea had turned into Ray's stupid plan by shouting, "I don't wear dresses!"

"It isn't about the dress," Ray said, trying to be practical. "It's about the pockets. Aimee's dress has pockets." Unable to move her, he took a different tact. "We don't have time for this crap! Aimee stepped up to the plate and generously offered. You're holding up the show and you're hurting her feelings."

"Give me the dress."

"She'll need your pants."

"If I give her my pants, I really will be wearing a dress."

"Brandy!"

She relented and the men left the room, offering the girls privacy.

The idea, from Ray's old shop-lifting days, was to borrow clothing (with big pockets) from their fellow inmates and over-dress;

one shirt over another, a jacket over that, a coat, Brandy's hand bag, a carpenter's apron or, maybe, Socrates' tool bag. Whatever fit (with big pockets), stuffed with as many wine bottles as they'd hold.

Of course, the size differences made for an interesting look. Brandy's jeans became culottes on Aimee. The reporter's dress, with nifty wide pockets on the hips, developed a train when Brandy put it on. Without hesitation, Aimee ripped the bottom off for the cause. Brandy recognized the sacrifice, adjusted her attitude, and got into the spirit of the crazy adventure. Once both had covered enough of their persons to pass as decent they let Ray back in to ready himself.

Luis entered, bare from the waist up, carrying his button down shirt in one hand and T-shirt in the other. Frowning, he tried to hand over the tee. Ray frowned too. "Pockets," he said, shaking his own on his left breast. Then he barked at Aimee, "Tell him I need pockets." Before she could, he snatched the button down from Luis' other hand. "And tell him I need his pants too."

Luis' were similar to what Ray'd worn as a kid in the States, a style somewhere between 'painter's pants' and 'cargo pants'; baggy, with huge pockets on the hips, the rump, and on the legs. Ray stripped off his jeans then waited with flagging patience for

Luis. His refusal to participate was exposed, by the much larger Ray, as a waste of time and the trouser trade was accomplished.

———†———

Thanks to Luis' late father, and the remnants of his dead winery, Father Trevelyan turned the chapel kitchen into a microbrewery. The priest pumped and poured, Aimee corked, while Luis dried and stacked. The assemblage of glass bottles, pails, and all of the chalices they could find had taken a long time to fill. No one bothered to estimate the gallons. Enough water to bathe the Pope - and wash the feet of a good many Cardinals - collected in the kitchen waiting to become something other than water.

Trevelyan had, of course, removed his vestments while they worked. He'd looked a little formal as it was, with Aimee more awkward than usual in Brandy's small pants, and Luis a sight in T-shirt and boxers. With the bottling done, the priest was donning his vestments again, to ask the blessing, when Brandy and Ray waddled into the kitchen. To put it kindly, they looked like over-dressed hobos.

"If you have anything with pockets, Clive," Ray announced, throwing his own too-big pants to Luis (and a rope for a belt). "It's your turn to contribute to the cause."

For a moment, the priest looked dumbfounded, then thoughtful, then nervous. Finally he said, "The, eh, only thing I have with, ah, pockets is my cassock. They don't usually come with pockets, er, but I had them added so I'd, eh, always have candy, ah, with me for, eh, the children, the altar servers and, eh, er, I have a sweet tooth. . ."

"Give," Ray said with his hand out.

"I, eh, er, I've never. . . eh, oh, without it."

"I need pockets," Ray insisted. "Whatever a cassock is God'll understand."

Trevelyan nodded, though he wasn't sure he agreed, and asked Luis to give him a hand as he pulled off the liturgical vestments he'd only just put on. Luis held the chasuble and alb, while Trevelyan began the laborious process of unbuttoning his cassock. Soon, down to black pants, shirt sleeves and clerical collar, the priest hesitated, not so much reluctantly as thoughtfully, before he passed the garment to Ray.

Both halted mid-exchange, as Luis' gave the priest an earful in excitable French. When it subsided, Ray looked from the ex-con to Trevelyan. "What was that all about?"

Trevelyan blushed. "He said. . . things I don't care to repeat. But he wants to know the point. He says you are racing blindly into the Devil's Bed. . . "

"The Devil's Bed?"

"It is what his mother called the unhallowed graveyard of the Templars. The resting place of Satan's servants. He says you are risking your lives and your souls. . . and asks for what?"

"Because," Brandy said, "we're running out of plywood. Tell him we have to try."

"His father tried all of his life and his family are all dead. He did what he thought was right and went to prison. He's afraid you go to your death. . . for nothing."

"Nah," Ray said flippantly.

"Have faith, my son," Trevelyan told Luis. "In the end, the reasons for everything will be revealed."

"Oh, no!" Ray held the cassock up to Brandy. "What were you whining about? We're both wearing dresses."

The priest winced. Hurt, he tempered the moment. "Did you want the collar too?"

Ray grunted. "It'll clash with my neck." He wrestled the cassock on, over the other clothes, which proved to be a chore. Then, examining the parade of buttons, asked, "Don't you guys believe in zippers? Must be fifty of these suckers."

"Thirty-three," Trevelyan said, "the number of years Jesus spent on Earth."

"You made that up!"

"I didn't!" the priest yelled in exasperation. He wasn't done. "Luis Socrates – Ray Kramer. Ray – Luis. While the rest of the world goes about its business, you two can sit around and yell, 'Bullshit' at each other. You'll get along famously."

Silence. Then Brandy and Aimee roared with laughter.

"What?" Ray asked innocently, fighting to rotate the cassock's sleeves over two shirts and a jacket. "What'd I do? Did the priest just say 'Bullshit'?"

"I'm confident God believes in you, Ray," Trevelyan said. "Even though you don't believe in anything."

Trevelyan put the alb and chasuble on again and returned to his duties with precise and choreographed movements. He donned his stole, begged God for the eternal life Adam and Eve had so carelessly chucked away, and made the sign of the cross over the collected water.

"I exorcise thee in the name of God the Father almighty, and in the name of Jesus Christ His Son, our Lord, and in the power of the Holy Ghost, that you may be able to put to flight all the power of the enemy, and be able to root out and supplant that enemy and his apostate angels; through the power of our Lord Jesus Christ, who will come to judge the living and the dead and the world by fire."

The priest crossed himself.

Ray, looking even more ludicrous than before in Trevelyan's long black cassock, stepped forward. "Well, let's hope that does it." His tone, while not mocking, was less than enthusiastic.

"Not so fast," Trevelyan said. "This isn't holy water - yet. It's just been prepared through the exorcism of the salt. The water still has to be blessed."

Ray 'harrumphed' and threw up his hands in frustration.

Trevelyan, frustrated himself, sighed, "Ray, considering what you two are about to do, along with anything I can give you, you might want to take a little faith with you."

Brandy took her fiancé by the arm and led him to the side of the room. Trevelyan returned his attention to the 'prepared' water.

"God," he prayed, crossing himself. "Who for the salvation of the human race built your greatest mysteries upon this substance, in your kindness hear our prayers and pour down the power of your blessing into this element. May this your creation be a vessel of divine grace to dispel demons and sicknesses, that everything it is sprinkled on in the presence of the faithful will be rid of all unclean and harmful things.

Let no pestilent spirit, no corrupting atmosphere, remain thereafter. Let whatever troubles the safety and peace of the faithful be put to flight by this water, that health, gotten by calling Your holy name, may be secured against all attacks. Through the Lord, Amen."

———†———

Back in the nave, a nervous Aimee pointed to several cases of bottles and asked the Americans if they were ready to arm themselves. "No," Ray said. "Not until we decide which way we're going out."

They scanned the chapel while they listened to the continued scratching and thumping of the Templars and their minions.

"Well, you certainly can not just walk out the front door."

Ray, afraid Aimee was losing her nerve again, raised what he hoped was a calming hand. "No. Not without a diversion."

"What diversion?" the reporter demanded, having taken the hand as a command she 'shut up'. "These things are only interested in blood. Nobody has any to spare."

"*Je peux vous aider.*"

Startled, they turned to find Luis carrying in another case. "Luis," Brandy barked, "one day your sneaking around is going to catch up with you."

He laughed at the translation. Then Aimee passed on the rest. "He does not know if you can get to the cemetery or what you will do once you are there. But, Luis says, he can get you outside without being seen. And without risking someone as, eh, *appâts*, what is your word... bait."

"We're all ears"

"He says, I know a short cut."

Eighteen

The verbal tennis match, French and English balls flying at once, Luis to Aimee, Aimee to Brandy and Ray, and back, with an occasional word from Father Trevelyan and a rare word from Felix, tending Eve, was something to hear and follow.

"Using the Templar history, and their curse, previous owners intended to restore the castle and grounds for tourists after World War II," Luis said. "There is a well on the far side of the castle, beyond the wall, part of that construction. *Eh bien*, the well was as far as they got. The project was abandoned, the property sold, the well forgotten."

"What has this to do with anything?"

"There is a tunnel from the dungeon to the well. This is how I escaped from the Templars... that first night. Down the well and into the dungeon where I hid."

"The Templars don't know about it?"

"It did not exist when the Templars were alive. I told you this was my playground. I know everything there is to know about Castle Freedom."

"This is fascinating," Ray said. "But how does it help us? The castle is on the other side of the courtyard."

Aimee, frustrated with Ray, passed the question on with attitude of her own. Luis signaled it was all right. "There is another tunnel that runs between the chapel and the castle. An ancient tunnel not part of the renovation."

Ray's shoulders dropped, and the ire disappeared from his eyes, as he flatly asked, "Where is it?"

Brandy laughed and slapped Ray's arm. "Let me guess." She did; correctly. The tunnel from the chapel to the castle started - in the ossuary.

"No," Ray said, shaking his head with finality. "No damned way!"

There's nothing like someone else's discomfort to bring real humor to a tense situation. So it was that Ray's dread of returning to the ossuary enlivened the mood of all as they gathered around the trap door entrance to prepare.

Aimee offered to assist Brandy in filling her many pockets, and handed her a bottle of holy water, asking, "Would you care for a nice claret?"

"Not a claret," Brandy said as she slid the bottle into the pocket of her borrowed apron. "With any luck, it'll be a *clear out*."

Both girls laughed... and a goofy game was born.

"A *pinhead noir*?" *Giggles*. And a bottle went into a jacket pocket.

"How about a heady *Mar-a-lot*." *General groan*. Into Brandy's bag o' plenty it went with the others.

"*Char today*?" A dead silence then *riotous laughter*. Father Trevelyan entered, in shirt sleeves, carrying a white bundle, curious about the boisterous activity near the altar. He soon caught on and, despite himself, began laughing too. Even Luis was laughing; probably because they were.

"Hey, beer drinker," Brandy chided Ray, "why don't you join the fun?"

Lacking their 'culture', the biker wasn't getting the joke. Not only wasn't it funny, it wasn't in good taste. With an occasional guilty glance at Felix and Eve in the corner, Ray loaded his pockets in silence.

Trevelyan unrolled the item he carried, his linen alb, and displayed it upside down. The neck and sleeves had been tied closed. He laid his braided cincture over it and approached Ray. "If your hands are going to be free, I thought this might make a fairly workable sack – if you don't over load it."

"You sure, Clive?"

"Not in the slightest, heaven forgive me. But half measures now are not the answer. I just hope it works."

Not counting her stuffed bag, Brandy had nine wine bottles in her layered clothes; one in her shirt, three in the pockets of Aimee's dress, three in the apron pocket, and two in Aimee's jacket. Not counting his, now filled, handmade alb bag, Ray had twelve bottles secreted on his person; two tucked inside his shirt, two in the pockets of Loup's sweat jacket, two in Luis' athletic jacket, four in the pockets of Luis' pants, and the remainder in the priest's cassock. Trouble was, while each layer increased their carrying capacity, it also constricted their movements exponentially.

Brandy nodded, ready to go, then asked for the torches she'd fashioned earlier. Luis objected and Aimee delivered the news. "You can not take them. . . the torches."

"Why?" they demanded.

444

"Were you to get through, the light, the smell of the burning torches would have the Templars on you in a second. But, Luis says, you would not get through. The tunnels are small. Ray will be fortunate to fit. There is no room for the torches."

"It isn't our playground," Ray said angrily. "We can't make the trip in the dark. We'd break our damned necks."

"Luis says you can take a candle. But cover the flame and extinguish it in the dungeon before you enter the well."

They reluctantly agreed. Accepting the candle Aimee offered, Brandy told the reporter, "Keep an eye on everyone until we get back."

Ray handed Luis his worn little black book and told Aimee. "It was in the pocket of his pants. In case he gets bored while we're gone." When she passed it on, Luis nodded. "*Merci.*"

Brandy hugged the Father. Ray shook his hand and thanked him. Trevelyan promised to pray for them.

Fighting back tears, Brandy told them all, "Take care of yourselves."

"We'll see them again, Brandy," Ray said with determination. He pointed at Luis, then at the trap door, and told Aimee, "Have Luis secure it tightly behind us."

"What if you need to come back?"

"If we can come back, they can follow. Just secure it, will you?"

Luis hesitated.

For some reason the chopping at the doors and windows, the howling of the gendarme vampires, the chanting of the Templars, which had gone on ceaselessly, now sounded especially loud and frantic. Perhaps, Ray thought, it was him and not them. "Look," he told Aimee, "I can't argue for something I don't want to do. Just tell him to block the door, huh? If we need back in, we'll knock."

He rapped twice, twice again, and twice - a third time - on the altar. Aimee nodded her understanding. Luis did too.

Ray shouldered his handmade 'bag' and, *chinking* and *clinking*, followed Brandy down into the ossuary. As the couple disappeared below the floor, Luis closed the trap. Then, with Aimee's help, he shimmied the heavy communion table over it.

Trevelyan, frowning at the necessary desecration, didn't get to disapprove long. Felix's shouts from the corner housing Eve's table bed demanded the priest's attention.

"Father! Father!"

Even at that distance, the terror was evident in Felix's eyes.

"Want to light my fire?" Brandy asked in the pitch black.

"Heck of a time to ask." Ray lit Brandy's candle. For the second time that night (and the second time in a generation), a flame burned and shadows danced among the seemingly endless skulls and bones in the ossuary. A shiver ran down Ray's spine.

"I thought you weren't coming down here again," Brandy teased.

"Rub it in. Have a blast."

Brandy moved, candle flickering, bottles chinking in her clothes and shoulder bag, toward the undiscovered side of the ossuary.

"Go slow," Ray said as he followed. "Be careful."

"Well, if they break, all we have are pockets full of water."

"Yes; and broken glass."

Brandy slowed and the chinking of the bottles softened. "Be careful."

"Good advice. Besides, they're our only defense."

"Careful. You sound like you actually believe."

On the far side of the chamber, they found the tunnel door as Luis described. Unlike the sturdy replica at the front of the chapel, this door was eaten by time, moisture and wear. And it led to... what.

Rusted hinges groaned as Brandy eased it open. Moisture and mold assaulted her senses. She slipped her candle in, like sticking a toe into a pool, and the flame flickered wildly. More skulls lined the sides of the tunnel as far into the darkness as either could see. The air was heavy, wet and evil, and mold clung to the stone and lay on the bones.

Brandy and Ray turned to each other – breathing rapidly. In the candlelight, her eyes glistened with danger and excitement; his glowed with resolve.

"Well," Ray said, "here goes nothing." He crouched to make an entrance.

"I'll go first," Brandy said, laying a hand on his arm.

"Why should you go first?"

"It's my idea. Besides, I'm smaller. You could get stuck."

"That's the dumbest thing I've ever heard."

"This whole idea is the dumbest thing I've ever heard."

"It's your idea. You just said so."

"Yeah," Brandy said.

"I love you, Brandy."

She slapped him hard across the face. "If you loved me... you wouldn't have been trying to buy another tattoo."

"What?"

"You heard me, Raymond. God, I just hate you sometimes."

"You hate me because I wanted another tattoo?"

"No. I like your tattoos. I was going to get you one myself... after our wedding... if there was ever going to be a wedding."

"If? I'm not getting this..."

"You said you wouldn't buy any more without talking to me first."

"Tattoos?"

"What were we talking about? You promised you wouldn't buy any more without talking with me."

He looked back into the ossuary, forward into the tunnel; at the remains of hundreds of corpses. He thought of the Templars above. He thought of their friends trapped in the chapel. Then he stared at Brandy. "You're bringing up the tattoo now?"

"When should I bring it up? After we're dead?"

"No, hell, no. Bring it up now."

She ducked and followed her torch. Ray laughed. "It's not funny," she said over her shoulder. Hunched low, knees bent, still laughing, Ray followed Brandy deep into the musty tunnel.

Nineteen

Life and death, as far as Father Trevelyan was concerned, was in the hands of the Almighty. We *puny humans* had little control over death and no knowledge of the day or hour of its arrival. That said, the priest knew Eve's hour had come. He didn't take the time to don vestments. Trevelyan kissed his stole and draped it about his neck without the usual prayer.

He separated the couples' hands, pulled Felix gently aside, and took Eve's in his own. He whispered in her ear. "Are you truly sorry for each of the sins you have committed?" He repeated the question - and felt a feeble pressure as Eve squeezed back.

Aimee held Felix. Luis (in the gallery) watched from the rail. Both silent; helpless.

"God the Father of mercies," Trevelyan said, "through the death and resurrection of his Son, has reconciled the world to Himself

451

and sent the Holy Spirit among us for the forgiveness of sins; through the ministry of the Church may God give you pardon and peace, and I absolve you from your sins in the name of the Father, and of the Son, and of the Holy Spirit." Trevelyan pulled a vial of blessed olive oil from his pocket and anointed her head and hands.

He tipped a flask gently against Eve's lips. "The blood of Christ," he said solemnly, and helped her sip.

"The host!" Felix pulled away from Aimee and grabbed the priest. "What about the host? She can't eat. Is her soul in danger if she can't eat?"

"It's all right, Felix," Trevelyan assured him. "Where the blood is, the body must be. The communicant who receives either receives Christ entirely."

Felix relaxed and Trevelyan pulled his hand free. He leaned over Eve and said, "May the Lord Jesus Christ protect you and lead you to eternal life."

————————⊹————————

No preacher's word, no line of scripture, could so completely convince someone of the existence of the soul as the act of watching it leave the body. Eve Molyneux was there, a beautiful young woman, wounded, wracked with pain; and then she was gone. Felix held her - and watched her go.

Aimee looked on, feeling helpless. Luis, at the rail above, turned away. Father Trevelyan took Eve from his arms and completed the anointing. Felix watched without seeing, shaking and heartbroken.

Trevelyan placed the vial of holy water at the feet. He folded a crucifix into her hands, rested them atop her stomach, and covered her (and her flaming red hair) with the pall that had been her blanket. He put a comforting hand on Felix, but the young man pulled away. Not from anger; there was no emotion at all. He simply pulled away, silent and alone, and disappeared into the vestibule.

The priest let him go.

"Nnnnnoooooo!!!"

Felix's hysterical scream reverberated through the chapel.

Trevelyan ran for the vestibule and reached it in time to see the desperate young man pulling the batten off of the chapel door. "Felix," Trevelyan yelled, "Don't!"

With madness in his eyes, Felix swung the wooden slat. The priest blocked it with his arm, cried out in pain, and fell. He heard the heavy door open, heard Felix scream and, through a blur of tears, saw him disappear outside.

———†———

Felix raced down the steps and came to a stop in the courtyard in front of the chapel – seething. His chest heaved. His hands were clenched, trembling fists. Tears ran down his cheeks. Then Felix seemed to wake; the insanity passing.

He heard labored breathing, the hisses and growls of predatory animals, the wet smack of salivating lips. He stared over his shoulder at several gendarme vampires, and one of the Templar knights, clinging to the exterior of the chapel, at the windows, on the bell tower, like bats on a cave wall. The other Templars, and the rest of their evil progeny, were spread about the courtyard. Fifteen feet away, the leader of the Templars glared. An otherworldly silence enveloped all.

Felix realized where his rage had led him. Then realized he didn't care. With a scream of hate and despair, he ran at the Templar's leader.

The knight drew his sword as Felix threw a shoulder into him. He lifted the creature off his feet; drove him backward and down. The sword flew, hit the ground, and sang –

steel on stone - as it sailed across the courtyard. Felix came to rest on top of him and
scrambled onto his knees to straddle the
creature. He drove a fist into the knight's
chest, using the red cross on the mantle
as a target. Again and again. The rotted
garment tore, rusted chain mail exploded
into the air and fell like metal rain. The
creature's mummified skin yawned gray-
blue beneath. The skin tore, the dusty
ribs snapped and broke. Felix's fists disappeared into his chest. The Templar's skeletal mouth fell open - and a hideous, guttural
laugh emerged.

Felix looked up from the laughing horror. The others had moved in; a crowd of
dead and moldering knights with fiery red
eyes, their tunics splashed in blood, bearing ancient weapons. Behind them, like hye-
nas waiting for the lions to finish, the gendarme vampire-things hovered and hissed.
Felix saw the horrors but couldn't register
them. His mind, having taken in all the terror it could hold, shut down.

Beyond the circle, the Templar chaplain lifted their leader's sword from the
ground. He stepped into the group of undead knights as they renewed their chant.
Their blasphemy grew to a fever pitch. The
knight threw back his cloak and raised the
sword.

Felix screamed!

The chaplain brought the sword around with relish.

＊

"It doesn't have anything to do with a tattoo."

Ray followed Brandy, and her candle, unable to believe what he was hearing, shaking his head in surrender. He envied the skulls lining the tunnel walls around them. Just now he wished he was dead too. "You just said. . . "

"If you loved me you wouldn't lie to me. If your word doesn't mean anything to you how can it mean anything to me?"

"You're right."

"Shut up. I don't want you to agree so I'll stop talking. I have a right to talk."

"Of course you have a right to talk. I said you're right. Brandy, you're right! My word has to mean something. I'm sorry."

"No more lying? About anything?" Brandy stopped in her track. "My God," she whispered. She reached back to Ray. "What was that? Did you hear that?"

'That', Ray knew, had been a scream.

The journey through the tunnel, from the chapel to the castle cellar, was slow going at best. With the exception of Luis Socrates, rats and spiders appeared to have been the only living things to have traveled this space in centuries. Great orb webs filled the passage (some torn away where Luis had recently passed). In various spots, the ancient piled bones and skulls had toppled and fallen in heaps. And Brandy had been chewing him out the whole way. (Not that he didn't deserve it.)

Then came a muffled scream above their heads. He saw Brandy's terror in the candlelight and did his best to hide his own.

"Was that a scream?"

"I'm not sure what it was," he lied.

Yes, it was a scream and Ray knew it. But he didn't know whose. He didn't know why. He was too frightened to guess.

Aimee was the first to hear Father Trevelyan's shouts. She found him, in agony, on the vestibule floor. "*Sacre*," she cried, helping him sit. "You have broken your arm!"

Luis, hearing the uproar, hurried to the vestibule. He was mortified to see the chapel door standing open and hurried to close it. But, before he could, he caught a glimpse outside – and it was as if time had reversed itself. It was the night that his mother and sister died, and here he was again helplessly watching the blood-thirsty killers.

He saw Felix attack a Templar; watched them fall. He heard the mummy laughing from the ground. He saw the others close in. And, unable to look away, he saw one of the knights decapitate Felix. Luis, his hands white gripping the door, yelled from the pit of his soul to release his horror and rage; for Felix, for Eve, for his parents, his sister, for his lost Micheline.

"I'm all right," the priest said, a thousand miles away. He didn't sound all right. Somewhere closer he heard, "Help Luis. Close the door!" Luis suddenly remembered the here and now and knew his friends needed him. "I have it," he told Aimee as he threw the chapel door closed.

No sooner was the locking bar back in place than the pounding started again.

Aimee guided Trevelyan into the nave, and to the sanctuary, as she called out the materials she'd need for a splint. Luis hurried to collect them.

The priest offered no resistance and seemed resigned – to everything. "A life in hiding. Back in Cornwall, here in Paradis," Trevelyan said wistfully. "A cowardly life in hiding." Tears rolled down cheeks now showing their age. "Waiting, I told myself. I was waiting for the proper moment.

To see... something. To experience... anything. To join the world. Just as soon as the fear was gone." Father Trevelyan, cradling his broken arm, sagged onto the steps. Defeated, exhausted, trembling with pain or fear (Aimee didn't know which). She braced his arm and held him while he cried.

"I guess I waited too long."

Twenty

A large web barred their path and wavered in the candlelight. A clammy current of air brought goose flesh to Brandy's arm. The damp of the tunnel deepened to a cloying mustiness. She pushed through the web and, only then, realized its floor dropped away and the passage opened into black nothingness. "Hold up," Brandy called back in a whisper. "We're at the end of the tunnel. Let me see where we are." She bent, as her overstuffed clothing allowed, and extended the candle beyond the mouth of the tunnel. It flickered with the foul damp air and Brandy peered through the gloom.

"It looks... dungeon-y," Brandy whispered.

"Dungeony?"

She nodded. "It's a wreck."

Ray, still crouching, didn't care how it looked. His calves, the backs of his thighs and his ass cheeks screamed with shooting pains. He just wanted to stand. "If there aren't any vampires or alligators. . . let's go."

Brandy almost stepped out - when something told her to look again. She lowered the candle and saw the tunnel opened into the cellar near the ceiling, seven or eight feet above the floor. She gasped.

"What's the matter?"

"At the risk of sounding cliché; that first step's a doozy."

Brandy turned her fanny to the mouth of the tunnel. She set her monster bag and candle to the side and extended her hand to Ray. "Lower me."

Ray did and, when she was fully extended, let her drop the last few feet to the floor. He handed down her bag, the candle (incredibly still lit), and his bag. Mindful of the breakables in his pockets, Ray nursemaided the hem of his cassock over the tunnel's edge and dangled himself. His height brought the floor closer; an easy drop. Brandy took up bag and candle. Ray, squinting through the gloom, laid his hand on her shoulder and allowed himself to be led into the cold stone enclosure.

That's just what it was; a stone box that, in its day, was inescapable and impenetrable. Massive, squat arches, built of round river stones in white mortar to support the weight of a fortress. The fortress was gone, the mortar discolored and in patches fallen away over the centuries.

"You can almost hear the ghosts of the old prisoners."

Brandy lit his face with the candle. "Let's hope that's what you're hearing," she whispered. Then she laid a finger to her lips. "We'd better be quiet now. They can reach us if they hear us and Luis says they have good hearing."

Ray raised his hands; a silent oath.

The dark made the dungeon appear larger than it was and crossing was hazardous. They slipped and tripped over broken floors, rotted wood splintered and jutting, and dislodged and broken stones exposed by time, coated with slime owing (probably) to the old well. It stank, not of the grave, but of low tide and Brandy knew they were close. She found the far side of the enclosure and the tunnel to the well where Luis said it would be. She examined it, stifled a laugh and whispered to Ray, "You're gonna love this."

He followed Brandy's firelight to - a rabbit hole. Ray sagged, physically and mentally, as his earlier complaints about the tiny ossuary tunnel faded to mist. Brandy lowered the candle to the hole.

"Don't!" Ray grabbed her arm.

"I'm just trying to see what's ahead."

"It doesn't matter. The light could give us away. And we're going regardless, aren't we? It's moonlight from here on out." Brandy nodded. "Follow me when we get outside and stay close. We'll circle the back. . . "

"Do you think we can outrun them dressed this way?"

"Maybe we don't have to." Ray hesitated. "When we were on the balcony discussing the car keys, I heard them. The horses, I mean. I heard them whinnying and got to thinking, maybe we could use them."

"Templar horses?" Brandy said doubtfully. "Dead horses?"

"Dead," Ray agreed, "but they don't need keys."

"This is all too. . . I can ride but can you?"

"I can ride anything on God's earth."

"Can we get to them?"

"A minute ago you were wondering if we could outrun them for a half-mile. Now you're doubting we can outrun them for thirty yards?"

"I'm wondering why we're doing this at all," Brandy said.

"It's your idea."

"Yeah. I know." Brandy reluctantly extinguished the candle.

In the dark, they agreed they were ready and started for the well. Ray led now, through the hole and short tunnel, crawling, with Brandy on his heels. It was horrid going, blackness and slime, with only their labored breathing and the soft clink of the wine bottles as accompaniment.

Moonlight, reaching into the well, exposed the end of the tunnel. Ray reached it, peeked out, and was slapped in the face by a rising dankness. His stomach rolled, but he kept going. He reached into the well and ran his hand across the stones. . .

"Gaaaaah, it's slimy!"

"Ray, *shhhhhh!*"

. . . searching for the cavities described by Luis; specific stones omitted during construction that created a ladder in the well wall. Ray grabbed hold. He found his footing. "Be careful. It's slippery." And, with the cincture around his wrist and the alb bag over his shoulder, started up.

The full moon starkly lit the top five feet of the well interior and bathed the shaft around Ray in a blue glow. As he climbed, he looked below to just make out Brandy as she poked her head from the dungeon tunnel, and above to see a million stars glisten in the night. He neared the top and Ray felt the cool fresh air. Another step and he took in a deep, delicious lung full. At the top, he reached for the rim.

A vampire grabbed his wrist.

Ray screamed, startled, and lost his grip on the ladder. He would have fallen had it not been for the hold on him; a hold so tight he feared his wrist would snap.

Several hours earlier, his attacker had been Aurore Vasser, the little sister of the *Gendarmerie*. Then, for a short while, she was dead. Now, staring down with a voracious look in her brilliant yellow eyes, hissing like a snake, she was something else altogether.

"Ray!" Brandy's cry echoed from below.

Ray kicked up. He caught his feet on opposite sides of the well, braced them as best he could on the slime, jammed his back against the wall and bridged his body with all the pressure he could muster. At the same time, he clutched the vampire's wrist and yanked down with all his might. The vampire fell into the well on top of him. Ray dropped one foot, rolled and shoved the grasping creature down past him.

"Look out!" Ray yelled as she fell screaming.

Brandy pulled back into the tunnel and just avoided being hit as the vampire hurtled past her. The monster disappeared into the dark. Then a splash reverberated up from the depths.

Ray dug into the walls, righted himself and scrambled up out of the well. He called to Brandy and, hearing she was safe, told her to follow. She slipped from the tunnel and started up the slimy ladder. In the dark below the vampire surfaced. Though Ray couldn't see her, and Brandy was too busy to look, they had no trouble hearing. She was screaming and slapping the water like a cat thrown in a river. Brandy reached the top and Ray hoisted her, and her bag o' plenty, up over the edge.

Outside of the vampire in the well, it appeared they were alone. Both knew it wouldn't last long. "She's going to bring them down on us." As if in answer, the screaming and splashing stopped.

But any hopes they had were dashed when it was replaced by a series of *snicks* below. The vampire was crawling up the inside of the well.

Ray pulled one of the bottles from the cassock pocket. "Might as well give one a try." The creature, as it scaled the slippery wall, was nearly invisible. But Ray could clearly see her reflective eyes. Targeting them, he pitched the bottle into the depths. It broke on the stones above her and rained down. The vampire hissed as the holy water soaked her. Then, unharmed, continued her climb.

"I knew it was all bullshit," he said. "We're screwed."

He scooped the alb bag up and, taking no pains to be quiet, heaved it over his shoulder and into the well as if it were trash.

"Ray!" Brandy reached - too late to stop him.

Halfway down the shaft, the bag hit the vampire in the head. A lucky accident, it knocked her off the wall and sent her, angry and screaming, plummeting. The vampire, bag, and bottles splashed, crashed and splintered in the cold water of the pit.

"Are you out of your mind?" Brandy cried, still whispering. "We need that holy water. Not to mention the noise!"

There was noise. The well roiled; splashing, scratching, an angry hiss echoing as the gendarme-thing escaped the water and started up again.

"They don't work," Ray said, too loudly. "It's a joke. You and that priest are a couple of kids."

"No!" Brandy shoved Ray from the well. She saw the eyes of the hellish creature below, coming on, and drew one of her own bottles.

"Brandy!"

"No!" she screamed again. "I believe! I believe!" Brandy hurled her bottle into the pit.

In the moonlight, in the well, it smashed against the creature's head. Shattered glass flew. Holy water splashed. The vampire shrieked. As if soaked in acid, she clawed at her blinded eyes. She dropped from the wall and, by the time she hit the water, burst into flames. Then followed a massive explosion. Ray's holy water, like so much floating gasoline, ignited across the surface and rose in a ball of flame.

Brandy and Ray ducked away as flames, smoke, heat and the acrid smell of burning flesh erupted from the well. Brandy took a deep breath; exhaled slowly. She tugged her layered clothing into place. Then she picked up her purse and told Ray, "You've got to believe."

Tongue-tied, Ray could only nod.

The well was on the far west side of the castle. Brandy moved to the edge of the ruin wall, in shadow, and looked to the courtyard. Ray remained, dumbstruck and unmoving, by the well. She pulled him into the darkness beside her.

Twenty One

Aimee carried a full case of bottles into the nave. Father Trevelyan, still on the sanctuary steps in a cloud of depression, hugged his broken arm. She plopped the case down beside him and asked, "Do you believe in these things? These holy waters? Do you think they will work?"

It took him a moment then, barely audibly, he said, "I don't know."

"I did not expect you to know, Father. I wondered what you thought."

When he didn't answer, Aimee plunked down beside him. (Brandy's jeans climbed nearly to her knees.)

"Forgive me, Aimee," he said. "I don't feel much like talking."

"You feel like crying." It was not a question. "I told Brandy I wanted to cry. She agreed; said she felt like it too. But she would not let me. She said there were things

471

to do. She is risking her life to do them." She stood and stretched her hand to the priest. He didn't take it, but looked past it to Aimee. "I can not let you cry either," she said. "Not now. There are things to do. Brandy and Ray need our help. We need your help."

———

Brandy and Ray crouched (as their clothes allowed) at the mouth of the alley running between the castle ruin and the stable. They had a clear view of the Templars feeding on Felix and the undead soldiers, like parasites, awaiting their turn.

Whether they were seen or heard first neither Brandy nor Ray knew but one of the Templars stood, stretched a boney finger their direction, and alerted the others. The rest of the blood-drenched knights rose from Felix's corpse to stare. And, as they stepped away, the gendarmes dove on the body - to drink the dregs.

Brandy swallowed. Ray inhaled deeply to keep from vomiting. Both knew it was best not to react. But Brandy promised herself a world-shaking breakdown in the near future. If only she could promise herself a near future.

"On the left." Ray pointed, without being obvious, at two Templar horses just off the courtyard. Brandy caught a glimpse and nodded.

But the Templars began to spread out. Two (as if they'd read Ray's mind) headed for a spot between them and the stable. Once there, Ray knew, they'd prevent escape to the north and, worse, cut them off from the horses. The others would flank them.

Ray could have kicked himself for underestimating them. Whatever else these things were; they were soldiers. And, if Clive was to be believed, well-trained soldiers at that. He knew, and Brandy knew as well, it was now or never. Both tensed to dash for the horses, when. . . .

Across the courtyard the door on the chapel balcony burst open and Father Trevelyan rushed out.

He was a sight even at that distance in clerical collar and shirt sleeves, with his arm in a sling, standing beside the four-foot crucifix at the rail. He held a smaller crucifix, awkwardly, in his bad hand and carried a wine bottle in the good one. Then he shouted, "I command you, unclean spirits. . ."

The Templars turned from Brandy and Ray, to Trevelyan's shouts, while the gendarme things began to shriek and race about the courtyard. Several jumped on the walls of the chapel and clung there;

howling. All of them, the mummies and their vampire offspring, stole glances at the priest. But the crucifix prevented their staring or drawing too near.

"Whoever you are," Trevelyan shouted, "along with your minions attacking these servants of God, by the mysteries of the incarnation, passion, resurrection and ascension of our Lord Jesus Christ, by the descent of the Holy Spirit, by the coming of our Lord for judgment, tell me by some sign your name, and the day and hour of your departure."

The Templar leader had apparently heard the speech before. He decided Trevelyan was a gnat and turned back to Brandy and Ray. He drew his sword and started forward. The other knights followed.

"It was nice while it lasted," Brandy said. She quietly drew a bottle from her apron. Ray, for all the good he thought it would do, pulled one himself.

The Templar knights advanced.

Then came the sound of smashing glass and a high-pitched shriek.

One of the gendarme vampires was on fire. His feet were in flames, his blood-stained pants spattered with holes, and black smoke rolled off his legs. The creature jumped around, trying to extinguish himself, screaming. Shattered glass and a puddle of bubbling holy water bathed the cobbles beneath him.

On the balcony Trevelyan stood with his mouth agape – startled by the results of his actions. Then he smiled and lifted another bottle above his head. He threw it into the courtyard; smashing it at the feet of the same beleaguered vampire. The flying shards of glass were shrapnel as, wet from holy water, they ripped through his legs. The splash hit him and the vampire burst into flames. He screamed - and flopped over like a rag doll.

"I command you to obey me," Father Trevelyan shouted, working it. "I who am a minister of God despite my unworthiness; nor shall you be emboldened to harm in any way these creatures of God or any of their possessions." More breaking glass as another bottle busted. Something undead howled.

"Depart transgressor. Depart, seducer, full of lies and cunning, foe of virtue, persecutor of the innocent. Give place, abominable creature, give way, you monster, give way to Christ, in whom you found none of your works. For he has already stripped you of your powers and laid waste your kingdom, bound you prisoner and plundered your weapons. He has cast you forth into the outer darkness, where everlasting ruin awaits you and your abettors."

Brandy was agog; Ray laughed. The priest was creating a diversion and having a good time. "In the name of the Father, the Son and the Holy Spirit."

The Templars had backed away. Their minions were running like hell.

Brandy and Ray raced past the two nearest Templars, who swung, missed them and clashed swords. Ray pulled out two bottles, one in each hand, while Brandy jumped into the saddle of one of the horses.

The knights extricated their weapons and turned on Ray. One swung his sword and Ray blocked the blow with a bottle. Glass and holy water flew. The knight backed away; wanting no part of it. Emboldened, Ray spun and hurled the other bottle at the one-armed Templar who'd been making a nuisance of himself all night. He defended himself with his stump. The bottle bounced, hit him a glancing blow on his rotting chest, slid down his mantle, off his boot and onto the ground without breaking. The holy 'grenade' rolled away intact.

"Ray!"

"I'm trying!" he screamed, jumping on the other horse. "I'm trying to believe!"

Brandy shook her head. She slapped the reins and her horse took off. Ray snapped

his and the horse reared on its hind legs
– nearly throwing him. He kept his saddle, though he didn't know how, and rode
it back down to four hooves. Then he held
on as the horse bolted - following Brandy
from the courtyard.

Francois de Raiis pointed an undead claw
after the humans, shrieked, and went for
his own horse. He leapt into his saddle,
spurred his mount and rode out. The Templars' chaplain likewise took to his saddle, dark cloak flying in the breeze. The
knights who, seven centuries earlier had
been Jules Lefebvre and Geoffrey de Charney, found their saddles and joined in the
unholy chase.

Brandy's plan to avoid undue attention was a miserable failure. Four demon
knights, blood drinkers all, were hot on
their trail in the full moon light.

The two remaining Templars, whose
horses had been stolen, returned their attention to the chapel - and to the blood-rich
humans still inside.

Brandy rode hell-bent for leather in the
field beyond the chapel cemetery. Ray rode
behind. He told himself he was guarding her
flank but, truth was, Brandy was a better

rider. His ego could cope; his nerves not so much. Behind, pounding hooves closed in.

Just like that, feverishly spurring his mount, the Templar leader rode abreast; his animal matching strides with Ray's stolen horse. The American looked from the mummy to the field ahead and back. The creature took his reins in one clawed hand and raised his sword with the other. Ray reached beneath the flapping skirt of Trevelyan's cassock, pulled a bottle of holy water from a pocket of Luis' pants and lifted it toward the knight with all the menace he could muster. Eyes blazing hell fire, the grinning Templar slashed at Ray, who ducked in his saddle swinging blindly. The sword hit the bottle with a *clink-smash*.

Ray closed his eyes as an explosion of water slapped him. Glass shards stung his face like rock-salt. Sanctified water showered down on the cloth hood covering his mount's head. The horse, or whatever it was masquerading as a horse, shrieked in unimaginable pain. The soaked hood, and animal's brittle mane, parchment hide and skull beneath ignited in fire and a huff of smoke. It burned like dry kindling then melted like candle wax. The horse's hellish whinny vanished – as did its head.

Everything switched to slow motion. The Templar shrieked and pulled away while his mount bucked, whinnied and kicked up dirt. Ray shouted in pain and horror. Ray's horse ran on. . . without a head. Then the creature's corpse faltered in mid-stride and pitched forward and down like a ton of bricks.

All returned to normal speed. Ray, in anguish, shouted Brandy's name as the velocity of the event hurled him forward from the saddle. He met the ground with a tremendous thud, his lungs dumped air, his face collected dirt and weeds in a skin-rending slide.

It took several minutes after the fall for Ray to realize he wasn't dead. And then only because he ached so much. He gasped repeatedly for breath before catching one. Then he raised his head off the ground, opened his eyes, and wished he was dead.

The leader had regrouped with the others and all four Templars were riding back in his direction. Their chaplain brandished their damaged standard, the gold cross flashing in the moonlight, as the mummy used it to beat his mount's haunch. The horse screamed, breathed hellfire and transferred the beating to the soft ground beneath its hooves. The others rode beside him; one swinging the spiked ball of his flail above his helmet, the other holding the reins in his teeth as he notched a bolt into his crossbow. The leader switch-backed behind them like a cattle driver spurring them on.

Ray picked himself up. Which, layered in soaked and torn clothes, broken wine bottles, and cramping muscles, was no small chore. It felt as if he were climbing out of quicksand. He stood at the end of a trail of debris; moldered armor, an abused saddle, rusted weaponry, bits of bone, patches of hide, and the burned and decayed muck of what had been the horse.

Disgusted, but too numbed to react in disgust, Ray saw the Templars racing for him with murder in their undead eyes. He ran, instinctively at first, until his senses returned. Then he felt the fool, beating feet in Trevelyan's cassock and looking in his mind's eye like Anthony Perkins as Mother. The night was cool, the ground spongy, the going slow. The Templar cemetery Ray remembered to be just over the rise may as well have been a thousand miles away. He would never reach it on foot. The Templar horses, whinnying, snorting great breathy clouds, kicking up soaking clods of earth, were nearly on top of him - when something flashed in Ray's periphery.

He heard a shout. But, unlike the cackling of the living skeletons, this was an exuberant shout of triumph. Then racing in from the side, cutting off the Templars, the shouter came into view.

Brandy saw Ray fall, turned on a dime and rode back. Now she leaned from her saddle and, without her mount breaking stride, wrapped an arm under Ray's, shouted, "Jump!" and kept on riding. Ray landed in front, draped over her horse, with the hard edge of the saddle in his gut. Had he not screamed, it would have knocked the wind out of him. But Ray was screaming like a bitch.

The Templars screamed too. They reined in their mounts, turned in Brandy's wake, and started the hellish chase anew.

Sagging like a sack of seeds, his head and feet by a stirrup on either side of the horse, Ray felt stupid... and relieved, and alive, and proud of and grateful for Brandy Petracus. From his ridiculous position he shouted over his shoulder, "I love you."

Brandy bit her lip and drove the horse on in silence.

————

It was quite the ride; the moonlit ground racing by beneath, the ancient leather saddle digging into his guts (despite the layered clothes), the thundering motion of the undead horse, and the occasional boney elbow in his back and lash from the reins across his shoulders as Brandy drove the animal on. Ray thought he'd puke.

She saved his stomach the bother by reining up near the fence of the Templar burial site. Brandy leapt from the saddle. Sucking air, Ray lifted his head and saw why. One of the Templars, swinging a flail, was on the right and dismounting. The other three were hard on his heels.

Ray shoved himself off the saddle putting Brandy's horse between them and the knights; all four now on foot. He pulled the last bottle from his pant leg, shouted, "Head's up," and hurled it over the saddle. It hit the knight in front, the one with the flail, flat against the red cross on his chest – and broke.

Splinters. Splash. Eruption. The other three Templars backed away. Their horses screamed and were off to the races. His heavy flail fell to the ground and the knight howled as smoke, fiery immolation and, finally, nothingness followed. Gore, smoke, remnants of mail and a couple of old weapons were all that remained. "Yes!" Ray shouted throwing his hands into the air.

Brandy hadn't waited. She was already on her way over the cemetery fence.

"You missed it," Ray shouted, starting after her. "You should have seen it."

He failed to notice the chaplain, striding over the gory remains of the first knight, and coming up on him from behind. He heard, but failed to recognize, the sound of a long blade being drawn from its scabbard. He saw Brandy turn and heard her scream his name. But, for an instant, Ray didn't understand why.

Twenty Two

Father Trevelyan was up to something.

He left the balcony, energized, having successfully created a diversion for Brandy and Ray. But there was more to it. He was still on a mission; a man with an idea. He ran past Luis, downstairs, looking to share that idea with Aimee.

Luis secured the balcony door then sat on the gallery rail. He didn't intend to overhear their discussion but wasn't about to sit in a corner with his fingers in his ears either. He split the difference, watching the door with one eye and listening with one ear.

"It is possible, you see," Trevelyan said, "they cannot take the sunlight."

"Take the sunlight?" Aimee asked.

"Abide it, yes. I've been putting together a mythology in my head. Trying to decipher what laws govern these creatures. The common thread I've witnessed is that the Templars live on blood but thrive on evil. Conversely, they are unable to remain in the presence of, or survive contact with, physical manifestations of the powers of good."

Aimee looked a question and Trevelyan rephrased it. "The powers of God."

"More superstition?"

"Superstition is my profession, Aimee," the priest said. "Superstition and the supernatural. Examine the evidence. These creatures, and those they spawn, are evil personified. Yet they do not spring from evil. The Templars were not merely knights, they were monks. They were in life devoutly religious men. They still recognize good, they simply can't abide it. They feed in a bastardization of the Eucharist. Prayer stimulates them to courage but theirs are chanted blasphemy. They wear crosses but cannot tolerate images of the crucified Christ. They recognize sanctified ground but cannot enter. And they are literally burned by holy water."

"And?"

"And," Trevelyan said. "Now I'm wondering whether, eh, the sun might save us."

"The son? The son of God?"

"No! Well, yes, obviously. But, no. I mean the sun. The rising sun. Daylight."

"The sun is holy?"

"*Ahh.* I don't know. That's my question. The sun is a symbol of purity," the priest explained. "In the Book of Revelation, Jesus said, 'I am. . . the bright Morning Star.' In 2nd Samuel 23 it says, 'And he shall be as the light of the morning, when the sun riseth. . . for this is all my salvation. . . ' The power of God flourishes in the light. I cannot help but wonder if the Templars know it."

"Even if what you're saying is true, what does that mean to us?"

"Well, perhaps, eh, it means that, ah, if we can survive until dawn, we'll survive."

Luis turned an idea over in his head. He made up his mind.

Only after he'd chosen a course of action did it occur to Luis how quiet the chapel had become. The Templars and their minions had been pecking and scratching at the doors, walls, and windows all night. Just a moment earlier, one of the damned things was on the balcony roof. Now all was quiet; too quiet.

A shudder went through the chapel. Again, a violent vibration. Then a thunderous crash followed and the gallery shook as if in an earthquake. Luis grabbed the rail.

Aimee called out from below, "What was that?"

Trevelyan joined Aimee, holding his sling and arm to his chest, and shouted, "That felt as if. . ."

Luis interrupted him, shouting that the building had moved. Then it happened again, a second shudder, second crash. With a shower of mortar and dust, a jagged crack appeared from end to end in the gallery wall behind him. "*Mon Dieu*," Luis said under his breath. Then he shouted that he thought the balcony roof had collapsed!

"How could it collapse?" He heard Aimee shout. "Luis? Luis?"

But he heard something else, as well; scratching at the balcony door. What in hell could have collapsed the roof, he wondered? What could be at the door?

"Luis!" Aimee called excitedly.

The scratching was joined by a frightened cry. Luis couldn't decipher the words.

"Luis!" Trevelyan was shouting as well.

"*Je vais bien!*" he shouted, letting them know he was alright, and wishing they'd shut up. Then he yelled for them to stay downstairs as the gallery might not be safe. And asked them to be quiet as he was trying to hear. . . something at the door.

"Don't open the door!"

He wasn't going to. He only wanted to see. He slowly approached the door, heard more scratching and, barely audible, a weak voice. Luis laid his ear to the door.

"Help. Help me!"

It suddenly occurred the voice might belong to either Brandy or Ray. They were, after all, outside with those things. Slowly he lifted the batten they'd made to bar the door. He gripped the handle and slowly turned the knob, creating the slightest crack.

Had Luis opened the door fully, he'd have seen that the balcony roof had indeed collapsed. More accurately, that it had been made to collapse. The main pillar, to which the ossuary crucifix was secured, had been yanked out and pulled down to the ground. He never got the opportunity. Instead, as he opened the crack, the door was kicked. Back on his heels, Luis found himself staring at the maniacal nightmare vision of ink, metal studs, and blood that once was Jerome Rousseau, the tattoo artist.

"Bloody hell!" Jerome screamed. Then he laughed insanely. "I can not fucking believe that worked! I would not have opened that door in a million fucking years!"

He grinned with a wide, bloody mouth. His huge black pupils swam in electric yellow eyes. His T-shirt was ripped to shreds with only the stretched collar ring and a portion of one sleeve still in place. He was covered in bite marks with huge chunks of flesh torn away. The aesthetic design of his 'tats', head to waist, was blown to smithereens. His wounds oozed something akin to blood yet he seemed almost giddy.

"Barking mad, isn't it?" Jerome asked, too loudly, in a voice that wasn't his. Red spit flew as he shook his head wildly. "Barking mad! The whole bloody thing!"

Jerome threw his claws out, snarled, and leapt on Luis. They staggered back and fell against the rail. Luis gasped for air. Jerome weighed nothing at all but this vampire-thing atop his chest weighed a ton. The tattoo artist forced Luis' chin up and away. He felt Jerome's acrid breath hot against his throat. He saw the nave ceiling climb into shadows above. Then he heard the wooden rail beneath him snap and give way.

They fell - vampire over victim.

Father Trevelyan screamed, "Good Lord!" Aimee shouted, "*Mon Dieu!*" Both had a fraction of a second to get out of the way.

Luis landed face down. Jerome, like a drunk driven from a public house, sagged awkwardly against an iron candelabrum. Aimee screamed for the priest. Trevelyan screamed to heaven. Both ran to the unmoving Luis who, thank God, was still alive.

There came a strange sound behind them; deep, guttural, gagging.

Trevelyan turned and saw Jerome back on his feet. The vampire had not been leaning on the candle stand; he'd fallen on it. The carving at its apex had been driven through his throat and impaled him. The vampire grabbed the upright base, still jutting from his neck, lifted it with a grunt and turned - swinging it like a club.

Now all three were screaming.

The vampire swung awkwardly in the priest's direction. The weight of the stand threw him off balance. He landed on his back. The candelabrum clanged to the floor jacking Jerome's neck with a horrendous crack. The vampire screamed, spitting gore.

Trevelyan grabbed a bottle of holy water and shook it over this hell-spawned version of the tattoo artist. Smoke curled. Jerome screamed, flailed, bubbled and burst into flames. "God help you," the priest screamed. "God help you! God help us all!"

Aimee cried at the top of her lungs. For Luis, whom she coddled on the floor in her arms, and in fear for Father Trevelyan, who stood mortified before Jerome's burning remains.

Both were startled by another scream from above. Another of the gendarme vampires had entered and stood at the broken gallery rail – shrieking.

Brandy's scream hadn't come in time.

The Templar chaplain drew back his long blade – painted with Ray's blood. Ray toppled over the fence into the cemetery. His wound, like one delivered to his sister days before, intended to disable not kill (the dead don't bleed), had done its job.

Gasping, Ray tried to crawl, while the three knights moved toward the cemetery gate – delighting in the sounds of their rapidly pounding hearts and the smell of his freshly flowing blood. Brandy tried to help, but Ray was heavy and seriously hurt. They struggled away from the fence and to the foot of the lone undisturbed tomb at the far side of the enclosure. Behind them, Brandy saw the Templars filing into the Devil's Bed.

No. No!

If Luis was right, if this was the Devil's Bed, then their fight had been in vain. If all that slept here served Satan, they had no hope. That she would not believe. Like the occupant of the tomb beside them, Brandy had hope.

She gripped the weather-worn lid. Unlike the others, engraved with curses and insults, this stone merely bore a date of death and a name; Jacques de Molay. She gritted her teeth and pushed with both hands.

Grunting in pain and fighting to breathe, Ray propped himself at Brandy's elbow and shoved with her. With their combined effort the lid screeched and fell to the ground.

The moonlight revealed the mummified corpse of the Templars' Grand Master. His gray skin was stretched and dried from the ages. Unlike the others, Molay seemed less one of the rotted dead and more like an aged museum piece. The long beard and mustache Brandy remembered from the painting in Trevelyan's study was scorched but intact, as was his balding head and stern elfin face. A large wooden shield, white with a bold black cross, lay atop the knight's chest – as if to protect him in the grave.

Brandy heard a metallic click and Ray's breathless attempt to shout a warning. She wrestled the shield from the mummy's hand and spun round as a *twang* sounded.

A loosed crossbow bolt struck the shield and stuck with a dull thud as Brandy dropped it in front of Ray. Behind the shield, he looked up gratefully and wearily. While, across the graveyard, the Templar grinned. The archer was playing with them.

Ray took the shield from Brandy and tried to defend them while she turned back to the tomb. Under the shield, on the knight's chest, she'd revealed his weapon; the golden handled treasure Father Trevelyan had referred to as the sword of the Savior. With bloodied hands, Brandy lifted the sword and with more effort than she'd imagined necessary handed it to Ray.

The Templars closed in.

Ray searched the pockets in his many soaked, torn and bloodied layers. Empty. He'd used, broken, or wasted all of his holy water. And the Templars were still coming. Ray tried to lift the sword. "Brandy," he whispered fighting for breath. "I can't do it. I can't lift it."

She knelt beside her fiancé as the dark cloaked knight drew near.

"It's all right, Ray," she told him, fighting back tears. "It's all right."

The Templar reached for her.

The new uninvited vampire hopped atop the broken gallery rail. He hissed, perched on his haunches, and readied to leap.

From the nave, Trevelyan pitched his arm up and over his head, spritzing holy water in wide arcs, into the air and at the monster, in the shape of a cross. "Abominable creature, give way," the priest screamed. "You monster, give way to Christ!"

In his disheveled shirt, his arm in a sling, the left lens of his glasses cracked, the gray tufts at his temples splayed wildly, teetering on the edge of sanity, Trevelyan threw the vial. The vampire ducked and hissed. Aimee grabbed the Father's crucifix and hoisted it into the air. The creature barked, covered its face and dropped backward off the rail. It disappeared into the gallery.

Aimee raced into the hall and took the stairs two at a time with the crucifix before her like a shield. The vampire was on the top step, descending, when Aimee got there. The reporter held the crucifix up, locked her elbow, and continued forward. The creature hissed, clawed blindly covering his eyes as he retreated, and abandoned the gallery for the balcony. Aimee slammed the door closed.

She secured the locking bar and fell against it. Eyes closed, she caught her breath. Then Aimee smiled as it dawned on her how she'd held her ground. She ran to the rail to tell Luis. She looked below, to the floor of the nave, and her smile vanished.

Jerome's corpse had not only gone up in flames, but had set the floor, candles and the broken pieces of railing on fire. In the swirling smoke Aimee saw the priest trying to extinguish it.

He grabbed a wine bottle from a case on the floor, uncorked it and shook it at the flames. The fire died, until a splash hit the vampire's body, then it flared brilliantly. It took a moment for the priest to realize his mistake but, when he did, Trevelyan tossed the bottle away. Holy water, evidently, made a beautiful weapon and a damned poor extinguishing agent. On second thought, he grabbed a hanging pall and, slapping one-handed, tamped at the flames while stamping the embers with his feet.

"Father, are you all right?"

"It's all right. Be careful of the railing. Don't come near the edge. I've got this."

Indeed, despite his handicap, the fire appeared under control and mostly out. Still the smoke, clearing below, rolled up to sting Aimee's eyes. She waved it away, coughing. "Father," she called in growing alarm, "Father, where is Luis?"

Breathing heavily, Trevelyan followed her eyes around the chapel.

Aimee joined the priest below. "Where is Luis?"

"I, eh, er, don't know, Aimee. He was there a moment ago. I was watching you. And then the fire. I, eh, don't know."

Aimee's heart began to race. She hurried to the vestibule, ran back into the hall, then headed for the kitchen calling for Luis. There was no response and Father Trevelyan watched after her in growing fear.

Twenty Three

The dark cloaked Templar, eyes blazing red, bloated black tongue wagging, grabbed at Brandy - while she grabbed the sword of the Savior.

She grunted and spun, swinging the weapon with both hands and all of her strength. The blade sang a low-pitched song as it cleaved the air, generated a sickening thunk as it met the dried flesh at the mummy's throat, a nerve-rending snap as it parted the second and third cervical vertebrae and, a breathless instant later, a muffled plunk as the chaplain's decapitated head hit the weeds and rolled to a stop on the ground.

The momentum created swinging thirty-two pounds of forged steel threw Brandy off her feet. On her butt, on the ground, she swallowed hard, taking in her handiwork. The skull of the dark cloaked Templar lay on its side in the tall grass, grinding its teeth and blinking its red eyes. Brandy rose, uncorked a bottle, and showered the corpse. Then, without waiting for the results, she dragged the sword back to the tomb.

She waved the open bottle of holy water, warning back the two remaining knights, and sank to the ground beside Ray. He groaned as she took him in her arms.

"I love you, Ray," she said, fighting not to cry.

"And you're... sorry... you slapped me?"

"No. You deserved it."

Ray laughed a pained, breathless laugh that became a cough. Tasting iron, he spit blood into the grass. "It was a good fight, baby. It was a good fight."

Brandy held him, covered his wound with the flat of her hand, and kissed him. "I was wrong," she said. "There's nothing in this grave but a corpse. I was a fool to even... I am so sorry for everything. I..."

"You don't have time for that. You've got to get out of here. You gotta run."

Brandy looked at the hovering Templars. She looked at Ray. She looked at the mummy lying in the tomb... and she shook her head angrily. "No! I'm not giving up."

"Brandy, please... Get back to..."

"I'm not giving up!" She ran the back of her hand across her cheek, to wipe away the tears and streaked herself with a war paint of Ray's blood. "I'm not giving up. Not on this... and not on you."

The Templars, wary of her holy water, hovered watching; the disabling of the big human, their chaplain's immolation at the hands of the girl, and now this pathetic love scene. Amused, the knights laughed hideously, the tall, and the archer. Their laughter melted into a demonic chant which, like a drum beat before a battle, led them forward toward Brandy and Ray.

———✝———

Aimee stood shaking, tears running down her cheeks, staring at the sanctuary floor. The Communion table had been pushed aside and the trap door to the ossuary stood open. Father Trevelyan was beside her, holding her up and holding her back.

"I found it this way," the priest said. "He's gone outside."

"Why," she cried. "Why would he do that? He wouldn't panic. He wouldn't run!"

"Of course not. He didn't just run away."

"Then why?"

"He must have overheard us. He's not convinced we can hold on in here until the sun rises. He's gone to do something about it."

"He can't go alone." Aimee tried to pull away and Trevelyan held tight.

"Luis is doing what he thinks he must," the priest said. "If he wanted you with him he would have asked. He certainly would have told you he was going. He wants you safely in here. That's the point. Besides, an old man with one arm cannot defend this place by himself. I don't mean to sound selfish, Aimee, but I need you."

She looked to the priest then around the chapel. And she listened. The prying, the scratching, the chopping continued. Her tears flowed freely as she listened to the undead creatures holding siege. Her heart ached and she quietly said a prayer for Luis.

It had been a quick trip through the ancient ossuary, the tunnel under the courtyard, and the dungeon of Castle Freedom; a trip Luis had made a million times. He did it in the dark. He did it on the run. Most of all, he did it on account of Aimee. The awkward but beautiful reporter was the first woman Luis had looked at since the death of his beloved Micheline. After all the heartache he'd been through, Luis no longer had any notion of what love was or if it even existed.

He knew only that he must do something to give Aimee, and the priest, a fighting chance of being alive when the sun came up. That meant getting those monsters away from the chapel and keeping them away and busy with something, someone, else.

There were few options for weapons. He had several of the Father's crucifixes in a back pocket (of Ray's baggie pants) along with his little worn book, three bottles of holy water – all he could carry, his fear for a group of strangers who had in one night become friends, and his feelings, whatever they were, for Aimee.

Luis entered the small tunnel, then the well, and knew instantly something had gone wrong for the Americans. The well pit smelled of smoke and burned flesh. Fear grabbed him. His mind took off, wildly imagining what had happened here. But he stopped it by sheer force of will. He didn't know. Nothing had changed.

Luis popped up from the well and, though he couldn't see them, heard the monsters at work. He made his way along the western wall, followed the curve and continued along the wall to the north. Ahead lay the courtyard, the chapel, and the shadowy forms of the Templars and the gendarme vampires, fervently scratching at the building; aware the night was nearly gone and desperate to get in.

In the distance, beyond the chapel and bell tower, jutted the hazy black zig-zag of the timber's treetops – and the deep blue of the night sky as it readied to receive the day. *'The west yet glimmers with some streaks of day'*. It was a line from the great Bard's Scottish play, spoken by a traveler hoping for the Inn by sundown. Luis' hope was akin; a prayer not for the last glimmers of sun, but for the first; not for a staving off of the night but for its end.

He'd had no time to plan. He knew only that he needed to act, to get those things away from the chapel, and to create a diversion. He lifted a bottle of holy water above his head and scanned the courtyard for a target. Then he heard a faint noise, a pebble falling, sand raining down beside him. He turned to the wall on his right and saw bits of ruin falling away. He looked up for the source of the debris. . . into the yellow eyes of a gendarme hanging upside down above him. The creature cocked his head, twisted his gray lips in a hateful grimace, and hissed.

Luis bolted and, as he ran, screamed as long and as loud as he could. If this was it, if his time had come, he would do all he could to draw the attention of as many of these things as he could. So he screamed.

The creature, momentarily taken aback by Luis' outburst, recovered and sprang from the castle wall. He landed upright in the grass and took chase.

Even behind the bizarre reflective eyes, and at that ludicrous angle, Luis recognized the vampire behind him. In life, he'd been Tristan Maigny; not a man to mess with. Which was, of course, why Luis always made it a point to mess with him.

From grade two, his *enseignement secondaire* at the age of 15, he'd played scofflaw to Maigny's law man and the chase had been on. Sometimes his old nemesis prevailed and he wound up in cuffs. Sometimes Luis escaped to start all over. Maigny thought himself the victor with Socrates' manslaughter conviction but the celebration had been premature. It was ironic, Luis thought, that even death hadn't ended the chase.

With Maigny on his heels returning to the well was out of the question. The courtyard with its Templars was also out of bounds. The stable was his only option and Luis ran for it... ran for his life.

The stable was originally a ponderous structure, sixty feet long, fourteen high, with stone walls and a slate roof, housing knights' horses and work horses alike. It fell into disrepair and was rebuilt, many times throughout the ages, but was again flagging. The northern end, once opening into pasture land, had been all but destroyed by fire during its World War II occupation. It stood only because of support poles hammered into place. These held off a collapse but did little to prevent the sag which eventually doomed the north wall. A stretched tarpaulin was jerry-rigged in its place.

The south end, on the other hand, had been fully restored by Luis' father for his beloved mule. Now buzzing black flies, filthy scattered straw and a maroon stain on the floor of his stall were all that remained of Zorion. His father always said his mule had earned a dry place to rest after a hard day's work. He certainly deserved better than to be hacked to death and carted away like so much rubbish.

There wasn't an instant to mourn or to hide. Maigny, the vampire, burst through the crack in the partially open south door. He spotted Luis on the run and leapt over the stall railing – airborne and headed straight at him.

The Templars, inching forward, had begun their awful chanting again:

*"Diabolus   quod   Hierarchies'   of
Abyssus."*

Brandy kissed Ray and helped him gently back down in the grass.

Then, rising to her knees, she turned her attention to the opened tomb. She spoke to the mummy of Jacques de Molay lying within. "You... you were imprisoned with them but were not one of them."

She reached into the tomb, her hands covered in Ray's blood, and grabbed the knight's skull on each side of his wiry gray beard. The blood matted the mummy's hair, filled the creases of his stretched flesh, oozed into the gaps in his grinning teeth and dripped into his mouth. "You suffered with them but were not of them."

"Lucifer, quisnam to order totus."

Brandy was crying; desperate and terrified. Tears raced down her cheeks, mixed with the blood smeared there, and fell like rain on the corpse. "You bore the torment of their curses. You died with them. But you were an innocent man; a man of God!"

The lead Templar waved the other toward Brandy. The archer nodded and drew a dagger from the scabbard on his belt. He raised the weapon and started forward.

"Beelzebub Leviathan Sonneillon. Tribuo nos vox."

Brandy ignored it all; the terrifying chanting, the shapes moving behind her, and the portent of death each promised. She spoke to the mummy in the tomb, wailing, "You stood strong. You believed. You shouted, I will hope in the resurrection!"

"Plumbum nos in victoria super nostrum hostilis."

With everything she had in her, Brandy yelled it again. . . "I will hope in the resurrection!"

The eyes of the mummy of Jacques de Molay shot open.

Twenty Four

Brandy screamed. Although she and Ray had risked their lives for it.... Although the resurrection of the wrongly convicted Templar knight had been her hope. Still Brandy was startled and still she screamed.

Then Molay turned his eyes on her. They were not the blazing red slices of hell that made up the eyes of the other Templars, nor the dead black islands floating in yellow swamps like their vampire minions. Despite being sunk in deep orbital caverns, with gray skin stretched over a skull-like face, these eyes, these 'mirrors of the soul' were soft and warm, light brown with green flecks like shining chips of diamond.

Behind her, Ray tried to stop the encroaching archer but, injured as he was, was easily thrown aside. Then, his dagger glinting in the moonlight, the knight hissed acidly and reached for Brandy.

Molay sat up in his grave, reached beyond the startled girl and grabbed her attacker by the front of his rotted mantle. He yanked him forward, bringing their two screaming skulls together.

Jacques de Molay remembered.

In life, seven centuries before, Geoffrey de Charney had entered the Templar Order at his right hand. The Grand Master had taken him under his wing, instructed him in the Lord, in the ways of the Order and in combat. Had turned him over to his friend, Francois de Raiis, to serve God, the Pope, the King and France. Raiis and Charney had betrayed them all.

Molay howled with rage. From his supine position, the Grand Master threw Charney over his sarcophagus.

The younger Templar, if age could mean anything after seven hundred years in the tomb, slid to a landing against the cemetery fence. He righted himself, a chore beneath armor and cloak, rose to a knee, then stood. His dagger was lost in the tall grass. The archer drew his sword.

Molay came out of his tomb and lifted his sword of the Savior from where Brandy laid it beside the grave. Then, almost casually, Molay threw it with one hand; flat and underhanded. The weapon impaled Charney, while the weight of the blade and force of the blow knocked him backwards. The knight toppled and the point of Molay's sword, protruding from his back, pinned him to the ground.

Brandy jumped to her feet and, by the time she'd reached the disabled creature, had yanked two bottles of holy water from the pockets of her jacket. She stood over the pinned knight and slammed the bottles together. Glass shards flew, blessed water rained down. Charney's unsettling scream was drowned out by the sizzling eruption of flesh and the explosion of fire which immolated the knight.

✝

It would be difficult to imagine the eyes of a Templar any brighter, redder, more terrifying then what they'd witnessed throughout the night. But those of the leader now burned with all the fire of hell behind them. He stepped toward Brandy.

Ray tried again to move her way but had to stop, yelling in pain. Not from the stab wound in his back, though that hurt like hell, not from the collapsed lung or the internal bleeding, both of which he had, but from something jabbing him in the groin. He fought with Trevelyan's cassock, damned dress, worked his hand beneath and wrestled the twist from his pants pocket. Then he pulled out the object stabbing him; the crucifix he'd taken from the ossuary.

The relief was instantaneous. Better still, Ray held the crucifix up before the approaching Templar. The mummy reacted as if he'd jabbed a hot poker into his red eyes - and violently backed away.

Brandy took the gold hilt of Molay's sword in both hands, jerked it from the ground, and out of the charred muck that had been the Templar archer. She lugged the weapon back and, terrified, lifted it to the knight standing beside his sarcophagus. Molay took his sword of the Savior and, swinging it over his head, turned on the knight that Ray was holding at bay.

The Templars squared off.

Jacques de Molay, Father Christmas reborn, with bald dome, matted white hair and beard, brown flecked eyes, wearing his trademark black cross on mantle and cloak. Raiis, hell incarnate, dried gray flesh over ancient bone, salted-black wiry hair and beard, red eyes matching the blood-soaked, rotted tunic and cloak emblazoned with the cross of the old Order. They strode toward each other and clashed swords.

They pushed off and swung on each other again. Molay missed. Raiis' strike landed. The Grand Master's mantle tore but his chain hauberk flexed round the blade and the soft gambeson beneath absorbed the blow. Raiis delivered a blow to Molay's leg. The Grand Master went down and defended from one knee while he fought back to his feet.

Molay swiped mightily at Raiis; the weight of his weapon and force of the swing taking him past his opponent. Raiis saw the opening presented by Molay's miscalculation. He turned his sword and drove the hilt into the Grand Master's gut.

Brandy had dropped back at Ray's side and held him, ducking and flinching, as the knights raged at each other yards away. Despite her fear, Brandy couldn't help but be amazed by the entire outrageous affair. Two dead men battling to - what? Their death? No. It was something more. The shadows of two men, their souls resurrected after centuries of waiting, were battling for eternity. Brandy grabbed Ray under the arms and, ignoring his windless groan of pain, dragged him back from the tomb and further out of the way of the battle.

That battle continued from one end of the burial plot to the other; singing swords cut the air, mail crashed, grunts, groans of exertion, and hellish howls rose and fell. A sword struck the wrought-iron fence with a clang and vibrating hum. Another landed on the side of a raised sarcophagus with a violent crack that sent marble chips flying. Francois de Raiis fell over a raised tomb and struggled to get back up. Jacques de Molay fell into an open grave and struggled to get back out.

Finally, to Brandy's horror, it appeared Raiis had the upper hand. Molay was driven to his knees again and the evil knight appeared about to deliver a last blow. He laughed maniacally as he raised his sword.

Brandy shouted, "Our Father, who art in heaven, hallowed be thy name."

Raiis paused, turned on her and hissed. From his knee, Molay rotated his sword and jammed it straight up into Raiis' throat.

"Thy kingdom come. Thy will be done on earth as it is in heaven."

The evil Templar, kabobed and gagging, dropped his sword. Putrid fluids, black in the light of the fading full moon, escaped his mouth as if it were a fountain. The Grand Master rose to his feet and yanked the blade out. As Brandy prayed on, Molay spun the sword once around his head, leveled it, and drove it back into Raiis' flesh with supernatural might.

"Lead us not into temptation but deliver us from the evil one."

The blow decapitated the demonic Templar. Molay found Raiis' head in the grass and lifted it by the hair. The eyes still blazed, the lips peeled back and sneered, the teeth snapped so viciously the entire head bobbed in the Grand Master's hand.

Brandy held Ray but her attention was on the surreal scene before her. The resurrected Molay placed the living skull atop one of the grave coverings on the ground, upright on its neck and still-snapping jaw. There it bobbed like a wind-up Halloween decoration. Then the knight grabbed the heavy stone lid from his own tomb and, with an audible intake of breath and an otherworldly grunt, lifted it high above his head.

Mesmerized, Brandy whispered, "For thine is the kingdom, the power, and the glory forever. Amen."

He brought it down with all his might on top of Francois de Raiis' decapitated skull. With a monstrous crack and trailing crunch the hellish thing was smashed to splinters and sent to a richly deserved oblivion.

Brandy felt it - as if a dark veil had that moment been lifted from her soul. Yet somewhere outside the graveyard she knew the evil still lurked.

Jacques de Molay found his sword lying near the quickly decomposing corpse of the evil knight. He lifted it, kissed the golden grip and slid the elegant weapon back into the scabbard on his belt. Then he turned and faced Brandy and Ray with gauntleted hands on his hips. Molay stepped toward them and extended his hand to Brandy. She took it and he helped her up, off of Ray, and to his side. Then, ignoring his complaints, Molay lifted Ray from the ground and slung him over his shoulder. The big American, struggling to remain conscious, had no strength to fight the Templar.

The knight carried Ray through the wrought-iron gate and out of the cemetery. Brandy followed wordlessly.

———

The vampire, Maigny, cleared Zorion's stall with his leap but missed Luis. The young man hit the dirt and rolled into the stall to avoid the attack, then was up and running again. The creature recovered quickly and took chase deeper into the sagging middle section of the stable.

There, beneath dust-covered tarps, lay the stored wine-making equipment from Anibal Socrates' failed venture; unused oak barrels stacked to the sagging roof, hand cranked presses (of rusting metal), chemicals (settling and separated), hand-bottling devices (claimed by spiders). And on the opposite side, under a second set of tarps, bottled wines and full casks from Socrates' first and only crop. They'd been stored there en route to a final resting place in the old castle dungeon because the village withheld the permits to sell them and his wife withheld her permission to drink them. Now they'd never make the last leg of that journey.

The human and the vampire tussled amid these relics; Maigny frantic for his sustenance, Luis desperate for his life. Socrates kicked the monster off of him into one of the tarp coverings and both heard the shuffle and rattle of encased bottles beneath. The vampire rose and, enjoying himself monumentally, whipped the edge of the covering away to reveal the wine. The vampire took the treasure in with his glistening yellow eyes. He grabbed a bottle by the neck, pulled it free and smashed it on the side of the case. Shards flew, wine spilled, and he brandished the jagged weapon.

Luis stared at the crouching vampire, and his improvised blade, and wondered if this night's battles would never end. In that instant of sadness, he instinctively reached for the comfort of the worn little black book in his back pocket. Not to read, just to feel it and know it was there. The pocket was empty; his Shakespeare missing.

Only then did Luis realize it didn't matter. Nobody could have worshipped the Bard that long without also carrying him in his heart. As he crouched, eyes trained on Maigny's broken bottle, he drew courage from Henry V, saying aloud, "Once more unto the breach, dear friends, once more. . ."

Maigny laughed. "Shakespeare." He waved the bottle and, with a grating voice and a nasty hiss, spit back one of his own. "If you prick us, do we not bleed?"

Luis was livid. How dare he profane The Merchant of Venice.

The vampire lunged.

Luis ducked, pivoted, retreated. Maigny slashed and stabbed coming on. Down the length of the sagging stable they danced, Luis ducking blows and throwing anything not nailed down, the vampire viciously swiping, beside him one instant, hanging from the teetering ceiling the next.

Providence, as Father Trevelyan would have called it, Luck as he and Ray would say, brought Luis backwards to a stool, a dust-covered table and the stretched tarp that served as the north wall. Cornered with no escape and driven by terror, Luis stepped over the first, tripped backward over the second and fell through the last. The day's first glorious rays of sunshine shot through the hole in the canvas.

The light swatted Maigny as if he were an insect. In seconds the screaming vampire, and soon the stable, was in flames.

Twenty Five

The vampire creature that once had been Antoine Beauvais was desperate. His sole motivation for attacking the chapel throughout the night had been an insatiable hunger. Now, though his thirst for blood was as great, a new reason had taken hold. Fear. A desperate fear of the rising sun - and its murderous light.

It caused the monster to risk immolation and jump the accursed ossuary crucifix as it lay broken on the ground. He cleared it, feeling the threat of its *inglorious heat*, and chinned himself on the balcony. Carefully, for the railing broke as the crucifix came down, he mounted the balcony and slipped beneath the collapsed roof.

He crawled beneath the debris, found the door and, hissing and scratching, tried to force entrance. Part of the roof fell away, slivers of sunlight painted the back of Beauvais' hand, and it flared. He howled, pulled it into the dark, and beat out the flames. Fear became panic as the vampire fought to enter while trying to hide from the blow-torch rays of the sun. The more he struggled, the more the crippled roof fell away. The more the roof disintegrated, the more he was exposed. His foot caught fire and, howling, Beauvais put it out. His hand caught again – and on.

Despite his frenzied efforts, and because of them, the balcony, the roof, and the door to the gallery were soon ablaze. Still pounding and screaming, Beauvais was on fire again.

———

Aimee and Father Trevelyan saw the smoke gathering in the gallery ceiling and knew the balcony was on fire. But what could they do?

It was outlandish; a raging fire before them, gallons of water immediately behind them, and they were helpless to put out the blaze. Every drop was blessed and every time it touched a vampire, a Templar, or anything unholy, it started a new fire or worsened one already burning.

They shared looks of terror but before they could act were interrupted by the sound of all hell breaking loose in the ambulatory. They ran into the hall and found the problem in the locked office.

Dust danced on a white beam emanating from the hole in the door - as if the room were filled with light. The reporter and the priest crept up. Looking past Brandy's crucifix, jammed in the hole, they saw the office window, shattered the night before, was now completely broken out with sunlight streaming through.

The day was here (to drive away the demons). They'd made it!

Then a shriek startled both. The scorched face of Fulke, Petit's driver a lifetime ago, glared through at them. Blood shot through his yellow eyes, ran from his mouth. Smoke curled off of his head and shoulders. As quickly as the monster appeared the crucifix forced him away.

The vampire was in agony and had nowhere to go. The sunlight, the crucifix, blinded and burned. Desperately the creature averted his eyes, grabbed the holy icon and yanked it from the door. His hand burst into flames. Screaming, he threw it as he fell back into the pool of sunlight. Fulke exploded in flame. The fireball burst out to the courtyard and in to the hall.

Trevelyan and Aimee fell, clutching each other, to the ambulatory floor as the door was blown off its hinges over them. The concussion died, the screaming stopped, but the blaze raged. Smoke and flames poured from the office while the priest and reporter crawled to get away.

Then came a high-pitched shriek from the nave. Aware they were the only two in the chapel, Aimee and Trevelyan stared at each other in disbelieving horror. The scream came again – a woman's scream.

━━━┼━━━

Luis was grateful. Repeatedly over the last three days, he'd faced death and escaped. He'd just done so again. Maigny had come *this close* to having him and he'd turned the table (or at least fallen over it). The vampire had gone up in flames. And he'd taken the stable with him; aided by his father's wine casks exploding. Luis was grateful. But gratitude was difficult to show with your back peppered with burning wood splinters.

He howled and tore his shirt off. It helped but wasn't a cure. That would take soap, water, antiseptic and time. All of which would have to wait. Luis still had some surviving to do.

He wandered from the collapsed inferno that had been the stable, his ears ringing, into the courtyard. He was stunned, smarting, his eyes filled with smoke. It didn't occur to Luis that he'd left the frying pan for the fire. As his vision cleared, he found he was standing not ten feet from one of the Templar mummies; the same dagger-throwing bastard who'd killed a soldier from twice that distance the night before.

Over that knight's shoulder, Luis saw a second creature, the one-armed Templar, hanging on the chapel tower, kicking frantically at the bell chamber louvers. The knight was panicked. The opposite slats were already broken and he had merely to crawl around and slip through, but the creature may not have seen this... for smoke billowed from the tower as if it were a chimney.

Luis' eyes followed down the roof to see... "*Mon Dieu, no!*"... the balcony had collapsed... the north side of the chapel... roared with smoke and flames. Suddenly it hit Luis as no vampire attack could... Aimee Laurent was inside. Aimee was dead.

Just as suddenly nothing in life mattered anymore. He saw the Templar in the courtyard draw a dagger. He didn't care. Luis simply waited. The knight slowly raised his hand, blade pinched between fore finger and thumb. Then his hand began violently to shake. The first rays of sunlight reached the north end of the courtyard, and Luis, and the Templar. It bathed the knight's stretched flesh. Puffs of smoke curled up from his face and hands. The gray skin blackened and, even at that distance, was heard to sizzle. The Templar convulsed and coughed a dry scream that came - not from the struggling Crusader but - from the pit of hell. His dagger clattered to the cobblestones. The knight's body vaporized while his cloak, mantle and armor, along with his ancient weapons, fell smoking in a heap as if someone had kindled a campfire with museum relics.

The golden sun rose like a searing blowtorch.

The one-armed Templar fell from the bell tower and landed prone and spread-eagled on the roof. The creature began to undulate and sizzle like an egg cracked on a hot rock. Soon, like everything else, he burst into flames. Then gravity provided the final insult as the Templar's helmet and halberd slid down the chapel roof and, respectively, flipped and dropped off the eave. Thirty feet below, the spear impaled the ground like a javelin, while the helmet struck a large courtyard stone and, dented and oblong, took a wobbling bounce and clattered away like a kicked can.

Luis stood numb. Then he began to shake. Then he began to cry. Finally, as the chapel fire raged, he began to scream - for his lost Aimee.

So completely devastated was he, Luis failed to notice the bloodied, reanimated Loup scramble up from the darkness beneath the collapsed balcony into which he'd crawled. He was upon Luis before he could react, had knocked him down and was atop him, yellow eyes dull in the light, black irises glistening with hate. Luis would have been done for – had it been an attack. But it wasn't at all.

The sun was burning him to a crisp and Loup, despite being ravenous, was trying to escape it. Luis, standing between him and the castle ruins, the only close structure not aflame, was in the way. Smoking and screaming, Loup crawled off of Luis and raced for the castle.

Suddenly Luis, on his back on the ground, had a reason to live. He'd sent Micheline's killer to whatever lay beyond. He'd rebuilt his life. Now he'd lost everything – again. Before he surrendered this existence, he would send all of Aimee's killers to a richly deserved hell. Luis rose and chased Loup into the castle.

On the far side of the ruined foyer, he found the warning tape down, melted as if cleaved by fire, and the *NE PAS ENTRER* sign lying on the descending steps. Luis followed the curved stairs into the cold earth and, at their base, took a deep breath to steel himself. One of the heavy wooden doors to the dungeon was ajar.

—✝—

It came again, a woman's scream above that echoed all around, the hall, the stairs, the nave. But there were no women save her, Aimee knew, alive in the building. She and Father Trevelyan tried to use the stairs but the gallery was engulfed. They turned back through the hallway, now raging with fire, and raced for the nave.

The place was a disaster, flames, smoke, heat, broken glass, broken doors and rails, torn banners, scattered candles, spilled water, bottles, buckets and chalices, blood, ashes, a burned corpse. Through the choking smoke they turned to see blood streaks smeared across the floor from the far corner, tracking up the wall into the gallery... as if something had climbed...

Suddenly Aimee was screaming.

The door to the balcony was open and on fire. The gallery was on fire. One of the gendarme vampires was at the rail on fire and shrieking. Behind him, crouched and crying on the floor was Felix's once gorgeous, now undead, girlfriend, Eve Molyneux.

Twenty Six

The evil that led Eve back from death had walked her up the wall and bid her open the door to the monster that once was Beauvais. And, having done so, left her with nowhere to go.

Eve's beauty was gone. She was pallid, sickly and destitute, with bright yellow eyes and black pupils. Her shaking hands fanned the billowing smoke and fought to shield her from the brilliant rays of sunlight that stabbed through the door. She was crying, bleeding, screaming, and her once shocking red hair was now shockingly on fire.

"Eve!" Trevelyan shouted as he started for the ambulatory door.

"No, Father," Aimee screamed. "Father! There is no Eve!"

He stopped and stared, wondering what in God's name was wrong with Aimee and

527

knowing, at the same time, she was right. Debris fell and the fire raged beneath the stairs, merged with the inferno in the hall, and forced Trevelyan back into the nave.

The gendarme thing had, by then, either jumped or fallen from the gallery and, in flames, was crawling across the chapel floor toward Aimee. She was frozen in place – staring. Above, Eve had stopped shrieking and fallen over dead again.

The fire was unlike anything the priest had experienced. The oppressive heat beat him to the floor. Brilliant orange, red, yellow and white flames danced around him. The smoke reached the vault and curled back down in great black swirls, devouring the daylight – and stealing the air.

Trevelyan choked and sputtered, struggling to breathe. He heard Aimee gasping as well. The smoke would soon have her, would soon have them both. But the vampire would not. Beauvais stopped crawling and slumped to the floor.

Foolishly, perhaps because he was dazed and oxygen deprived, Trevelyan grabbed a bottle of water from one of the crates, pulled the cork with his teeth and shook it at the fire. The flames laughed at his effort – until a splash landed on Beauvais' burning corpse. The reaction was devastating; as if he'd thrown gasoline. The flames flared brilliantly, burning Trevelyan and driving him back.

Aimee, holding her breath against the increasingly superheated smoke, stumbled to the front doors and wrestled the batten free. She threw the door open and gasped at the exchange, cool autumn air rushed in at her feet, black smoke poured out the top of the door and Aimee fell to her knees for a breath.

Straining through the smoke, she was stunned to see the priest, outlined by flames, still deep in the chapel. "Father Trevelyan," she screamed. She coughed heavily, gasped for a breath. "Father Trevelyan!"

Aimee took in a breath of clean air, held it and ran back into the nave. She reached Trevelyan, confused, rubbing the smoke in his eyes with the smudged back of his good hand. She grabbed the priest and, crouching, led him back toward the open door – just visible beneath the smoke. Both were coughing horribly.

Aimee stumbled from the front door of the chapel holding Father Trevelyan and helping him to hold his injured arm and sling tight to his body. A cloud of smoke rolled from the doors behind them as they fell together to the cobblestones.

Brandy's mind wasn't working. She saw the billowing smoke and knew something was on fire but couldn't put two and two together.

It couldn't have been the castle. With the exception of a few supporting timbers, a couple of doors, scattered debris and rotted flooring in the dungeon, the castle ruin was entirely made of stone. Their candle was innocent, she knew. And, though the lady gendarme's immolation caused a surprising explosion, the fire had been contained within the well.

The few outbuildings had stood for hundreds of years unmolested but only God knew what happened in the time they'd been gone. At that, her heart leapt in her chest, for Brandy finally accepted the reality that it was the chapel burning.

The mummy of Jacques de Molay, with Ray thrown over his shoulder, moved steadily across the field in the direction of the smoke. Brandy, at their side, tried to hurry but the knight stayed her with his free hand. Ray couldn't talk and the Templar didn't but Brandy got the message. There was danger ahead. Molay wasn't going to allow her to run into it.

She tried to steel herself as they topped the rise but, to her surprise, that was as far as they got. When they reached the chapel cemetery Molay simply stopped.

———— ╀ ————

Just after sundown the previous night, one of the Templars had initiated the gendarme massacre by throwing two daggers. One struck Maurice Delvit in the chest, the other in the back. Either would have been fatal had the knights not gotten to him first. But they did and they drank his precious life blood. After rising from the dead, Delvit removed the blade from his chest and joined the others assaulting the chapel. Now the vampire that once was Colonel Blanc's driver no longer needed to get in. The humans had opened the door.

Delvit hid from the dawn, as best he was able, in the back of the gendarme van. From this shadowy recess, beneath an unrolled tarp, he watched as black smoke poured out... followed by the lady reporter and the old man of God. They stumbled, choking, from the burning building and fell gasping on the ground.

He knew the sun would destroy him if he remained there. And he knew the castle had a deep, dark cellar. More than that, the vampire knew he was starving. He slid the van's side door open and, blocking the sun with the tarp, emerged. He raced, shrieking against the pain, across the courtyard, toward the reporter and the priest. His eyes were on the girl; his thoughts were on her blood.

Aimee's face was smudged with ash. Her eyes teared from the smoke. She was coughing and trying to catch her breath. But there was nothing wrong with her ears. She heard the creature and, at the same time, she saw a bottle of Trevelyan's holy water lying, unbroken, on the courtyard stones.

The vampire let the tarp fly into the breeze and reached for her. Aimee jumped for the bottle. She grabbed it as he grabbed her. Screaming, smoke curling off his blistering face, Delvit pulled Aimee up toward his gaping mouth.

"Of this. . . ," she screamed, "I am so sick!"

Aimee smashed the bottle across the vampire's face. Blood and teeth flew. Delvit screamed as his torn features began to melt and his chest to burn.

As Trevelyan hurried to Aimee, the creature spun round gurgling. It was then the priest saw the dagger protruding from his back. Repelled and energized, he gritted his teeth, reached with his working hand, and yanked the knife free. He leveled the blade at the nape of the shrieking monster's neck and swung.

The screaming stopped. Delvit's head, all but decapitated, flopped forward onto his flaming chest. Then the burning mess dropped in a smoking pile.

With a shriek of unused metal, Luis pulled open the doors to the dungeon. A ray of sunlight sliced into the dark like a dagger and dust, recently disturbed, danced. His burns were soothed by the cool of the cellar as Luis followed the light in. He panned the depths with squinting eyes and hollered, "Loup? Loup Wimund?"

Somewhere in the darkness, to his left, he heard an angry hiss.

Then the vampire hit him like a great predatory cat, the second time within an hour he'd been bowled into by one of these things, and drove him back over a pile of debris and into the dark.

Charred, bleeding, and desperately hungry, the Loup-vampire snapped at Luis' throat. Little was left of Loup's scorched hair but Luis clutched what he could to keep the monster at bay. Then he bent his knees, worked his feet between himself and it and, with all he had in him, kicked Loup off.

The sunlight shone brightly now, on the courtyard, into the castle ruins, and down the dungeon staircase. What had, a moment before, been a sliver in the doorway was now a swath of holy light pushing into the dungeon. Driven by Luis' kick, Loup stumbled backwards across the room, through the patch of light, and fell whimpering into the shadows on the other side.

Luis pulled himself up, strode into the light and, in French, told the thing crying in the dark, "I don't know if you are Loup or not. I don't know what you are. I think of the times I wanted to hurt him, Loup... Yes, even kill him."

The whimpering ceased and there came a rolling growl from the dark. Yellow eyes followed Luis as he paced the light.

"But I am not here for Loup Wimund... I am here for the evil that now lives within him. The evil that has taken everything I hold dear; killed everything I loved." A tear rolled down Luis' cheek. "My mother, my sister, my father... and Aimee. It means nothing to you. But I loved my family. And I loved Aimee Laurent."

Luis stopped his pacing and stared at the eyes in the dark.

"Even they were not enough. Felix, Eve, the priest, the Americans. All dead." Luis shouted, "All dead!" He paused as the echo died. "Hide in the dark as long as you like," he told the creature. "The daylight will only grow brighter... and hotter... and I will not leave until you are back in hell."

Loup growled and leapt from the dark. He landed on Luis - grasping and snapping. Luis used the vampire's weight against him, taking him over his head and onto the sun-lit floor. He came down atop the Loup-thing and held held him there, snapping, kicking, scratching, howling until the vampire burst into flames. Despite the searing pain, Luis continued to hold him, pinned in the light, struggling, teeth grinding, muscles aching, as he burned.

How should she feel? Dear God, how should she feel?

Brandy stood beside the chapel cemetery, alive, when all night she felt on the verge of death. Ray, like a child in the Templar's arms, was badly injured and fighting to stay alive. The sun was up on a glorious new day but black smoke and flames poured from the chapel, meaning all of the friends they'd left behind were dead and gone.

What was it she'd told Ray? She used to feel too much. Now she felt nothing at all. It was better to be alive. It was better Ray was alive. It was terrible - about the others. She knew this; knew she should feel devastated, or happy or sad or... She felt nothing. It was as if she were hollow.

The smoke poured from the chapel. Heavy clouds of black smoke billowing up in the morning breeze and blotting out the sun in the western sky. Ash and sparks danced past and rained down.

Brandy watched as the Grand Master laid Ray in the tall grass at the edge of the cemetery. The bearded knight studied him for a moment then rose and stared at her. The green flecks shown in his soft brown eyes. Brandy began to cry. She reached for him but Molay avoided the touch and stepped back. He pointed to Ray as if relinquishing his care and turned away.

Brandy knelt and cradled Ray. His breathing was labored. Sweat covered his brow. His blood still flowed from the wound in his back and through his chest; bright red to cover the dried stains of maroon already marring his layers of clothing. Brandy kissed Ray's forehead.

Molay stepped to the brink of the cemetery. He cocked his head listening (feeling?), and perhaps, Brandy thought, getting the same sense she had, that the last of the evil had taken flight. He looked longingly into the graveyard.

In life he was a dedicated knight in the Crusades; in the service of the Lord, the Pope and the King. An innocent man, wrongly accused of foul crimes, put to death by greedy, power-hungry men. Molay now declared his innocence by the only avenue open to him. He stepped forward into the cemetery and onto hallowed ground.

Brandy and Ray watched through tear-filled eyes, fearful but unable to look away, as the Grand Master strode forward.

The knight passed the weathered, moss-covered grave markers. He came to a stop within arm's reach of the same whispering, winged angel and cross that so startled Luis in the thunderstorm that first fateful night. Molay drew his sword of the Savior and, to the wail of approaching sirens, lifted it to the blackened sky. Here and there the clouds of whirling smoke thinned and javelins of brilliant sunshine pierced the veil. The light flashed across the outstretched blade throwing glints of silver like fireworks.

The Templar convulsed. The sword fell from his hand and impaled itself in the ground forming, by hilt and handle, what an imaginative mind could well have seen as a shining cross. Then Molay fell to a knee, gasped quietly and toppled. A moment more and all that remained was a smoldering suit of armor and a handful of dust.

Twenty Seven

Brandy neared the courtyard with Ray heavily on her arm and came to a halt – aghast at the chaos. It looked as if the Crusades had just been refought.

The chapel was in flames and, between rolling clouds of black smoke, the damage from the siege was glaringly obvious. The doors had been hacked and rammed, the walls were pitted and scarred, arrows and crossbow bolts littered the courtyard. Though she couldn't see it from there, Brandy knew several windows were broken on the other side and could only guess how the balcony and kitchen looked. Everywhere ancient weapons, a crossbow, daggers, maces and flails, a halberd and swords, lay scattered as if a museum had exploded.

Not to mention, or even think about, the bodies.

The last thing Brandy expected to see in the midst of the death and destruction was a limousine but, as she looked up, a deep blue BMW pulled in behind the row of police cars. Marcel Fournier climbed wearily out and surveyed the tumult with disbelieving eyes. He'd bought the castle for a song, ran his Templar tour for a tidy profit, and now owned nothing but devastation.

A fire engine, its lights flashing as its siren went mercifully silent, wound around and wheedled past the gendarme vehicles giving the firefighters aboard an eyeful. The doors on Colonel Blanc's car stood open, the windows shattered. The body of a soldier, face down in blood and broken glass, lay sprawled across its hood.

The engine came to a stop between the castle ruin, smoke curling up from below, and the burning chapel, totally engulfed, with the remains of the stable blasted to hell beyond the courtyard. Two firefighters emerged from the rear of the cab pulling on their gear and air packs. They looked about, then gaped at one another, wondering where to begin while in the distance other sirens wailed.

The fire chief climbed from the passenger's seat – king of all he surveyed. His was not an elected position, but a selected one; appointed by the local magistrate. It should come as no surprise that, when called upon to fill that important office, Judge Pierre Dupont chose himself. Who else in Paradis, he'd been forced to admit, had the courage, knowledge and authority necessary for the job?

Dupont wore a huge white hat, like an overturned basket, which, coupled with his amazing mustache, left little to see of his puffed red face. But there was plenty to hear. He shouted orders and watched his men scurry. One grabbed an axe, the other flaked hose onto the ground from the engine's bed, while the driver threw the engine into 'pump' and made his way to the side-mounted controls.

The other sirens died away as a tanker truck and a white (and blue and orange striped) ambulance arrived and pulled around the growing lot of cars. The tanker continued on to the first engine while the van stopped short, anticipating a quick exit.

Soliveres climbed out and strode for the rear doors, and their medical equipment, without bothering to look around. On the other side, Aldric (and his pimples), jumped from the ambulance pulling on a pair of blue latex gloves. Mouth open and eyes agog the young attendant surveyed the courtyard. He barely saw the raging fires and scrambling firefighters; they were background.

Aldric was taking in the bloodied bodies, the dismembered bodies, the scattered burnt clothes lying with the aspect they once held bodies, looking for someone alive to treat.

Soliveres joined him, bitching that he'd had to get the equipment himself. He hurled the heavy medical bag at Aldric, barely gave him a chance to catch it, then followed with the oxygen kit. "Who do you think you are?" Soliveres demanded.

In less time than it takes to tell, three men erected a portable reservoir. They dumped a thousand gallons of water into this pool then ran a supply line from it to Dupont's engine. The men joined the engine crew, fighting the fires, while the now-empty tanker lumbered away to refill.

Firefighters with a charged hose advanced on the chapel. The fire had spread and orange and red flames now danced in the smoke at the open door.

On their right, south of the chapel, Aldric saw a small woman supporting a large, wounded man; the Americans from that bloodbath at the village hotel. Everything these people touched, apparently, caught fire. Both were oddly dressed, filthy, and looked to have been beaten. Aldric hurried to them.

His partner didn't notice him go. He couldn't. The older ambulance attendant had finally looked at the courtyard. His color vanished, his breathing became rapid and shallow, and Soliveres passed out.

Despite the language barrier, Aldric got his message through, and Brandy lowered Ray to the grass. The patient fought an oxygen mask at first, but soon gave in, as the young medic hurried to stabilize him. Aldric dug into his bag, absently suggesting Soliveres cut the patient's clothes (and failed to notice there was no reply). When Brandy asked if his partner was okay, Aldric followed her gaze to see Soliveres unconscious on the ground. "*Eh, bien.*" Waving good riddance, Aldric returned his attention to Ray.

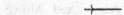

On the north side of the chapel, Aimee had cried herself dry on Trevelyan's chest. The heartbreak and guilt at being one of only two survivors was more than she could endure. But not even Aimee could cry forever. She was used up. Silently she and the priest watched the firefighters trying to save the chapel.

Dupont rounded the building and was flabbergasted to see the young reporter and an injured priest sitting on the cobblestones. When his questions received no answers, he chased them away. Then, for the first time, Dupont saw that side of the building. A huge crucifix lay shattered on the courtyard. Beyond it, the windows were broken, the balcony collapsed in a burning heap, and black smoke rolled from what was once the gallery door halfway up the chapel.

As Aimee and Trevelyan followed the chief's order, retreating to the fire engine, the reporter spotted something on the cobblestones and picked it up. It was Luis' little worn black book. She held it to her breast and began to cry again.

A revived Soliveres joined Aldric while Brandy stood vigil at their elbows with alarm in her eyes and growing fear in her heart.

"My God," the humbled medic whispered. He kneeled in the grass taking scissors to Ray's cassock. "What's happened here? What could possibly. . . ? Who would do this to a priest?" He cut the vestment to reveal a jacket and beneath two more shirts. Soliveres and Aldric traded silent questions.

Beneath the bloodied layers they found their target; a gaping stab wound to the right upper quadrant of his back, through to the chest, bubbling blood. Aldric slapped a jellied gauze on Ray's back and the chest wound began a rhythmic sucking. He applied a second patch on his chest and the noise stopped. The pair worked on; tearing sterile packages, readying plastic tubing, flashing needles.

Brandy kissed Ray's hand and whispered through her tears, "I'm sorry."

Ray pulled the oxygen mask down, despite the medics' protestations, and opened his eyes to exhausted slits. "You're... sorry... about what?"

"About... the whole tattoo-thing," she said sheepishly.

"You're sorry... about the tattoo?"

"No!" The sheep (a wolf in fleece) vanished. "You lied to me. I'm not sorry about the tattoo." The sheep wandered back. "I'm sorry about the tattoo-thing. About bringing it up... I mean... when I brought it up. It probably wasn't the best time."

Ray winced as Aldric slid an IV needle and catheter into his arm. "Forget it," he told Brandy. "Your timing is so much better now."

Both laughed; Ray in pain, Brandy in tears.

Aldric signaled they needed to go.

―———

Clutching Luis' book to her chest, Aimee looked up through tears to see medics rolling a cot from south of the chapel to an ambulance. Despite the blanket, IV and oxygen mask, the big patient was easily recognizable as Ray Kramer. Brandy was walking at his side.

"They're alive," Aimee whispered. Then it dawned and she turned to the priest on the tailboard and shouted, "They're alive! Father! Brandy and Ray. . . they're alive!"

Soliveres eased Brandy away from the cot. Then he and Aldric collapsed the mechanism and rolled Ray into the van.

As Soliveres followed the cot in Brandy was grabbed from behind. She spun, ready to fight, and peered into Aimee's shrieking, elated face. Both screamed. Father Trevelyan walked up a moment later and Brandy fiercely hugged him. Only when he grimaced did Brandy realize how broken, burned and exhausted the priest was. She apologized, wiped her tears and asked, "Felix and Eve?" The Father shook his head. She turned to Aimee and saw the worn black book in her hands. "Luis?"

Aimee began to cry. Brandy took her in her arms.

The blazing chapel, the hustling firefighters faded from Fournier's reality as he stared at Felix's body in the courtyard.

The fire chief (magistrate?) saw him in *his* fire scene and, stroking his mustache, strode over to move him out. As he drew near, Dupont recognized Fournier as the driver of the car that had overtaken his engine on the mountain. He cleared his throat and demanded to know why he'd cut them off. Didn't he know the law? Didn't he know who he (Dupont) was? Didn't he hear him talking?

Fournier laid his jacket over the corpse and, when his trembling knees failed him, sat down on the cobblestones beside. The chief barked again. Fournier, tears streaming, stared at the pompous ass from his place on the ground but made no response.

Neither did he respond when Father Trevelyan sat down beside him and began to pray over Felix.

Neither did he respond when Aimee shrieked. . .

Twenty Eight

✚

Father Trevelyan finished his prayer then sat, exhausted, between Felix's body and the fire engine. Fournier was still there, still crying and, it seemed, not happy with the priest's presence. He said something, said it again with a forceful gesticulation, then shouted over the din. Trevelyan wasn't getting the message. The priest just sat giving Fournier his full attention but no satisfaction.

On the other side of the engine, Luis stepped, blinking, through the front arch of the castle. He wore tennis shoes and Ray's baggy, scorched pants but was naked from the waist up and badly burned. He sat on the steps as if waiting for a taxi.

Aimee saw him and thought her eyes were playing tricks. She pulled away from Brandy and shrieked in delight. Then, shrieking again, ran to Luis, fell on him and kissed him desperately giving in to feelings she had steadfastly denied.

"I thought you were. . . " Tears ran down her cheeks. "Where have you been?"

"I told you," he said through gritted teeth. "I know this place."

"You tried to save us?"

Luis waved it away. "Just wanted to get you a story."

She hugged and kissed him until Luis, his eyes wet with pain, begged for air.

Brandy watched their reunion, sharing their happiness without jealousy. She looked at Ray as the medics worked and realized that, though she was frightened, for the first time in a long time she was happy too.

Only after Aimee let go, and let Luis breathe, did she see how badly he was burned. His hands were blistered. His stomach, chest and face, beneath the smudges of ash, were splotched in brilliant patches of red. His black hair was singed a dull brown and wound in brittle curls. She helped him up and toward the ambulance.

Soliveres had Ray almost ready for transport, Aldric was seeing to Trevelyan's arm and - thankfully superficial – burns, when

Aimee walked up with Luis. The young medic took one look and blurted something to his partner in the back of the ambulance. Soliveres yelled back in exasperation.

"What's he shouting about?" Brandy asked.

The priest joined the conversation and, when an agreement was reached, translated. "With Ray, they have room enough for only one more. We agreed it should be Luis. I assured them we'll make our own way to the clinic."

"How?"

"Marcel. . . M. Fournier has offered to take us."

"I'm not leaving Ray. And I'm not going with a drug dealer."

"I'm delighted to see the old Brandy," the priest said, then added, "but you have no choice regarding Ray."

With a boost from Aimee and Aldric, Luis was assisted up and onto the bench beside Ray's cot. Aldric followed him in and began pouring sterile water on his burns.

"As for, eh, Fournier's. . . eh, drugs. . . he's leaving that business."

"He's giving up dealing. . . "

Trevelyan shushed her and led Brandy from the ambulance. "Yesterday was emotional for Fournier as well. Felix's leaving injured him more than any of us would have guessed. It was, he said, like losing a son. Then last night he was stupidly caught, how would Ray say it, with his trousers down? He thought the *Gendarmerie* were coming for him. When they passed by he had an epiphany of sorts. He paid his men off and, he claims, spent the night dumping his, eh, product into the canal. He described it as pathetic; a scene from a bad opera."

"Last night," Brandy said. "I thought I'd seen everything. Now I've heard it."

"Oh, it's stranger still. Fournier has always made it plain I was his enemy. And, for years, I wondered why he hated me so. His mother, it seems, wanted him to be a priest – and he took that out on me. Now he thinks he's been called."

Brandy gawked across the courtyard at Fournier, still at Felix's side. "He's giving up dealing to be a priest?"

"He's given up drugs," Trevelyan said. "The priesthood, eh, is a matter between Fournier and the Lord. But, ah, he has offered a ride. Shall I tell him we're ready?"

For the first time Brandy noticed the object in her hand, Luis' little worn book. When Aimee spotted him and ran, Brandy somehow wound up with it. Only now did she flip through the book's pages. A quizzical expression crossed her face.

"Brandy," the priest asked again, "shall I tell Fournier we're ready?"

"Not yet." She joined Aimee at the ambulance and held up the book. Luis saw it and beamed. But, when he reached for it, she pulled it back. "It's in English," she told him flatly.

"*Quel*?"

Brandy shook her head. "Oh, no."

Ray peeked over his oxygen mask, saw Brandy's face, and laid back down. He knew the look. Thank God it was aimed at someone else.

"You can read English," Brandy told Luis. "You've been reading English long enough to wear it out." She wagged his Shakespeare at him. "That means... you speak English."

He looked innocently from Brandy to Aimee, and back, then smiled. "Yes," Luis said with perfect clarity. "Of course."

Aimee's mouth fell open. "*Vous... parlez anglais*?" She swore; and repeated it in English.

"I never said I didn't." He pointed at her. "You said I didn't speak English."

"I did not think you could. You left me translating for you all night."

"I didn't ask it of you."

"You didn't trust us?" Brandy asked.

Luis' smile faded. "After five years in prison, you too would be slow to trust. Besides," he added, nodding at the cot, "Ray was not friendly when we met last night."

Ray groaned at something Soliveres did then peeled back his mask. "I'm sorry," he told Luis. Both managed weak, pained smiles as the medics continued to paw at them.

"Well, you're not in prison anymore," Aimee told Luis.

Aldric said the ambulance could wait no longer. He offered the women a chance to kiss their men *au revoir* and they wasted no time in doing so.

"Behave yourself," Aimee told Luis.

"Where is the story in that?"

Brandy kissed her fiancé's forehead and whispered, "I do love you, Ray."

"Should we get married, after all?"

"Yes. Yes! But you need to hold on."

"No worries. After last night, I want no part of being dead."

Brandy nodded her understanding, then confided in him, "I used to feel too much. Now, I just feel so much!"

They climbed from the van, assisted by Trevelyan and, of all people, Fournier. The ex-drug dealer, less foreboding with eyes swollen from crying, escorted the women and the injured priest to his car.

On-lookers, from the village, neighboring farms, passing motorists, had gathered. They'd filtered in behind the emergency vehicles and were blocking the egress. Realizing no gendarmes remained to remove them, Aldric implored the chief for help. Dupont, tugging his mustache, chased them back.

Aimee and Brandy, in Fournier's car, watched the ambulance enter the throng. "*C'est fini?*" Aimee asked. Brandy mulled the question, one she actually understood and, despite her tears, smiled. "The night is over, Aimee. The horrible night is over. But no, thank God, it's not the end. Life is just beginning." Fournier's BMW followed the van over the drawbridge and away.

The crowd turned back to the burning ruins; chattering, laughing, crying. Some stared in wonder. Some shook their heads at the tragedy. A handful secretly wished they'd witnessed the events first-hand. But dotted throughout the crowd were those few who, though they neither knew nor cared to know the details, were certain of the inspiration for the chaos. They crossed themselves, kissed their rosaries, quietly prayed, and could be heard to whisper, "*La vengeance des templiers, les chevaliers de l'ombre.*"

They were witnesses, they knew, to the vengeance of the accursed Templars; the knights of darkness.

Dear reader,

We hope you enjoyed reading *The Devil's Bed*. Please take a moment to leave a review, even if it's a short one. Your opinion is important to us.

Discover more books by Doug Lamoreux at https://www.nextchapter.pub/authors/ doug-lamoreux-horror-mystery-author

Want to know when one of our books is free or discounted? Join the newsletter at http://eepurl.com/bqqB3H

Best regards,
Doug Lamoreux and the Next Chapter Team

You could also like:

The Melting Dead by Doug Lamoreux

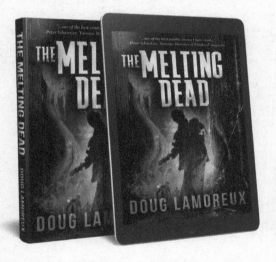

To read the first chapter for free, please head to:
https://www.nextchapter.pub/books/the-melting-dead

About the Author

Doug Lamoreux is a father of three, a grandfather, a writer, and actor. A former professional fire fighter, he is the author of four novels and a contributor to anthologies and non-fiction works including the Rondo Award nominated Horror 101, and its companion, Hidden Horror. He has been nominated for a Rondo, a Lord Ruthven Award, and is the first-ever recipient of The Horror Society's Igor Award for fiction. Lamoreux starred in the 2006 Peter O'Keefe film, Infidel, and appeared in the Mark Anthony Vadik horror films The Thirsting (aka Lilith) and Hag.

Other Books by Doug Lamoreux:

- Corpses Say the Darndest Things: A Nod Blake Mystery

- The Melting Dead

- Dracula's Demeter

- Apparition Lake (with Daniel D. Lamoreux)

The Devil's Bed
ISBN: 978-4-86745-107-6 (Mass Market)

Published by
Next Chapter
1-60-20 Minami-Otsuka
170-0005 Toshima-Ku, Tokyo
+818035793528
4th May 2021